BLOOD AND IRON

BLOOD AND IRON

T.M. JOHNSON

Library of Congress Control Number: 2015912068

ISBN:	Hardcover	978-1-5035-8969-8
	Softcover	978-1-5035-8968-1
	eBook	978-1-5035-8967-4

Print information available on the last page.

Rev. date: 07/30/2015

To order additional copies of this book, contact:
Xlibris
1-888-795-4274
www.Xlibris.com
Orders@Xlibris.com
714196

To *Julia Ann Watkins*

From you I received this love of writing and storytelling and to you I dedicate this novel. Although you are no longer with me, I kept you in my heart throughout this entire process. Your hand guided me through my ups and downs in regards to writing. When I stumbled you caught me. When I faltered you urged me forward. Thank you for being my inspiration. I hope I made you proud.

ACKNOWLEDGMENTS

THERE IS NO WAY POSSIBLE that I would ever be able to describe how thankful I am to have so many people supporting me in so many different ways. However, I will attempt to try. First and foremost I would like to thank my parents, Darryl P. and Jackie Johnson, for financially supporting me and always encouraging me to follow my dreams. I appreciate it more than you know. I would also like to thank my brother, Darryl E. Johnson, for allowing me to share this wonderful story and my ideas with you during its infancy stage. I know I annoyed you sometimes but I truly mean it when I say you played a major role in the creation of *Blood and Iron.* A world of thanks goes out to my English teachers Amanda Bross and Rachel Cronin for always being that helping hand to guide me through the mechanics of storytelling and language arts. Your support means more than I could ever express. I want to thank my friends, Evelyn Mendoza, Taylor Brown and Erika Ventura for always being there for me no matter what. You guys have stuck by my side through many things and I can't tell you how much it means to me to have people like you in my life. And last, but certainly not least, I would like to thank my amazing team at Xlibris publishing. You all took me from Tiffany Johnson to T.M. Johnson and brought my wonderful novel into fruition. I am grateful that you saw something special in my story just as I had.

PRONUNCIATIONS

Characters:

(King) Acheros......Uh-kair-ous
Aldous......Ull-dus
Aoife......Ee-fa
Bacchus......Ba-cus
Crichton......Cry-ton
Diatomin......Dy-uh-toe-min
Guryon......Ger-yun
Instobv......In-stuh-biv
Karuli......Kuh-ru-li
King Araun......Ar-un
Lyrrad Meeklea......Ly-red
Mi-kli-uh
Maille......My-lee
Meenoah......Mi-no-uh
Miew......Mi-ew
Moira......My-ruh
Parthena......Par-theen-uh
Teta......Tet-uh
Tiqo......Ti-co
Tyblant......Tih-blant
Van Crion......Van Cry-un
Yion......Y-un
Zakai......Zuh-ky or Zuh-kay

Places:

Belle (Palace)......Bell
Eijack......Ee-jack
Herec.......Hare-eck
Honudo.....On-u-doe
Iclin (Forest)......Ick-len
Iraquin.......Ear-uh-quen
Islocia.....Iss-loh-see-uh
Kion.....Ky-on
Kreni.....Kren-ie
Larnach......Larn-ick
Naif.....Ny-eef
Qingkowuat....King-co-watt
Qualmi.....Qual-mi
Sythos.....Sih-thos
Ville Morte.....Vee-lay mort
Ynafit.....yeh-nuh-fit
Yenyun......yen-yun

Born from the fires of hell, cradled in the arms of steel.
Forced unto suffering, from those who suffer the least.
Lips sealed, mind molded with cement.
I pledge to those who know not of my existence.
I shall die for those who will dig my grave.
With Valor and Grace. Destruction and Pain.
I fear the corners of a circle, licking blood from my sword.
Though death has accompanied me, I stand for another day.

CHAPTER 1

I RESEMBLED THE MESMERIZING WAVES THAT rushed to shore, soaking my feet. The salty water reluctantly resided to its edge until pushed over the brink again. Graceful destruction. Terrorizing beauty. Sporadic obedience. Out in the distance a seagull pursued its meal, plunging into the immense aqua marine, lucky not to be captured by the vast waves.

As the water soon returned to the shore, chilling my toes, I inhaled the salty air swirling around me. The ocean—a porcelain blue elegance that battered all that refused its might! An intimidating force portrayed with leisurely attributes. And to those who encountered its enchanting ferocity were fooled by a sleek body and dimples. They did not see the mavericks brewing just along the horizon. They did not see the strength of the current until it dragged them under. When the chaos ended and the sea was calm, the water swayed peacefully again. A dangerous tranquility.

Ten years I lived on this beach. Ten years I watched the waves come and go and come and go. The Royals required plays to entertain their desires. Mine were satisfied with the quiet rhythmic romance of the water and beach. At times the waves would blow kisses. But when their desires surged, they met each other with crashing dynamism igniting in a rough pattern that still depicted disheveled loveliness.

"It is not often that time is so calm that you may take a moment to observe great beauty. It is this frame of peace that must be salvaged and forever cherished," Meenoah, the eldest elder, spoke as she stood beside me. She was a round woman with weathered bark-colored skin. A bushy mound of gray hair, tied into four thick braids, flowed down her short stature. She was dressed in colorful woven cloth, which matched the eccentric wooden jewelry dangling from her ears. Her eyes, pale blue, saw not only the present but the past, and maybe even the future. She was the wisest woman I had ever had the pleasure of encountering. I respected her.

"It is not time that is unperturbed in a moment of peace, for peace lurks in the background; rather, the timekeeper has noticed something beyond what lies before him. He sees the north, the south, the east, and the west. The sky and the ocean. The people and their faces. That is what should be salvaged. The moment in which you see faces," I replied, continuing to stare out into the waters.

"Do you see faces?" she asked as I felt her turning to look at me.

I paused, and then replied with the simplest answer I could fathom. "When I am able to see my own is when I will be able to see others."

From behind me, to the left, I heard the soft shuffle of feet running through the sand. "Meenoah! Meenoah!" the tiny adolescent voice cried. I turned to see Little Teta, in all her innocence and ragged beauty, coming our way. Gasping, she took deep breaths, Meenoah and I both noticing the fear and panic in her eyes. "Six . . . of . . . them!" she said between breaths. "Coming . . . towards the village!"

"Return to your mother, Teta. Tell everyone to stay in their homes until the bell sounds, especially the children," Meenoah instructed the girl. "Go, now!" Teta nodded before running off toward the village.

Before Meenoah began speaking I had already shed the sheep's blanket I had draped over my shoulders. Walking into the little shack I constructed from dead wood and boulders, I went to work, strapping daggers onto my belt.

"Return in peace," Meenoah muttered just outside the little shack, for it only was able to accommodate one.

When I was finished I turned to face her. "I shall return." Then I was gone.

* * *

With one hand balancing myself on the branch, I peered through the thick wall of leaves. The forest stood silent with the exception of the subtle twist of branches and hums of the winds sifting through the leaves. I mirrored the softness of the forest. My breathing and heart slowed so that I could hear for inconsistencies. The metallic rasp of iron. The discreet pounding of horse hooves. It didn't take no more than a minute to finally hear them coming. Six soldiers of the Royal Army road horseback to destroy the Qingkowuat village. Kerts have been scarce lately, and the quota for finished goods only continued to increase. The Qingkowuats were two weeks behind in paying their dues. Their punishment: death.

The soldiers finally came into view, directly underneath the branch I was perched on. I allowed five to pass before I made my presence known.

Swiftly gliding down from the branches, as quiet as an ant crawling across the ground, I landed on the sixth soldier. His horse, startled by my sudden appearance, took off, which caused us to fall to the ground much louder than I anticipated. Before the other soldiers realized what had happened, I had him pinned to my chest with one dagger at his throat while he struggled beneath my immobile grasp.

"Release me!" he spit, clawing at my arm. I jabbed him in the throat with the handle of the dagger to quiet him. He choked on his words for a while until finally he only gasped for air.

For a moment the other guards seemed rattled by the attack. Frozen in place they stared at me, intimidated. Unfortunately that stare faded into amusement. The leader of the guards came toward me.

"Do not move any further or I will kill your mate!" I hissed, angling the dagger so that it would easily stab underneath his helmet and deep into his throat. The head guard stopped his ascent. He took off his helmet, handing it to the guard to his right.

The head guard was not a muscular man but, rather, a man who asserted power. The average person would be intimidated by his layers of armor but not I. I saw through his iron façade. Though poised gallantly on his steed, he would easily crumble when faced with a real opponent.

"What is your name, girl?" he asked, sharpening the point of his chest-length beard. His long brown hair sank down his back, matted from the uncomfortable fit of the helmet. He was indeed a Royal, judging from the cleanliness he reverberated.

"That is not of importance," I replied, pushing the dagger fractionally closer to the soldier's throat. Again he tried to pull my arm away. His attempts failed. "I will allow you all to leave. None of you will be harmed if you go now. The refusal of my offering will result in death. The choice is yours."

The head guard pondered my notion for a fraction of a second. "Girl, you are clearly outnumbered. Yes, you have one inadequate hostage. However, the odds are against you. Five trained men to one woman?"

"Do you wish to die today?" I asked the guard whose life I held in the palm of my hand. He shot a worried glance at the head guard before responding.

"I am not the one who will be dying today!" the captured guard screamed.

"Release him, girl. Do not hurt yourself. I am sure he will forgive your crudeness and spare *you*," the head guard said, sounding bored.

"Will you leave this village in peace?" I asked, giving them the opportunity to escape with their lives.

"No," the head guard replied before laughing senselessly. The guard to his left handed the head guard a scroll. "It says here that this village owes the kingdom five carts of grain, two herds of livestock, and another five carts of cloth."

"As you can see I do not have any of those items, and neither does the village," I replied.

"Then step aside! We will raid the village until it has met its demands. If the village has an insufficient supply, well, that will be handled accordingly." He smiled wryly.

"You will not pass into that village," I said, inching the knife closer. "Leave now."

"Watch me," he replied. "Guards, forward march."

Like slicing a soft apple, the guard in my arms fell beneath me. The other guards froze in place, paralyzed by disbelief. *Big mistake.* Swiftly I danced over the fallen guard, pulling out two more daggers. With a quick thrust of my wrist, the knives sailed through the air. With unworldly precision the daggers went underneath their helmets, penetrating the jugular, and killed two of them instantly

Another guard began to charge as the two guards' bodies fell to the ground, scattering their horses.

Kicking his horse, he charged forward, pointing his sword at me. I counted the strides until we met. *One, two, thre*e . . . Like water through a crack I slid underneath his steed and latched onto its tail.

For several seconds I was being dragged, the guard unaware of my presence. Deliberately I took my final dagger and struck his horse in the rear by pulling myself up using its tail. The horse toppled over almost immediately. The metallic cry of bent metal underscored the guard's fall.

Standing, ignoring the several tiny slits along my bare back and thighs, I walked over to the guard. The panicked horse made his leave while the two final guards watched in bewilderment. The downed guard on the other hand was trapped by his own armor. The horse had collapsed on his legs, denting the iron so that the guard could not bend his knees to stand.

Grabbing his sword, which had been thrown several feet, I returned to the guard and held it over his head. "Are you prepared to die today?"

"I will not die today!" he yelled, looking up at me. "Especially not by you!"

One quick plunge of the sword silenced his hopes. I turned to the two remaining guards who stared wide-eyed and distressed. To them I must've appeared to be some sort of beast. My clothes were already worn and torn from their lack of material, the more important body parts receiving cover; blood began to dry on my bare limbs. They did not see fear in my eyes; they saw nothing. An empty black hole with nothing to lose and nothing to fear.

"I'm willing to give you forty kerts in hopes that you will leave in peace," I said, wiping the blood from my hands. "Considering that the harvest has been dry and the disease that swept the livestock, I'm sure you will understand the Qingkowuats' need for leniency."

The head guard, still traumatized, took a minute to recompose himself into his iron façade. "Forty kerts is a fair price." I tossed him the bag of gold before retrieving my daggers from his fallen companions.

Qingkowuat village had one of the largest human populations with the exception of Lárnach. Unlike Lárnach, the capital of Islocia, the Qingkowuats lived in unbearable poverty. The average weekly income for a family of four was two kerts. It cost four kerts to buy one loaf of bread. The price of grain was continuously raised due to the lack of harvest. It had been a dreadfully dry growing season. There was only enough grain for families to salvage in hopes to last them a few days. Most of the men left the village and went to Lárnach in hopes of finding work. Children were forced to work, leaving behind a forgotten childhood. Meenoah and the four other elders, Tikqo, Instobv, Yion, and Miew, did their best to reach the kingdom's quotas. Unfortunately, they hardly ever did. They hated seeing their people starving . . . dying.

The Qingkowuats, however, did not have the worst situation. Many of the other villages suffered far worse than they did. When the guards collected empty revenue then the price they had to pay were their children. The children who were "collateral" were either jailed or forced to work in the mines at Honudo—the coldest region discovered. Though that was only a rumor. No one would ever dare step foot in Lárnach. It terrified us all. It is believed that when the guards took the children, many of them died before their villages could reach their impossible quotas. The elements, disease, starvation, or the guards killed them by the hundreds. Parents were never notified of their child's death, not even when their quotas were met. I knew how much Meenoah loved her people, and because I respected her I vowed to defend them at any cost.

It didn't use to be just me who promised the peace and preservation of the Qingkowuats. There were six of us. Two were killed, one was captured, another quit, and the other two . . . no one ever heard from them. They just one day disappeared; that was the official story. I saw them packing the night before. I saw *him* preparing to leave in the dead of night. Without me. *Gabriel...*

"Excuse me," a quiet voice said from behind me. Before I allowed my anger to fume, I turned to see Little Teta walking awkwardly beside me as I made my way through the village. "Are . . . the bad men gone?"

I stopped, just as I was about to turn and head for the coast, and kneeled down beside her. She winced at my presence, probably from the set look on my face. Up close I saw the hidden beauty of the little girl buried underneath famine and filth, and even more so I saw the innocence that was portrayed in her bright blue eyes. "Yes, the bad men are gone."

A small smile tugged at the corners of her mouth. "Thank you." She reached for my hand, kissed it quickly, and then scurried away toward her older brother Zakai who waited for her near their mother's shop. Their mother, just as beautiful as her children, smiled at me before pulling the curtain down to close an already empty shop.

"Arianna," Meenoah said, coming up from behind me. Rising from the ground I turned to face her. "Your pay. Ten kerts. I understand that it is not the twenty we promised you." Distressed, she toyed with one of her long gray braids. "Miew went to the kingdom to collect more gold. He was denied by the Royals."

"I shall resolve this." I nodded, taking the money.

"This is not a problem you can solve with the deadly end of a sword," she replied, lowering her voice. "The kingdom owns every blade of grass from the coast to every stroke of wind to the clouds in the sky. They own us."

"What is there to do?"

"I don't know." Though she tried to hide it, I saw the fear that flashed through her eyes. She felt the pain and distress of all her people. She too was hungry. She too was starved for revolution.

"I will wait until the harvest to collect my pay," I said, handing over the bag of kerts. She reluctantly took the bag and then nodded thanks. I continued my lonely walk back to the coast.

A merciful killer.

CHAPTER 2

I DO NOT UNDERSTAND WHY PEOPLE cower at the thought of death. Or why they fear its grasp and hostile whispers. I do not understand why people refuse its hand when facing the inevitable. They'd rather allow pain or the harsh truths of life consume their being instead of surrendering into death's comforting arms. I have eight years behind me, and I realize death's blessings. I realize that in life, pain is unavoidable. I realize that pain tends to cease when you walk in the shadows of death.

"Get up!" the voice growled. Beaten senseless and broken beyond repair, I whimpered on the ground. Blood was my bed, pain my blanket. Hours and hours and hours I fought this devil! I fought. Begging for my own life! Begging for survival! "You worthless child! Get up! Fight back!" I could not. I could not rise. I could not win.

"Take my life if it pleases thee!" I cried, choking on my own blood. "I hand it over!"

"Death?" I heard the soft cry of a sword being drawn. "Death is too easy. Death is too merciful. I am not a merciful man."

"I cannot fight you anymore! I have failed you! Living, I shall not!" Tears, the last ones I'd ever cry, splashed onto the sand that clogged my windpipe.

He slid the sword across my back, not cutting me; its coolness was a relief to my sore limbs. Kneeling down beside me he laid the sword so that I saw only my reflection. The battered child who cried the pain away stared back at me.

"Is this who you want to see? Is this who you want to be?" He hissed, grabbing me by the hair and forcing me to look closer. "If so, take the sword from my hands and welcome death! But welcome it on your own terms."

I considered it. I considered ending it all. I considered a pain-free beginning.

"Only the strong can die honorably. The strongest never see an ending to their own life but to others. The weak are already dead. The weakest take their own life. Which are you?"

I grabbed the sword . . .

"Arianna!" The sound of an outside voice quickly jolted me back to reality and away from my past. "Good grace, girl!" Hineson hurriedly dumped a bucket of water on the weapon I was welding. Steam permeated the small shop, tearing me completely away from the leftover memories that clung to my mind. "Wu' you like tuh kill us all, aye? You alls most burnted de ho damn shope!"

"Apologies," I muttered, accepting the cloth he handed me. I wiped down the iron rod that was still simmering from the heat.

"You alls right?" Hineson, an enormous, greased-covered bald man with a deep mountain accent, worked the blacksmith shop. It's rare he had any customers, considering no one could afford to buy a sword. Actually, the majority of his customers were wealthy merchants who dared to venture into the forest and dirty their hands with the commoners. I respected Hineson for his caring disposition. Though, I never quite understood how a man who lives in a famine bowl could still be so unearthly large.

"I am fine." Lifting the rod, which stood at five feet, I handed it over to him. "Would you mind smoothing it out for me? I'll pay you."

"No churge reqired." He smiled a dazzling set of yellow and black teeth. "You my best customer, I's give you a discont."

"Much appreciated, thank you," I replied as he went to smoothing out my weapon. I placed five kerts in his bowl; it only cost three.

"What dis here fo?" He asked, dipping it into cool water.

"Hineson"—I grabbed a rag to dry it off—"I promise that when it is in your best interest to know, I will tell you," I replied dryly. Giving a stern nod, he handed over my weapon: a five-foot iron pole, four inches in diameter and approximately twenty pounds. "Thank you again."

"You come back and sees me soon, ye hear?" he said while handing over my sheepskin sack. "'Tis lonely here."

"I shall return." I walked out of his shop and into the winter rain. The village streets were empty as people found shelter in their leaking homes. The homeless were probably outside one of the elders' homes, begging for their children to be allowed in until the rain stops.

Walking through the streets I saw the suffering of the families who stripped out of their tattered clothes and used them to patch the holes in their roofs. I saw the sorrow in a mother's eyes as she watched her children cower beneath shops and drink the runoff from the rooftops. I saw these miserable people who were a stone's throw away from death. But because my soul is black and heart alone, I do not care for the weak, I do not care for the strong, I do not care for the dying, and I do not care for the living.

* * *

"Prick!" I growled just as the dagger proficiently pierced the handmade target in the middle of the tree.

Completely surrounded by thick layers of forest and peacefully alone, I practiced precision and skill with my weapons.

It was in that frame of time that I demanded solitude while battling with internal conflicts. It was that place where I was free to express emotions beyond the subtle smirk or curt nod. It was that opportunity for which I spent time with myself, to give to myself, so that one day I may be able to give to others what was lost to me.

"Arrogant bastard!" I muttered, whipping three knives through the air and into their targets. I threw another one to the left. Another to the right. One to the front of me and one behind. "You left me!" They all hit their marks perfectly. "With nothing! You left me!" I reached for another knife in my belt and felt there was only one left. I allowed my mind to wander as I contemplated my next move.

Battles are not won; lands are not conquered unless thou hath conquered thyself and mind.

Standing before me was Doubt, Reason, Mercy, Fear, Loss, and Love. They bared their teeth and drew their swords in my direction. So I drew mine. They stood in multitudes, all with the same goal—to destroy me.

I would not allow it.

"I am not to die by the hands of the weak, but I am not to live under the thumb of the strong," I shouted as the warriors before me prepared for attack. "If my life escapes me then so be it. I was born to die, but never was I created to summon defeat and shake its hand! No! I am not a prisoner to my body but that of my mind. Never will I bow to choices composed by the defeated. I am strong! Stronger than any man coated in armor because I believe that deep within me lies a power far greater than any crown! Far greater than any merciful death!" I was willing to test that theory.

They charged. We fought.

Reason attacked first. Their blades were sharpened to a point where it sliced the air into millions of pieces. Crowding around me, I pierced my sword into their justifications, ignoring their tedious explanations, and stabbed through their chest, which is the cause of the actions. I exiled Reason and all its counterparts.

Doubt soon followed. It was not a matter of uncertainty as I removed their heads one by one until there was a sea of doubtlessness. Their little knives never broke my skin. Their lack of conviction was swept away with the blowing wind.

A thin layer of sweat coated my body as Mercy and Loss came at me from both sides with Fear stalking just behind them. Mercy, with their compassionate eyes and forgiving features, paused. They searched for terror in my eyes and for distress to ravage my body. Mercy thrived only if fear was present . . .

Suddenly, a surprise attack from below! Fear clawed, bit, scratched, and tore at my guarded soul!

"Cursed be the wretched that break when bent!" I struck fear in its heart, watching a black ink pour from within them. They died slowly, painfully. "I *am* beyond the might of those who dispense terror."

Mercy soon died quickly.

Loss combined with Love. Together they created an extremely powerful offender that stood six feet taller than I. Love, with its intensity. Loss, with its destruction. Both so potent and so dangerous, people feared them. Luckily, my fear lies dead.

We charged each other.

Dropping my sword, I flung myself forward, grabbing onto its mountainous head. The beast, which destroyed many lives, released a volcanic roar that shook the earth! Bits and pieces of Love clung to my being, my mind betraying me. "I am not weak to which I accommodate the betrayal of Love! Or the deception of Loss!" Grabbing my last dagger, I looked the beast in its eye. I saw all that could be given and all that will never be. I saw the suffering by the naïve and vexatious laugh of the deceitful! I refused this weakness. "It is I who must destroy you!" With both hands I grabbed the dagger and plunged it deep into the iris of agony! "Never will I allow you."

My enemies fell before me. Surrounding me. Capturing me. But never defeating me. It is not by death that I have won, but by the will to stay strong and survive. Though my mind betrayed me. *He* betrayed me! For some inexplicable reason I felt I had not fully conquered my enemies. Images of *that night* flooded my mind. *Him leaving me . . . With nothing but a tattered soul and empty heart . . .*

"Ahhh!" Grabbing my hair, I sank to the ground, cursing his name! Every muscle in my body tensed as the memories intruded. "To hell with your pitiful soul!" I screeched to the heavens. "To hell with your condemned mind!" A barrel of screams and curses filled the forest around me. I punched the ground several times; I ripped up roots and clawed at my own flesh. "Ahhh!" I screamed until my throat became raw and the muscles in my cheeks began to burn with soreness. I did not calm until the sun had nearly fallen and the sky portrayed peace. Sitting in the middle of the forest, out of breath and broken, I gathered myself into my merciless mask of indifference and picked up my new weapon. I called it my *boe*. It's Crectian—the ancient language of the Qingkowuats—for *savior*.

I twirled my boe in my hands, getting a feel for it first, noting its weight and dexterity. I'd only need to swing it with little force to drop a man twice my size. "Come and get me," I muttered to myself, happy with what I had created.

All of a sudden, a loud snapping of a fallen twig and the soft rustle of metal had me directing my attention to the forest. Though I could not see through the black spaces created by the trees' shadows, I knew I was no longer alone.

They walked in unison, all of them. With flashing swords and recently polished breastplates. Crimson capes draped down their backs as the Royal Standard waved frantically in the breeze. The Royal Army had not forgiven our earlier encounter. They stood a thousand strong, all determined to take me prisoner or dead.

One soldier stepped forward with a scroll in his hand. He removed his helmet before speaking. "To whom this may concern, you are being charged with high treason, obstruction of justice, unlawful manslaughter, and the killings of four Royal officers. You will be taken in immediately and imprisoned until further justifications are decided."

Eyeing all of them as they surrounded me, I asked nonchalantly, "What if I refuse?"

He skipped several paragraphs before responding. "Your refusal of arrest would result in forcible removal from your current establishment. Possibly death."

Surrounding me was an impenetrable wall of armor. Every one of them prepared to fight to the death. Their skill did not compare to mine; their number, on the other hand, spoke volumes. They had swords; I had my bow. My other weapons lied scattered along the forest floor. I was a drop of rain, and they were the rushing waves of a fierce ocean. But that did not deter me.

"I choose death." I smiled.

The guard put on his helmet. "So be it."

They charged. We fought.

CHAPTER 3

FROM THE TIME I WAS born I was given a knife. When I was able to understand, I was ordered to kill.

Never was I asked if this was my life's choice. Never was it considered that I could be beyond death and killing. For my Conqueror molded me into the being I am. My limited adolescence was cradled in the arms of steel, and I was birthed from a womb doused in flames. My crib, where I developed, was a harsh, barren wasteland. Silk linen and feathered pillows were that of imagination. The Conqueror said I had no use for such childish things. My belly was full, but not of food. Hate and rage tasted better than sand. And when I was given the option to satisfy the lion trapped in a cage too small, I was to kill for it. Bakeries, homes, nursing mothers, and children with their sweets. I was bred to be ruthless and forever unforgiving.

The Conqueror, however, ate four meals a day. He slept on silk linen with six feathered pillows. He had coverings to protect against the jagged rocks or the scorching sand. His clothes, I remember, were leather and fine thread from top to bottom. My clothes consisted of rags to cover my chest when I began to flower, and so were my undergarments. The rest remained bare. I barely survived many winters and many summers. Because there was a drought, it did not mean I was allowed to think about water. I was ordered to be obedient. I was trained to kill. The Conqueror was the bow, and I his arrow.

"Ask yourself this, girl." The Conqueror paced before me. I stood on the edge of a cliff with my ankles hanging over. My toes clung to withered blades of grass as a gust of wind nearly knocked me right off the cliff and down into the sharp rocks a hundred feet below. "Is this moment, for which you stand before me and before death, the end or the beginning? Are you strong or are you weak? Life or death? Do you choose fear? Or do you choose indifference?"

The muscles in my legs began to burn as I steadied myself on the edge. I could not slouch; I could not cross my legs; I could not move. Straight as a board with a stern face were my orders. Twelve hours he made me stand like this. No food, no water, no bathroom breaks. Twelve hours. And I would stand twelve more if he asked me to. I obeyed his every command. He is in fact the Conqueror. How could I refuse him?

"I do not own myself," I replied. "I haven't for a while now."

"What of this statement defines this moment?" he asked.

"All of it."

"Have you chosen indifference?"

"Who am I to decide?"

Slowly, like treading water while wrapped in several layers of wool with boulders tied to my ankles, my body began to awake. Feeling no longer rested in the soft thud of my heart, it now spread to the edge of my body. I began flexing my muscles, checking their maneuverability. I felt a sharp pain pierce my wrist as I stretched my fingers. The more I pulled, the more pain I caused myself. *Shackles.* I was shackled to a wall. The rust was cutting into my wrists, and I felt the heavy chains locked on my ankles. Luckily my clothes were still intact, for the most part. Looking around I could not see anything. There were no windows, no source of light. Only sounds. I figured that somewhere alongside the far wall was a door. The occasional murmur of voices seeped through the cracks. There was a rhythmic trickling of water off in the distance of the cell. Meaning, I was underground.

I began counting the drops of water to keep the time. After around three thousand, my mind got lost in itself . . .

How many times are you going to convince yourself that this life is worth living? It'll only take one time to die. That seems so much easier.

"Shut up!"

Come on then! Do it! Let's finish this once and for all. Three times you've tried and failed. I know how you can get it right this time.

"Stop, stop talking!"

I can't stop. I am you, you are me. If you hate yourself so much then do it. Accompany death to the stairwell of hell. Bask in the arms of the exiled. Smell the burning flesh of those who've tried but could not succeed.

"Ahhh!" I let out a bloodcurdling scream, hoping to silence the voices. "Enough please!"

Enough? That is exactly the point. You have had enough. I am not going away—we are not going away. Succumb to us, succumb to you. This is all of which embodies you. Unless you choose death.

"I am worth something!"

You are worth the weight of a single grain of sand.

"Stop, please!"

You know exactly how to silence the voices of reason. I've asked. Now I will command you. DO IT!

A sudden rattling of chains outside the cell restored my conscience. I could not form words from the mumbling in the hallway, but based on their speech patterns I knew they were of higher class. It was safe to assume they were the same guards who found me in the forest. *Interesting.* Why hadn't they killed me? Unable to do anything further than have my heart beat and breath escape my lungs, I decided to rest. Something deep within told me I would need my strength later.

* * *

Days must've gone by. My stomach began dissolving itself, and I could smell the stench of my own filth and waste. The rust had broken my skin hours ago; blood ran down my arms and soon began to dry by my armpits. My breathing became labored from lack of fuel to my body. I swallowed slowly, trying to fill my stomach with anything tangible. There was a horrible burning sensation with every gulp. Not even saliva could satisfy the fire blazing down my throat. I could no longer sleep. I felt the weight of drowsiness, but I could not surrender to it. My mind wandered aimlessly, causing my body unrest. On the inside I struggled with the conditions, but my exterior portrayed nothing less than triviality. But I soon understood that it would only last for so long . . .

"Ahhh!" I couldn't control myself. Everything inside me snapped like some invisible cord that had reached its limit. Terribly exhausted and deathly depleted, I sagged against rusted shackles. "Gaaaaahhh! Ahhh!" It took every muscle in my body to breathe. *In, out, in, out, in, out, in, out!* I worked so hard that I became light-headed from the strain. Hours ago my mind got lost in the silence! No longer able to bear the endless depths of solitude, I made friends with the drops of water and enemies with the shadows.

Thinking I could relieve my mind of this pressure of darkness, I bashed my head against the wall. *Once, twice, three times!* My vision became blurry, and I clung to whatever bit of consciousness I could hold onto.

"Ahhhh!" The edges of my mouth felt as though they were being ripped apart from the force I used to get the sound out. I tasted blood on my tongue, the dryness finally cracking. For a moment I reveled in the moistness. The metallic taste was rather inviting. But it did not suffice. Not for long.

I pulled on the shackles, trying to free my wrists. The skin around it became so infected that I could no longer feel it. Fresh blood didn't even come out. Using everything I had, I heaved against the chains, my muscles burning. "Ahhhhhhh!" It did not budge. Again I tried. And again I failed. I had no strength left in me. I had no will.

"Only the strong can die honorably. The strongest never see an ending to their own life but to others. The weak are already dead. The weakest take their own life. Which are you?"

There was only one way to escape this. Unable to control my body and mind, I struggled for reason. I clawed at some inclination for an end! Approaching footsteps, the opening of the door, or the silencing of my heart. I was not so fortunate. Though wrecked and depleted, my heart did not cease. Though starved and horribly restrained, my heart continued beating. "Take me now!" I screamed to the heavens. "Finish me off! Welcome me into Satan's arms if need be! Take me now!" I regretted the words that spilled from my soul. I did not favor defeat, and I certainly did not idealize death. But I was not in control of myself. Emaciation and distress were selling my soul. "Have mercy on me!" I cried, tearlessly sobbing. "Ah!" I broke my scream with another bash of my head. "Ah!" I felt the warmth of my blood running down my neck as I did it again. "Ah!" My entire body tensed as I heard the shattering sound deep within my head. "Ahhhhh!" A deep rugged sound of pain poured from me as I pounded my head against the wall until I could do nothing more than hang by my wrists and ankles.

I needed sleep. My mind could not rest unless it was completely off. I needed sleep. I craved sleep. But I was not indulged. The feeling of lethargy hung onto me like a blanket of cement. It covered me completely while taunting me with the possibility of an escape. I would try to force my eyes shut, but they would only force themselves open. Hunger and thirst were comforting compared to the lack of rest my own damned body refused me! "I want to sleep!" I begged my body to allow me seconds, mere seconds, of peaceful release. I pleaded with my mind to calm itself if only for a minute or two.

I did not sleep. I never came close.

Drawing in a single breath was comparable to breathing underwater. It was too difficult. I no longer had the strength.

For a long while silence roared around me, filling my ears and emptying my being. Darkness joined the silence as they battered me. It tore me apart and stripped me of any ounce of sanity I might've had. I was drowning in their might and fettered to their will. For a moment I considered accepting defeat. How easy it would be to bow to loss and gaze upon what could've been. Closing my eyes, I pondered the thought.

"No," I murmured barely above a whisper. "No!" I said it again only louder. "I . . . will . . . not . . . accept . . . this fate." I will cheat it.

With all the remaining strength I had, I sucked in a mouthful of air and held it. Ignoring the roaring in my ears, I listened for the drops of water. *One, two, three . . .* The pressure in my chest built with every passing drop. *Sixteen, seventeen, eighteen . . .* I fought against the urge to breathe. I fought against the fortress of doubt. *Forty-five, forty-six . . .* My lungs burned for air; they pleaded for release. I gave them no leeway. *Sixty, sixty-one, sixty-two . . .* My heart began to slow, conserving the dwindling supply of oxygen. Air soon filled my ears beseeching for any sort of escape. Silence and darkness spun around me as I became less and less coherent. I could not feel the sharp bite of hunger. I could not feel the terrible confinement of my wrists. I could, however, feel the inexplicable buildup of pressure in my head and chest. *Seventy-four, seventy-five, seventy-six . . .* My body fought for control I would never give. My lungs demanded relief I painfully ignored. *Eighty-nine, Ninety . . .* I felt it happening. *Nine-five, ninety-six . . .* My entire body swelled up like I was to pop. *Ninety-nine . . .*

Finally.

All the discomfort went away.

As did I.

* * *

"Dead?"

"No response, I assume so!"

"Pity, I wanted to ruff her up a bit. Teach her a lesson."

"She killed fifty of our most well-trained men in that field. I believe her to be the teacher, dear friend."

"O' shut it! We still captured here aye?"

"A thousand to one seem like a fair fight to you?"

"Yes!"

"Sure, mate, why don't you ask the fifty bodies we buried the other day? Or the hundred or so wounded. Tell me what they think, why don't you."

"Didn't I tell you to shut it? We got a job to do—focus on that."

"Alright? But why is that you think you're in charge?"

"I'm considerably older than you, chap. Enough of that mumbling. Help me unchain her!"

"How long has she been here? She's disgusting . . . filthy."

"I am not sure. No, no, unhook her ankles first."

"The mice have begun to pick at her."

"They must've been drawn by her scent. Vermin adore the company of other vermin."

"She's a vermin?"

"Might as well be—she defended them. Don't feel pity for her now, do you?"

"I guess not. Here, I'll catch her body."

"Why bother? She won't feel it."

"Respect, mate."

"Do you coddle your rubbish before tossing it out? Same concept here."

"She'll be easier to carry."

"If this little thing is really that heavy, we can just drag her."

"She's beautiful."

"Shut your mouth right now! I could have you hanged for such a slip of the tongue! No woman is more beautiful than the queen herself. You know the law."

"Apologies, Jeroh. Never again will I speak ill of the queen."

"Good. Watch your feet. Here she comes!"

"Ew! Did you hear the sound her head made? I told you that I could've caught her."

"She didn't feel it! Toss her over your shoulder and let's leave."

"I should have worn less armor. I can hardly bend."

"What did I tell you about the mumbling? Hand me your sword and shield."

"Much appreciated . . . she's rather warm for a corpse."

"Are you going to pick her up or hold her hand the entire time? Come on, let's go. I'm not here to be your patsy all day."

"But she's still warm. Maybe she's—"

I lunged.

For a moment we were nothing but tangled pieces of body parts and metal. The other man, Jeroh, fumbled with his sword before beginning to charge at me. I pushed the younger one aside and then turned my attention to Jeroh's oncoming assault. Dodging his swing, I dipped below his arm and forced him onto the wall. With a quick pull I snapped his wrist. His cry pierced the air as he fell to the ground. Grabbing his mane, I slammed his head against the wall until he spluttered over his words and became unconscious.

I turned to the remaining guard. He cowered in the corner, barely able to hold the sword steady. I watched as he trembled, fear dominating him. A small gash was on the side of his head, a bit of blood dripping onto the floor. He was rather young. Too young to be a soldier yet too old to be a squire. He had childlike eyes, lost and afraid. Though he held a sword and carried a shield, I knew he was not yet a man.

"Calm yourself." My voice came scratchy and rough. "I will not harm you."

Incredulous, he eyed his fallen comrade. "I-I cannot set you free. Not if I want to live."

"I do not want to be released." I cleared my throat, stepping closer to him.

He tensed up, pointing his sword at me—an empty threat by all means. "What is it you want?"

"A few cups of water," I replied, kneeling down to his level. He pointed the sword so that it was at my neck. His hand quivering so desperately, I knew if he went for an attack he'd surely miss. Gently I removed the sword from his hand. "And some bread."

Breathing heavily, undeniably terrified, he replied, "I think that can be arranged."

CHAPTER 4

FORTUNATELY, I WAS GIVEN AS much water as I required, and they even allowed me several slices of bread. Unfortunately, I was once again handcuffed and escorted, only this time four guards surrounded me. Each well equipped to take me down, need be.

Once I was finally able to leave the dark cell I noticed that I was indeed underground. The soldier who I spared, who I now know to be James, told me I was brought to Ville Morte, a prison based in Lárnach, capital of Islocia. I had never ventured farther than the Iclin Forest just outside the Qingkowuat village. I had gone my entire life only hearing stories about the great kings and queens who ruled their kingdom. Never had I planned on coming here. Especially not under these terms. It has been said that Ville Morte sends its prisoners to fight to death if their punishment cannot be decided. It has also been said that the monarchs' beasts are set free to eat the bodies left after the duel.

The guards and I made a turn down another stone-walled tunnel. We passed several heavy wooden doors that I knew led to a cell similar to the one I had been in. It was dark in the tunnels, the only source of light being the torches that clung to the walls. The shadows they created danced before us, toppling over themselves to salvage any hint of darkness. They too basked in the imminence of fear. "Where am I being taken?"

"Bite your tongue, vermin," a guard to my left hissed, shoving me forward. I stumbled, accidently falling into the guard in front of me. He turned and slapped me across the face. It hurt more than usual, considering he was doused in his armor. "Walk on!"

Rage fumed inside me. It took every bit of restraint to hold myself back. They believed that numbers ensured their safety; I wanted desperately to prove them wrong.

The guard behind me, to my left, stuck his foot out, causing me to stumble into the guard ahead of me. Again. This time he used the handle of his sword and thrust it into my gut. I coughed up my lungs while the guards behind me snickered. When I was finally able to breathe again, I stood up slowly and looked the guard in front of me dead in the eye.

"Walk on!" he ordered. I stood still. He stepped closer; the stench of wine and musk battled with the smell of my own filth. "I said, walk on." He voice lowered, menacingly. This man was rather large. I saw his arms and stomach spilling from the parts his armor didn't cover. He had a matted red beard with bits of rubbish clinging to the ends. His eyes, a dull blue and glazed over from a night of drinking, tried to penetrate my soul. He was to no avail.

Ignoring his tone, my eyes sliced through his overstated ego, and I felt as though I towered over him. Even though he stood a few inches taller than me. He was not the opponent he believed himself to be. I saw right through his façade. And he knew it.

"Walk on!"

"No."

Shock and a bit of fear flashed across his mask of indifference. I did not bow to his command; I did not give in to him.

Swallowing his uneasiness, he stepped forward so that his mouth was at my ear. "No one knows of your existence here. I own you. And it's ample time that someone taught you some manners." He stroked his finger along my thigh.

I leaned in closer to his ear and replied, "If it is death you want, I will most certainly oblige you."

Suddenly he grabbed me by my throat and squeezed as hard as he could! I gasped for breath as he looked me in the eye. With his other fist he punched me in my gut, still choking me! He did it again before releasing me. I fell to the ground, my lungs grabbing desperately for air.

"Walk on." He laughed.

Enough was enough.

I took my chained hands and slammed them against the knee of the guard to my left. With a loud crack he fell to the ground. Taking full advantage of the other guard's disbelief, I retrieved the fallen guard's sword and began my assault. In a matter of seconds I had slayed two of the guards, leaving only the filthy red-bearded bastard standing before me.

No longer hiding behind his numbers, he now quivered before me. I watched as nervous sweat dripped from his ghastly beard. I watched as piss trickled down his leg. I watched as his composure fell into bits and pieces. The soldier he claimed to be was no longer in this tunnel staring back at me. That man was long gone.

"I wouldn't do that if I were you," I hissed as his hand twitched for his sword. He took an involuntary step back just as I stepped forward.

"I apologize for my rudeness," he replied, continuing to step back. I matched his pace, making sure to only be a few feet away from him.

"Where are you running to?" I cooed, stalking after him. At that moment he stopped right underneath a torch. It took me too long to understand what was about to happen.

All of a sudden the torch was being thrown directly at me! I knocked the flame away with my sword just as the guard came charging at me with his sword drawn.

"Die!" he bellowed, swinging for my head. I ducked below him and went for his legs. He sidestepped just in time for me to miss his kneecap. He swung at me again. I held up my handcuffs to shield myself. His sword hit a loose chain directly, freeing me. I dodged another plunge of his sword and was able to strike his arm. Blood spilled from his armor as he let out a pain-bearing wail. I did not pause for his agony. I continued my attack. I struck his other arm, kicked his sword out of his hand, and forced him to the ground. He tried to surface, but I finished him off with a few haymakers and a final roundhouse kick to the face!

He lied there gasping in pain and hanging on to life by his fingernails. I knelt down to his level. Blood dripped from his face and created a puddle on the floor. He was broken. "Mercy," he pleaded, choking on death. "God . . . has mercy . . . on a dying . . . soul."

"I am not your god. And I have no mercy for a dying man." With that I slit his throat and watched the life drain from him and seep into the cracks.

It wasn't too much longer when I heard another group of guards approaching. I hadn't seen them yet, meaning, I had just enough time to calculate another attack . . .

"Good grief! What the hell happened here?"

"Fucking massacre . . ."

"You—no, not you—you! Check to see if any of them are living. Hurry!"

"What about the girl?"

"What girl?"

"The one slouched against the wall."

"She probably tried to escape. Leave her last. Hurry now, check our men!"

"Dear God! They're all dead."

"Bloody mess."

"How?"

"Why?"

"Who?"

I lunged from the wall, immediately killing the guard closest to me. Now that my eyes were open I counted seven guards. With only a second's worth of hesitation, they all charged.

In the end I killed four and was, once again, apprehended. Except, this time, I was escorted with a knife to my throat. The only reason I hadn't killed all of these guards was because the previous mental and physical tortures from my cell had taken a toll on me. With every thrust of my sword there was an irrefutable bite of soreness. Which was to be expected, considering the amount of stress caused to them.

"What is it we will do with her?" the guard behind me asked.

There was a pause before a response. "Throw her in the lion's den. Drown her. Hang her. I do not care as long as she is dead!" Presumably, the head of the trio responded.

Another pause. "Why not feed her to the arena?"

"Excuse me?" We made a sharp turn, which then led us into another stone-walled hallway.

"Make her fight in the arena." The question, which nobody had asked, hung in the air until he answered it. "She murdered four guards in cold blood. Show her how it feels!"

"She is a female."

"We throw children in there! Against grown men!" I am not one to weep for the weak, though hearing that certainly started a fire inside me.

"The arena?"

"Yes!"

We stopped marching as the trio pondered the notion.

"The arena . . ." He eyed me. Looking me up and down, he wrote his assessment on the comical look plastered on his face. "She will not last the drawing of the swords. Hald and Geraul will have a nice appetizer before the real feast."

They all laughed as we began walking in the opposite direction.

* * *

"Go on! Move it!" They thrust me into a set of hidden stairs that led up into the first pitcher of sunlight I had seen since I was captured. Once I had reached the top of the stairs I was forced to shield my eyes from the nauseatingly welcomed rays that burned the days in that cell away. When I had almost adjusted to the deadly light, I noticed the ground rumbling below me. Looking up I saw the masses of people cheering and applauding . . . for me?

Dazed, I absorbed my new surroundings. I was standing on a sand field stained in blood. There were a handful of lifeless bodies scattered around as well. Encompassing me were thousands of Royals losing their minds in the hype of this "sport" I assumed I would be participating in. They were all dressed in their most colorful best and were seated in a stadium that seemed almost the size of a peasant village. It stretched up like the clouds and spread wide like the sea. When I had almost made a full turn, partly dizzy from all the noise, I noticed a secluded area where only a few sat. It was raised a little higher than the other seats, and there were several guards on the outskirts and a few standing behind the center of the seclusion. Homing in on the center of this "private party," I saw the child slaves chained to their post!

As quickly as my brain had made the connection, I planted my knees and face to the ground and bowed down. *I can't believe it!* Inhaling the sand, I braved a second look. *It can't be!* She sat there. Magnificently beautiful, power dripped from her brow and spread throughout the entire arena. Doused in the brightest colors and outlined by the most precious gems and metals, she sat high up as to underscore her might! She was indeed the most majestic, prevailing, poised, and elegant being that had ever touched the earth. Let alone my eyes. Directly to her right and left sat two enormous male lions. Their golden fur shined in the sunlight like a flame at night. The massiveness of these animals was almost as intimidating as the godlike person they guarded.

"Get up," a voice to the side muttered. I rose slowly, dusting the sand from my bare legs, arms, and belly. "I'm the Tyblant," a short stocky man said while coming up beside me. "It means game keeper!" he clarified, noting my confusion. "Do as I say if you want to live." He then stepped forward and spoke to the audience. "My lords! My ladies! It is today of which the hand of life and the hand of death clash together to assume dominance over the lives of these withered souls. It is now that evil and its twin"—he turned and winked at me, causing an eruption of laughter from the crowd—"fight to the death!" Applause poured throughout the arena. The Tyblant held up his hand to silence the crowd. "Those who fight today do not despise who is against them. But love that of which is being fought for. Freedom! And their love of our most astounding monarch. Queen Ophelia Valkiria Asphodel Acheros of Islocia!" The entire stadium exploded into shouts and screams of delights toward the queen. Unable to stare too long, I saw her smile and issue a practiced wave of gratitude.

"Fighters!" the Tyblant continued. "Make you presence known!" He walked toward me and whispered, "Salute the Grand Royals then bow again to the queen after you state your name."

I stood in the middle of the arena as it suddenly became very quiet. Only the yawn of one of the royal lions occupied the unexpected silence. Looking up at the fierce kings, I mumbled, "I guess it wasn't a rumor after all."

"What?" the Tyblant hissed. "Never mind that, I do not care. Introduce yourself!"

I said nothing.

"Please!" He desperately looked at the restless crowd as the silence carried on.

I stood silent, watching as the lion licked the dried blood from its teeth.

"It seems our first contender is nameless." He forced a laugh to lighten the mood. "Moving on. Our next opponent hails from the Rhine village. A ravaged and revolting place that welcomes the slaughter of infants and arrests civility."

The audience's attention now turned to the opposite side of the arena. Ascending the stairs was man with muscles rolling along his arms, down his abdomen, and in his lengthy legs. He stood several feet taller than me, weighed a hundred pounds heavier than me. Our age was equal. My ability to kill unmatched. He eyed me with his pale eyes with a shadow of a smirk plastered over his chiseled face.

He spoke. "My queen." He bowed and then saluted the Grand Royals. "I am Crox Donan! Hear me roar!" Again the audience flew into a frenzy as he imitated the royal lions. He pointed to me. "Death to you!" I understood the game now.

Skepticism took the place of the sun as it shined bright around me. Now that my opponent was known, I was no longer favored to be victorious. Doubt, accompanying incredulity, suffocated the emptiness the air filled. The weight of their disapproval did not affect my stride. I did not falter nor did I hesitate. I sauntered into position. I would be released back into my comforts, the forest, only if I were to win. I understood. I understood that my life depended on me being victorious. Therefore, there would be one victor; it would be me.

"Death determines the victor! Each will be afforded one weapon." Crox was handed a sword while I was thrown my boe. The guards must've seized it from the clearing after they captured me. "There are no rules binding them, except they must stay within the arena!" The Tyblant moved to a safe place along the edge of the arena. "My Lords! My Ladies! It is time! I give you . . . *Les Combats*! May blood fertilize this hallow ground!"

With the sounding of a bell, it began.

Crox Donan resembled an ape as he charged at me. His movements fueled by rage only made it so much easier to calculate my attack. He would not be able to comprehend the slight crouch in my stance or the position of my weapon. No, he is only thinking of an obvious place to strike.

Closing my eyes, I counted the strides until he was within an arm's reach.

One . . . two . . . three . . . four . . . five . . . six . . .

Opening my eyes, I blocked the swing of his arm just as he was to strike. In that same second I shoved him back a few feet using my shoulder to move his large body. Incredulous, he paused for the slightest hint of a second. I, on the other hand, did not wait. Taking my boe in both hands, I struck his jaw! Shocked, he stumbled backward, silencing the crowd. I advanced. Again I struck his face and then his stomach. He did not have time to counter my attack! I hit him again before he crashed to the ground. Finally I allowed him rest.

Rising, he cupped his bleeding jaw and drew his sword. "Death to you! Death to you!" Crox charged at me, controlled by anger, steered by embarrassment. It was my turn to return his earlier smirk.

He swung wide, giving me the ability to duck beneath his blow and plow him in the stomach. I landed a few more gut blows before sliding under his legs, creating a cloud of sand. Anchoring my boe in the ground I quickly pulled myself upright, prepared for his next attack. He turned quickly, wielding his sword! In one swift move I gripped my boe, swung around, and landed a kick to his abdomen! I did not hesitate to yank my boe from the earth and rapidly beat him senseless.

Head!

Stomach!

Shoulder!

Knee!

Stomach!

Leg!

Stomach!

Knee!

Repeat!

Blow after blow, he took them graciously. I spun backward, giving him time to stagger about before he truly registered his pain. With my next move I hit him in the stomach; he bowed forward. Perfect. His face was level with mine. Using the tip of my boe, I thrust it up into his chin with as much strength as charging bulls; his feet left the ground! Within seconds his body came back to the earth but not before I finished him. Allowing the boe to slide to the end of my hand, I cocked back and swung! His head the ball, my boe the bat. A deafening crack accentuated my victory. Crox Donan was no more.

A cold hush swept the arena. The crowd no longer showed their vigorous joshing or stereotypical mockery. I stood before them no more than a soldier and no less than a woman. Pleased, my boe as my cane, I strolled to Crox's body and wiped away his blood using his bare chest as a towel.

I addressed the crowd.

"I am Arianna Korinthos!" I bellowed. "He is not my first kill. And he is certainly not my last!"

I began walking away from the middle of the arena when the crowd announced their delight in their new victor! Pausing, I basked in the uplifting ambiance and then turned to face the queen.

She held up her hand and all went silent. Again I bowed to her and laid down my weapon. The queen whispered to the slave to her left and then sat upright on her throne.

"Her Grace would like to see more." The young slave spoke eloquently as the queen eyed me from her perch. "Send out . . . three more prisoners."

Just as the last word fell from her mouth, three more men just like Crox Donan charged me from the corner of the arena.

Taking a deep breath, I counted.

One . . . two . . . three . . . four . . . five . . . six . . .

"Her Grace is pleased with your accomplishments. It has been many moons since such a competitor has come forth." The slave bent to listen to the queen before speaking again. "It seems Her Grace would like to invite you to dine with her. If you so accept, she would prefer more appropriate attire." More whispering from the queen. "My apologies. Her Grace does not request your presence. She demands it."

Kneeling, I replied, "It would be my honor to accompany you, Your Majesty."

The queen simply replied by nodding her head in approval.

"My lords and my beautiful ladies! Her Majesty, the Queen, bids her good-bye!" The Tyblant returned to the middle of the arena. "May God forever lay their hands on your gracious shoulders. May your days be long and filled with grace. Long live the queen!"

"Long live the queen!" the crowd replied in unison. The queen smiled at the crowd before leaving with her posse of polished clones and armed guards. The audience cheered for her departure, longing for her return. It wasn't often that the queen left her palace. I have not the slightest idea as to why.

"Milady." A guard came from behind me, grabbing my elbow. "It would be in your best interest to accompany me to the palace."

"Why is that?" I asked, pulling free.

"It is feeding time," he hissed just as the royal lions were beginning to be unchained.

The Belle Palace was the most remarkable site I had ever had the pleasure of seeing. Larger than an entire country, more magnificent than diamonds and gold. It was the most beautiful thing I had ever had the pleasure of gazing upon, with the exception of the queen.

"Beautiful, isn't she?" the old man sitting across from me said. The horse-drawn carriage dipped into a hole before returning to the gravel path. "King Ano Domonic, the one who suggested the design, wanted to break away from the traditional architecture of the stone castles. He wanted beauty and grace. He wanted something elegant yet asserted power. The queen at the time, Josephine Armio Domonic of Yenyun, wanted a beautiful courtyard to raise her children in. A courtyard so magnificent that only the Gods could admire it. If you were to stand upon the palace you would see the intricate swirls of the hedges and beautiful placements of the plants. Yohn Palácies was the architect. He worked seven years on the palace. And once it was complete, he marveled at his work for two days before the king summoned his death."

I turned to look at the man. He gazed out of the window as the carriage made its way to the front of the palace. He was not a guard nor was he a Royal. His clothes were heavily worn and certainly less than fine linen. He didn't have a weapon with him, but the guard to my left certainly did. At the time I was unsure as to why.

"Why did he have him killed?"

He paused just as the carriage began passing under a row of trees with white leaves dangling overhead.

"Angels' Teardrops," he said, catching a fallen leaf and twirling it in his fingers. It was then that I noticed he was in chains. "King Diam Fiton named them just before his beheading. He claimed that the leaves were the millions of innocent souls that the Acheros family *will* and *have* destroyed."

"Why was the man killed?" I asked again, though that wasn't my only question.

"King Ano wanted to be the only one with this particular design." He sighed just as the carriage pulled to a stop in front of the palace.

The door was opened by one of the many guards standing around the front steps to the palace. Just as I exited the carriage, the man said, "Good days to you." And then he was gone.

I pondered his words for a little while but was soon interrupted by a cheerful pale-faced Royal. "Milady," he said, walking down the steps. His clothes were so . . . different compared to the rags and sheepskin of the Qingkowuats. They were pointy at the shoulders and tight around his skinny waist. His inky black hair was shoulder length and glistened in the sun; never have I ever seen such a feminine man. "I am Jepson Forthtude of Lárnach Islocia. It is my pleasure to escort you today. Her Majesty is looking forward to dining with you this evening."

I responded with a nod, feeling extremely lascivious in my attire. I looked down at my short cloth skirt that barely covered my rear and my makeshift bra that was see-through when wet. And how could I ever ignore my bare toes while everyone who surrounded me at that moment wore pointy coverings for their feet.

Jepson's eyes lingered much longer than mine did as I finished assessing myself. I shifted restlessly to regain his attention. "You are . . ." He cleared his throat. "Second to the queen, milady." He continued staring before finally recomposing himself into his cheerful, rather than lustful, being. "Harrison!" he barked, turning to face one of the guards. "Bring a robe for our lovely guest. Immediately." Harrison nodded once before charging into the palace. Jepson turned back to me with a sinful smile. "We wouldn't want to upset Her Majesty."

It wasn't long before Harrison returned with a long red silk robe to cover me. I fastened the belt just as he placed some fancy coverings on the ground.

"Shoes are required in the palace," Jepson said, noting my confusion.

"What is it they are called?" I asked. "Shoos?"

He chuckled. "O', my dear. You certainly have much to learn. Lucky for you, that is what I am here for." He continued chuckling as we made our way into the palace. I followed him up the steps as all the guards outlining them saluted us.

CHAPTER 5

As expected, the palace's décor was elegant beyond words. Bright beautiful colors decorated the sky-high walls; large glass openings allowed the sun to pour into the palace like wine at a wedding. Everything was pristine, from the picturesque flowers assorted on vintage vases to the soft swirls created by the marble floors. The architecture on the outside seeped its way into the cement walls, creating a sophisticated and embellished look. The palace was more amazing than any home in Lárnach! Nothing could compare! Not the castles along the coast or the mansions in the mountains. It was pure perfection.

"Beyond words," I muttered, gazing at the monarch's paintings aligning the walls.

"Yes, yes, it is," Jepson agreed, offering me his arm. I obliged and he guided me through the rest of the palace. "You see, milady, the Belle Palace was meant to symbolize the monarchy. It is strong, beautiful, assertive, and unworldly. No one, not even the Grand Royals of Astinian—the most wealthy city—could ever commandeer any worthy comparisons to the Belle. Her Majesty and the monarchs before her understood that. As you should too."

"I understand." The rest of the tour consisted of crystal chandeliers glistening from the ceiling, priceless artifacts, and several Royals mingling in their designated social areas. Jepson explained that there were seven hundred rooms that were able to house around twenty thousand Royals. He also said that there were 2,000 glass coverings—windows—1,250 fireplaces, 67 staircases, and more than 1,800 acres of park. The palace was prominently immense in stature and perceptibly spacious. Ten horses could fit comfortably aligned next to each other from wall to wall in the hallways. It was indeed impressive.

Just as we ascended one of the sixty-seven staircases, we stopped in front of a room. He motioned for me to walk in, but I hesitated.

"Milady, this is Rye Beddon." He acknowledged the girl who stepped out from the room. She was not a Royal, for she wore a plain gray dress that did not compare to the Royals', but her hands were clean. Her eyes never left the floor, and I noticed Jepson did not talk directly to her. "She will dress you and care for you for the duration of your stay. I'll see you at dinner. If you need anything, ask any of the slaves. They are at your disposal."

"Slaves?" I eyed Rye Beddon and noticed she was wearing similar clothing to the other young girls cleaning and caring for the Royals. "Slaves . . ."

"I bid my good-bye." Jepson bowed once before sauntering away.

Once I got into the room, Rye Beddon undressed me with tender fingers, filled a large porcelain tub with hot water, and bathed me from head to toe. At first, I wasn't too sure about this sort of treatment, but she reassured me with her tender smile that she would pose no threat to my life.

As she was bathing me, she used these slippery bars with relishing scents to wipe away the blood and grime from my twenty and four years of uncleanliness. When the washing was complete, she helped me from the bowl and stood me in the middle of my large and immaculate room. Nude as a newborn, I watched as she pulled several layers of clothing out of one of the many closets along the far wall. Rye did not look me in the eye nor did she speak a single word, unless I spoke to her first. Her moves were quick and practiced as she slipped a silk under garment over me before presenting the actual frock. It was the same color of the sky just before it rained; light grey. Never had I worn something so elegant or stunning in my life. For years I was subjected to the rotten fabric I was able to sew together. For years I was forced to slaughter sheep and wear their hide for clothes. For years I wore rags; now I wore *real* garments.

"I do not have kerts," I said just as she was about to put the finishing touches on.

She looked at me quizzically before saying, "Need no kerts, need no kerts."

Once we were done she brought a large mirror into the room so I could marvel at the beautiful woman before me. This woman did not resemble the killer she truly was. Her long, dark-brown hair flowed just past her shoulders and created a sheath around her beautiful face. Her lips were tipped red, complementing her sharp hazel eyes. Continuing down her stature, she had enticing curves from her breast to her hips, the gown covering her thin figure and toned legs. The woman before her was indeed beautiful . . . from a distance. Up close, someone could see the scars that marred her arms and legs. Up close someone could see the suffering and pain from the many years ago that she tried so desperately to tuck away. Up close someone could see the devilish gleam in her eye and the swiftness of her deadly hands. Up close this woman was not beautiful—she was lethal.

"*Plus belle que la beauté* (More beautiful than beauty)," Jepson muttered, standing just outside the door. Rye Beddon bowed once for the Royal before scurrying out the room. "Milady, it would be my honor to escort you to the queen's court."

"I was under the impression I would be dining with the queen," I responded, turning away from the mirror and leaving the woman behind.

"Unfortunately, milady"—Jepson licked his lips as his eyes approved of my gown—"Her Majesty cannot denounce her busy day. She will meet you in her meeting chamber. Once we arrive she will dismiss the congregation for the day and head for the dining hall. There, we will dine with the rest of the selected members of court. Come with me." I took his arm and we headed out the room.

"Why was I bathed?" I asked as we started working our way down the marble steps.

"You now mingle among the lords and ladies of Islocia. It is only right that you are treated as such. Also, you had a bit of an odor when you arrived." He winked, eyeing me suggestively. "Dining with the queen is as great an honor as any. Considering your background, I assume you would want to know how to dine with royalty?" I nodded and he continued. "It is not only the queen you will be dining with. The Grand Royals, who are the queen's most appreciated associates, and King Charles H. Araun of Kreni. Also Lord Jamison and his squire Thompson Arch will also be dining with you. Lord Jamison is head of the Royal Army. Do not mistake him for the head of the Shadows—"

"What are the Shadows?" I asked as we made our way down another extravagant hallway.

"They . . . protect the monarchy in ways the Royal Army can't. It's certainly none of your concern," he replied quickly. "Moving on!" He continued talking about plates and silverware and etiquette, but my mind did not follow. How could it? This was all incredibly unreal! I went from watching the waves to fighting an army to being imprisoned to fighting for my life in the arena for the queen to being bathed and dressed without lifting a finger to being invited to dine with royalty. Simply unheard of! Was I being set up for death? Did the queen have some ulterior motive that resulted in my humiliation? Would I ever return to the forest again?

"My dear," Jepson whispered, tugging on my arm, "remember you must bow before your queen whenever you are in her presence."

Forcibly dragging myself out of my thoughts, I noticed we were no longer dancing through hallways and sidestepping child slaves. We were in an entirely different realm! The room stood several dozen feet tall, covered in magnificent drawings of battles and victories and castles and angels and kings and queens and wealth and prosperity! Gorgeous colorful glass windows manipulated the sun's rays into beautiful beams of wonder. A long, red, silk carpet started at the entrance of the room and flowed up to the stone steps that housed—

Poised gallantly in her royal attire and radiating power, the queen sat upon her golden throne. Those who stood before her, on either side of the carpet, bowed beneath her might. The queen, with her pale skin, brown eyes, and plaited auburn hair, stared down at her subjects who surrendered their souls to her. To the left and right of her were the Grand Royals standing a few steps away. Two guards stood directly behind the golden throne while another dozen aligned the steps.

I bowed before the queen. My queen.

"Rise," she commanded in her assertively high-pitched voice. Immediately everyone rose to their standing positions in unison. "What is it you have brought me, Jepson?"

"My most honorable queen"—Jepson bowed his head—"your guest has arrived."

"Approach." She waved us forward.

I began walking forward and felt every eye in the room glued to me. There were no whispers or snickers present; the silence was filled with hushed gusts of winds and the soft thud of my coverings on the carpet. When I reached the steps, the guards aligning it drew their swords!

I stopped.

The queen looked me over for several long minuets, her thin face portraying nothing short of indifference. The silence dragged on as she signaled me to turn around as if she were memorizing every inch of me.

"Jepson," she said, still looking at me, "I am famished. It is time to eat." Then she took her leave.

* * *

Like every other room in the palace, the dining hall was no exception to the rule of extravagance. This room was large and wonderfully decorated. There was a large wooden table that stretched from one end of the room to the other, seating over forty people. Jepson called it the Porcelain Room. I could easily understand why. The table was decorated with three silver candle sets placed equally from each other. Also on the table were white plates imported overseas coordinated with their napkins and silverware.

"You will be sitting in the middle. The seat at the head of the table nearest to the window is where Her Majesty will be seated. Nearest to her will sit the Grand Royals. The seat opposite to the queen will be where His Majesty will sit. Nearest to him will be Lord Jamison and his squire as well as a few other high-ranked guards. That leaves the middle seats for us. I will be sitting directly across from you. Watch what I do when we begin eating."

"That's quite a lot of information," I said, eyeing the arrangement.

"I have an overwhelming feeling that you, my dear, can handle it." He smiled. "A slave will enter the room and ring a bell, signaling us to position ourselves by our seats." Just then a short, chubby boy draped in rags entered the room and rang the bell. The Royals moved into place; I did as I was told and luckily found my seat on the first try. We stood for a few minutes without any hint toward us taking a seat. I eyed Jepson, and he shook his head just as I was about to pull my chair out. Then another child slave came out, only this time he played a horn instrument thing.

The queen entered the room and stood in front of her chair. We all bowed our heads in respect. The king then entered and stood before his chair. Again we bowed.

The king was not what I was expecting him to be. He was a tall, muscular man with a perfectly aligned brown beard that started from his temples, curved around his lip, wrapped around his chin, and ended at a perfectly tipped point. His rusty brown hair was shoulder length and tied back into a masculine ponytail. The king's gentleness matched his soft green eyes almost perfectly. Though blessed with the title of being a monarch, he was not a man you would fear when standing before him. He was a man you would respect. The king had to be two decades older than the queen, who I believed matched my age. The stresses of running an entire kingdom showed in the king's sandy, weathered skin.

The king motioned for the queen to take a seat. When she sat, he sat; and when he sat, we finally sat.

Standing behind the chairs were twice as many young slaves as there were guests. It was quite an odd feeling being waited on hand and foot. Especially by children.

"Excusez-moi, le vin est maintenant servi!" the boy who rang the bell said. I looked over to Jepson, completely lost in translation. He smiled understandingly and shaped his hand like a cup and pretended to drink from it. "If you would like some wine, please gesture to the servers."

Two frail girls dressed in pale-gray dresses entered the dining hall with a leather sack full of wine. They went down the rows and filled every cup that wanted it. I did not. I needed a clear mind if I was to accurately assess the situation and the characters involved.

At the top of the table, surrounding the queen, were the Grand Royals. All female and all very similar to the queen. They all wore layers of tight clothing underneath what seemed like heavy dresses. Though they did look beautiful in them. The Grand Royals continued a conversation amongst each other. They all seemed so delicate and so fragile; obviously their money bought them their power. At the end of the table to the left of the king was Lord Jamison. Lord Jamison was an impressively muscular man with icy pale-gray eyes and shoulder-length silver hair, although he wasn't old. He had a stern face that mirrored that of a person who was smelling something quite awful. His squire sat across from him, a short child of a man with a playful tone to his voice. Going down the line were a handful of guards all built and armed. Even the one sitting next to me. Probably the most well-trained and deadliest guards in all of Islocia.

"Is it me or is there a vermin at the table?" one of the Grand Royals asked, silencing the dining hall. "Don't pretend like I was the only one who could smell it!"

The other Grand Royals giggled at her comment, sipping their wine and lowering their inhibitions.

"Your Grace, why is it that you have brought such an abhorrent creature to dine amongst your most esteemed lords and ladies?" She laughed, eyeing me over the lip of her glass. "We must be sure to clean her place setting thoroughly. Certainly we would not allow her to spread her diseases and filth to *us*!"

"Clarice!" the woman across from her chided in mock empathy. "Do not chastise the poorly bred; rather, the *breeder* should endure your tongue lashings. Only an incompetent beast could produce something so wretched—" The knife that was originally tucked inside my napkin sliced through the air, cutting the end of her comment short as it breezed past her ear and pierced the wall behind her.

"That you are alive does not mean I lack the ability to kill you!" I hissed, reaching for my fork. The guards surged from their seats and drew their swords. Still, I continued. "I am no virgin to death. Your head on my plate would satisfy me just as much as the meal they are about to present. Do not allow your mind to stray from that. Because the next time I ponder your life, I will not miss."

The dining hall sank into silence, all eyes on me, awaiting my next move. The queen stared at me utterly entertained. *I'd hate to disappoint.*

Swiftly I took my fork and stabbed the guard next to me. During his moment of disbelief, I grabbed him by his head and cracked it against the ceramic plates, shattering them. I retrieved his sword. Lord Jamison hurled himself over a chair and stood only a few feet away from me, both of our swords drawn. I charged first. Our swords clashed together, sending sparks onto the table and burning the gold tablecloth. Lord Jamison was indeed a skilled fighter. The other guards were about to join in, but he waved them off. "She's mine!"

His moves were unpredictable, and I had less than a second to mimic his strikes. We did our dance around the table, knocking over chairs and spilling the wine. I was tired of this game; I knew I could win. He swung for my head; I dipped below it and pushed his arm into the air, leaving his chest wide open. With as much strength as possible I tackled him to the ground. My dress constricted my moves, but I was able to climb on top of his chest. I hadn't realized he still had his sword. Simultaneously our swords ended up at the other's throat.

"Enough!" the queen ordered. "Enough. Lower your weapons."

Lord Jamison inched his sword closer to my throat; I did the same to his. The other guards lowered their weapons, but I did not and neither did he. We were deadlocked.

"Lord Jamison," the queen said sternly. "Lower your weapon first. She will follow."

He hesitated a moment longer before eventually throwing his sword to the side and throwing his hands up in surrender. Satisfied, I rose from his breastplate and leaned my sword against the moaning soldier I had defaced with the plate and returned to my seat. Lord Jamison's squire rushed around the table to help him up. Once upright, he tucked his sword away and returned to his seat as well.

"Now that that is settled. Lady Aren"—the queen said to Clarice, Aren being her last name—"apologize to my guest. As will you, Lady Dynia."

"My sincerest of apologies," Lady Aren muttered, slurring her words and finishing her glass of wine.

"I most certainly apologize," Lady Dynia followed. Everyone who had plastered themselves to the wall during the scuffle slowly and cautiously returned to their seats.

They awaited my response.

"I'd like a glass of wine now." I smiled, lifting my empty cup. "And how about one for my friend here?" I gestured toward the bleeding, grousing, gurgling guard.

For that, I was awarded a sinful smile from the queen.

* * *

"You asked for me, Your Majesty?" the room the queen had called me in was large and elegantly furnished. I had received word that she had wanted to speak with me toward the end of the day. Naturally, I assumed she was going to ask me to leave the palace and return the dresses she had bought for me. My behavior at the dinner party most likely assured my leave of luxury.

Her Majesty was lounging poetically on a large chaise with one of her dozen or so ladies-in-waiting reading her a sonnet. When the queen heard me come in, she raised her porcelain hand to silence the reading and smiled indulgently at me. "Lady Korinthos, please come in," she said in her loving, soft voice. With her right hand, she stretched it out toward me, and with her left she waved off her ladies.

Puzzled, I waited outside the room, not sure if she were speaking to me. I was no Lady—why had she called me that?

"Come in, come in." She was looking right at me as she was speaking, but she had not said my name. I was only Arianna. Not a Royal who deserved a title as grand as Lady anything. "Lady Korinthos," she said the name again, slower. "*You* are Lady Korinthos. Come in. I will not ask again."

Accepting the invitation, I entered her lavish room and stood a few feet in front of her. Her Majesty eyed me skeptically but managed to maintain perfectly composed. "Good afternoon, Lady Korinthos. Thank you for joining me."

I nodded appreciatively. "The honor is forever mine, Your Majesty. Although I am confused. Why are you calling me outside my given name?"

A soft, trilling laugh escaped her as she stared at me. "Dear girl, do you not recognize the compliment?" My silence told her I did not. She continued. "I am giving you the title Lady Korinthos. You are now an official member of my court."

"Your Majesty . . ." I gasped, my hand trembling. A member of court? Me? Yesterday I was Arianna Korinthos; now I am Lady Korinthos? This must be a dream.

She smiled a very diplomatic smile and offered me wine, but not without saying, "Pour mine first, then help yourself." Obediently I did as I was told, still shell-shocked. There had to be some sort of mistake . . . I was not worthy enough to be a Lady of Queen Ophelia's court. I was nothing compared to the Royals.

After a few moments of silence I thought that perhaps that was all she needed from me, until finally she spoke again. "I wanted to enjoy a moment of your company. I know that this transition must be very overwhelming to you."

Releasing a shaky breath, I smiled anxiously, not wanting to offend her by not saying the right thing. "I've never been more appreciative, Your Majesty. Thank you." I shifted restlessly on my feet, wondering if she would ever offer me a place to sit.

"Don't flatter me, my dear," she replied simply. "Your comfort means a lot to me, Lady Korinthos."

There it was again! That title! So prestigious . . . so honorable. "The fact that Your Majesty has taken interest in in my well-being is plenty enough comfort for someone of my . . . background," I said nervously, toying with the glass in my hand. More silence stretched between us, the awkwardness settling in. *Lady Korinthos . . . Lady Arianna Korinthos?* If only the Conqueror could see me now. Lady Korinthos. There were millions of things running through my mind! I wanted to thank her, kiss her feet, anything to show my appreciation! But I had to think logically now. Why would she give *me* this title? What value could I have to a monarch?

Her Majesty, ever so clever and lofty, asked, "Is there something more you wish to say?" The queen was every bit the monarch people expected her to be. She was self-assured, calm, and graciously accepting. She had the warmest smile that made me want to open up to her and let my guard down.

Sighing, I replied, "Your Majesty has been exceedingly gracious by allowing me all these luxuries . . . I'm wondering . . . why is it that you believe I deserve it. It was merely a fortnight ago that I was nothing more than a mere slave to the forest and then the arena."

Her response was quick and to the point. "You proved yourself to be very useful to me. Therefore, I wanted to reward you."

I thought for a moment, not entirely convinced. "The dinner would have sufficed. The rooms, the dresses, everything else . . . it seems a little overindulgent."

Nodding, she smiled. "Lady Korinthos, you will soon learn that in this court, among these people, for every one friend you acquire there are ten enemies lurking alongside you." She held my gaze, her brown eyes searching for understanding. "Loyal relationships are important to establish." I wanted to blush at the compliment, but her words continued. "However, I understand that your . . . circumstance . . .

isn't conventional for this court. Many of my councilors have relayed their distress at your presence and recent title—"

"I never meant to cause you any duress!" I was quick to explain, but she cut me off politely.

"As queen I am awarded the opportunity to ignore them. I like you, Lady Korinthos. You're not like these other plaster-faced, money-hungry degenerates that I allow to be in my space. No, you are real in a way that the Royals are not. I need a little more real in my fairytale life."

"Your Majesty . . . I don't know what to say . . ." The thought that Her Majesty held me to such a high standard flooded me with immense joy and satisfaction. The fact that I had come from squalor and despair to being raised to the queen's favor was . . . unheard of.

"You need not say anything," she replied, clearly satisfied with herself. "Remain loyal to me, and I will forever remain content with you."

Lady Arianna Korinthos, protector of the monarchy and Lady to Queen Ophelia Valkiria Asphodel Acheros of Islocia. Naturally, I was skeptical and wanted to turn the offer down, but Her Majesty was persistent and assured me that I would become a very valuable resource to her and all of Islocia. How could I refuse such a grand offer? I left my skepticism in the past and embraced the bright future that was laid before me.

The ceremony took place in *La Grande Galerie,* surrounded by all of the Royals. Never in my life had I found such a purpose. My queen brought me to the balcony of the palace and presented me to the kingdom. Crowds of people applauded and cheered for *me*. Even Her Majesty dipped into a curtsy. Lord Jamison, dressed in his best armor that mirrored the shine of his silver hair, reluctantly acknowledged me but was respectful when I was brought upon the twenty thousand guards of the Royal Army. They saluted my acceptance and bowed to me as if I were truly a Royal.

For months on end, I lived as one of the Royals. Fancy clothes and fancier food, overpriced jewelry and cheap conversations filled my life. The Grand Royals finally accepted me after I stopped a thief from snatching Lady Dynia's diamond necklace when we were making a rare appearance through the kingdom. I also learned to deal with the Royals who lived in the palace, and I conquered my dislike for cleanliness. Rye Beddon remained my handmaiden. I never lifted a finger to cleanse any part of my body. Hell, I didn't even dress myself. Jepson continued to remind me of the proper palace etiquette, and I learned new things from him every day. Although it was slow, we were soon becoming close friends.

My queen, who I irrevocably adored, treated me not as the vermin Lady Aren perceived me to be but as a friend and respected soldier. I followed her around every day and everywhere, from the time her twelve handmaidens dressed her to the time they undressed her for bed. When we were in court I stood proudly beside her as she spoke amongst her advisors. When we ate I sat to the chair to her left. My living arrangements moved from the common Royals' to the Grand Royals' apartments, which were close to the queen's.

Her Majesty showered me with gifts and praise. She was so happy to have me, and I was unbearably honored to be in her presence. She even threw a party just for me! My queen ordered the best wine, the best food, the fanciest attire, and the most renowned musicians. I had a chance to mingle with society's most acknowledged Royals and even spent time with the king. I learned that he is a kind fellow, so full of life yet very wise. I liked the king, I respected him.

However, I loved my queen.

In my mind, she could do no wrong. Everything she did was in the best interest of the kingdom. It was with a heavy heart that she sentenced bad men to death. She loved Islocia more than she loved herself. Queen Ophelia would die before she caused unjust harm to her kingdom or the people she vowed to protect. She was hardly the vile monarch the villagers pictured her to be. She was gracious and kind. Loving and admirable. I would die for my queen if she asked me to. I'd certainly kill for her.

CHAPTER 6

IT WAS MIDDAY, AND I was just on my way to riding out into the courtyard to check for any infractions before the queen went on her stroll, when I heard Jepson call me from the stairs. "Lady Korinthos. Walk with me. Her Majesty wishes to speak with you."

Immediately, I obliged and followed behind him. For a few long minuets it was deathly silent; only the metallic rasp of armor from the guards following us and the soft thud of our coverings filled the air. We walked through *La Grande Galerie,* and once again I was mesmerized by the beauty and elegance in the hall. I thought my queen would want to speak with me here. Instead we made our way into a different room, a room I hadn't known existed.

"Le salon de la Paix," my queen said, standing in the middle of the room. My queen was gorgeous with her bright red gown that tightened at her waist and flowed like water over the marble floors. Her gown was complemented by her heart-shaped headdress encompassed in gold thread and artistic designs. It was impossible not to stare; she shined as if the sun was plastered behind her. Probably from the gems hanging exquisitely from her neck and ears. "It is one of my favorite rooms in the palace." I surveyed the room, always dumbstruck by the massiveness and the unworldly attention to details in the antique allegories painted on the ceiling. It was nothing compared to *La Grande Galerie,* but it was another beautiful aspect of the palace.

"It is beyond words, my queen," I replied, staring at the two golden lions in front of the fireplace. They were obviously meant to represent Hald and Geraul, the royal lions from the arena. I turned to my queen when I noticed the silence that suddenly cloaked the room. "Your Majesty? Is everything alright?"

Her beautiful pale face did not depict the powerful rejoice that elated a room. It was now crumpled underneath the hand of sorrow and the bitter taste of agony. My queen was weighted by a burden so heavy it altered her entire persona.

"I love this room. So much history," she said somberly, turning to face me. "Do you see the oval painting above the fireplace? That is King Louis XIV handing out olive branches to his conquered enemies. It is a sign of peace. Look at the ceiling. Do you see the doves pulling the chariot? The chariot is carrying Islocia. Following behind the chariot is glory and immortality. It is also a testament to peace. I love my home. I love Islocia. It is a country of peace and serenity."

"You have done all Islocians proud, my queen," I responded, acknowledging the crafty artwork on the ceiling.

"Not all . . ." She bowed her head, overcome by shame.

"What do you mean?" I took an involuntary step closer. The guards behind me drew their swords. Her Majesty waved them off and patted her cheeks with a handkerchief.

"Lady Korinthos . . ." She began walking over to me. As she got closer I saw the suffering in her tears that *almost* fell. "Someone is trying to destroy my home."

"I will slay any man who defies you!" I vowed, kneeling before her. It had been quite some time since I unleashed that part of my past; however, I knew my skills would always be unmatched.

"I cannot protect Islocia on my own." She sobbed tearlessly. "I know that I have given you this title of nobility and have asked that you shed your past . . . however . . . I believe I might need you. Will you help me, Arianna?" My heart melted as she said my given name. It was a sign of friendship. "Will you help me save Islocia from the wretched claws of dismay?" She touched my shoulder.

"I vow it!" I felt my muscles ache with the need to stretch and showcase my skills. Any harm that could possibly threaten my queen would be slaughtered upon my arrival. Adrenaline shot electricity through my body, I becoming restless.

"Will you destroy the pestilent few who resist the kingdom and therefore resist *me*, their queen?"

"I vow it!" I was already calculating how long it would take to change out of my dress and into my natural attire.

"Will you"—she reached for my hand and helped me stand—"sacrifice the few inconsequential innocents in order to ensure and preserve the prosperity of the many who have a strong deference in the monarchy?"

"Death to all who defy you, my queen," I promised. "I vow it."

"We shall see. For I am willing to test your loyalty." Again, she dotted at her dry eyes.

"With all due respect, Your Grace. You have not brought me a challenge I have not conquered."

She smiled quizzically, her mood suddenly shifting, "Are you questioning my capabilities?"

"No Your Highness," I replied, returning her smirk. "I am simply reminding you of mine."

* * *

I am not one to weep for the weak. I believe that life selects the strong by demolishing the inadequate. It is not man's decision to be less than man. But it is life's decision to determine who will carry on. Life's decision. Not man's.

Blood poured from the skies and drenched the soil. Piercing screams hugged the flames that burned the huts to the ground with people still inside them. Death clung to the atmosphere sending men, women, and children into the arms of the deliverer. Bodies accumulated in the multitudes as the guards raced through the village. They slayed the weak; they demolished the inadequate. A fifteen-minute slaughter is what she called it. The guards are allowed to do whatever they please until the fifteen minutes are up. All at my queen's insistence.

"Vile vermin of the Naïf village," my queen preached, standing on her royal stool. A few of the Grand Royals had made the long trek to Iclin Forest: Lady Aren and Dynia. They stayed idle in their carriage, watching the events unfold as if it were the most entertaining thing they had ever seen. It was nothing more than a show to them, and I was brought along to add to the amusement. "This plaque of suffering was brought upon you by your own doing. Accept this consequence in hopes that God and his angels will forgive your insolence towards *my* throne—"

A woman's scream turned my attention away from my queen. Lord Jamison's squire had the woman by her hair and dragged her into the hut. I will never forget the sinful smile on his face or his dark eyes that were waiting to release wicked and detestable torture onto the woman. I will never forget the fear that wrecked her body and the hint of tolerance in her eyes.

"Guards!" my queen shouted. "Gather up all the villagers, and bring me their leader."

"Your Grace . . ." A gasping guard ran over to the queen. "Some of the villagers are on the run. Do you want us to retrieve them?"

Though the skies rained blood, and the screams fueled the flames. Though death surrounded us and innocence was lost, my queen pondered his notion as if she were taking a stroll through the courtyard. Then she turned to me and smiled. "No, continue to gather the villagers. Arianna will capture the escapees."

"Yes, Your Grace." The guard saluted her before returning to his task.

"If need be"—she continued talking to me—"kill them."

I nodded once. Again she smiled as I took to the forest.

Running at full speed, I sifted through the forest undergrowth. I wouldn't allow my mind to think of what was happening behind me. My queen had to protect her kingdom; therefore, certain things had to be done in order to assure her reign. Right?

The jagged hedges and grabby roots caught at my feet, tripping me. They were slowing me down so much that I knew I would never catch them in time. So I took to the trees. The bark dug a little deep into my skin as I hoisted myself up, but pain was rather easy to ignore. Once at the top of the tree, I began gliding from tree branch to tree branch. The forest moved past me in a blur. It was nothing but splotches of green and streaks of brown.

When I knew I was gaining on them, I began listening for them . . . the soft frantic beating of a panicked heart, rough naked feet running over thorns and getting caught in the roots hidden by the brushwood, and the hushed gasp one makes when they're exerting themselves. I was trained well enough to silence my body on command. They would never hear me shift in the trees. They would never hear my heart beat over theirs. And . . . they would never see me coming.

I continued making my way through the branches, hoping to catch them before they made it to the edge. If they were smart they'd head toward the river and follow it north. If they weren't smart then they'd continue straight and be cornered at the cliff.

It didn't take long until they were in sight. I knew it wouldn't have taken long to capture them. A moment, maybe two? I was prepared to do what Her Majesty asked of me. No matter the cost. However, the escapees weren't who I was expecting. There was a small boy, maybe six years of age, running behind who I assumed to be his mother with an infant swaddled in strips of cloth in her arms. The mother continued to look over her shoulder, waiting for any indignation of a pursuer. She never thought to look up in the trees.

"Faster, Jacob!" she called to the boy. "You must go faster!"

"Mama," he gasped, trying desperately to keep up. "Mama, slow down."

She looked back at her son but did not falter in step. The infant began to fuss, and she went faster.

"Mama, slow down. Help me," the boy sobbed. But his mother did not stop. "Help me, Mama, help me."

I jumped from my branch just as they were a few yards ahead of me. The mother saw me and made a dead sprint toward the river. I ran after them, easily catching up to the boy. I would've grabbed him if the satin lace of my coverings hadn't got caught in a shrub. I tumbled messily to the ground, snagging my arm on a thorny bush. The boy sped faster until he was only a foot or so away from his mother. When she turned to look back at me, an emotion flashed across her face. I couldn't recognize it right then, but it must've been the reason she turned and ran toward the cliff with her son following close behind her.

"Hurry, Jacob!" she screamed, dipping below a low branch and jumping over a fallen tree. "This way, Jacob. Hurry!" The boy followed his mother adamantly. They were out of sight in seconds; only the muffled shrieks of the infant could lead me to them.

I ran as fast as my damned coverings would allow me! My queen would be highly disappointed if I couldn't capture the escapees. Jumping over boulders, gliding over the ground, I charged through the forest. It wasn't long until I caught up to them. The mother was dragging the little boy with one hand and struggling to carry the infant in the other.

Suddenly, the ground had turned to sand. I was no longer avoiding the roots of the trees; I was no longer ducking beneath the low-hanging branches; streaks of brown and blurs of green no longer surrounded me. Only the gray sky above and the ugly depths of the unknown lie ahead. We were at the cliff.

"Stop!" I shouted, watching the mother continue to run for the edge of the cliff.

"Jacob, hurry!" The boy's feet were hardly touching the ground as she dragged him faster and faster!

"Hey, stop!" I shouted again. She turned and saw me coming and dragged the boy harder. His foot slipped on a loose stone, and he fell from his mother's grasp!

"Mama!" he screamed, lying in the dirt as she continued running. Tears filled her eyes as she turned back to look at her son. "Mama, help me! Mama!" The infant began crying as she slowed and contemplated going back for her son. But I already had him. He didn't put up much of a fight; he only reached for his mother. "Mama!"

She stopped and turned to look at me. Gasping and sobbing, she watched her son struggle in my arms screaming for her to rescue him. She did not move. Her boy, her little child that she gave life to, called for his mother! She did not move toward him. Instead she took a step back.

"Stop!" I said over the shrieking boy. "I will not harm you. Come back this way."

She took another step back. Now she was dangerously close to the edge! Only two strides away from certain death!

"Stop!" I said again, stepping toward her. Her eyes darted from her infant to her boy. The agony and sorrow that painted her will haunt me until the day I die. Sobbing, she reached for her boy, and he screamed for his mother.

"Mama, save me!"

Closing her eyes, she turned from her child and took those two strides . . .

"No, no, don't!" I screamed, pushing the boy down and running to the cliff's edge. "No!"

She jumped.

I watched as her body plummeted down the side of the cliff, hitting every jagged rock with brutal force. I watched as she wrapped herself tightly around her crying infant, doing her best to shield it from the pain. I watched as the rushing waves of the deep and the serrated boulders below shredded her into millions of pieces before washing her and her baby away. I watched as a mother not only took her life but the life of her child's while leaving one behind . . .

"No, Mommy, no!" The boy pushed the pain out in a broken cry. "Come back, Mama . . . Come back!"

* * *

The boy and I made our way back to the village. He did not make a sound the entire journey. I understood his change. I understood the corpse that now replaced the boy he was an hour ago. I understood the desolate eyes of one who has experienced a loss that pain cannot even measure.

"Guards!" We exited the forest and entered the village. Sidestepping a few bodies, we walked into a crowd of what was left of the villagers. My queen was on her stool. "Bring me the man in charge!"

Two guards pushed the beaten man into view. He fell to my queen's feet, groaning in pain.

"The quota for this village was not met. That means *my* kingdom will not have enough resources because of the inadequateness of *you*," she hissed menacingly. "You have failed your queen. Punishment for such a crime is death."

"I am already dead!" The man shouted, rising shakily to his knees. "And you are not my queen."

One of the guards took the handle of their sword and beat him across the face with it. A part of me was glad the little boy was too short to see the callousness of the monarchy.

"What a relief it is to know that you are prepared to die." She smiled, watching the man's life slip into hell. "You shouldn't put up much of a fight then." My queen signaled the two guards to hold the man up by his arms, keeping him on his knees. Another guard came into view. He had a rope in his hand. The guard put the rope around the man's neck and dragged him to a nearby tree. The queen signaled for all of us to follow. As we stood in front of the tree, the guard threw the rope over a low branch and forced the man onto a stool. The guard looked to the queen for instruction. She nodded.

"Papa?" the little boy whispered, stretching to see the man's face. He had pushed past the other onlookers and had unfortunately made it to the front. "Papa!" The man looked up at his son one last time before the stool was yanked from beneath his feet and the rope caught tightly around his neck. "No, Papa, no! Papa!" His father writhed frantically as his body hanged from the tree. Slowly, his body lost its strength, his face turned blue, and his attempts to breathe ceased. He was dead shortly after.

The boy went to run to his father, but I grabbed him, holding him in place. He cried in my arms and beat his little fist into me, his body now fueled by hatred and loss.

"You!" My queen pointed to a man in the crowd. "You are in charge of the Naïf village. Be sure they meet their quotas. Which, by the way, is now doubled. If the quota is not met by the end of the month"—she let the threat hang in the air before continuing—"beware of the *Shadows*."

The guards began loading the carts with all of the villagers' food and supplies. They were literally left with nothing—only ashes of their homes and the dead members of scattered and broken families. My queen climbed into her carriage without a care in the world. She was actually rather content with herself.

I released the little boy from my grasp and headed toward the carriages. Looking back at him I noticed he hadn't moved. He stared aimlessly into the distance, wondering where he belonged now that his family was gone. I understood that feeling as well.

"Be sure to wash your hands before you touch anything," my queen snapped just as I was to climb into the carriage. "For now, walk alongside us."

"Your Majesty . . . it's quite a few miles until we return to the palace," I said, noting that many of the guards rode horseback and I was without a horse.

Shrugging, as if not affected by my words, she shut the door right in my face. The carriage driver whistled for the horses to move; and the caravan, with me beside it, began its trek back to the palace.

CHAPTER 7

PACING BACK IN FORTH IN my room, I went to my door and checked to see if anyone was in the hallway. It, unfortunately, was still empty. "Damn it!" I muttered as I continued pacing. Three days ago I summoned him. Three days and it took two for a reply! The note said that he would be here after dark, yet he was nowhere in sight. I waited at the palace steps for hours before I decided to wait in my room.

Once the queen and I had returned back to the palace after the raiding of the Naïf village, I couldn't help but notice the pearly white trees that lined both sides of the driveway to the palace. *Angels' Teardrops.* The man in the carriage had told me that's what they were called. He explained that they were the innocent lives the Acheros family would destroy . . . I hadn't understood him then, but when I was walking past them I felt my heart ache in the worst way possible. I felt as though I had been a part of something that was not what it had seemed to be.

After many long hours researching and questioning who the man was, I finally was able to discover who he was and where he was. I needed answers and he seemed to have them. I had to go through over thirty or so people before I retrieved his information. And it took a few days of loitering before he decided to make the trip here.

I went to check the hall again. It was deserted. My queen and the Grand Royals were getting fitted for their evening gowns. Jepson told me mine would be sent to my room. Ever since the raiding of the Naïf village I haven't seen much of my queen. Instead of speaking directly to me I got messages and orders from Jepson who sometimes refused to answer any of the questions I had. Which is why I asked to speak with the gentleman I met when I first arrived here.

There was a commotion in the hall just as I went to pour myself a drink. I shuffled over to the door and listened.

"I've been summoned," I overhead a male voice say.

"It is my understanding that you were never to return to the palace!" a different voice interjected. By his thick accent I knew it was Jepson speaking. He sounded tense and barely spoke over a strained whisper. "Her Grace will have you killed!"

"It is my understanding that tonight is the eve of my execution. Presumably, no matter what my doings are, I will be dead upon the morrow," the man countered.

"No sooner shall the sun rise. There be no business for you here. There be no need for you to stir things up with your derogative accusations and blasphemous ideals!" Jepson hissed.

"Yet here I stand. Called upon for a consultation," the man replied. I chuckled at his response.

"Gods be damned!" Jepson shouted exasperated. "What possible reason would someone have to consult with the likes of you?"

"Considering the monarch upon the throne, I assume another member of the Acheros family has been bathing in the blood of innocence again," the voice countered nonchalantly. "It only be just that I am the one to explain."

"Watch your tongue or have it cut out!" Jepson snapped. "Who has summoned you?"

"Lady Korinthos," he replied. "It seems Ophelia's pet has wandered out the back door and dug up a few bones."

"Enough of this! Leave now or be forcibly removed!" Jepson ordered.

There was a soft chuckle before the man replied, "My dear friend, you have changed not at all. You have no authority in this situation. It is my understanding that Lady Korinthos is ranked higher than you. Which means if she asks me to leave, then I must. But if you ask me to leave, I will not."

There was a long silence before Jepson responded. "I beg of you to be honest for once!" Exasperated, he said, "If not for me then do it for your conscience. Before you are laid to rest."

"My hands are clean," the man replied. "What dirty rag have you dried yours with?"

Jepson muttered something in his native tongue before allowing the man entrance. I heard their footsteps approach my door. There was a pause and then a knock. I counted to ten before opening the door. Too my surprise, Jepson and the man weren't alone. Two guards stood behind the man. For one moment I didn't understand why until I saw the shackles on his hands and feet. Then I remembered how he had worn them when I had first met him. It seems Her Grace had me transported to the palace in the same carriage she transports her prisoners.

"Good evening, Lady Korinthos." Jepson bowed. "Do you mind if you and I speak for a moment?"

"I'll see to it that we speak later," I replied, gesturing for the man to come in. The guards were about to walk in behind him when I stopped them. "It's alright, gentlemen. I can handle myself."

"We have strict orders to stay with the prisoner at all times," one of the guards protested.

"Boy, you two sure make me feel important," the man mumbled sardonically.

"I am Lady Arianna Korinthos. Protector of the Monarchy and Lady to the Queen. When I say I can handle myself, I mean it. Or would you like a demonstration?"

"Please do," the man murmured.

"Apologies, milady," the guards replied. They bowed once as I shut the door.

The man walked into the middle of my room and whistled in appreciation. Then he turned to face me, and I saw a smile tug at the corner of his mouth.

"You are the most beautiful woman I have ever had the pleasure of being with," he drawled, looking me over. "I see why Ophelia keeps you in rags. She hates competition."

I picked at my gray dress, thinking it was one of the most beautiful things I had ever worn. "I have worn many rags. This, to me, is fine linen."

"Interesting." He smiled, taking a seat at the small breakfast table near the window. "I assume you're new to this 'royal lifestyle'?"

"I've lived here for several months now," I replied, walking over to him.

"Yeah," he chuckled, reaching for a glass, and then paused. He looked down at his cuffs and then at me. Understandingly, I poured him a glass. He nodded in appreciation. "You're new to this."

I sat across from him and waited for him to settle in before I began asking my questions.

"Why is it you have brought me here?" he finally asked after I refilled his glass twice.

"I have many questions," I responded, tapping my fingers on the glass table.

"Ah, I see," he said, looking into his glass. "No one in the palace is willing to answer the questions that can't be satisfied with canny remarks."

"Are you willing to answer them?"

He paused before responding. "Twenty years ago Ophelia had me arrested for treason. I was found guilty and was sentenced to two decades in jail before I was to be executed. She told the kingdom I was selling lies about her and the Acheros family. It wasn't lies that I was selling—it was the facts the monarchy wanted to hide. It was the coldhearted truth about what was done behind palace walls! You see, I used to be Jepson. I was Ophelia's eyes and ears when her back was turned. I did it for her and the monarchs before her. I knew everything that was going on. Just as Jepson does now. At the time, Jepson was a rank below me. I knew all the dirty secrets and was sick of letting them just get away with it! I wrote down every infraction I saw or overheard and then sold it to other Royals, hoping it would eventually weaken the Acheros family. Unfortunately I was caught riding out in the middle of the night." He paused, toying with his glass. Then he looked back up at me. "I have no problem with what I did. I conquered all my demons. I've washed my hands and cleaned them thoroughly. So to answer your question, Lady Korinthos, if I am willing to go to jail for the truth then I most certainly have no issue discussing it with you over a couple glasses of wine."

I leaned back in my seat, absorbing all the information, and took a sip from my own glass. "Let's start with your name."

"Lyrrad Meeklea of Kreni," he replied.

"Pleased to meet you, Lyrrad." I reached across the table and shook his hand. "How long have you lived in Islocia?"

"Sixty and nine years. The first fifty were spent living in the palace. The royal family at the time was the Fiton family. King Diam Fiton and Queen Jacqueline Elizabeth Fiton. They were magnificent." It'd be hard to miss the longing and admiration he felt for the fallen monarchs as he spoke into his empty glass.

"How did the Acheros family take control?" I asked while offering to refill his glass. He waved me off and continued staring into his cup as if he were watching his memories.

"Commodus Aurelius Acheros," he said the name as if his mouth was filled with poison.

"My queen's father?"

"Yes, *your* queen's father," scowling at his cup, he replied. "The man believed himself to be more than man! Bloody coward if you ask me! Releasing a full attack on a kingdom, knowing our army was down. King Fiton had just returned from war, the battle of the Somme, with barely any soldiers left. Commodus knew he could never defeat King Fiton when his army was strong and prepared. Commodus knew that if they met on the battlefield he would be slaughtered. So he attacked before the king had removed his battle armor."

"King Acheros? What was he like?"

"Psychotic!" He spit before I could even finish asking the question. "It has been said that Commodus killed a hundred lions in one day, a giraffe just for fun, decapitated an ostrich to scare political opponents, killed his sparing partners, and slayed prisoners for game. Commodus was so convinced he was Hercules that he declared himself a *god* to the kingdom."

"What happened to King Fiton?"

Somberly he looked up from his glass and out into the window. The moon shined bright on him, and I could finally see he was rather old. Lyrrad was a man of many years, for his skin hung loose on his face, marred by memories and prison. His gray hair grew unruly and clung to his pasty skin. The stars danced off his black eyes before burning in the intensity of his gaze. "*My* king was beheaded immediately after Commodus took control."

"And what be it your fate?" I asked.

Sighing, he turned to look at me. "I was to serve the beast and water his seeds."

"Ophelia."

"Not exactly," he replied, toying with his cuffs. "Ophelia was a one of forty-two children of Commodus and his ten wives. Only one woman was considered the queen, and that was his first wife, Anne Marie Asphodel of Islocia. Anne gave Commodus three children. Twin boys and Ophelia. The twins, Cain and Abel, fought constantly. They never liked each other and they only lived for six years because of it."

"What happened to them?"

"One day the two boys were fishing in the river when Cain pushed his brother over the edge of the boat." He spoke as if this story was boring rather than tragic. "Abel grabbed onto Cain as he fell into the water, and both boys tipped the small wooden boat over, and because neither of them could swim, they drowned. Commodus hardly took the time to mourn the loss of his only sons. He blamed Anne for birthing such hostile creatures and set out to find a new mistress. Ironically Commodus didn't have to far to find Lady Amelia Grace Irene of Islocia. Lady Irene was the most beautiful woman Commodus had ever encountered. Instantly the rugged king fell for the pristine noblewoman. She was in every sense perfect to him and was admired by all of Islocia immediately. Unfortunately, the king could not marry Lady Irene, for it so happened that Lady Irene and Anne Marie were sisters. The Laws of the Land denied any man who has married before the right to marry another woman related to his previous wife. It was a law King Fiton put into place."

"Why?" I asked.

"I believe it was because King Fiton's brother, Prince Worren, tried to divorce his wife to marry his wife's sister. King Fiton was very fond of Princess Lucinda, Prince Worren's wife, and denied his brother that right and secured Lucinda's rightful place in the palace," he said, speaking to himself rather than to me.

"Interesting," I replied.

"Anyway, it soon came to be that Commodus refused Anne Marie of any royal treatment and instead gave it to Lady Irene. He showered her with gifts and love while he worked to rewrite the Laws of the Land. Because, as you should know, the Laws of the Land can only be rewritten by the seven monks who live in the Todon Monastery. All seven monks must sign the new laws. As you should also know, Commodus had eventually killed the seven monks so that now the

Laws of the Land are to be examined and executed by the reigning monarch. But at the time it was very unfortunate for Commodus because the Todon Monastery was in an unknown location, and he knew that the monks came to visit every ten years or so. He did not want to wait. He also knew his enemies were aligning themselves to overthrow him, and Commodus did not have a son to take his place! So he rushed to get Lady Irene pregnant. Lady Irene gave birth to a girl. Commodus was disappointed but also vowed to love the little girl, for she was pure of heart."

"When did he get his other wives?"

"When Lady Irene became infertile after an illness she caught from the soiled drinking water. He did not want to risk dying without having a son to follow in his footsteps, so he gathered eight women and forced each of them to birth eight children. Many of the babies died at birth, and some of the women grew ill over time. Still, Commodus got enough children for him to feel secure in his bloodlines, although they weren't royal. Only Ophelia and her half-sister, who was also her half-cousin, were pure royalty. However, Ophelia's claim to the throne was much more valid than her half-sister's because her parents were the King and Queen. Her half-sisters parents was a King and noblewoman which made her eligible but not first in line for the throne." he answered, standing up. He walked over to the window and gazed out into the endless night. I wondered desperately what he was thinking. So many questions raced through my mind, but I had to start from the beginning in order to understand the present. My reward would only be attained through patience.

"Why was it eventually only Ophelia?"

"A deadly fever swept across Islocia, killing thousands, including the royal family. Only Ophelia and her half-sister were unaffected by the disease. They were visiting their father at his summer palace in Yenyun. Their mothers were with Commodus as well. When he learned that all thirty-eight of his children had died, he cried to the heavens. Not because he was mourning but because he no longer believed himself to be a god. He thought that he was cursed, so he blamed Anne Marie and Ophelia, for they were not pure of heart," he replied.

"Why was Ophelia not pure of heart?"

"Lady Irene had snow-white hair and ocean-blue eyes. Women who were born with those attributes were seen as angels. Angels are pure. Ophelia's half-sister was born with snow-white hair and ocean-blue eyes as well. Commodus was most pleased with himself." He chuckled before returning to his solemn tone.

"What was the outcome? Why Ophelia?"

"Are you asking why she is queen?" I nodded, unwilling to interrupt his answer. "Unfortunately, I do not know the details to finish this particular story. No one in the kingdom was there to witness the fall of Lady Irene and her daughter. All that is known is Commodus was killed in battle, and the heir to the throne was somehow Princess Ophelia."

"And what was the fate of Ophelia's mother?"

"Anne Marie was beheaded."

"Why?" I asked.

"Commodus believed her to be the reason for his awful luck. He decided if he could not divorce the snake, he will simply cut its head off. And that he did, in front of the kingdom and on display for the gods. There was a festival for her death. Everyone came to celebrate except Ophelia, who was to sit off to the side and mourn her mother while Lady Irene danced the night away with Commodus." He coughed after clearing his throat. I offered him more wine, but he denied it and asked for water. I poured him the water, watched as he took a long, slow sip, and waited for him to continue. He went back over to the window and stared off into the distance. "I do not know much else about the underlying events that led to Ophelia's rise. But there is someone who does know the truth."

"Who?"

"*Your* king."

"King Araun?"

He nodded. "Fill the king's glass with an abundance of wine and learn the truth about *your* queen."

I pondered that, knowing I hadn't spent much time with the king. "Tell me more about King Araun."

Shrugging, he replied, "I only know the basics of your king. He was born in Kreni, son of the late Lord Edvard Araun. When he was thirty he was told he would marry one of the daughters of Commodus. At the time he had a choice between Ophelia and her half-sister. As

I have told you, Commodus needed a man to run his kingdom. Lord Araun was a strong and intelligent boy. He came from a rich and powerful family too. Ophelia did not care for him much, but it has been said that he chose to marry Ophelia's half-sister."

"Why didn't he?"

Again he shrugged. "I am unsure of how those events unfolded as well. I'm sure Ophelia was jealous that her half-sister received so much attention from the prince. They were a perfect age for each other. One young and vibrant and the other mature and steady. Ophelia, however, was almost the same age as the prince—"

"What?" I interjected. I had always thought the king was much older than my queen. I remembered his weathered skin and graying beard. The stresses of running a kingdom are certainly taking a toll on his weary appearance. The only thing left of his youth were the lingering muscles that framed his arms.

"O' yes," he replied matter-of-factly. "Your queen has seen many days."

I remember seeing my queen as youthful in appearance and spirit. She had a perfectly pale complexion and beautifully combed auburn hair that sat upon her head. She mirrored my age.

"How can that be?"

"The queen wears layers and layers of white lead mixed with arsenic powder. In her early years Ophelia caught the small pox from a gentleman she was very fond of. He unknowingly brought it to her and it marred her face. Her father now saw her as rubbish and no longer allowed her to leave her room. So she did what she could to cover the scars. Eventually the paint mixture began eroding her face, so over the years she has to apply more and more to hide the effects." He returned to his seat and finished drinking the rest of his water. He smiled at me as he watched realization and understanding settle. "You knew none of this?"

I shook my head, choosing to stay silent.

"*Your* queen is not the polished gem you believe her to be. Have you heard about the famine sweeping the kingdom? I doubt she has told you of the Shadows as well?" he inquired.

Again I shook my head.

He chuckled, leaning back in his seat. "It seems Jepson has been doing a very good job at keeping you tame."

I slammed my fist on the table. Standing, I growled, "I am no animal for someone to put on a leash and escort around! That will be the last time you make a mention of that."

Snickering, he countered, "You are right. Ophelia has you in a noose rather than on a leash. And she is continuing to tighten it without you even knowing. Spoiling you with gifts and fancy food. But make notice that eventually she will certainly hang you out to dry if you're not too careful. For she's an Acheros."

Allowing my temper to fade out, I sat back down. Taking a deep breath, I asked, "What are the Shadows?"

He answered, "They are the reason for Ophelia's reign. No one ever sees them lurking in the shadows until it is too late. I assume Ophelia has taken you on a raid?" He waited for me to nod my head before continuing. "The Shadows are the ones who continue killing after the Royal Army's fifteen minutes are up. They are the ones who tear children away from their parents and throw babies into the flames. The Shadows are the 'secret police' of Islocia. Those who follow your queen never know of their existence. Those who resist your queen . . ." He pondered how to explain it. "I'm sure you understand how this works. The Royal Army has laws that the Shadows do not have to follow, for they are—"

"Undocumented," I finished, realizing where he was going with this.

"Exactly," he confirmed. "They only take orders from one man who is given orders by your queen. He is the highest ranked individual next to Ophelia."

"Who is he?"

"Only your queen can answer that," he replied.

"It's not Lord Jamison?" I asked, wanting to know more.

"No, Lord Jamison is only in charge of the Royal Army," he replied, looking at the door. "It will be time for me to depart soon."

"Not until I get my answers," I replied loud enough for the guards outside to hear. Turning back to him, I asked, "You mentioned a famine. What famine?"

Sadness covered his face as he turned away to look out the window. "Ophelia places unbelievably high quotas on the kingdom. Specifically, the peasants. As you should know the harvest has been less than profitable. Villages hardly have enough food to feed their families. And yet, *your* queen asks for more food than they can give. If starvation and malnutrition isn't killing all of the peasants, then the Shadows are. They're raiding the villages and stripping them of all their resources, just like the Royal Army, only the Shadows never stop. Before you left whatever village you hail from, food was scarce, yes?"

I nodded.

"But there was still food when you left?"

I nodded again. "Of course I knew food was scarce, but I assumed it was only because of a dry harvest . . . not the quotas."

"Stupid girl. Villages have nothing. Of course the harvest was bad. There was hardly any time for the crops to grow before quotas were announced." He held my gaze. "People, *your* people, are literally dying to feed *your* queen."

I allowed the room to fall into silence as I listened to his words. Listening, not believing. I couldn't believe him. My queen would never allow her people to suffer. She loved Islocia. How dare I listen to this man denounce my queen? How dare he show such disregard toward her! Lying about the monarchy is forbidden.

But why would he lie? What would he gain? If what he is saying about my queen is true, then something should be done, right? But how to know if this is true is the question. Her Majesty did slaughter an entire village without even blinking an eye. But that was to help Islocia, right? Not for her personal gain.

"I do not need you to believe me, young one," he said, reading my thoughts off my face. "If you seek the truth, find it for yourself. I can only offer you my knowledge and experience."

"Fair words." I nodded, deciding to take his advice and find my own evidence. Noticing how the time had passed, I knew that soon he would have to leave. I'd probably never see Lyrrad ever again, for I knew his days were numbered. "When is your execution?"

"Tomorrow at dawn." With sad eyes, he turned to smile at me. "I was alive to see the rise of the Acheros family. It saddens me that I will not live to see their fall."

Just as he stood from the table, there were two knocks at the door. "Lady Korinthos, the prisoner must return to his cell."

He began walking toward the door, but I grabbed his elbow. "Is there anything I can do for you? Anything at all?"

Placing his hands on my shoulders, he replied, "I do not fear death, young one. I have washed the blood from my hands many years ago . . ." There was another impatient knock at the door as he continued, "I do, however, fear that the children of Islocia will continue to bow to *your* queen as she holds their lives in her hands. I fear that they will never see an end to the Acheros reign. I fear that pain and suffering will fill their cups and empty their souls . . . You can do me no favors. But know that my biggest regret, as I watched the Acheros family consume Islocia, was not doing more to end them. My silence took part in the deaths of millions. Until I chose to take a stand."

"What can I do then?" I asked impatiently.

The door opened with the guards standing outside of it. They grabbed his chains and forced him out the room! He turned to look at me and replied, "What you believe is right for *your* people."

Then he was gone forever.

* * *

Music filled the air, pouring out the palace windows and into the streets of Islocia. I watched as the Royals spun each other around under the crystal chandeliers, sidestepping passing slaves and laughing the night away. The mood was festive, and everyone appeared carefree and exuberant. Even my queen attempted a playful smile as she sat at her table watching the party rather than enjoying it. I was to stand next to her as well as Jepson. Neither of us exchanged more than three words to each other, but I was sure Jepson had told my queen about the meeting with Lyrrad. Try as I might not to think about his parting words, they rang in my head louder than the music. I wasn't sure what he wanted from me.

"Lady Korinthos?" my queen called, still looking out at the dancers. "Are you enjoying yourself?"

Nodding graciously, I replied, "Yes, Your Majesty. Most certainly. Thank you for inviting me." She smiled appreciatively and ended the conversation with her head bobbing to the music.

The music dipped into an upbeat waltz as I noticed the king, looking ravishing in his gold tunic and pointed leather shoes, make his way over to us. He smiled warmly to his queen before nodding once to Jepson.

"I do believe this to be a party, my dear." He spoke to me, offering his arm. "Do come and join me for a dance?"

I looked down at my queen for permission. She did not bother to look back at me. Instead she waited several long seconds and then turned to the king. "I find it interesting that you asked *her* to dance." She smiled sardonically. "As if she is the only woman in the room. Or is she the only one you see?"

"I don't reckon you would care too much for a dance," he countered, narrowing his gaze.

"Perhaps not." She shrugged innocently. The king took that as his cue to reach for my hand until she grabbed his arm. "But it would be incredibly polite to acknowledge *your* queen first."

Sighing, he took a step back, bowed, and then reached for her hand. "My dearest queen, would you honor me with a dance?"

She yanked her hand away and waved him off. "No."

"Lady Korinthos?" he asked me again, obviously reining in his anger. The Grand Royals who were seated nearby whispered in disapproval. No matter, I smiled politely and accepted his arm. His weathered face lit up with joy as he escorted me away from the queen's table.

"Are you enjoying yourself?" Spinning in a circle and placing one hand at my waist and the other in mine, we danced while the Royals made extraordinary efforts to get out of our way. The glistening chandeliers spilled sparkling rays of light onto the dance floor, making the event all the more elegant.

"Yes, Your Majesty," I answered, following his lead. I stumbled once before I picked up on his moves. He chuckled at my correction.

"You dance quite well, my dear," he said, stopping and releasing me. We both took a step back. He bowed to me, and then I curtsied to him, and we came together again and continued to dance. "Who taught you to move so fluidly?"

The Conqueror, but I could not answer with that. The only reason he taught me to dance was to flaunt me in front of his friends. I was no more than a pet he liked to use and abuse at his leisure. However, I wasn't his only treasure.

"My father," I replied, looking away from his soft emerald eyes. King Araun was so much different from my queen. He did not have this hard exterior and cold demeanor. He was warm, kind, and unbelievably charming. Gripping his muscular frame, I reveled in his grace. He moved like water over a stone and dazzled the court with his smile. Though several years my senior, he looked almost boyish with his chocolate mane pulled back in his signature ponytail while the dynamics of his beard introduced a playful, sophisticated side of him. His somber emerald eyes lingered on me for a moment longer than it should have, but I did not mind. He was, in fact, the king.

"Do you love my queen?" I had no idea where the question came from. And regretted it immediately! I turned my head quickly away from him and hoped that the music had drowned out my question. It hadn't.

Pausing, absorbing the question, without missing a single beat, he answered, "It is not love that runs a kingdom. It is a powerful bloodline."

"I assume that she is not one to love as well?" I asked, barely missing his toes as we glided around to the melody of the song.

"Yes, she does not love me. And I do not love her." His eyes left my face and gazed at the ceiling.

"Have you ever loved?" I pushed, hoping for more understanding.

The king slowed our dance until we stood absolutely still. The music had not begun to stop as he released me from his grasp. "Thank you for the dance. Until next time." He kissed my hand before leaving me.

Just as I was to follow after him, I heard a piercing scream come from my queen's table. I turned to see her in a fit of rage, staring at the food the slaves had placed before her.

"What the hell is this?" she screamed, tipping over a plate of bread. All eyes were on her as she barked at the slave who pinned his knees to the ground in submission.

"A-apologies, Your Grace," he sobbed, raising his hands in defense. Angrily she grabbed her empty wine glass and threw it at his head, barely missing him. "It's all we have considering the b-bad h-h-harvest."

"You call this food?" I had never seen my queen so tense. Her face no longer depicted the perfectness she radiated. Her cheeks were tinted red, and her eyes were like jagged icicles in search for blood. "I will not eat this!"

"Apologies," the slave said again. "But it is all we have tonight. We ordered food from the other villages. Unfortunately that won't arrive until the morrow, Your Grace."

"You dare feed your queen rubbish?" she hissed, knocking over another plate of food. "If I wanted to get on my knees and eat like a dog, I'd be attending the party of a commoner!"

"Apologies!" he quivered, continuing to surrender himself to her. "It is all the food we could find on such short notice, my queen. The other villages have no food for themselves, let alone any food to spare."

"Is that my problem?" Her question hung in the air as silence overtook the room. "Those vermin do not deserve to eat. I am the queen of Islocia!"

"What can I do to fix this, Your Highness?" He braved a look at my icy queen.

She walked down the few steps to where the slave bowed to her and said, "First, you will be punished immediately. Take him away!" The man sobbed as she signaled to the guards. "You!" She pointed to another slave who had, like all the others, plastered himself to the wall, praying to remain invisible. "Throw out the food. The party is over!"

"Wait!" I heard the words before I realized I was speaking against the queen. She turned to look at me; her gaze did not soften. "I understand that Your Grace does not wish to eat the food. But considering that, at the moment, food is limited, it might be wise to do so anyway."

Stalking over to me until we stood toe to toe, I saw the intensity in her eyes and burning rage that hummed behind her glare. "You dare speak against your queen?"

"No, Your Majesty. I'm concerned for your well-being and the well-being of Islocia," I replied, looking back at her. "If you refuse to eat the food, fine, but do not waste it in a time of famine. Those plates of food could feed two villages!"

"No," she said sternly and slightly surprised I knew of the events outside of the palace. I assume she was hiding the famine from me so I did not speak against her; my knowledge on the subject had her intimidated. *Why would she hide something like that from me*? "And that will be the end of this discussion."

She began to walk away. "But, Your Grace!" I called after her.

Turning to face me, she growled, "You're lucky I obliged your rude outburst, Lady Korinthos. It is only out of respect that I did not have you killed where you stand."

Taking deep breaths to calm the insult, I retorted behind clenched teeth, "Thank you, my most forgiving queen."

"Don't let it happen again—"

"Your Highness," I continued, pushing the issue, "there are people, your people, *starving*. And you refuse to see things outside of the palace walls! My queen, you have never gone days without food. My queen, you have never endured nights where your stomach begins to consume itself. For that pain is real, and Islocians, the people you vowed to honor and protect, are dying in order to host your party. They are dying in order to feed your friends." Though I didn't say it, I knew I was only trying to convince myself that my queen was not the demon Lyrrad believed her to be. She cared for her people; she would not desert her people. There is heart inside of her.

"You would be wise not to speak ill of your queen," Lord Jamison interjected.

Turning to him I said, "I speak truth and logic. No more than what any of her advisors presumably do. Never once have I forgotten that she is my queen." I turned back to her. "But I also know that if you deny *your* people today, then you have a hand in the death of millions of Islocians. And I do not believe that to be *my* queen. I believe you to be the mother of Islocia. Not its executioner."

She smiled, cocking her head as if she was examining me. "You have so much passion for an issue I assumed impassive to someone as yourself. It seems your talk with Lyrrad Meeklea has changed your perception of . . . *life*?"

"No, but your decision tonight will certainly change my perception of you," I growled just as her guards began drawing their swords.

"I never knew your opinion was so heavily valued amongst *us*." She smiled, keeping a close eye on her guards that were too far away to save her, had I decided to strike. "It's comical that you believe I would entertain suggestions from someone of your background."

"I have lived as a commoner and as a Royal. My knowledge supersedes those who have been sipping gold their entire lives," I replied, not backing down.

She shook her head, braving a step closer to me. "That is where you are wrong, my dear. You see, you are still a commoner. You just happen to be *my* commoner. The only difference being that when it rains I allow you back into my house. Every other commoner is chained to the fence while you, Arianna, you are chained to my throne."

"I am not so low, in the eyes of dignity, that I am to be compared to a dog!" I snapped.

"No, but you are a bitch. Nonetheless"—she raised her hand to silence me just as I was to retort—"I refuse to continue listening to this hypocrisy, Arianna. You pronounce me a murderer, yet you are a murderer too. There are far more deaths on your hands than mine."

TETA AND ZAKAI

CHAPTER 8

THE FAMINE THAT ENCOMPASSED ISLOCIA was so detrimental that the peaceful Qingkowuats turned to savagery as they clawed, bit, fought, and killed each other for food. The plentiful farmlands that once raced along the coast were stricken bare. Any hint of vegetation was quickly devoured by the famished people. Children, who were originally first to receive food, were shoved aside or beaten by the adults. The water in the wells became so heavily contaminated by disease and smut that it will forever remain a murky brown color. Yet the people still drank it. Bodies fell by the day and clogged the dirt paths. The elders did everything they could to provide some sort of relief to their people, but they were to no avail. There was no food to be given to anyone, even themselves.

A woman, Maille, who was mixed in a large crowd of starving people begging outside the elders' hut, slowly made her way out of it. She knew that no food would be given out today. She and her children would not eat again. Her only option was to go to the burial ground and dig up some of the bodies that hadn't already been picked over. She could not bear to tell her children what the meat was; she could only watch in silence as they ate a family member, a friend, or a neighbor. But even the body parts she acquired were not nearly enough to satisfy the three of them. For the people they ate were just as skinny as they were.

Walking out into the middle of the dirt road, she surveyed her village. Many of the huts that once stood proud were torn down by the Shadows who raided the village a few weeks earlier. They came without any warning and showed the villagers no mercy. They took all the food they could find, killed most of the men who had stayed in the village, and even ripped a few infants away from their mothers. God knows what happened to them . . .

Maille and her children, Teta and Zakai, did not sleep in their hut anymore. They spent the days searching for food, and at night they slept high in the trees because the Shadows liked to slither into the village and do wicked and detestable things to the women and girls.

Suddenly, a child darted out from the shadows and caught a mouse that had scurried onto the middle of the road. Maille watched the savage girl with wild eyes and willowy limbs begin to eat the mouse where she had caught it. The little child was smart to finish her meal fast before someone was to notice. Maille even considered taking the mouse from her and giving it to her daughter and son. Unfortunately she did not have the strength to do such a thing. Not at the moment. Maille hadn't eaten for four days, for whatever meal she acquired was immediately given to her children. She was weak and indescribably malnourished. Her skin hung loose on her bones, her hair was dry and falling out, every bone could be seen if she was to stand nude, and she was depleted beyond words. The humming her stomach made as it begged for food ceased once it too realized food was no longer an option. So it began feeding on her muscles, making her very frail. She could no longer climb up the tree where her children slept. Maille was forced to make her bed in the bushes beneath it.

Maille watched the child run back into the shadows and continue walking toward the woods. For a second, without volition, Maille wondered what the girl would taste like now that she had a mouse in her. Quickly she erased the thought altogether! She hated thinking such awful things! For she knew someone would think the same of her sweet Little Teta. Lately her mind had been taking control of its own decisions without her doings. Sometimes she forgot how to stand, sit, talk, or move. Once for an entire day she sat on the side of the road, dazed and confused, wondering how she had gotten there. Other times her thoughts would make her believe that she was at the harvest festival and there was a bouquet of food before her. She believed that she and her children were eating a massive meal and that the famine was merely a dream.

"Mama, wake up!" Maille turned to see a little boy beside his mother who lay on the side of the road. She was very ill and her eyes were sealed close. The boy did not want to accept his mother's fate, so he continued prodding her to wake up. "Please, Mama, wake up. I am hungry. Please, Mama. Please." Maille knew the boy's mother would not be waking up. Looking up into the sky, she prayed to her angels that her children would never have to see her dead. She did not want them to ever endure the unbearable pain that little boy would soon be forced to acknowledge. She wanted more for her children.

After her prayer, Maille had finally made it to the forest. Although it was not a strenuous walk, it did take a lot of energy out of her. She instantly plopped down into the bushes, paying no mind to the thorns, and tried to rest her eyes. Nighttime would soon be falling, and she would have to stay awake to keep an eye out for the Shadows.

As Maille slipped into unconsciousness, she dreamed of the harvest festival again and hoped that it would soon be reality. That's what kept Maille going. Hope. It was the only thing she could give herself and her children. *Hope.*

"Come now, Teta, I can hear Mommy calling," Zakai said while holding his little sister's hand as they trudged through the swamp. Zakai had been carrying his sister through most of the thick murky waters; her little legs were not strong enough to push through it. Now they had to march through the hot, dense mud that could suck them underneath the earth in an instant. Unfortunately, this was the safest path to get to the forest, but it surely was not the most comfortable. The swamp air was thick as it pushed through their nose and filled their little lungs. Bugs, never minding personal space, teased the children by landing on them and biting their flesh before flying away only to return another second later. Many times, Zakai looked up into the sky and wondered why the sun was so mean. He never complained in front of his sister, o' no. He did not want to cause her any unnecessary distress. But still he wondered why the angels ignored him and his family in their time of need . . .

"I cannot hear her," Little Teta replied, yanking her big brother's hand. "Why can you hear Mommy but I cannot?"

Zakai smiled to himself as he listened to his little sister's sweet high-pitched voice. The little child was so innocent and pure that he prayed she would stay this way forever. He adored his sister and admired her tenacious and caring attitude. She did not see the world they lived in as a harsh, baron wasteland; she saw it as something beautiful and exciting. Teta could find beauty in the darkest alleys and dirtiest streams, a trait many adults would die for. She made an effort to smile every day, no matter how hungry she was or how much pain she was feeling. Sweet Little Teta could make the rain stop falling and the sky a little bluer. Zakai loved that about his sister. He loved it so much that he and his mother hid the harsh truths of their lives from Teta just to keep her smiling for another day.

"You cannot hear Mommy calling because your ears are too little," he said while helping her over a fallen log.

Frowning, she replied, "My ears are not little!"

Zakai could not hide his smile as he watched his sister toy with her ears. "Worry not, Teta. One day your ears will grow to be as big as mine. And once they do you will be able to hear Mommy calling."

"Promise?" She pouted.

Smiling, Zakai said, "I promise."

Adoringly, Teta smiled at her brother, showcasing her yellowed and decaying teeth while patting her ears. "I'm going to have ears as big as Mommy's someday!" Swinging their hands, Teta hummed a sweet lullaby as they continued through the swamp. Soon they would reach the forest, and from there it's only one hundred trees until they were with their mommy again.

"Zakai?" Teta asked after her lullaby was finished for the third time. "Why is there no more food in the village?"

Sighing, he thought for a second and then responded, "Well, Teta, the royal people must eat more food than we do. And the food has been very sick for a long time, and in order to feed the royal people, they had to take food from the villages."

"Why do the royal people get to eat but we do not?" she asked, sidestepping a spider. For a second, Teta wondered what it would taste like.

"Well, the royal people are very fat. And they need to eat more or they will get sick and die from not having enough food," Zakai explained.

"Why must we take care of them?" she continued asking.

Honestly, Zakai had no idea why the Royals had the right to eat while everyone else starved. He thought it to be exceedingly unfair that the Royal Army came to their village and took all their livestock and all their crops, leaving them with nothing. But the boy was smart—he knew you could not argue with the proclamation of the queen. For she was chosen by the angels to be a keeper of this land. Zakai and his family just had the unfortunate luck to live during Queen Ophelia's reign.

"The Royals are very important, little sister," he replied just as the forest came into view.

"Are they more important than us?" she asked, looking up at her big brother.

Nodding, he said, "They are much more important than we are."

"Why?"

"Because . . ." He contemplated for a second. "They have more kerts than there are blades of grass in Islocia."

"Why does that matter?" she asked, not letting go of the subject.

"Because . . ." Again, he thought of what to say. "The queen likes lots of kerts. Gold is her favorite color, as Mommy says, and the royal people have lots of gold, and that makes the queen very happy. We want a happy queen."

"What does this have to do with food?" Teta asked inquisitively.

"Well, we do not have any kerts. Meaning, we cannot make the queen happy. Therefore, we do not deserve to eat. The Royals do have kerts, and they *can* make the queen very happy. Therefore, they do deserve to be fat and eat our food."

"Why do they have kerts but we do not?"

"I do not know," Zakai replied, unable to think of a solid answer.

"How do you get more kerts?"

"I don't know." He shrugged.

"How do the royal people get their kerts?"

"Teta, I do not know." He sighed, wishing he could be more for his sister.

"If I found a gold coin, would we be able to live in a big castle?" she wondered aloud.

"Maybe, little sister," he said solemnly. "Maybe."

"I'd buy a gold castle and invite all the villagers to live in it! I'd even invite the queen! We could eat bread and drink tea. Would that make her happy?"

"Yes, Teta." He sighed, squeezing her hand gently. "I'm sure that would make her very happy."

When they had reached the edge of the swamp, Zakai had to dig his little sister out of the mud and wipe the thick substance off of her. Once she was relatively free, he searched her back for leeches. Luckily, he only found two today. There were several scars from the other creepy crawlies on her boney back. Zakai sucked in his breath as he noticed he could see more bones today than yesterday on his sister . . .

Zakai would not let Teta see the bugs when he found them, which is also why he had his mother take the leeches off of him when he got to their tree.

"Are you ready, Teta?" Zakai asked after wiping the mud off of him. "We must hurry. I can hear Mommy calling."

"I cannot hear Mommy calling!" she whined, grabbing his hand again.

"That is because we are not close enough yet. Come, Teta. Mommy is calling for you," Zakai replied.

Teta lead the way as she dragged her brother by his hand. She did not know the exact way to get to their tree, but she knew Zakai would tell her when they needed to go a different direction. She released her brother's hand to crawl under a log. Once that was accomplished she retrieved her brother's hand and continued forward. Meanwhile, Zakai counted the trees and marked the landmarks he had memorized. They were eighty trees and two turns at the boulders away from their mother. He prayed that their mommy had food for them. They could not find any this morning, and there were no edible critters in the swamp . . . except for the leeches that still clung to his back.

"Can you still hear Mommy?" Teta called over her shoulder as she tugged her brother along.

A little winded, he said, "Yes, Teta. Mommy is calling for you. We are getting close." He continued counting the trees as Teta led the way. Just as they came up on the boulder, Zakai saw a brown object shift between the bushes. He stopped immediately.

"What are—" He hushed Teta before she could continue asking her question.

Zeroing in on the bush, he waited for another sign of movement. After a few long seconds the leaves rustled and he knew there was something in there. He gestured for Teta to stay where she was and remain quiet while he stalked silently over to the bush.

Peering in, he saw the furry creature frantically nibbling on the roots, trying to consume its meal as quickly as possible. Zakai understood the need to eat what little food he could acquire as fast as he could. For he knew savages lurked in the shadows, waiting to pounce on helpless prey. Today, Zakai was that savage.

Quickly Zakai dove into the bush, scaring the poor rabbit. It tried to escape the predator by dipping underneath the bush and darting out of it. But Zakai was quick! Hunger fueled his attack as he lunged for the animal again. He missed but got close enough to corner it against a big boulder. Zakai saw the fear in the animal's eyes, but his heart did not ache for it. He needed to feed his family. Picking up a stick he charged at the rabbit, pinning it to the wall with his stick so he could wrap his fists around its neck. The attack was quick, precise, efficient, and lethal. The rabbit tried to free itself from his grasp, but Zakai would not release it.

Emerging from the boulder covered in thorns and carrying the writhing rodent, Zakai held up his prize to his little sister. He did not notice the agony in her eyes; he did not see the terror that suffocated her frame. It wasn't until he snapped the squirming animal's neck that he noticed the frightened tears that streamed down her face.

Quietly sobbing and slightly quivering, Teta looked at Zakai in complete horror . . . Never had she seen her big brother act so violent.

Realizing what he had done, he apologetically reached for his sister who instinctively flinched away. "Teta . . . if I hadn't . . . well . . . there's no food . . ." How could Zakai explain his actions to his younger sister? How could he explain it to himself? "Stop looking at me like that, please. I know what I have done."

It wasn't difficult for her to look away from him. For a long moment all they could do was stare at the ground. Zakai did not want his vulnerable, sweet, innocent little sister to see something so vile. His need to eat overcame his sense of compassion. Though he would not have spared the animal, he would have spared his sister from the sight of it . . .

"Come, Teta," he finally said as he reached his hand out to her, unsure of what to do or say. "I hear Mommy calling for you."

"Mama!" Zakai called down from their tree. "Mama, come quick!" Maille pulled herself from her restless sleep, forcing her eyes open only to close them immediately. The sun was relentless as it branded its beams across her face. God knows how long she had been lying there . . . a day? Maybe two? Zakai had been bringing her whatever food he could find and had to serve her water. For she was too weak to bring it to her lips. She hated that her children had lost out on a childhood, especially Zakai. Teta was young enough to forget these awful events once the harvest pulled through next year. But Zakai, he will always remember how his mother couldn't even take care of him when he needed her most. Which is why she closed her eyes and ignored her son's cries. Too afraid to disappoint him more.

"You will be alright, Teta, I promise," Zakai cooed as he rocked his sister in his arms. She coughed into his chest and hugged him tighter, her sobs merely painful whimpers. Teta had caught a fever a day or so ago, and Zakai had been doing anything he could to keep her well—bringing her the cleanest water he could find, searching for food, and wrapping her in his clothes at night to keep her warm. Unfortunately Zakai was just a boy and could do nothing for his little sister, except comfort her as she became sicker by the day. Their mother couldn't even help them, for she lay at the bottom of the tree crying herself to sleep every night. She no longer prayed to her angels; instead she cursed the heavens and denounced the queen, begging Satan to welcome the queen into the fiery pits of hell. Zakai always tried comforting his mother, but it was to no avail. He wished his papa was there . . . He would know what to do. Zakai wondered aimlessly about where his papa had gone and if he'd ever see him again. Teta does not remember their papa. He left for Lárnach when Teta was only three years old. He promised to return one day, but before he could return, he vowed to send all the kerts he made back to them. The kerts never came, just like his papa never returned.

"I . . ." Teta coughed again. "I am thirsty, Zakai. Please . . . I need water." Zakai sighed down at his little sister and obliged her, although he feared the water was what was making her sick to begin with.

The rabbit they had eaten a few days ago was old and very thin. All the streams near their village were infested with disease and filth, yet they were still forced to drink it. People dropped dead every day because of the water; even the animals became sick from it. Still, Teta and their mother picked off the meat and even ate the organs of the rabbit. However, Zakai refused to eat the rabbit because he wanted his family to eat first. His mother tried to convince him to eat it, but he respectfully declined.

Yesterday his mother had thrown up blood; Teta broke out in a nosebleed and caught a fever a day or so later. And Zakai was forced to take care of them. A boy who was suddenly forced to become a man.

He loved his family. He loved his mother and missed how she used to sing every night just before bed. He missed when she used to smile and buy him and his sister sweets from neighboring shops. He missed how she held him after a nightmare and wiped his tears when he cried. He loved his sister and missed how her eyes sparkled whenever they found "treasures" beneath the rocks near the swamp. He missed how she laughed; the sound was so sweet and joyful. He missed when they would play pretend and Zakai was the knight and Teta was the princess. Their castle was the big boulder hidden deep within the forest. Zakai would tie together flowers and place a tiara on her head. Teta would find a pointy twig and knight him on their castle. He would ride the winds of innocence and adolescence while defeating foes in honor of his princess. But once their mother started calling and the sun would tuck itself in for bed, Zakai would lay down his sword and grab his sister's hand and lead her home. That's what kept Zakai going—the possibility to retain the past and sink into everlasting happiness once again. It's a shame that he did not appreciate it more when he had the chance.

"I will get you some water and food if I can find any." He paused and then hugged her. "Don't leave, little sister. I promise I will be back shortly." Teta gave him a puzzled look, not quite understanding what he meant. There was no way she could make it down the tree by herself! She barely had the energy to stay awake. But Zakai did not want to explain, so he kissed his sister on the forehead before making his way down the tree. Once at the bottom he grabbed his mother's hand and squeezed. She stirred but did not fully wake. "I love you." He kissed her forehead too and headed toward the swamp in search for food and water.

A few hours later, Maille woke to the sound of terror. The ground rumbled violently beneath her; the sky, which was once clear, was crowded with gray clouds while freezing rain pinched her skin. Shouts and cries poured from the village, and the scent of death clung to the air. For a moment she was confused; she saw nothing around her that could match such terror. The forest was calm and nothing was aloof. Looking up into the tree, she saw Little Teta cuddled against a branch, trying desperately to sleep.

Though tempted to convince herself that it was all in her head and to go back to sleep, Maille *felt* that something was off. She had to go check it out.

Slowly, as her bones fell into place, she stood just as a loud boom came from the village followed by louder pops. More wails and cries escaped from the village. She looked back up in the tree again but only saw Teta. Frantically looking around, she did not see Zakai. *Where was Zakai!*

Instinctively, Maille thought to run toward the village to retrieve Zakai and hide him up in their tree. But before she left, she looked back up the tree at Little Teta and knew she could not leave her alone. If something were to happen to both Maille and Zakai and Teta was left alone in the tree, she would not survive. She had to give Teta a chance.

Louder rumbles and screams attacked the serenity of the day. Quickly Maille climbed the tree, ignoring the bite of soreness from lying on the ground for long. Once she reached the top, she hugged Teta to her chest before climbing back down. Though Teta weighed a little more than a loaf of bread, Maille struggled to carry her.

When they got to the ground, they began heading toward the village. As they got closer and closer to the village, the terrible awful noises grew more and more panicked. Maille fought the urge to run and hide with her daughter. The thought of Zakai alone in this terror fueled her decision to continue on. She did not want to fail him again.

"Run!"

"Help!"

"Please don't take my baby!"

The sight that assaulted Maille as she entered the village will scar her for the rest of her life. Bodies, chopped into pieces or burned, covered the ground as soldiers marched through and destroyed what was left of the Qingkowuat village. Unable to move, let alone comprehend the situation, she watched the people she loved fall.

It was not the sight of death that shattered her heart. It was not the sight of her village crumbling right before her that tore at her soul. It was the sight of children being ripped away from their parents' arms. It was the sight of babies being tossed into the flames. It was the sight of those damned carts being filled with the purest of innocence God and his angels could create. Maille's heart shattered as she thought of Zakai's fate . . . If her son was anywhere near the village the soldiers would have dragged him away by now. Never to be seen again.

"Hey, you there!" Maille tore her eyes away from the horrific scene and turned to see three guards coming her way! She took a step back, and they began to run toward her. Teta whimpered in her arms, and it was as if Maille remembered she was there! If she could not save Zakai then she will at least get Little Teta to safety. She had to! Maille did not want to fail another child!

She dashed into the forest just as they began to chase after her. Dipping below branches and gliding over fallen trees, she tried to outmaneuver the guards. Teta sobbed in her arms from being jostled around and clung to her mother tightly. The guards were close behind them, but they were no longer in sight. Maille could only hear their armor that rubbed together as they continued to follow her. She had to get to their tree! Teta would at least be safe there, and Maille could continue running until the guards got tired. Adrenaline powered her angst and quickened her pace!

Finally! Their tree was in sight, and the guards were still out of sight! Quickly, as fast as her depleted body would allow her, she held Teta to the tree.

"Climb, Teta!" Maille urged, looking over her shoulder to be sure the guards were still out of sight.

Teta cried, unable to grip the tree, for she was too weak. "Mommy, I can't!"

"Teta, you must climb! Please!" Maille heard the guards getting closer. Pushing on Teta's rear, she shoved and shoved, trying to get the little child to climb. "Teta, climb!" Maille was too weak to climb the tree with Teta on her back again and knew that time was running out! "Climb, baby! Please!" Teta gave it all she had. But try as she might, she could not get up the tree.

"I'm sorry, Mommy," Teta began crying and held tightly to her mother's arms as Maille lowered her form the tree. Maille looked back at where she heard the guards and cried as well; not only could she not save her son but her daughter too. She stood in the middle of the forest, helpless.

The guards were getting closer . . . Maille could only do what she had to do.

"Teta, baby girl . . ." She kneeled down and looked at her daughter. Her words rushed out too fast for the child to understand, but Maille did not have much time. "Run straight, Teta. I will follow, I promise. But I need you to run. No, don't talk. Do this for Mommy. Run, Teta! Run as fast as you can."

"Don't leave me, Mommy, please!"

"Teta, Teta! Stop! Do this for me." Maille could see the guards in the distance. "Run, Teta! Run!" She shoved her little girl in the direction she told her to go. Teta stumbled but caught her feet and started to run as fast as her little legs would let her.

The guards made eye contact with Maille . . . She closed her eyes and counted the seconds until they reached her. She could not bear to turn back and see Teta, so she prayed she was out of sight. Maille just had to fend off the soldiers as long as she possibly could to give her baby a chance.

The guards had found her . . .

The first guard was surprised as she threw her whole body at him. With the small piece of wood she found off the ground, she tried to aim it at his neck. Her stick broke against the armor, so she continued to beat him with her fists. Unfortunately the other guards reacted to her assault quickly and pulled Maille off the fallen guard. They forced her to the tree, slamming her head against the trunk and then let her body fall to the ground. Maille was dizzy and filled with unbearable pain for a few seconds until she heard a sound she had wished she would've never hear again. A sound that was supposed to be far away . . .

"Mommy!"

Maille turned and saw Little Teta running back toward her! "No, Teta! Run!" But the guards had already seen the little girl, and one of them went to grab her. They had captured Teta . . .

"NO!" Full of rage, Maille lunged at one of the guards. The guard closest to her grabbed her by the hair and slung her to the ground! Dissatisfied with that, he continued to beat her from head to toe.

Teta watched in utter horror as her mother bled before her very eyes!

"Mommy!" she called and reached for her hand. But another guard snatched Teta's hand away and laughed at Maille's weak attempt to do anything about it. All she could do was cry and watch her daughter continue to reach for her . . .

Teta tried to escape the guards' hold on her, but Teta was too weak, too little, and too helpless.

"P-p-please, no. Not my baby." Maille reached for her daughter again, but the guards were already walking away.

Maille lay, defeated, in a pool of her own blood and watched as the guards took her child away. "Mommy!" Teta cried in the distance. "Mommy, help me! Mommy!"

* * *

"Get off of me! Get off of me!" No matter how hard Zakai kicked and scratched the guard holding him, he could not break free. "Get off! Help!" The terror that raked the village drowned out Zakai's wails. Try as he might to block the images of the dead that lay slaughtered all around, he couldn't seem to break away from the sadness that overwhelmed him. The guards made no effort to hide their delight in Zakai's sorrow. They teased the little boy for crying his pain away.

"Shut up, you vermin!" the guard to Zakai's left snapped. "You're getting on my nerves." The guard had Zakai by his wrist and was dragging him toward the big carts that were stuffed with weeping children.

"I want my mommy!" he sobbed, trying to yank his hand away. The guard only tightened his grasp on the boy. "Get off of me! Help! I want my mommy!" Any other day, Zakai would be embarrassed about crying for his mother, but today was not any other day. He was scared and rightfully so. It was a little less than an hour ago when he was scavenging the swamp for fresh water and food for his mother and sister. All of a sudden he hears loud popping sounds coming from the village, followed by screams of fear and agony. Curiosity overcame him and went to the village to see what was going on. He regretted it almost immediately after seeing what his village was once. The immense amount of blood that spilled from the villagers had turned the ground dark red. He saw mothers trying greatly to fight against the soldiers who stormed their huts and ripped their children away. Fathers did what they could, but there were so few, and weeks of malnutrition had weakened any attempt at revolt. The soldiers plowed through the village almost effortlessly. Zakai even saw a guard take a woman to the ground and do unspeakable things to her . . . He threw up at the sight and prayed his mother and sister were safe. Unfortunately while he was throwing up what little remnants filled his stomach, a guard had noticed him. It was too late for Zakai to run away, for the guard was on him in a second. "Your mine now, vermin!" the guard hissed. Completely trapped within the guard's grasp, Zakai could not escape! So he did the only thing he could do. He spit in the guard's face! Surprised and equally disgusted, the guard dropped Zakai, and he was able to run! But poor Zakai was caught almost instantaneously. Angry, the guard grabbed Zakai by the hair with one hand and punched him in the stomach with the other. Gasping for breath, Zakai lost consciousness and fell limp in the guard's arms. The next thing he knew he was being dragged away toward the carts.

"Get off of me! Help! Somebody, please help me!" But no one could. His village lay in shambles; nothing remained standing. Even the elders' huts were torn to pieces . . . the site broke Zakai's heart.

"There!" The guard shoved Zakai into the filthy carts that were already packed too full. "Vile vermin." Zakai bounced against a few kids before he finally got his footing. Looking around, he noticed that he didn't recognize any of these children. They were thin and covered in rags, but they were not from the Qingkowuat village. As he continued to look around, he noticed he didn't see his sister either.

His heart began racing. "Have you seen a little girl? Very small, curly sand-colored hair, blue eyes?" Nobody answered him so he asked again. "Have you seen a little girl? Very small, curly hair, blue eyes?" The children around him resembled solemn statues that couldn't possibly grasp what was happening to them. "Please, anyone! I need to find my sister!" Panicked, he grabbed the little blonde girl next to him and asked the same question. "Have you seen a little girl? Very small, curly hair, blue eyes?"

The girl shook her head slowly without even making eye contact. Instead she stared off into the distance with a grim look that matched all the faces of the children in the cattle carts.

"Have you seen her?" He grabbed another kid but was saddened to get the same results. "Please! Has anyone seen my sister?"

"Hey! Quiet down!" one of the soldiers standing guard by the carts snapped.

"I need to find her! And my mother!" Zakai sobbed but was ignored by the guard. Defeated he cried. *Maybe they're safe! Maybe it's a good thing that she's not here because it could mean that they went to get help!* But Zakai knew all too well that that was not the case. So he continued to cry.

He cried for himself and what lay ahead of him now that he was alone. He cried because he didn't have his mother to hold him and tell him that everything will be okay. He cried because his sister wasn't there to make him smile. He cried because he no longer had anything to live for . . .

"Help, help!" Zakai heard the tiny voice, which only made him cry more. The sound reminded him of his little sister. "Help, help!" Again he heard the high-pitched squeal and realized that another child was about to enter the cart. Though all the children were deathly thin, space was certainly limited. Zakai was so smashed that he could only breathe in the terrible stench of waste that piled against the ground and the children that stood around him. He wanted to sit down, but there wasn't enough room to. He could only stand, like crops being transported to the market.

"Help, help! Mommy!"

Zakai wished his mom was here. What he would give to hold her hand and kiss her cheek. He was terrified on his own; he wanted the protection his mother guaranteed and craved her affection. She made everything all right, even the darkest of situations.

"Mommy, help me!"

He wanted to close his ears. The sound of a little girl begging for her mother touched him in a way he didn't want to be touched. It made him think of Teta. O', how he missed his little sister. What he would give to just hug her or play pretend. Right about now Zakai wished he were a knight so he could fend off these devils draped in impenetrable iron and restore his kingdom. He longed for his princess too . . .

"Please don't take her!"

Wait! Zakai snapped his head up and began looking outside the carts. *I know that voice. That's Mommy's voice!* He didn't want to believe it, but it was true! That was his mother's voice!

"Mommy!" the high-pitched squeal screamed.

Teta! Zakai strained his neck to search for them. Though his brain told him not to get his hopes up, his heart told him he was right! And he was!

There! In the middle of the village was his mother, bruised and bloody, on her knees with her arms outstretched toward the guards. The two guards were walking with Teta! They had her by the arm and were easily pulling her away from Zakai's mother.

"Don't take her, please!" Maille screeched, crawling toward the guards. "Please!"

"Enough, you vermin!" The guard not holding Teta went to Maille and slapped her across the face. She fell back two feet and lay limp on the ground. "Get rid of her! Now!" Another guard came into view and held up what looked like a metal tube with a wooden handle. Zakai had never seen anything like it! At the end of it was a long, sharp sword. And it was pointed at his mother!

"No!" Zakai pushed through the children in the cart and jumped down. The soldiers guarding it weren't prepared and paused just long enough for Zakai to run past them and head straight for his mother. "No, not my mommy!" Without thinking, Zakai shoved the guard with the metal tube and ran straight into his mother's arms. She embraced him immediately! "I love you, Mommy. I love you, I love you." His tears soaked her blood-stained clothes.

"Shh, it's okay, baby. It's okay," she replied weakly. "I love you too."

"Enough of that!" As quickly as Zakai was in his mother's arms, he was just as quickly taken away from her again. "Take this back to the carts. Take both of them."

"No, not without my mommy, please!" Zakai reached for his mother.

"Hurry up and put them in the carts! This is taking too goddamn long!" the guard holding Zakai barked. He turned and locked eyes with Maille, who could barely hold herself up. The guard's eyes were as dark as his soul, and he showed no emotion whatsoever. Still he said, "Leave her be."

The guard with the metal tube didn't lower his weapon. "What?"

"I said leave her be! That's an order!" He didn't break eye contact with that guard until he put the tube to his side. Then he turned back to Maille. "The rest of you will leave her be!" He ordered and then whispered, "She's lost enough already." Maille was too overcome with hate to thank the guard. She'd rather be dead than watch them take her children away from her.

"Mommy!" Maille's heart sank as Teta continued to call for her. "Mommy!"

"Let's go, boys. Wrap it up here, we're heading home," the guard who had spared Maille said to his soldiers.

As the raid ended and the guards marched back into line, Teta and Zakai were being escorted back to those dreadful carts. Maille watched powerlessly as the two most important things in her life were being taken from her . . .

Once loaded into the carts, Zakai grabbed his sister's hand and refused to let go. Unable to control her emotions, Teta held on tightly to her big brother and cried into his chest.

"What's going to happen to us, Zakai? Where's Mommy?" She sobbed, burying her face in his chest.

Zakai could not answer Teta's questions and could only empathize with her fears . . .

"We'll be alright, Teta." Zakai placed his head on top of hers and looked back at his mother for the last time. She tried standing to run after the carts but fell back to the ground. After two times he knew she would not be able to rise again . . . "Teta, do you remember when we used to play pretend?"

She nodded, too sad to verbally respond.

"Do you remember what I always used to say when the bad guys came to get you?" Zakai asked, swallowing past the lump in his throat as he tried to hold back his tears. When she did not answer, he said, "I said, 'I am your knight in shining armor. And you are my princess. To the death I will fight for you. For all my life I will protect you. I will never lay down my sword and accept defeat. And with God's good grace and angel wings, you, dear princess, will soon be queen.'" He kissed his sister's forehead as a tear dropped onto it. "I will never leave you, Teta. Nothing will happen to you, I promise." The carts began to move, and Teta and Zakai left their home, their mother, and everything they ever knew.

Maille's Poem

O' when the trumpets sound and the earth rumbles beneath my feet.
Through the dense marsh and forest Satan subtly creeps;
to wreak havoc amongst the inadequate and destroy the will of the wise.
I fear the worse for this most unwelcomed surprise.

O' when the trumpets sound and the earth rumbles beneath my feet.
I see the lives that fall before a beast far too powerful to see;
beyond the wrath of oppression and the destruction of man.
I fear for the innocence that once fertilized this land.

O' when the trumpets sound and the earth rumbles beneath my feet.
In my arms I protect thee through the pain and suffering brought upon by me.
I shall bow for no being unless a being shall bow for me;
for a mother knows nothing more than the love of her child and the hatred of Queens.

O' as the trumpets depart, I am left alone without a heart.
They took you, my loves; there was nothing for me to do.
And for that I lay down my life, in apology for you.

O' as the trumpets descend, I soon realize that this is the end.
I manage to crawl beneath a willow tree and pray for God's good mercy.
He obliged me, my loves, and took me by the hand;
He allowed me leave of this most insufferable land.

O' as the trumpets sound and heaven's gates open up to me.
The angels and I weep for those who could not be set free.
My loves, I am waiting for you to come to me. But for now I will simply watch over thee.

O' when the trumpets sound for you, it'll be my hand to pull you through.

CHAPTER 9

"AM I STILL ON PUNISHMENT?" I snapped at Jepson who had made the stupid mistake of opening my door.

Three weeks I had been put off to nothing more than my room. I was prohibited from dining with the Royals, talking with the Royals, even looking at them! Not that I ever got the chance. The queen never said a word to me after the dinner fiasco a few weeks ago. The only orders I received were from two armed guards escorting me to my room.

"*Madame,* I am merely the messenger." Jepson smirked as he invited himself in. He surveyed my living corridors for a moment before turning to me. "You should be more grateful, Arianna—"

"It's Lady Korinthos to you!" I corrected.

"Her Majesty has been most gracious with your... accommodations," he finished, completely ignoring me.

"Gracious?" Was he serious? "Her Highness sent me to my room as a parent would direct a child in need of reprimanding."

He chuckled, taking a seat at my dining table. "And to think Her Majesty was worried you would not understand the depths of your punishment. It seems you understand it completely."

The smug look on his face enraged me entirely. "Be mindful of that tongue of yours, Jepson. I assure you if you offend my intelligence again I will not respond with a *hollow* threat."

A little rattled, though he tried to hide it, he stood from the chair and stepped a few more feet away from me. "You must agree that this is a beautiful room. Aren't you a little grateful?"

"Of course I am grateful for what your queen has bestowed upon me, Jepson," I replied, moving toward him. He had his back to me and was looking out my window.

He chuckled and said, "She sends you to your room for a little while and already she's not even considered your queen anymore."

"It was not my intention to speak ill of Her Majesty," I corrected. "Nonetheless, our relationship has surely declined. For she has me behind these plastered bars and locked away in a furnished cell. Her Majesty has no regard for me anymore. I am simply nothing more than an inconvenience."

Turning to face me, with his pale, thin, pointy features, he shrugged in agreement. "A beautiful inconvenience nonetheless." He winked and then gestured toward the pitcher of wine on the table. "I wonder if you would be good enough to share some of your wine with me. It seems I'm a bit parched." I nodded and he said, "Would you mind pouring me a glass?"

"Jepson," I replied, walking to sit at my dining table, "I do remember you having the ability to pour your own drink." He followed shortly after I had settled in, and he took a seat across from me.

"No matter how true your statement is"—he reached for the glass with that god-awful smirk on his face—"I must say I prefer others to handle such mundane duties. There are far too many important things for me to handle than something so domestic. Besides, I know how worthless you must be feeling, so I wanted to allow you to do something that will make you feel useful. Seeing as at the moment you contribute absolutely nothing to *your* queen or to this kingdom." He filled his glass and raised it towards me, smiling, "But do not fret, Lady Korinthos. I shall fill my own glass. Cheers."

I understood where Jepson's new sense of righteousness birthed itself. From the looks of his new fancy attire and pointy shoes, I see the queen has been spoiling him. It must be reward for leaking Lyrrad's secret meeting with me. I also assume his rank was raised or I was demoted. Either way he had power over me, and for the time being there was nothing to be done about it. I understand why he basked in his temporary victory over me. Even though I did think we were friends. He taught me nearly everything about the palace and was very courteous and openly flirtatious with me in my early weeks.

His attitude changed once the queen granted me a higher status than he. Jealously ate at Jepson for months. It carved this futile game he believed me to be taking part in, a game being manipulated by the queen with the results already predetermined. In the end there will be no winner, only two losers.

"Jepson, now that your ego has doubled its size, I do inquire as to what this visit entails," I said just as he finished half of his glass.

"Déjà ennuyé? Oui?" He snickered, running his finger around the lip of the glass. "You could not grant me five more minutes to witness your dismay?"

"O', but dear friend, was it not you who spoke of the many tasks that have been placed upon your shoulders? I assume you wish to return to your duties as swiftly as possible," I countered, pushing the wine away from him just as he went to pour himself more.

"Trust me, *camarade,* I find no pleasure in having to babysit you. Especially not in this smelly room. You should really consider opening a window," he chided, crossing his thin legs. The amusement in Jepson's eyes made me want to dismember him piece by piece. "I understand that, at the moment, you can't do much of anything for yourself, so I will attempt to ignore your inadequacies."

"What do you want?" I snapped, no longer wanting to continue playing this game.

"Are you not having fun anymore?" He smiled, flashing his pearly white teeth.

"Jepson, if that smug look on your face is the assumption that I am envious of you, you are sadly mistaken," I replied casually.

Sighing loudly, he tapped his fingers on the wooden table, contemplating his next move. When he came up with nothing, he shrugged and said, "Her Highness wishes to speak to you. She has someone she wants you to meet."

Fed up and skeptical, I countered, "Jepson, I have allowed you the room to express your crude acknowledgments, but I do attest that the game is over. In honor of our previous relations, I do ask that you state the true reason of this visit." I knew Jepson had an agenda and his time frame was running out. Her Majesty would soon realize my importance and things would go back to the way they were.

"I speak of no farce," he replied as if offended by my accusation.

"If what you say is true, then why hasn't Her Majesty come to tell me herself?" I asked, pushing to my feet. "It would be the courteous thing to do."

"Lady Korinthos, I was sent here by the queen to relay this message to you," he replied, continuing to sit.

Now it was my turn to throw some dirt on him. "O', I see. To think I believed your social status among the Royals has changed. Turns out you're still the queen's bitch boy who runs her messages and wipes her ass. And you thought I was the one who smelled?"

Jepson's entire body clenched up as if he were about to burst at any moment. His breathing quickened, and his face turned bright pink! I was going to laugh at his inability to withstand such chiding and venomous banter, but I decided to enjoy the view instead. I had had to endure his verbal berating, so it only seemed fair that he had a taste of mine.

For several minutes he fumed, but soon the pinkness in his cheeks returned to their pasty white color, and he aligned himself back into his perfect posture. "I will overlook your condescending tone, Lady Korinthos. I understand this has been a difficult time for you."

"When shall I expect your absence?" I said, hating how calm he now suddenly was. "Hopefully soon."

Standing from his chair, he sighed again and then headed toward the door. I followed behind him, hoping that he would leave me in peace.

He stopped with his hand on the door and turned to face me. Giving me a once-over he smiled, tilting his head to the side. "Childish ridiculing aside, Lady Korinthos, I do miss you. Please, meet with Her Majesty. I'm sure she misses you too."

"Good-bye Jepson," I snorted, forcing the doors open. There were, like always, two guards standing outside my door. Jepson casually stepped through the threshold and paused again.

"She's in *Le salon de la Paix.*" He smiled again before turning to walk away with his own personal guards. *"Au revoir!"*

Hell would have to freeze over for me to accept such an improper summit.

* * *

Curse my curiosity! Standing a few feet away from the entrance to *Le salon de la Paix*, I thought of what this summoning from the queen could mean. For weeks Her Highness has locked me away and pretended as if I no longer was of existence! Why, all of sudden, has she requested me? It had been several minutes after Jepson's departure that I decided to go meet with her. Curiosity had gotten the better of me. For all I know this could be a trap! What's to stop her from killing me? Nothing is more important to the queen than the queen herself. She proved that at the dinner party! Throwing out food in the midst of a famine was not the worst of it! The worst part was she wouldn't even allow the peasants the scraps. She placed three armed guards to guard the discarded food just so the poor could not salvage any of it. It wasn't until the food was rotten did she relieve the guards of their task. For what? I am unaware of her intentions. She has failed her kingdom, and therefore, she has failed me. Yet here I stand, about to walk into the dragon's lair and face this "impeccable" beast.

I braved that first step.

She was sitting on her throne, draped in her beautiful blue gown that ran to the floor. Though I only stood in the entrance of *Le salon de la Paix*, I could see her gems glistening in the sunlight. Her Majesty was beyond words! More beautiful than beauty itself! It was a shame that the queen's appearance did not mirror her reign.

"Arianna . . ." She said my name in the same tone a guard would address a prisoner. Cold and stern. She had turned to look at me, and I noticed how bright white her face was. Its aroma slapped me before I realized the queen had put on several layers of paint to counter against her eroding flesh. Her face, though made up with color, was without emotion. She had only looked at me for a second before turning to stare ahead once again. I assumed it was my cue to speak.

"To what do I owe this summit, Your Grace," I said while remaining outside the room.

"I prefer to speak to you in private. Please come in." Her tone softened just enough for me to feel comfortable joining her in the room.

None of the rooms in the palace ceased to amaze me; *Le salon de la Paix* would be no exception. It seemed a lifetime ago that the queen and I had met here on friendlier terms. I had faith in the monarchy back then; now I doubted its objectives wholeheartedly.

"You come before me as if I have all the time in the world to deal with these litigations," she snapped just as I stood directly in front of her. Her Highness's thrones were always placed so that no matter who she spoke with she never had to stand to stare them down. Even her chair at the dining table was raised higher than everyone else's. The intimidation was there but I did not crumble beneath it. Not this time.

"Apologies Your Majesty," I replied with a hint of sarcasm, though I soon regretted it. Berating the queen would not work as well as it had with Jepson. She would shut me out completely, so I have learned. In order to calm the beast, you must appease it. "Please forgive my crudeness. I must be out of practice."

Her features softened a little more as she believed I was giving in to her tactics. "I feel as though there is a hint of repugnance in the mention of your punishment. Do you believe me to be unfair?"

"Not at all, Your Majesty," I replied without missing a beat. "My time alone has given me the space to think of my actions and crave repentance. I most certainly wish to prove myself to you once again."

For a moment she did not say anything, only assessed my response and determined if it was truth or a façade. Then she said, "That is the exact reason why I summoned you. I agree you must prove yourself to me again. Therefore, I no longer require you to be by my side, Arianna."

"But, Your Grace—"

She held up her hand to silence me. "I do, however, need you on other areas in and around the kingdom."

"I shall do whatever it is you ask of me," I vowed, remembering when I once meant it.

She smiled. "I would expect nothing less of you, Arianna. You're a rather resilient girl. Which is why this task is perfect for you. I know you will not let me down. Others in the past have failed me. I do not condone failure, Arianna. It is punishable by death."

"I, Your Majesty, expect nothing less from you," I bowed my head, absorbing her threat. "What is the task you require of me?"

I heard footsteps behind me just as the question settled between the queen and me.

"There is someone I would like you to meet." She gestured toward the man who emerged from the shadows. The man was tall and lean. His skin reminded me of snow as it ran over his limbs and tightened around the veins in his hands. His body was cloaked in black clothing that highlighted his fair complexion. The brown hair that rested loosely atop his head barley passed his ears—so unlike the Royals. The devilish gleam in his blue eyes hinted to a dark side that was hidden behind his charming smile. He was a beautiful man.

My breath caught as he neared. He extended a smooth hand to me, but I did not oblige. I was lost in him.

"Delicious, isn't he?" The queen drawled, knocking me back into reality. I dare not look away from his enchanting eyes that could lure me into hell. He stared deep into me, as if undressing me to the bone. Fear was not the dominant emotion cascading along my limbs; it was awe and a bit of wonder that had me drowning beneath his gaze. "Arianna, I would like to introduce you to Islocia's most prized possession."

Finally I accepted his hand; he wrapped his other hand around mine and smiled down at me. "Her Majesty gives me too much credit. She sees only the surface of a very complex being." He smiled indulgently at her. "I am Adok. Adok Calder of Hellec."

His accent was mesmerizing, thick but easily understood. I wanted to smack myself for not being on guard with a stranger, but I liked this new feeling he aroused in me. It is a feeling I had not felt in a very long time. "P-pleased to meet you. I am Arianna Korinthos of Islocia."

"The pleasure is all mine, Lady Korinthos." He bent and kissed my hand, his lips maybe lingering for a moment too long. I should be frightened; I should pull my hand away. But I wasn't afraid and I did not pull my hand away.

"Adok has been away for too long. I sent him to Honudo to oversee the, how to put this, clog in the jails. Now that they are efficient again, he has returned to make our jails here just as efficient." If not overwhelmed by Adok's larger-than-life presence I would have questioned the queen's very general explanation. But I did not do that either. I could only stare into the eyes of this man who had me under siege.

"I have requested your assistance, my dear," he replied, lifting his lips from my hand. "The queen tells me great things about your impressive control."

"*Control?*"

He never stopped smiling at me as he slowly released my hand. "Yes, dear. She says you are swift and agile. Never missing your mark.

You kill when you are told to and never lose a night's sleep over it. I find that very astonishing. Especially in a woman such as yourself." His tongue, unconsciously, darted out and licked his lips. O' what the sight did to me . . .

"It seems the queen is giving *me* too much credit." I returned his smile and I watched his eyes dance. "Do you deem me fit to attain your request?"

Those eyes of his . . . how they melted into me . . . slowly looked over my body. He stared at my feet and gradually went up to my face. I felt his gaze caress me slowly, tenderly . . .

"You, darling, are perfect," he replied vehemently. "Dear Queen, you failed to mention how beautiful your soldier is. I see why you keep her locked away in the palace."

"I did not notice," she dismissed. "A girl is a girl no matter the cloth that drapes her."

Leaning forward, he whispered, "A girl is not who stands before me. I only see a woman. A very beautiful woman." He kissed my ear.

Shocked, my brain scrambled for comprehension but found none! It did the only thing it knew to do, and I quickly stepped away from the perceived danger!

He chuckled as I blushed. "She is more timid than I was expecting."

The queen replied, "Lady Korinthos has spent very little time in the company of attractive men. I believe that to cause her dismay and terrible gawkiness towards you."

Utterly embarrassed, I mentally beat myself to a pulp. *If the Conqueror saw your behavior he'd have you burned at the stake! Emotions are a weakness—you are not weak!* I had to gain control of myself again. I was a warrior, a soldier as he put it. I must prove it.

"It is not often the queen is wrong," I began, finally regaining myself, "but in this instance she is making an exception for herself. In regards to my stumble, I apologize. The queen has had me on punishment. My ability to assess a person and determine if they are a threat or not is on the fritz. I assure you, Lord Calder, I am more than you can handle. Physically and mentally. There is not a task you can force upon me that I cannot complete. That, I promise."

His eyebrows raised and his smile widened at my assertion. "We shall see. I do warn you, Lady Korinthos, I am a dangerous man. Your arrogance and sense of invincibility has never been tested the way I plan to test it. You trust that your character will only bend but never break." He chuckled to himself and shot a quick glance at the queen. "Dear girl, I believe you have just met your match."

It was my turn to snicker. "I have killed hundreds of dangerous men. All of them more intimidating than you."

"Is that so?" He stepped closer, smirking.

"Yes," I replied, returning his smirk.

"What is it that you fear?"

"Honestly?"

"Of course."

"Nothing."

He laughed cynically. "You should fear me."

"It was my intention to relay that message to you."

He laughed again and clapped his hands. "You do not find me the least bit scary?"

"You have not given me a reason to fear you."

"Not yet," he assured. "Many people fear me. Some call me the devil. Some say I reside in hell and find comfort in misery. I do not disagree."

This time I stepped closer to him. We were so close. Nearly touching. The heat from his chest mixed deliciously with mine. I could feel his breath spill onto my face. I was drunk in his scent. Whispering intimately, I replied, "Rumors and superstition do not amount to much. You simply reside in hell. But, Lord Calder, I was born in it."

I was prepared to continue this verbal game of tennis, but he stopped and merely smiled. Seemingly satisfied with my response, he began walking out of the room. "Come with me." Just as I was to make the first step, I stopped and turned to face the queen. She gave me no recognition, so I continued out the room and followed behind Lord Calder's swift steps.

"Where are we going?" A few paces behind, I fought to catch up. He didn't respond, only marched down the marble hallway. His hands at his back and his attention forward, he was a man with an agenda. We turned a few corners and went down several sets of stairs, and still he had yet to respond. "Lord Calder?" I said again, but he disappeared down another hallway. It was moments like these when I hated the immensity of this palace. Finding a person in the palace was equivalent to locating a speck of dirt on a beach. Unfortunately there was nothing to be done about the issue at the moment. I could only keep up my pace and follow. "If you were to walk any faster, you would be sprinting!" I joked as I finally caught up to him.

"If you were to walk any slower, darling, you would be standing still," he snapped over his shoulder.

A little taken back, I replied, "I meant no disrespect, Lord Calder."

"Doesn't quite sound right when you say that." He came to an abrupt halt just as he made it to the entrance of the palace. "Does it?"

Nearly smacking into him, I asked, "What are you talking about?"

"*Lord Calder,*" he said dryly. "For now on never call me that! No one does. Call me Adok or Calder. Milord will do too. Either of those work for me. Got it?"

"Yes, sir."

"Now that that's settled, follow me." He was just about to take off again, but I grabbed his sleeve. O' what fine cloth it was.

"Where are we going?" I asked sternly, not releasing his arm.

"It's a surprise!" He smiled wickedly.

"I hate surprises, Calder." I greatly disliked the way his name tasted. It was odd speaking a Royal's name instead of their title.

He looked down at his arm and then back up at me and smiled. "We are going to Lárnach. Your task awaits you, Lady Korinthos. Let's not keep it waiting too long." He gestured toward the palace doors. "Shall we?"

As if on cue, the two guards standing by the door pushed its heavy weight until it opened. The sun rushed into the palace, and the smell of the air nearly swept me off my feet. O' how I longed to be outside!

"We shall." Calder and I made our way down the steps to two saddled horses. And once again we were off! Calder was indeed a graceful rider. He resembled a ghost or mythical being! His long black sleeves blew wildly in the wind like several hundred crows flying in unison. His skin was so bright that it flashed as lightning did when it was angry. Not to admit fear, but to a passerby it would be quite frightful. It didn't help that his horse was also black.

The horses galloped gracefully along the dirt path toward Lárnach. Our escorts, two guards on horses, made sure our path was clear. Calder took the lead while I trailed closely behind. Had I known where we were going, I would have fought for the lead. Only out of respect for him did I lag behind.

We neared Lárnach, and once again I was in awe of the vastness of Islocia's capital! For years on end I spent my life hidden in the forest. It was my home. Now, as I gazed upon the tall structures and many stone buildings, I found myself feeling rather small. I had only seen Lárnach once; the queen did not let me travel outside the palace unless I was to patrol her gardens. I never understood why, but I loved this new opportunity!

Calder slowed his horse and I did the same. We began walking in silence and my curiosity fumed inside of me. What task could *I* be helpful with in Lárnach? My skills are better suited in combat or stealth, not engaging in communications with the upper class.

"Calder?"

"Hmm?"

"What is it exactly you need me for?"

He paused for a moment, thinking. "You are a frigid woman, so I hear. Ophelia tells me much about you in our letters." I was shocked he used her first name! I would be stoned if I ever disrespected her in such an unfashionable manner. Calder looked over at me and noticed my dismay and smiled. "I have known Her Grace since she was but a child. It is not so uncustomary for me to speak her name. Though I would not recommend you follow my path, my dear."

"I would never!" I vowed. He chuckled, and we continued our slow ride as we entered into the busy villages of Lárnach. Our escorts took the lead and cleared our path of Royals scrambling from expensive shop to expensive shop. Carriages that busied the streets were soon idling on the side of the road. Children busily played about while their mothers sipped tea and chatted amongst each other. I was amazed at the energy of the village. Everyone was smiling, and their gowns and clothing resembled their bright, cheery attitudes. Even the men smiled as we rode by. Harlots, who were dressed rather indecently, flaunted there attributes at Calder and the two guards who obviously enjoyed the attention. Trumpets sounded to the royal flag— red with a golden male lion's head in the middle— as we continued traveling through Lárnach. People cheered for us and threw roses at our feet. Calder offered them a wave while I blushed at all the positive attention. I could hardly hear my own thoughts at the roaring of the crowds. Men whistled in appreciation of me; but, insulted, I offered them no recognition.

"Just up ahead!" Calder said as we turned at the end of the road. "This is the town square." The street opened up and transformed into a large plaza with emphasis on the center of the town square. "This is where most of the town meetings or Royal Proclamations are held. Anything that the queen believes the public should know about is dealt with here."

"I assume there is a reason for that?" I pointed at the wooden structure placed prominently in the middle of the town square. The structure was tall with a scaffold at the base and gallows at the tops. Hanging from the gallows were eight ropes with nooses tied at the ends of them. Beneath the ropes were tall stools that seemed oddly misplaced. The height of the rope was perfect for men, so the stools seemed redundant in my opinion.

"Yes, yes, it is. There will be a hanging today." He nodded as we left the town square.

"I assume that to be my task?" I wondered aloud. It now made sense why he would need me. I do not falter at the sight of death and have no qualms killing evil men.

He simply responded with a nod, and we continued our ride in silence.

We ended up at an enormous castle almost the size of the Belle Palace! Never would I have believed that another structure could compete with the vastness of the Belle! The Belle's beauty could never be topped. What the Belle lacked in size, it made up for it in beauty and grace. This, however, was bland and unworldly unattractive. It resembled the common castles that were the norm for this day and age. I assume it was home to another member of the royal family.

"How many people must I meet before my task is delivered upon me?" I asked while dismounting my horse. One of the guards standing outside the entrance tied down my horse, and then Calder's horse.

"What do you mean?" Calder asked as he too dismounted.

"This is a castle, yes? Only royalty is blessed enough to live here, right?" I followed him to the front of the castle. "These walls are what, ninety or a hundred feet high?"

"It is two hundred and twenty feet by ninety feet. The walls are eighty feet high," he responded as if the question was common knowledge.

"Quite impressive! I have never seen a castle like this. Though it does not compare to the Belle." I smiled admiringly at the building.

"This is no castle, my dear." He signaled the guards out front to open the large wooden doors. They obliged and began opening it.

"What is this place then?"

The doors opened, and I wished they hadn't. Wails and screams! Cries of terror! The stench of rotting flesh and feces charged out of the building and almost tackled me to the ground. The guards were trying to scream over the poor souls who filled every crevice in the cells!

"This is the Bastille, Lady Korinthos." I felt him stare intently at me but I could not look away.

"It's a prison," I gasped, hardly able to speak.

"Yes," he replied sternly.

"There are no criminals in this prison . . ." I choked, swallowing past my alarm.

"It depends on how you look at it." His ghastly voice crawled up my skin, giving me the chills. He put his hand at the small of my back and urged me forward. Every step made my heart ache more and more. The sounds, the smells, the agony all got stronger! I could hardly breathe, which was not caused entirely by the disgusting odor. "They are victims, yes. But they all have contributed to the desecration of this kingdom. Therefore, they are also criminals."

"They are children!" I snapped, swiping his hand away and taking a step back. "How can you persecute the innocent?"

Just then, a guard pulled a young, thin sobbing girl out of her cell and threw her in the middle of the jail. She cried and tried to return to her cell mates who reached their boney arms out to her. The guard took off his helmet and used it to beat the little child . . . It wasn't long until her body was limp and bleeding. That same guard ordered two other children to clean up his mess and then shoved them back in their cell.

"Quotas were not met, punishments were delivered," he replied as if this was common sense. He seemed frustrated that I did not agree with him. How could he expect me to see it through his eyes! "You cannot weep for the weak, Lady Korinthos. Their only duty is to drag everyone else down with them! In order for a kingdom to succeed, it must demolish the pathetic. And if that means persecute the innocent then so be it! The needs of the many speak louder than the cries of the few. Get that in your head!" Rage piled up inside of me like no other emotion I had ever felt! My breathing quickened and my heart raced on! I was prepared to fight any man here! Slay any man here! *They* did not deserve to live! "Come now, Lady Korinthos." Calder placed his hand on my back, but I shot him a look so deathly that he quickly removed it. "You are not needed here at the moment."

Disgusted, I exited the Bastille and stormed to my horse. The guard tried to assist me, but I pushed him away and mounted on my own. I was just about to ride away when Calder grabbed my reins.

"We are not finished," he said behind clenched teeth. O' those eyes—how I once drowned in them—turned to ice, and now I hated them. I hated this man! I hated this place! I hated my queen for suggesting that this would be a suitable place for me to reside! I wish her to be damned! "You will leave when I dismiss you."

I did not reply. I was too consumed by anger to acknowledge him as my commander in chief.

He held my reins for a second longer, underscoring his intimidation, and then went to his horse. He mounted and signaled for me to follow him. Reluctantly I obliged.

We ended up back at the town square where a crowd of people surrounded the scaffold. The executioner stood off to the side, hidden behind his black hood. Calder and I stopped our horses at the rim of the exceedingly large crowd.

A flash of something shiny caught my eye. A guard on horseback was coming toward the gallows the same direction that Calder and I had just come from. My stomach twisted up around my spine . . . a great fear seeped through my body.

From the scaffold a gentleman appeared with a drum hanging from around his neck. As the guard on the horse came closer into view, the drummer began playing to the rhythm of a heartbeat . . .

Bum . . . Bum . . . Bum . . . Bum . . . Bum . . . Bum . . .

My fears had come true.

Following behind the guard on horseback were eight children marching in step to the drumbeat. Their tiny bodies were draped in heavy, rusty chains that kept time with the drum as they marched closer and closer to the scaffold.

I turned to look at Calder, but his eyes were intent on the children with a look of contentment smeared across his face.

Suddenly, the drumbeat quickened.

Bumbumbumbumbumbumbumbumbumbum!

All of the children ascended the stairs. Their bodies were so depleted that the only thing that held their bones together was skin. From where I was I could see the dirt that caked their limbs, the feebleness in their steps, and the sadness that weighted their eyes. They lined themselves to their own stools. The guard who was on the horse dismounted and roughly put the children onto their stools . . . The executioner walked by and put the nooses around their necks. Though the nooses were small, he still had to tighten them because they were too big to fit around the children's tiny necks.

Bumbumbumbumbumbumbumbumbumbum!

"Why was this task bestowed upon me?" I asked, unable to take my eyes away from gallows and the fearful children. "Am I still being punished?"

The executioner placed black hoods over all of the children. Some of the children, the youngest ones, were trembling so badly that the ropes shook the gallows. I could see liquid stains forming around their genital areas, and I could hear the sobs from where I was.

"Her Majesty feared that you had the intention to revolt against the monarchy. Your outburst at the party stimulated much repugnance towards your attitude and status among the Royals. Her response to this was to show you the power that she and only she possesses." The executioner returned to his original post where the lever that would release the floor beneath the children's feet resided. "God does not determine who is to live and who is to die. In Islocia, in this kingdom, every life is in the hand of the monarch. The innocent, the poor, the young, and the old. Yes, even you and I, are not safe from the wrath of Ophelia. You not only questioned your queen, you did so publicly. So yes, Lady Korinthos, this is your punishment."

I swallowed past a lump in my dry throat as I realized this was my fault. "She had me locked in my room until you came. She knew I would have figured out what was going on beyond the palace walls. I would have tried to reason with her. She thinks I would have caused another scene . . ."

The drumbeat halted, and silence flooded the town square. Even the cries and sobs of the children on the scaffold ceased. The only sound I heard was the hammering of my heart against my chest.

"Now you must pay witness to the power of *your* queen," he whispered.

The executioner released the lever.

The bodies fell five, maybe six, feet until the rope caught and snapped against their necks. Some of them died immediately. Others dangled for several long minutes, trying to resist the welcoming arms of death. The skies darkened, and the clouds began to weep for this tragic loss. For innocence, in its purest form, dissolved into thin air as the last warm body fought for its final breath . . .

CHAPTER 10

I'VE SEEN TWENTY-SEVEN HANGINGS. THAT'S two hundred and sixteen children suffocating as the queen released that damned lever twenty-seven times! She has killed more people within the week than the famine had within a month. Hell hath no fury compared to a queen as belligerent as she. Her mind may bathe in the decree of the Divine Right of Kings, but she cannot hide the bloodstains of her own people on her pristine hands! Though the words burn the insides of my mouth, I must say I do not love the queen.

Calder seemed pleased with himself. He has proven to be the devil he is so often called by those who cower at his presence. I, on the other hand, fear no man though Calder continues to try to rip my control away. He believes he is the one who can break me; I believe he is the only one who can come close.

Though I despise his occupation and wish him dead, I do not mind his presence. I cannot explain why, but I often find myself staring at him. I want, more than anything, to see him as only the one who supervises the legal death of children. But I cannot. In the palace walls he is exceedingly alluring. We danced at one of the few parties the queen allowed me to attend. He held me so close, maybe too close. I could still feel his lips at my ear and hands on my hips and the bottom of my back . . . No! I cannot think such things! I cannot remember such things! That man! That damned man deserves no such recognition! May hell drag him by his ankles into its awaiting flames! I want him dead! The only reason I still feel his touch is because his touch is the flame that fuels my rage toward every Royal! Especially those who condone the death of innocents! Curse him! I want him dead! I do not cherish his touch and crave his presence. If

I had the chance I would kill him myself. I want to, I do. I really do. I want him dead.

Right? That is what I want, I am almost sure of it. He is a bad man who kills for the enjoyment rather than for the pay. I see no sense of doubt or grievance toward the queen as she demands the slaughter of those who cannot defend themselves. Any man who preys on the weak is a *boy* who fears the idea of an even fight!

But he held me so close. He was so warm, so sure. Smiling down at me as if I were the only woman he saw . . . Kissing my hand so tenderly, touching me so softly, and looking at me so adoringly . . .

Lately my mind has been assaulting itself. It could not make a simple decision or contemplate things as they are instead of what they should be! I never give the guilty the benefit of the doubt! Though it is exactly what I do in regards to associating with Calder. I am meant to defend the just and stand up for those who cannot do it for themselves. Yet ever since I have arrived at the palace, I defend the wealthy and the corrupt and stand for nothing . . .

"Lady Korinthos," I heard a familiar voice call as I exited my room. Normally at this time of day, late afternoon, I would head to court and listen to the litigations of the daily crises among the Royals. I was running late, not that the queen would care. "May I escort you to court?"

"To what do I owe this most respected surprise, King Araun?" Smiling politely, I accepted his outstretched arm. It was not often that I was allowed to spend time with the king. Due to the matriarchal ways of the monarchy, King Araun spent his days hunting. From what I could tell he never saw much of the queen and hardly ever attended court. Jepson even mentioned that the king and the queen sleep in separate rooms on opposite sides of the palace. Even King Araun said he did not love the queen. I found it quite odd, but I was not one in the position to question much of anything these days.

"Lady Korinthos, it is most certainly my pleasure to escort someone as yourself." He patted my arm and we started down the hallway. The king is a strong man with muscles that still held their shape. The only sign of age he had was his wrinkles; still he had a handsome face.

"I must say, Your Highness, it is not often that one gets to dance with kings," I replied, acknowledging our dance a month or so ago.

"And I must say, milady, it was one of my greatest honors and fondest memories." The king smiled at me as we continued walking. For a few long moments we walked in silence. I wondered if he would honestly address his notion but did not want to pry. Unlike the queen, I sincerely admired the king. He was patient and fair. Strong yet gentle. "Today is a day worth remembering. So much beauty, wouldn't you agree?"

I smiled, knowing how rare it was to find a man who sees beyond what is before him. "Yes, Your Highness, I must agree."

"My dear, do you agree because your observation is honest or because I am your king?" He chuckled, eyeing me as a father would his child.

"I honestly agree. When I am allowed to see more than just the courtyard below my window I certainly take the time to admire such beauty," I replied honestly. "The only home I've ever known was the outside. I always had a blue, sometimes purple or black, roof over my head. When I was younger I convinced myself that the stars only shined bright for me."

The king stayed silent before saying, "My home has always been marble walls and shiny floors with gold trimmings. When I was a boy I was not allowed to play in the forest. Now that's all I find myself doing." He paused and then sighed before continuing. "It's quite comical the direction life will take you. Here I am, king of the most wonderful kingdom in all of the lands. I have everything I could have ever asked for. Well, every materialistic thing, that is. Still, I feel the hole in my heart every day as I wake up by my lonesome, eat at a table with only my plate sitting on it, and attend to a chore that is meant for sport and go to sleep to start the dreadful day again in the morning."

"I know of such a hole, Your Majesty. Though many are not as lucky as you, for you have a beautiful wife to fill that hole, yes?" I pondered aloud. We continued walking through the halls at a leisurely pace; he obviously was in no rush, so why would I be? "I believe God has blessed you quite well. Far too many have not had such fortunate upbringings as you have had. Fewer experience the generosity of a queen."

He struggled with what to say for a little while and then sighed. "Yes, I am incredibly grateful for my queen."

Silence filled the space around us as the awkwardness crept in. The solemn look in the king's eye told me he longed for something this palace and the queen, perhaps all the money in the world, could not provide. I was sad for the king, though I did not show it.

"Milady . . ." Finally the king broke the silence. "I wonder if I may inquire you for a moment."

"I mind not, Your Highness." We turned down another pristine hallway as we headed toward the stairs.

He thought for a moment and then asked, "Do you like me?"

"Of course, Your Majesty," I simply replied, "I like you a lot. You are a respectable man. It is quite admirable of someone of your stature and prestige."

He smiled his appreciation. "Kind words, milady. Very kind words." Again more silence and then he asked, "Do you admire your queen?"

I took longer to answer this one. "Of course. She is the queen."

He chuckled. "In the tone your answer was presented, I assume that line is well-rehearsed."

"Those are your words, Your Highness. I spoke only to appease the question," I said matter-of-factly.

"That you did," he noted, holding my arm tighter while we descended the stairs. "That you did."

To defend against the silence that would soon follow, I asked, "May I now inquire you?"

"Of course, milady." He smiled, slightly releasing me as he finished going down the stairs. "I am indeed a fair king."

"I must agree." I laughed at how his eyes danced when he spoke. "You are the fairest of them all. Mysterious and well-versed, but nonetheless very fair."

"Mysterious? Such an odd word to describe a king!" He laughed, playfully scolding me. "To what do I owe that title for?"

"I am merely stating facts." We headed toward another set of stairs and smiled at the Royals we passed by. "Who, may I ask, has pierced through your golden crown and fancy clothes? I do not believe that anyone has seen the king's heart."

"There is only one," he murmured, staring ahead into the distance.

"Who might that be?" I asked. The king did not acknowledge me and did not answer my question. Deciding not to push the issue, we continued our long walk to where the court was and left the question behind us.

After a short while down more stairs and hallways, I asked, "What was the purpose of those questions?"

He sighed audibly and continued to stare ahead. "I spend no time in your company. Mayhap it best I get to know you as the person, not the soldier who cradles the sword."

"Thank you." I could not mean words to mean more than those I spoke to him. He was absolutely a gracious and most loving king. I more than respected King Araun; my grip on his arm tightened.

We arrived at court a minute or two after his decree. Drudgingly I gazed upon my position next to Her Majesty's throne and reluctantly released his arm. I did not want to attempt to melt a glacier with a single torch. But orders were orders, and I was always one to follow them, so I must stand by the queen while she openly disapproves of my presence.

"I admire you, Lady Korinthos. You are beyond words, if I may say so myself." He brought my hands to his lips. "Mayhap when you are relieved you would join me in my apartment for a game of chess?"

Just then I felt a scorching hand at the small of my back. I did not have to turn to see who it was.

"Your Majesty," Calder hissed, anchoring me to his side. King Araun's features hardened as they stared down one another, their heights even with each other. "Lady Korinthos is late for court. Be it your doing?"

"Yes, I am the reason for her tardiness," the king snapped. "Be it none of *your* business. I am the king. Therefore, I do as I please." The king slowly released my hand. "Adok, if you would be so kind as to pass my apologies to your keeper? It would be much appreciated, dear *boy*."

Calder's sinister laughed chilled the space between us. "I will no longer be the one to keep you from your . . . *playtime*. Some of *us* have honest work to be done. So please, continue to polish your crown while others put theirs to work." Calder turned our backs to the king, a blatant sign of disrespect!

"Adok," the king barked his name, causing Calder to pause, "do remember that my crown is made of gold. And shines very prominently to all with the gift of sight to see." I felt Calder tense beside me as he felt the weight of the king's statement. He spoke to me now. "I look forward to our next encounter, milady."

"As do I." I tried turning my head to address him, but Calder held me firmly at his side with our backs still to the king. With nothing further, I heard the king walk away while Calder began shoving me down the hallway away from the court. We kept walking at a faster-than-normal rate, and he continued to squeeze me! I could hardly breathe! He forced me into a secluded hallway where no Royals and their slaves lurked about. It was only me, him, and his personal guard.

Before I had time to fully assess the situation, his guard pushed me against the wall! I struggled for a second before his guard pressed harder against me. Calder calmly, as if nothing was askew, approached me. Menacingly smiling at me, he said, "I do inquire, if I may, why you believe such behaviors as the ones you have presented are acceptable."

I fought the urge to take down his guard and break his neck! The guard crushed my arms to my sides and then pushed them above my head, so I was completely at his mercy. I hated it! I could kill him, right here and right now! I could damage him forever! All I'd have to do is wrap my legs around his back and slam him to me. The pressure on my wrists would subside due to his surprise, and then I would wage my full attack!

"You would be wise to have me released!" I growled, testing the guard's hold. He gave no leeway.

"Do not test my patience, Arianna, please." He shook his head with his hands behind his back. "I have been very kind to you and for the most part have ignored your indiscretions and lack of deference towards the queen. But I cannot turn a blind eye to *this*."

"Let me go." I had to stay calm, for I knew that assaulting a Royal would cause me more problems than I needed. "Now."

"Do not forget that you are here for the queen," he replied casually. His eyes were as razor sharp as his smile. Calder was a man who did not force fear upon someone; rather, he expected those at his mercy to quiver as if a natural reaction to his presence. He did not have to scream or yell to evoke fear. Just a look or a quirk of his lips could have you scrambling for death just to escape him. "I do not mind if you fancy the company of Royals, but I will remind you that there are things you are permitted to do and there are things you are certainly not allowed to do. If you continue to parade such carelessness in front of the very being that has clothed you then I will continue to treat you like this."

"Get off of me, now!" I yelled, ignoring his spiel. "Right now!"

"Do you understand?" he asked nonchalantly. I wanted to destroy him! I hated this man! I hated him! Damn him! I writhed angrily against the guard, but his hold was too firm. I screamed at Calder, but he continued to try to cut me with his gaze while this monstrosity of a guard held me in place.

"Have me released, you damned serpent!" I growled, thrashing against the wall.

"I said do you understand?" he asked again.

I had had enough of this. Stilling for less than a second, I bashed my head against the guard's helmet. Though it hurt me more than it did him, it awarded me the momentary pause I needed. Continuing in my assault, I pulled my arms free and slipped out of his grasp, and with all my strength I shoved him away from me. He stumbled for a moment, long enough for me to tackle him to the ground. Hastily he reached for his sword, but I stopped his advance. Snapping his wrist, I pulled the knife I had tucked away in my garter. I removed his helmet and quickly and roughly dug the knife into his neck and watched his life slip away.

Consumed by rage, I turned toward Calder with blood dripping from my hands and staining the pristine marble floors. With just my bare hands I could demolish this man. I wanted to, I needed to. But—though my mind was too overcome with hate, I was able to think—my fist would not save me. Only my tongue . . .

Standing before Calder, denying myself his death by my hands, I replied, "Yes, milord, I understand."

His gaze softened into an emotion I was too angry to define as he looked at my dripping hands. "You are not needed in court today. Go to the Bastille." He turned and quickly disappeared down the hallway.

* * *

How lucky I am to have such a steed that can lead me rather than me leading it. I was too overwhelmed with anger to direct it to the Bastille. How dare Calder! How dare him! And to think for a moment I considered him . . . no! No! Accurse the man draped in black!

Accurse the man whose skin is pale as snow! May he die a thousand painful deaths by my hand! Accurse he who smiles such a menacing smile! May his children be birthed from a polluted womb and his genitals decay!

I arrived at the Bastille, fuming, daring any guard to rattle my bones! No matter how much I hated Calder, I hated this place more! The rotting flesh and feces slapped me in the face every time I braved these wooden doors. The guards—how I wished them dead as well—drank until their noses bled! They would send their squires to retrieve the harlots who stood upon the corner, flashing their bosoms and flaunting their attributes. The harlots would then service the guards in the attic of the Bastille where there were no cells. When the guards got bored and they were done with their harlots, they would commit an evil so foul the devil himself cried.

The children in the Bastille ate only once a day, three days of seven. Most of the food was scrap from the Royals' feast or crops that had been spoiled from bathing in the sun too long. The guards knew how starved the children were and the lengths these children would go to feed. So what they would do to entertain themselves is place a turkey leg in the middle of the floor with two children on opposite sides of the food. The guards would then place their bets while they held the children back. Once they released them, all hell broke loose. It was horribly amazing to see what hunger could do to such innocence. Once I witnessed two brothers mauling each other for the "prized" turkey . . . I stopped the game before one of them died and gave them equal share of the turkey. Unfortunately their cell mates weren't as happy and beat the boys until they lay limp. The guards surely got a kick out of that . . .

"Lady Korinthos," the post guard bowed and tied down my horse. He signaled to the gatekeepers to open the doors, and I forced myself to go inside.

Screams, wails, cries of terror plowed into me, almost causing me to lose my footing. My heart always ached for these children, their suffering settling deep within me.

"Lady Korinthos!" All of the guards who were once lounging stood straight and saluted me as I came into view. I nodded them at ease and they dropped their arms. Sir Crichton came to me and knelt before me. It was a sign of respect, the way the guards saluted me, although I despised them.

"Sir Crichton," I acknowledged him. Once I did he stood, slightly standing over me. He was older than most of the guards but still kept in shape. His blond beard was trimmed and his golden hair flowed down his armor. The harlots' preferred Sir Crichton, for obvious reasons unseen. "Tell me of the day."

"Yes, ma'am." We began walking down the halls with cells stuffed with sick, hungry, dirty, and terrified children. "We received word that an enemy is gathering rebels to defend their way of life. My spy says they are planning to start here. They want to storm the Bastille and gather all the children. Certainly a mild threat considering the fear the monarchy has ensued but still, a threat is a threat. Should we add more security?"

"No!" I answered a little too quickly. Sir Crichton must not have noticed while he sidestepped a little girl's outstretched hand. "If such an attack is honestly brewing, I don't believe them to have the courage to storm through town. How long would it take the Royal Army to assemble? Minutes?"

"Yes, ma'am, but it is likely they could surprise us."

"Are you not the one who just stated that it was a mild threat? I have been told that the rebels have been planning such an attack for seven decades. We cannot afford to be frightful of every threat," I snapped.

"Yes, ma'am." He nodded although he most likely disagreed.

I had to look away from the little boy crying for his older sister who was locked in the cell on the other side of the hall. I could feel the sorrow in every scream but could do nothing about it. Sir Crichton did not seem to even notice such pain among these "prisoners."

"Is there anything else?"

He thought for a moment. "Yes. Four raids took place this week, and I need your signature so that the prisoners can be admitted in the cells." He pulled out a scroll and a feather with the point already tipped in ink. The queen suggested that I be in charge of all collateral retrieved from a raid. Meaning I must account for every child that comes through these walls . . . It seems Her Majesty continues to punish me. "Also, Lord Jamison has introduced new weapons. We used them on our latest raid and they are quite effective. I wonder if you would like to see them."

"What are they?" I asked, signing the scrolls. I tried not to look at the names of the villages, for I more than likely knew of the people that lived there. But a very familiar name caught my attention as I signed the final line.

"They are called—"

"When was this raid?" I cut him off and pointed at the line I had yet to sign. Next to that line was a name of a village I never thought I would see!

"The raiding of the Tyi village took place a few days ago. Why?" he replied, reading the scroll. "They caused no problems at all. It was a very easy extraction. So unlike the village before them . . ."

His words were drowned out as my mind raced! I know the Tyi village! They're merely a stone's throw away from . . . No!

"Crichton! Bring me the map of Islocia! Now!" I ordered. He paused only momentarily before leaving to fulfill my task. While he was gone I did not let my mind think the unthinkable! It could not be! The Tyi village . . . I know that village. I have been to that village!

"Here you are, ma'am." Sir Crichton returned, carrying the map under his arm. The map of Islocia was so old that it was drawn and detailed on cloth rather than on paper like the scrolls. But nonetheless, it was accurate for my purposes.

"Open it for me!"

Hurriedly he did. Unfortunately the Bastille was poorly lit, and I could not see what I needed to see. So I grabbed a torch that was hanging on the wall and brought it over to the map.

"Careful," Crichton warned. "Cloth is very fond of the flame."

I ignored him and began reading the map. My heart stopped. "I was unaware that the raids ventured to the coast."

"Why would they not?"

I suddenly became very warm; sweat began to dot my arms and chest. My breathing became sporadic and fast, but every deep breath poisoned my lungs.

"Those red flags drawn on the map . . ." I could barely hear myself over the cries of the innocent. "That is where the raids had taken place?"

"Yes, ma'am," he replied assertively.

"This map is up to date?"

"Yes, ma'am. I did it myself."

"Damn it."

"What's the issue, ma'am?"

Ignoring him again, I began scanning the children's faces as I passed the cells at a rapid pace.

"Lady Korinthos!" he called after me. It wasn't long until he caught up, slightly winded. "What is going on?"

"My village!" I growled, not bothering to look at him. I had reached the line of cells at the end of the hall and was momentarily glad that I had not found what I thought I would find. But my relief was short-lived as I turned around and saw the two children I hoped to never see there, in the cell. "You raided my village." Crichton did not know what to say as he followed my gaze to the sickly girl curled against her thin, protective brother. She was shivering against him and coughed blood on his shirt. The boy, with fear and sadness in his eyes, hugged his sister tightly.

Little Teta was the first to look up at me. My God, how awful she looked. Every bone in her body protruded through her thin, sickly skin. Her hair was falling out, her eyes had sunken in, and filth caked her entire body. She looked as if death was holding her hand, pulling her one way while her brother tried desperately to keep her here.

"Lady Korinthos . . ." Crichton began, but I silenced him with my hand.

"Leave me be!" I snapped, kneeling down to Teta's level.

He paused and then replied, "Yes, ma'am."

Teta lifted her head a little more to get a good look at me. She winced at the pain of the movement, which then jostled Zakai. Zakai turned to look down at his sister and then followed her gaze. He frowned.

"What are you doing here?" he snapped, scooting away from the bars that separated us.

"I did not know this would become of my absence," I replied softly. The boy was angry, yes, but it was understandable. No child should endure anything like the circumstances Teta and Zakai were in. "There is no justification for this Zakai. And for that I am sorry."

He sniffled and wiped angrily at a tear that had slipped away. "Your words do nothing for me. They do not feed my sister or unlock these bars."

"Zakai, I understand how you must be feeling—"

"Shut up!" he screamed, accidently jerking his sister. "Shut up, shut up, shut up! You have no idea how I am feeling! At least not anymore . . ."

"Explain . . ." O' how heavy my heart was as the weight of their grief was revealed.

"Look at your clothes, look at your feet! You even smell different!" He sounded so disgusted with me. His tears left tracks in the dirt on his face. "You forgot about us."

"No, I did not—"

"You were meant to protect us!" he cried, again wiping at his tears. "You were s-supposed to p-protect us from the bad guys!"

"I am so sorry," I whispered, reaching my hand in to comfort him. He kicked my arm away and moved farther away from me with Teta still in his arms. "I did not know about this. If I had I would have protected you!"

"Go away!" He kicked his legs though I was nowhere near where he could reach me. "Go away! This is your fault!"

"I am so sorry! Zakai . . ." He turned his head away from me. "Zakai!"

Teta raised her head again and opened her mouth as if she were going to speak. It took her moment before she could finally say, "A-Are you friends with the b-bad men?"

"Teta . . ." I sighed, defeated. Even a child as young as she could see the truths that lay beneath me. "I will make this right, for you." I spoke louder to get Zakai's attention. "I vow to you both, you will not be harmed! Do you hear me? I will make this right. Everything will be alright."

Neither of them responded.

Slowly I stood and looked at the two children one more time before I started walking away. It wasn't long until I found Sir Crichton waiting for me a few cells down the hall.

"Ma'am?" He asked, knowing I was to relay orders to him.

"Be sure that those children"—I pointed to where I had just come from—"get food and water every day, twice a day. Do you understand?"

"Ma'am, we have orders that the prisoners are only to receive such luxuries three days of seven," he replied.

If only looks could kill. "I'm overriding those orders." I stormed out of the Bastille, ecstatic not to be suffocated by the painful truths that were locked behind those wooden doors. The post guard untied my horse and I mounted quickly. "Sir Crichton! If my demands are not met, it will be your head. I mean that in every sense of the word." I didn't wait long enough for him to respond before I began racing toward the palace.

"I need to speak with Her Majesty immediately!" I growled at the guard who blocked my entrance to the queen's apartment. He was young, barely old enough to grow a beard, and shook nervously in his boots. Unfortunately, no matter how terrifying I was to him, he did not open the door!

"The queen has requested not to be disturbed for the rest of the evening." His voice quivered. "Come back in the morning."

"Open the goddamn door or I will tear you to shreds!"

Sweat dotted his brow as he tried not to meet my fiery gaze. "I c-c-cannot!"

"Tell her it's Lady Korinthos! She will understand!" I shouted, exasperated. Still the guard did not open the door.

"I have my orders." He tried gaining some of his confidence.

I threw my hands in the air. "Fuck you and fuck your orders! This is important. Open the damn door!"

"I will have you detained if you do not leave, now!" that damned guard barked. It must've been his first day on the job. Or he was filling in for the other guards who were at the pub drinking their day away. Either way he was alone.

"Open the door," I hissed an inch or two away from his face. "Now."

"N—" Frustrated, I took my hand and wrapped it around his throat and squeezed. It wasn't long until his face turned beet red to blue. He squirmed beneath my grasp, but the scrawny man could do nothing. His hands reached for his sword, but I grabbed it first. Using the handle I jabbed it into his chest until he passed out. I let his body drop roughly to the ground.

"Rule number one"—I threw the sword away from him—"if you're going to have a sword, use it as quickly as possible." I opened the door.

I was not in the right mind to admire the queen's massive and luxurious apartment. I was on a mission. It took me a long while to maneuver through her many apartments until I found her privy chamber.

Surprisingly, once I walked in, I saw Calder folded over the queen's bed while the queen toyed with the hair on the back of his neck. Though I found their closeness odd, I continued walking in.

"Arianna," the queen said, a little shocked by my intrusion. She removed her hand from Calder, who stood and greeted me with a stern nod. I did not acknowledge him as he did me. Her Majesty was dressed in her royal night gown and was still magnificently beautiful even before slumber.

"Your Highness"—I curtseyed—"I need to speak with you."

There was nothing but silence as the tension built between Calder and I. "Go on then—speak."

"I would like to speak with you alone, Your Majesty," I replied, not wanting to look at Calder.

She sighed and waved Calder off. "Very well then. It must be of importance if you have made such an effort to speak with me." She leaned over slightly to eye the fallen guard before turning her gaze back to Calder. "Lady Korinthos has required your absence. Please, humor her."

"But, Your Grace," he began to argue but stopped as she shot him a look I did not quite comprehend. Sighing, he bent down and kissed the queen's hand and murmured, "I will see you upon the morrow."

She smiled up at him from her enormous silk bed and ran her hand down his face. "Until then."

His features hardened as he got a look at me. He intentionally bumped his shoulder to mine as he passed me and headed out the door. He stepped over the unconscious guard as he closed the door behind him.

"Well now, Arianna. You have my full attention. What is so important that you must kill my night guard?"

"He is not dead—inadequate, yes, but alive," I corrected, stepping closer to her.

"What do you want? I am very tired and would like rest. It would be much appreciated if this encounter be quick." She mock yawned for emphasis.

"I will be quick, Your Majesty," I vowed, slightly bending my head.

"Good. Now speak."

"Your Majesty, were you aware of the village I was captured from?"

She pondered for a moment. "No, I do not recall it. Why?"

"My village was raided without my knowing. A few of my . . . friends are imprisoned in the Bastille. As you could imagine, I am a bit conflicted."

"I do not understand the issue." She shrugged impatiently.

"They are sentenced to be killed."

"Yes, and?"

How could she not understand! Even I without a soul can see the wrong in that! "I will not allow for them to be killed."

She cocked her head to the side, puzzled, and then smiled. "You will if I command it."

I hated her in that instance! I wanted to wrap those silk sheets around her neck and hang her from her window! But I had to stay calm. The queen responded best to words, not violence. "I understand that, Your Majesty. I am asking for you not to command me to commit such a travesty. Please."

She thought for a moment and then asked, "You are asking me to pardon criminals as to not disrupt your alliances with the vermin who are beneath you?"

"Yes," I replied, ignoring her last comment.

She laughed. "What is it that I receive for this agreement?"

"My devotion to you for the rest of my days," I replied, knowing I was selling my soul.

"O' please, Arianna." She chuckled. "I already have that."

"Your Majesty, I am begging you," I pushed, knowing how much she was enjoying herself.

She thought for a second and then said, "If I agree to this then how will I know which vermin to pardon?"

I replied, "Pardon them all."

She laughed hysterically.

"I speak a truth, Your Highness." I continued to press the issue. "I beg of you not to murder any more children. You have accomplished your goal and planted fear and misery all throughout the veins that run through Islocia. Not a single being will ever dare question your might! That I know for sure."

"You are asking me to spare the lives of criminals?" She rolled her eyes. "That is nonsense."

"Your Majesty, I have done all that you have asked of me. It would certainly please me if you would do the same for me. I am at your mercy, Your Grace."

"This is no small feat that you are asking of me." I could hear the enjoyment in her voice. She loved playing god. Calder was right. All of our lives are in her hands, and she can do whatever she pleases with them.

"I understand that, Your Majesty." I dropped to my knees and bowed to her. "That is why I asked you. You are a gracious and most loving queen. The people of Islocia willingly bow to your feet. I pledge my life to you, Your Highness. Please let the children of Islocia grow up and witness the rise of the greatest queen that ever lived."

"The greatest?"

"Yes, most definitely! I am more than honored to be at your disposal."

She smiled as her ego grew before my very eyes. "I cannot deny the truth."

"You are the best! But do not take my word for it. Listen to cheers and applause of Islocians who believe the same as I do. You are a phenomenal queen."

She chuckled, clearly satisfied. I had given her what she wanted; now she must return the favor.

"Give me time to think," she replied.

"But Your Majesty . . ." I had to keep trying; I promised Teta and Zakai that they would be all right. "Great queens do not need time to think. They naturally know what the right thing to do is. Prove to me that you are a great queen."

She mulled for a few minutes, visibly thinking the decision over. It felt like days until she finally spoke. "Very well then. I have made my decision."

"What's your decision, Your Excellency?"

"I have deemed your notion reasonable, Arianna. I will no longer order for the death of the prisoners in the Bastille."

"Thank you, Your Majesty!" I stood and went to kiss her hand. "Thank you, thank you! I knew you were a great queen! No, you are the greatest! Thank you!"

"Be gone now." She pulled her hand away and slid beneath her covers. "I need my rest."

"Thank you again, Your Majesty." She acknowledged my gratitude before drifting into a peaceful slumber.

CHAPTER 11

THE QUEEN MADE GOOD ON her promise, for none of the remaining children in the Bastille had been ordered to be killed after her ruling. Calder wasn't as enthusiastic about it as I was. He openly berated me and forced me to supervise the guards at the Bastille. A task he knew I hated. Nonetheless, I did as I was told and accepted his berating graciously.

King Araun and I had been spending more time together as well. When I was not busy at the Bastille, I spent nearly all of my time with him. He certainly was a very gracious and loving king. It was often that King Araun would tell me stories of him as a boy and as a young man. My favorite story he told me was about the time he was no older than a squire. It was his first time putting on armor and one of the proudest moments of his life.

The king and I would spend many hours walking all throughout the palace and the courtyard. We would go riding through the hills, always with an escort, and even made an appearance in the town square together. I admired the king and found him rather charming. He was always making me smile and I could not hide the hold he had on me. For reasons I could not fathom, Calder's hatred of the king grew as did his dislike toward me. The queen also grew increasingly distrustful of my relationship with the king and even made an effort to end it . . .

"You summoned me?" The day had barely begun to blossom when I received word that the queen wanted to speak with me. It had been a little while since I had spoken with her. I figured she would want some space between us ever since our little confrontation in her room a week or so ago.

"Yes, please come in." She hardly looked at me as she sat in her cushioned seat sewing while one of her maids played the lute. As I walked into the room, I nodded politely at her ladies, many of them Grand Royals, and waited patiently for them to be dismissed so the queen and I could talk privately. Her Majesty, however, began talking without awarding me that privacy. "Lady Korinthos, it is not in my nature to waste time, for it is very valuable to me. Therefore, allow me to be direct."

I nodded although she had still yet to look at me.

"I recall having a conversation with you, o' so long ago, about loyalty and trust. I distinctly remember confiding that such characteristics were very important to me and the security of my kingdom. Do you remember that?"

"Vaguely," I replied, annoyed with her simple speech. She was treating me like a child, again, and it burned my nerves to have to remain composed.

She continued, ignoring my snub. "I only allow loyal and trustworthy people in my company."

"Your Majesty, if I may . . ." It took everything in my being to remain polite. Even though I was in the presence of a monarch, I found it hard not to think improper and violent thoughts. "I have been nothing but exceptionally blind to everything you've done, regardless if I disagree with it or not. If that's not loyalty, I'm not quite sure what the word means then."

She snickered, her politeness nonexistent, "Watch your tone. Do not forget you are in my royal presence." I nodded an insincere apology and waited for her to continue. "My ladies tell me that you have been spending an unnatural amount of time with the king."

I shrugged. "I did not know my interactions were a source for gossip." I shot a glare at the ladies who had made an impressive effort to act as though they had not been listening to our conversation. "My apologies. I'll be sure to be more discreet."

She laughed humorlessly. "Discretion is not the issue nor is it what I'm looking for."

"So as to not waste any more of your time, tell me what it is that you want, Your Highness."

Finally she made eye contact with me. Staring up at me, not bothering to stand, her brown eyes smoldered as she replied, "Stay away from the king." It wasn't a request.

"As you wish, Your Majesty." She was just about to return her attention to her sewing when I continued to say, "However, if His Majesty requests my presence, it wouldn't be my place to refuse a monarch."

She sighed, clearly annoyed. "Be very careful with what you speak of, Arianna." I tensed as she used my real name instead of my given name. "Do not forget all that I have given you and all that I can, at any moment, take away."

After that, I avoided the queen and her ladies for quite some time. I found it easier to be amongst those less powerful than those of plenty.

"Your Majesty," I said as the king and I walked leisurely through the courtyard. There were four guards trailing behind us, a custom I had yet to get used to. To no one's surprise, on several occasions when I tried to stay away from the king, he had, in fact, requested my company. I happily joined him every single time. "May I inquire you?"

"Milady"—he chuckled, patting our linked arms—"you need not ask for permission. Please, inquire me."

I smiled, leaning into his hold on my arm. "Why is it that you do not attend the queen's court?"

We stopped at an old stone bench, and he gestured for me to sit down. In a moment or two a slave would bring us our midday tea. Enjoying time with the king was becoming a bit of a routine amongst us. Although it was obvious that many of the Royals disapproved of my closeness with the king, I found it comforting to have a friend.

"I do not attend her court because I am not needed." He accepted the tea from the slave, and I did the same when I was handed my cup. "Her Majesty is in charge of the kingdom."

"Why are you not? You are the king," I asked, taking a sip of my tea. I tried not to cringe every time I drank it, but I just couldn't acquire the taste. His Majesty, however, found the tea quite flavorful.

"Yes, I am the king, and that is all I am." He sighed. "You see, milady, Her Majesty is the heir to the throne. I am not. Therefore, her ruling is the only one that matters. She is queen in her own right."

"Then the purpose of your marriage is . . . ?" I asked, not quite understanding.

"Well, her father wrote a law that required a king and a queen to run his kingdom. If there was no king to assist the queen then the power of the throne would then be passed down to the next male in the royal family," he replied. "Do you understand?"

"Yes, but if I may, what responsibilities to the kingdom do you have then?" I found the monarchy all too confusing. How they made it work as swiftly as it does is a miracle all in itself.

"Were you never taught any of this?" he asked, finishing his cup. The slave returned and filled it again.

"Where would I learn such things?" I chuckled.

"I suppose that may be true. Silly of me to assume that all have been raised by gold." He smiled apologetically. "To answer your question, milady, I am here only to produce an heir to the throne."

"That is all?"

"Yes, in the kingdom I have no political power. And that is because I am technically a prince rather than a true king. A prince has no political power in his new kingdom and because I am not of the purest of royal blood, I am not a king. Her Majesty was gracious enough to allow me to keep the title of king once we wed." He shrugged. "Yes, the history of Islocia is very complicated."

"Yes, I agree, Your Majesty." I thought for a moment and debated whether or not to ask my next question. "If I may, why did you choose the queen when you were told you would wed one of the daughters of King Acheros?"

Slightly startled by my inquisition, he returned his cup to his lap and thought for a moment. "Where did you learn I had a choice?"

It was my turn to think. "An old man named Lyrrad Meeklea told me about the rise of the Acheros family."

"I see." He sipped his tea. "What did he tell you?"

"With all due respect, Your Grace, my question came before yours," I reminded him, knowing he would leave my question behind.

Sighing, he took his cup and mine and gave it to the slave. She bowed once and then scurried away toward her master; one of the guards escorting us through the courtyard. The king then reached behind me and plucked a beautiful white flower from the hedge that surrounded our bench on three sides. Gently he tucked the flower behind my ear and marveled at his handiwork. He said, "*Álainn.*" Which means "beautiful" in his native tongue.

"Thank you, Your Grace." I blushed, reaching up to touch his hand, which had not left my face.

"In regards to your question, milady, it certainly deserves an answer." He took his hand away from my face and returned it to his lap. "You see, the Araun family, my family was very wealthy. King Acheros wanted to increase his wealth so he formed an alliance with another powerful family—mine. The deal was I was to marry one of his daughters and become king and he would receive a hefty purse from my family."

"But, that doesn't answer why you chose the queen," I prodded eagerly.

His mouth had hardly opened before I sensed an unwelcomed presence. "Arianna!" Calder barked my name in the same tone a whip would crack a slave. A cold shiver ran down my spine as I prepared myself for what was to come.

I turned to look at him and was nearly blinded by his searing gaze. Calder always seemed out of place compared to the other Royals. The sun did not favor him as well as it did King Araun, whose aged skin looked nothing less than handsome under the sun's rays. Calder, on the other hand, was pale as snow and always wore black clothing. He reminded me of the shadows the trees make during a thunderstorm. Scary. Intimidating. Evil.

"Excuse me, Your Highness." I stood, knowing not to test Calder's patience. King Araun stood too and caught my pinky in his fingers. He then gave my hand a squeeze and smiled before releasing it.

I tried to keep the warmth of the king's smile with me as I approached Calder's arctic frame.

"Enjoying yourself?" he asked, slicing me with his fuming stare as I stood before him. He remained composed, as usual, though Calder spoke more with his eyes than with his words.

"Quite." I smiled, shielding the sun with my hand. The scowl that marred his face was comical but I did not dare laugh. "How often is it that one gets to dine with kings?"

Snorting, he began briskly walking away. Because I had not yet been dismissed, I was forced to follow. We hadn't walked more than twenty steps until he turned into a small opening that would surround us in a circular gate constructed by tall, luscious, green hedges.

"You like *him*, yes?" he asked, leaning casually against a hedge while two guards entered not soon after we settled in. They began furiously pacing around me in a large circle as a shark would its prey.

"If by him you mean the king," I said watching him and the circling guards, "yes, I am very fond of the king. I love the king."

He forced a laugh so hard that veins popped out of his neck, and his face no longer was white as snow; it was as red as blood. "*Love*? Dear girl, how stupid you really are. *The king*?"

"What do you want, Calder?" I asked, looking away, still keeping an eye on the guards as he continued laughing. "Considering this fatuous attitude I now have a better understanding of your need to remain composed when an audience is present."

Then suddenly it stopped. The cackling, the circling, the hate, the evil. It all stopped. The only sound being the distant chatter of the Royals who had also decided to enjoy this beautiful day. The sun was shining; the flowers had blossomed for the last time as the winter season began making its presence known. The only issue with this day being the shadowy man before me who had suddenly become very quiet.

When the silence dragged on for far too long, I looked up at him. His blood-red face had simmered back into its white perfection. He looked . . . lost. Like he was confused why he was here. His blue eyes were no longer hard as ice as he stared down at the ground. Then he looked back up at me.

"Calder?"

The guards were on me in a second! There was no time for me to do anything about it. Their hands were like iron grips holding me in place! They had me pinned to a hedge with its thorns tearing into my flesh. I tried to squirm free, but they held me so tight . . . too tight!

"Get off of me!" I wrapped my legs around the back of the guard's knee, the one who held my shoulders, and yanked as hard as I could! His leg buckled and we fell to the ground. For a second we were nothing but a tangled mess of armor and limbs! Then the other guard grabbed me by my hair and held me down. He had me on my back and held my arms over my head, completely overpowering me. The guard who had first held me had his legs shoved in between mine, keeping them far apart. His eyes caught fire as he noticed the slit in my dress had torn, making my waist area more visible. "Calder!"

"Shut up!" the guard hissed, pushing my legs farther apart.

I heard a soft cackle in the distance. "Simmer down, Kurt," Calder replied in that calm voice that sent shivers up my spine. "You will get your turn."

I feared the worse! Writhing and kicking and bucking my hips, I could not move this mass of iron! I screamed for help, but Kurt covered my mouth with his hand, suffocating me. He pushed down harder on my mouth. I tried screaming again, but the sound was muffled. Luckily, I realized his hold on my arms was weaker without his other hand! Bucking with my hips I slipped my hands out of his hold. Quickly I punched him in the jaw, glad he wasn't wearing his helmet. He rolled off of me, creating a cloud of dirt. I went to finish the job but was taken down by the other guard I had forgotten about! Once again I was pinned to the ground. One guard had me by my arms while Kurt straddled me again. They forced a gag in my mouth.

I tried pulling free but again I could not . . .

"You see, Arianna," Calder cooed, kneeling down to my level, "I own you. You are mine. You belong to me. You need to get that through your head, darling. Life in the Belle would not be this difficult for you if you knew where you stood in the eyes of the monarchs." He was so calm, so polite, and so malevolent. He spoke to the guards. "Stand her up!"

Roughly the guards had me on my feet with my arms bound behind my back. Calder approached.

"Do you understand?" he asked, rubbing his hand down my cheek. "Why do you keep doing this to me? It's quite upsetting."

I tried to attack him again but the guards held me firm.

"I don't understand your breed. You have all that could be given and still you want more." He sighed, shaking his head. "What more can I give you?"

I growled, wishing he was close enough for me to head-butt.

"You leave me no choice, dear." He smirked, pulling his hand away, "O' the skies will cry for you tonight. I believe it is time someone put you in your place. Lucky for you I have brought two strong, ruthless, soulless men who were more than eager for the task."

His burning eyes searched my face for fear. He looked so empathetic while he stared at me. Calder evoked fear so easily. Even from me . . .

With his index finger he drew circles on my thigh before moving it slowly up my leg. His breath caught as he reached my garter. Slowly, tenderly, he removed the knife that had saved me from a similar assault he had attempted. He tossed it aside and then returned his finger to my upper leg. He lingered too long on my waist before continuing to move upward. His vicious icy-blue eyes never left mine. He licked his lips as he reached my breast; he circled it once before moving to my collarbone. His ghastly finger did not leave a trail of fire behind it; it was as cold as ice. "So beautiful," he whispered so softly I doubted he spoke. His finger found my face. Slowly, slowly, slowly, he pulled the cloth out of my mouth. I remained frozen; the world had stopped spinning and all was silent. Calder traced my lips with his finger as I watched in awe. His gaze softened while his eyelids grew heavy.

Then . . . his lips crushed against mine . . .

It was rough, hard, and wet. His tongue darted in and out of my mouth over and over again. Both of his hands made it to my face as he squeezed my head. He slipped his leg between my legs while he forcibly stole my sanity. I was dazed when he pulled away, unable to think, speak—hell, I couldn't do anything but stare back at him. My tongue burned as if his kiss was poison.

His mask of indifference had returned. "Leave her be," he muttered before walking out of our circle that was surrounded by tall hedges. The guards tossed me to the side. I bounced off of the thorny hedges and fell to the ground.

* * *

I do not know how long I lay there drowning in my own thoughts. The sun had nearly settled, and the shadows created by the hedges blanketed me although it did not protect me from the chill of the night. Winter had slowly crept into Islocia and had found comfort in the twilight. As the sky darkened, winter was safe from the sun and could do as it pleased . . . It took the opportunity to prepare for the battle that would soon wage between autumn and winter. Soon, very soon, all the warmth that flowed through Islocia will be prisoner to the frigid victory of the winter season. At the moment, I was a victim of such a travesty. Unfortunately the cold was not enough to deter my mind from the day's events.

Calder had . . . no! I am merely dreaming. In a moment or two I will awake! This day had not happened . . . A cold breeze swooped in and sifted through my dress, telling me that this was in fact reality. I pulled my legs to my chest and tucked my head between my knees. If only I could just forget about it! If only the memory wasn't so fresh in my mind! If only I couldn't feel his lips on mine . . . If only I couldn't feel the helplessness that I was forced to succumb to . . . If only I could have fought back . . . Another chilling breeze clung to my bones, and I squeezed my knees tighter. Why hadn't I fought back? Why hadn't I seen it coming? Why hadn't I done more?

My teeth chattered loudly as I watched my breath turn to a white fog that vanished slowly before my eyes.

If only it were really that easy to disappear . . .

A few more hours had passed . . . two, maybe three. The darkness and cold swallowed me whole and gave no indignation as to when I would be released. I didn't mind . . . I had lost something . . . something I didn't know if I could ever get back. I was at his mercy; he could have ordered those guards to do the unthinkable to me, and there would be nothing I could've done to stop it . . . he took something from me . . .

In the distance I heard the sound of guards shouting and hooves thundering against the ground. At first I thought it was a trick of the wind, but the noises got louder as time grew on. It wasn't long until I saw the soft glow of torches make their way to the entrance of the cell Calder had locked me in.

"Lady Korinthos!" the guards shouted. I watched as a few of them continued on past me. I was hidden so well in the dark. I counted the horses that went by—one . . . two . . . three . . . finally the fourth one stopped and entered the circle of hedges. "Lady Korinthos?" I hid my head between my knees, not wanting to look this guard in the eye, partly because I feared who I might see and also because I was too ashamed. Calder had taken something from me today . . .

"Your Majesty! I have found her!" the guard shouted. Still I did not look up at him. I heard a few more hoof beats coming my way a minute or two later.

"Thank you, Sir Crichton." I tensed at hearing the name. Now I really could not look him in the eye. How shameful would it be to look the man who works for me in the eye in the state I was in? I could only imagine what I look like . . . Nevertheless, he had seen me, and now I am to be the laughing stock of the Bastille. "Go tell the others that they are released." I waited a moment until I heard Sir Crichton's horse disappear into the night.

"Arianna . . . ?" I heard the sound of the king's soothing voice near me. He must've gotten off of his horse because I now felt the warmth of his body from being so close to me. "Are you hurt?"

"Did . . ." My throat was raw from being battered by the cold air. "Did the queen send you?"

I heard him sigh. "Come now, my dear, let's get you inside." I looked up just as he was about to touch me and quickly moved away from him. I did not go far because I soon realized how stiff my muscles were from being blanketed by the winter breeze for so long. "My God . . . what did he do to you . . . ?" This time the king carefully reached for my arm. I was too cold to fight back again, so I let him wrap my arm around his neck while he o' so gently lifted me up off the hard ground. "You're shivering."

I was too numb to notice.

* * *

"Lucky for you, my dear"—the king handed me another blanket and brought a pot of tea over—"I have a fresh pot of tea that I had not yet had the pleasure to enjoy."

"Yes, Your Grace"—my tone was a cold as the outside breeze—"luck is certainly on my side today."

"Apologies . . .," the king replied sheepishly. "Please forgive my poor choice of words. I meant no disrespect."

I sighed, melting into the warmth of the fireplace and several layers of wool blankets. "No, no. It is I who should apologize. It is not my place to take such a tone with you, Your Highness."

He settled into the chair across from me. The king's apartment was grand. More than grand! It was astonishing. It was like a palace of its own. Lots of gold and silver highlights, and many gorgeous paintings hung on the decorative walls. Surrounding most of the walls were bookshelves stuffed neatly with books. Beautiful chandeliers glistened orange from the embers bouncing out of the fireplace. A small table separated me from the king, something I assumed he meant to have happen.

"If only we all could live as kings," I muttered, staring up at the high ceilings that were painted most beautifully. When I turned to look back at the king, I saw him mull over what to say. His mouth opened briefly, but he shut it and sighed. "How big is your room?" I asked, hoping he would not ask about me or . . . *him*.

"The apartment itself is immeasurable. It is merely a series of rooms connected by wide archways. Right now we are in the council study. It is where, if ever necessary, I conduct a meeting with the Grand Royals. Honestly, I only use this section of the room to study literature and read." He continued talking about minute details regarding the several rooms that make up his apartment. I did not pay him much attention, but I certainly enjoyed the noise. Something he obviously understood because he spoke loud enough for me to know he was talking but in a tone that suggested he didn't care for the topic. I liked that he kept talking only for my sake. His voice allowed my mind to forget what had happened to me. I was comfortable now that he was here. The world wasn't as painful with him.

"You play?" He caught me eyeing the chessboard that sat on the small table to the left of him. I noticed that he had already started a game with someone.

I nodded, seeing that the game was in fact over; white was in checkmate.

"Would you like to play?" He smiled, warming me further.

"Sure, but I must warn you, I'm pretty good." I smiled back.

"We'll see." He got up and retrieved the chessboard. "White or black?"

"White."

"Perfect." He returned the pieces to their rightful spot, and he gestured for me to go first. Once I had my first move he smiled and said, "I assume we are a playing a five-minute game, hmm?"

After several games and even more glasses of wine, I soon realized the king was exceptionally good at this game. He had beaten me every time in less than ten or so moves. Even after his fifth glass of wine he was able to beat me. I hardly came close. It had to have been well into midnight as we laughed and drank the night away. You would think one might enjoy chess in a quiet setting, but as the king drank more, the more boisterous and rowdy we became. We both needed a release and luckily we both had each other.

"Good grace, Your Majesty!" I laughed, swallowing a mouthful of sweet, crisp wine. "How did you get so good at chess?" I covered my mouth to hold back a burp.

"I spend many evenings by my lonesome, dear girl," he replied, reaching for a bottle and frowning once he realized it was empty. "Besides, it is the only instance in my life where the king is the most important character." He stood and raised his arms above his head. "All hail the king!"

A little dizzy, I surged to my feet and screamed, "All hail the king, all hail the king!" We laughed and sat back in our seats.

"Chess is my second love!" He laughed, falling back into his seat. How comical it was to watch the seemingly old king laugh like a child. I liked seeing him like this and noted that I never saw him act this way with the queen.

"O', dear King, then who is your first love?" I laughed, thinking we were laughing together but soon realized he had stopped. When I looked at him I saw that he was now very serious and looked so much like his age. The fire created deep shadows that filled the spaces between his little wrinkles. It no longer mirrored the festive atmosphere it had merely seconds ago.

"My first love . . ." He sighed, turning to stare into the fire. "What a pity you ask me such a question, and we happen to be all out of wine."

"Apologies, Your Majesty." My cheerful mood slipped away as I realized I must've opened an old wound.

The room was weighted in silence for a long moment before he spoke. "You asked me a question earlier, and I have yet to answer."

"There is no need to answer it." Though curiosity was eating at me, I could not harm the king further.

"I believe it is time you know the truth." He sighed, running his hands through his silky brown hair.

"Dear King, you will regret it in the morning," I replied, noting how much alcohol we had drunk in such a short amount of time.

He chuckled, leaning forward to pick up the bottle we had finished. "My dear, I drink maybe two or three bottles a night. It is the only way I can sleep right."

"Why?"

He paused and thought for a moment, absentmindedly stroking his beard. "The queen has taken something from me. She knows she has committed such a crime, which is why she spoils me so."

"I'm sorry, Your Highness," I said, not wanting to ask him to go on but not wanting him to stop.

"Lady Korinthos, I wonder if I may trouble you further and ask that you stay for a story," he asked with pleading eyes.

I could not refuse the king. "It would be my pleasure."

He smiled, taking a deep breath. "These walls listen to every word spoken behind them. We must be quiet for this particular story. It is forbidden to be spoken aloud."

"I vow my silence," I assured him.

Again he smiled, but this time he rose to his feet. He gestured for me to stand too, so I did. We were just about to head out of his apartment when he stopped. He left my side for less than a moment, and when he returned he had a wool shawl for me and placed it around my shoulders. He said, "I do not trust these walls." And then we were off. We hurriedly left his apartment and trekked down all the marble stairs as silently as possible. It was so deep into the night that all of the Royals were resting peacefully. Only a few torches were lit, and amazingly it was enough to illuminate our path to wherever the king had decided to take me.

"Your Majesty, where are we going," I whispered as he continued to lead the way.

"Hush, we must keep quiet," he replied over his shoulder.

We had to go down another several set of stairs before he slowed down a little. From what I could tell through the dim lighting, we were at the southeast end of the palace. I had never ventured past this area; no one really did, so I assumed that this was the spot where the king would tell his story.

"Take my hand," he said, reaching for it. "It is going to be hard to see from now on. I do not want you to get hurt." I did as I was told and grabbed his hand. The king looked over his shoulder as he brought me to a hidden door neatly tucked away beside an unused bookshelf.

"Watch your step, my dear," the king said, opening the door. "It's quite dark down here."

"Won't somebody see us?" I whispered, looking over my shoulder.

He shook his head. "The queen does not allow anyone passage through this area of the palace." I nodded and followed him down the stone stairs that certainly did not fit the beauty of the Belle.

Once we reached the bottom of the stone staircase, we were stopped by a heavy wooden door I would have never seen had not a small torch been hanging on its door. The king went to the door and knocked twice. After a moment the small opening at the top of the door opened, and two eyes stared back at us.

"It is me, Sir Simeo," said the king. "All is clear." And with that the small opening shut. From behind the door I heard several bolts and chains rattling until finally the door was opened. Standing before me was a large man, three times the size of any guard I had ever seen. He did not wear armor, only a leather tunic with a sword strapped to his side. His eyes were lifeless, as if he had seen every horrible thing imaginable all in the same day. No hair was upon his head, which told me he was not welcomed among the Royals. He was not a fat man by any means. He was tall, muscular, and intimidating.

"Who is this?" His deep voice rumbled as he looked down at me.

"She is a friend. You can trust her," the king assured the giant man. "Please, I wish to speak with her tonight."

Though I did not understand the hidden meaning in his message, Sir Simeo certainly did. He nodded and allowed us entrance.

"I will light the way for you, Your Highness." Sir Simeo grabbed the torch hanging by the door. His Majesty nodded, and we followed behind the large man. With what little light the torch provided, I noticed how grim and eerie this place was. It was cold, unbelievably so, which explains why the king gave me this shawl. Everything that surrounded us was made of stone. It reminded me of the jail I had been locked in the first time I came to Lárnach. It was actually a spitting image of *Ville Morte*.

"Where are we going?" I asked as we made a turn down a hallway.

"You're not scared, are you?" The king inquired, pulling me closer to him.

I snorted, "There is not many things that have the power to scare me."

"I know."

After a long while of walking over the slippery stones, we came upon another door. Sir Simeo knocked three times on this door, and once again another pair of eyes looked down at us. "All is clear." And with that the door was unbolted and opened for us. Another large man, the same size as Sir Simeo, stood before us. He did not speak and stepped aside for us to enter. I assumed we would be entering another series of hallways, but I was wrong. This doorway opened up into a dungeon. Never would I have guessed that the Belle could be so repulsive in its beauty. Beneath the marble floors and plastered walls was nothing short of a living hell. The dungeon was a wide-open space with torches hanging from the walls. Rats scurried freely, and the smell of musk had my stomach churning. No outside light was allowed in; one would go mad from being unable to tell the time of day. No guards patrolled this dungeon; only the large man who stood by the door was present.

"Wh-what are we doing here?" I asked, hearing my voice bounce off the walls. "Why had you brought me here?"

The king let go of my hand and stepped toward the opening of the dungeon. "These walls are a tad more forgiving."

I did not understand. When I was just about to speak, another voice cut me off. A voice that was neither the king nor Sir Simeo or the other man behind me. This voice came from one of the cells tucked away in the dungeon. The voice was soft and sweet. It asked, "Is that my king?"

The king turned toward me and smiled. I had never seen the king's smile reach his eyes before.

"I am here, my love," he replied, turning back toward the dungeon. I walked up to him and followed his gaze to an outstretched arm coming from the bars of one of the cells. "Come meet *my* queen," he said to me.

I followed him toward the cell, millions of questions running through my mind. *Who is his queen? Why must I meet her? Is she his first love? Why is she in here . . . ?* Once we got to the cell the king knelt down and grabbed the pale hand. He wrapped both his hands around it and kissed it. The other arm came out and stroked his face, and again he smiled a smile I had never seen before.

"I have missed you, my darling," the female voice said. I could not see her face from where I had stopped just before the cell.

"My love, I am here now. It pains me to not be able to be by your side every moment of the day," he replied, kissing her hand again. He turned to me then and gestured me to come over. Nervously I obliged him. I'm not sure what I expected to see in the cell, but once I did get a look inside I knew I would have never guessed it.

She was beautiful. Amazingly so. I gasped once I got a full look at her. She had a heart-shaped face with beautiful ocean-blue eyes and skin a shade a two darker than Calder's. Her hair, how strange it was, was not white but as close to it as it could get. It flowed all the way down to her waist, and despite her depleted condition, it looked beautiful. I never thought another human being could match the queen's beauty. I was mistaken. This woman was not caked in paint or doused in expensive clothing. She wore rags that matched the ones the people of my village wore. She was filthy, though still remarkable. Once I could pull my eyes away from her, I noticed the smut she was living in. Her cell was no bigger than a closet with only a bucket and a bench in it. She was crouched against the rusty bars so that she could touch the king. Her arms and legs were covered in sores and dirt, and yet she was still beautiful. It didn't take me long to realize who she was. She was the queen's sister. I remember Lyrrad describing her to me. White hair and blue eyes. She looked like no one else in the entire kingdom.

She looked up at me for a moment and then smiled back at the king. "It seems my king has had a glass or two tonight? I have never had visitors before."

"I needed to see you, my love. And she needs to know the truth," he replied, pulling himself closer to her and resting his head on the bars. She adoringly stroked his face and kissed his head.

"It is all right, darling." She smiled in his hair before turning to look at me. "Who are you to him?"

Slightly intimidated by this woman, I replied, "I am a friend."

"By whose demand?" she asked, piercing me with those tantalizing sapphire eyes. This woman seemed too old to be the queen's younger sister.

"My own—certainly not the queen's," I replied.

"I am the queen." She smiled. "Which makes you Lady . . . ?"

"Korinthos," I finished.

"What is your first name?"

"Arianna."

She smiled. "That's a very pretty name. Quite nice to meet you, Arianna Korinthos."

"The pleasure is all mine . . ." I waited for her to finish with her name, but she didn't, so I asked, "I'm sorry, but I do not know what to call you."

"Call me Your Majesty."

"She's kidding," the king said, lifting his head to look at her. "She is not too shallow in which her title comes before her name."

She laughed, continuing to stroke his hair. "My king knows me well." Then she turned to look at me. "I am Parthena Aurora Irene Acheros of Islocia. Daughter of King Commodus Aurelius Acheros and Lady Amelia Grace Irene Acheros. Sister to Queen Ophelia Valkiria Asphodel Acheros."

Instinctively I kneeled before her. "Quite an honor, Princess Acheros."

I heard her giggle. "You need not kneel for me, Arianna, and I am no princess."

Puzzled, I stood and asked, "How are you not?"

She smiled down at the king and then looked back up at me. Princess Parthena was so incredibly beautiful. "Officially, I'm dead." The king sighed beneath her and she kissed his forehead. "Would you like me to start from the beginning of my story? I assume that is why he has brought you down here."

I nodded.

"Have a seat, Arianna." She gestured toward the spot next to the king, "It is a long story." Instead of sitting right next to the king, I sat where I was standing. She didn't seem to mind.

"My troubles began the day my father met my mother. I remember her, my mother, being very beautiful and very charming. Men were constantly drawn to her, falling over themselves just to say a few words to her. I will never understand why my mother chose my father. He was strict, mean, and cold. Well, that's what I was told. To me my father was just strict but never mean. He loved me, I knew that for sure. Everyone in the kingdom feared my father, but my mother was fearless. She had tamed the beast. He did whatever she needed no matter the task. The only problem with this fairytale was his wife, Queen Anne Marie Asphodel Acheros, and his first daughter," she said, absentmindedly toying with the king's hair. I'm sure he had heard this story millions of times, but he didn't show it. He gave Princess Parthena all his attention as if he could hardly live with himself if he didn't. "For some reason he could not wed my mother if he divorced Anne, but that hadn't stopped him from loving my mother. When I was born I honestly believed that Ophelia and I had come from the same mother. We acted like sisters. I don't remember her hating me in my adolescent years. But then my mother fell sick and could no longer have children. My father began to panic because he did not have a male heir to the throne. It wasn't long until the palace was full of my half-brothers and sisters, thirty-eight to be exact. I loved every one of them. They were so cute and so unique in their own little way. Ophelia, on the other hand, believed we should not associate with them because they were not of *royal blood.*" She sighed, staring off into the distance. I could see the pain that tugged at her heart as she remembered a past she'd rather forget. For a long moment she didn't say anything; just silence and the inconsistent drip of water off in the background filled the space around us. "Once I had turned nine, all of my half-siblings had perished due to a disease that had swallowed Islocia. I miss them . . . My father blamed Anne and Ophelia for their deaths, and he told me to never associate with *vermin*." She cringed at the word. "After that Ophelia and I were separated. She was sent away somewhere, and I remained in the palace with my father and mother. We were happy. So, so happy." She smiled to herself. "When I turned sixteen my father told me it was time for me to marry. He said, 'My princess, your hand will no longer be mine and I will soon have to sign it over to a young fellow who doesn't deserve you.' That is when I met my king." She turned her smile to the king. He brushed his fingers over her lips and then kissed her softly. "I fell in love the moment I saw him."

"We spent that whole day together." He smiled, squeezing her hand. "It is a day I will never forget."

"Neither will I, my darling." She offered her lips for another kiss, and he vehemently obliged her through the bars.

Awkwardly I interjected, "Why did the two of you not wed?"

They did not respond right away; instead they stared at each other with sad eyes. For a while I wasn't sure if they heard me, but then Princess Parthena began to speak. "My father died a day before Charles, Lord Araun at the time, was to formally propose to me." Again another pause. "My father's death, without a male heir, left the throne to Ophelia. She was the oldest of his children and next in line to the throne."

"Did she deny your engagement?"

"Yes." Sadness weighted her as she stared desperately into her lover's eyes. "She took him from me. I begged her for him. Got on my knees before that tyrant, and yet she denied me. She did not want him. Charles was thirty, and she was nearly twenty and seven years.

My father had wanted me to wed an older man so that I would have time to produce as many heirs as possible. Ophelia was nearing the age of indifference. It wouldn't be long until she couldn't produce any children, yet she still . . . she still took my king from me."

"Why didn't you just say no?" I asked the king.

Deeply exhaling, he replied, "My family made a deal with King Acheros before he died. I was to wed the daughter that would inherit the throne. It was one of those situations in which I had no choice. Either I marry Ophelia and be miserable or dishonor a promise and wage a war between two families."

"King Acheros was dead. Wouldn't his death break that bond?"

"No, the Grand Royals knew of the decision. They would go to war on behalf of the king. You see, my family was very wealthy. When I married Ophelia the crown got quite a bit of money and my family got a higher status. The Grand Royals didn't want to lose out on the purse so they forced our marriage agreement," he replied somberly. "I never stopped thinking about Parthena. Completely and irrevocably consumed by her beauty and grace, I had to be with her. I made every effort to love and cherish Parthena when Ophelia wasn't looking. Even after I married Ophelia, I still spent all of my time with my *true* love. I couldn't, can't, live without her. She is the rhythm in my heart, the air in my lungs, and the soul to my spirit." He kissed her hands and then her lips again. She smiled as a tear ran down her cheek.

"Ophelia eventually found out about us." Parthena sniffled, swiping at another tear. It made me feel awkward watching other people cry, I didn't like what it did to my insides. "She . . . had me brought before the whole kingdom, stripped me down to my underclothes, and proclaimed me a traitor."

"She told the entire kingdom that Parthena would be killed for her crime . . . adultery," the king exclaimed. "No one in the kingdom knew that Parthena and Ophelia were sisters because King Acheros kept them locked in this damned palace all their lives. Therefore, Parthena was easy to forget about. No one would question the queen's motives." He paused as he struggled for his next words. "There is no pain comparable to that of the thought that I would lose my princess. I would rather find comfort in being burned at the stake than hearing such a horrid proclamation."

"At first I believed she really was going to have me killed. Instead she locked me away down here. But that wasn't the worst of the matter." Though it was dark I could see her sapphire eyes liquefy as she continued to open old wounds. "Ophelia"—her voice quivered with every word—"hung my mother the same day she damned me to this cell." She cleared her throat. "Then when she found out about the baby"—more tears—"she had it destroyed."

"What baby? Whose baby?" I asked softly.

Princess Parthena couldn't hold it in any longer. She began to sob uncontrollably, and the king's efforts to calm her were to no avail. He turned to me and said, "Parthena was with child when Ophelia sent her down here. The baby"—he swallowed past the lump in his throat—"*our* baby was the heir to the throne. Parthena was the princess, and I was the king. Ophelia could not produce an heir, thus making Parthena's child the next heir to the throne, and Parthena would then become queen regent. Ophelia would not let that happen . . ." Princess Parthena continued to cry as the king mulled over how to finish this tragic tale. "Ophelia . . . sent two guards into the dungeon . . . they . . ." Though he tried to hide it, I saw the tear that had escaped his composure. "They . . . shackled Parthena by her wrists and suspended her above the ground . . . they . . . took turns . . . beating . . . Parthena . . . until she . . . miscarried. I didn't find out until I came to visit her the next day and I saw...the blood between her legs and the bruises all over her."

I was shocked into silence.

I did not want to believe such bad things in regards to the queen. I could not believe she would have her own sister beaten. Her *sister*. I knew the queen was evil. I knew she thought only of herself. But I did not know her as this soulless portrait the king and Princess Parthena had just painted for me. I now understood the king's resentment toward the queen. He had every right to hate her!

"I was never permitted to visit Parthena, and I still am not allowed. Only during the night, when Sir Simeo and Sir Euit are on duty, am I able to visit my love. Sir Simeo has been a friend since I was a boy, and Sir Euit has much regard for Sir Simeo's opinions. I owe them both my life." He kissed Parthena's hands as she finally gained control of herself.

"Why not take her during the night and run away?" I could not bear the thought of seeing my king so sad. I could not bear the thought of him returning to his miserable life alongside a vicious queen. Something inside me had changed. Boiling rage spilled from my quickened breaths.

"As much regard as Sir Euit has for Sir Simeo, he will not allow me to take my love. Neither will Sir Simeo. They only promised me access to Parthena, nothing more." He sighed, brushing Parthena's hair out of her face.

"There has to be something we can do! The queen is not an immoveable force—she is human!" I didn't know what I was saying. All I knew was I was saying it and I meant it. Parthena did not deserve to be in this cell, and the king did not deserve the life he had—they both deserved better.

"Arianna"—he gave me a half-hearted smile—"on the throne sits a power that has no restraints and infinite hate. She cannot be verbally reasoned with and is too intimidating to take on alone physically. She *is* an immovable force. The only one of its kind."

Anger, rage, hate . . . I wanted her dead. "I do not believe that one can fear a *crown*. It is no more than metal-painted gold!"

Parthena replied, "Any person who believes they can summon God and place their feet on his back is a person you should fear the most. She has taken almost everything from me. I will not risk losing the one thing that keeps me breathing." She squeezed the king's hand tighter. "I can't."

"I cannot live without my heart," the king whispered, pulling Parthena as close to him as the rusty bars that divided them would allow.

Her hands ended up on his chest, and she replied breathlessly, "And I cannot live without my soul."

"I have neither. Therefore, I have nothing to lose," I muttered, though they didn't hear me.

Something had to be done. I could no longer stand by and watch the desecration of all that is good in the world. Something had to be done. I wanted the queen's head. I was going to get it.

CHAPTER 12

THERE WAS A MARTYR UPON the throne. How beautiful she was with the crown finally in its rightful place. For the first time the subjects of the monarchy cheerfully kneeled before their queen. For there was a martyr upon the throne. A soldier stood beside the throne. So strong and full of pride. A beast had been conquered that day. And though the foul demon attempted to corrupt the innocence, it had lost to the will of the determined. The proof of such an accomplishment was in the soldier's hand as blood spilled from it. The soldier was not wounded. Only triumphant. In her hand was the head of the demon . . .

"Arianna . . ." Straining to pull myself from my restful slumber, I heard the whispers of a familiar voice alongside me. Once my senses rebooted, I could hear the breathing and feel the dent in my bed that the person beside me caused. "Do not be afraid. It is only I." My entire body tensed at the sound of his voice. I wished to never hear his voice ever again! I wished him dead! May God mercilessly rain lightning upon him!

For a moment I said nothing to him. I remained lying in my bed, sheltered by fine linen and six feathered pillows. But I knew he would not leave me be until I acknowledged his presence. "Calder."

He sighed as I sat up and leaned against the headboard. "You say my name as if it were to poison you." He was dressed in all black, as usual, and his pale features never looked more revolting. His usually malicious blue eyes were sad as he stared down at his feet. "You must be so ashamed of me. I am ashamed of myself." He eyed me then, daring to gaze upon me in my risqué night attire.

"What is it you want?" I noticed he was without his guards this time. Completely at my mercy. Yet he doubted that I would do anything.

Again he sighed. "I have come to apologize." He paused and then braved another look at me before quickly turning away. "It seems my overwhelming attraction to you had gotten the better of me. And for that I am sorry."

At first I didn't say anything. I wasn't sure what his true intentions were. "Is that all?"

He smiled that sinful charming smile that had captured me the moment I met him. "So controlled. So direct." This time he was able to look at me. "I came here hoping you would forgive me. What I had done . . . what I did . . . Arianna, it was unacceptable. Such an abuse of power is frowned upon, as it should be. Therefore, I sincerely apologize." That pleading look on his face made me want to forget about all of his harsh and unworldly indiscretions. He came to me so raw and vulnerable . . . how could I not be lost in him? Those blue eyes cut through my shell and touched me in a way I had never been touched. The almost childlike awkwardness he had never shown before was enchanting. I didn't know what to say. My mind was working way beyond its capacity. "Can you forgive my troubled soul?"

Swallowing, my throat working, I opened my mouth, but no words came out.

"Have you no faith in me? Am I not the man who had you stumbling over yourself the first time we met?" He half-smiled as he stroked his hand along the edge of the bed. Slowly, o' so slowly, he inched it closer to my leg. I tensed when he began drawing circles on my thigh through the sheet.

"Calder?"

He whispered, "So beautiful." At first I wasn't sure if I was imagining him leaning toward me; he moved so smoothly and so slowly I couldn't tell—not until his lips were only an inch or two away from mine. "Can you forgive me?" Everything was moving at hyper speed. I felt my brain scramble for something to do or say. Calder, so captivating and vile, was inches from me. The man I had sworn to hate for the rest of my days was pleading before me. Try as I might I could not stop myself from longing for his presence and acceptance. So much so that I could only reply, breathlessly, "Yes."

In that instance he sealed his mouth over mine. I felt his hand slide up my thigh until it rested against my hip. The bed shifted as he moved to place his other arm on my shoulder . . . then my neck . . . I pulled away from him just as I felt the slickness of his tongue along my bottom lip. Gasping for breath I could not dare look him in the eye. For several long awkward moments it was quiet. Then he leaned forward again. Now both of his hands were wrapped around my neck and he urged me forward. Without even thinking I leaned forward. Again he kissed me. I didn't pull away when his tongue teased my lips . . . then it began dancing with my own tongue. I didn't know what I was doing; all I knew is that I was doing it. Slow, o' so slowly, he kissed down my chin and then to my neck. I sucked in a deep breath, unable to comprehend what was truly going on. My hands never left my lap as he worked his way back up to my mouth. He urged my lips apart with the thrust of his tongue. I felt his hands tighten around my neck, his body being assaulted by his uninhibited lust for me.

A moan escaped from between his lips as he pushed me onto my back. In one swift motion, Calder, in all his elegance and glory, climbed upon me. Licking deeply into my mouth, he forced my knees apart by placing his body between them. He began to grind on me then. I felt the tightly drawn satin bulge touch that sensitive spot between my legs. I gasped as he drove himself closer to that part of me. "Calder…" I was breathless with confusion. "No!"

He deftly ignored me and continued to ravage me. Although I had said no, my body reacted to his cues. I could not fight against him. His hands burned across my skin as he hitched my right leg up and then my left so that I was wrapped around him. "Undress yourself," he commanded, although it was only a whisper in my ear. With shaking hands I did as I was told, unable to control myself. He watched me intently as I removed my top garment and bared my breasts to him. A sinful smile filled his face as he untied his pants. My bottom garments soon followed my top. His searing gaze scorched me as he released his bulge and positioned himself to enter me. "Open."

* * *

I lay still for a long while after he was done. Though Calder had captured me and used me for his own gain, I allowed him to do so. I did not participate in the way he had wished. I did not stroke his cheek or beg him not to stop, as lovers so often do. He did everything. His sweat dripped onto me as he thrust himself deeper and deeper, but I did not indulge in the sensation. Throughout the whole act it was as if I were standing outside of my body and watching the events transpire. It was not lovemaking that I had endured. Not in the slightest. I watched him desecrate me . . . I watched him steal something I tried so hard to guard.

When he had rolled off of me, he kissed me once on the lips and then sat up and fastened his trousers. It was done. Yet I could not move. I lay there, staring up at the ceiling. Empty. So empty.

"I request your presence at brunch," he muttered in that same voice that had had me bending beneath him when we first met. Now . . . it made me want to cringe.

"As you wish," I replied in an almost lifeless voice. He was silent for a moment before I felt his eyes on my face.

"I shall meet you down there." He left me then . . . just as quickly as he had arrived. The doors to my room shut rather loudly as he exited.

Alone and baffled I sat, wondering what the hell had come over me. Calder was the enemy! He had taken something from me, yet I continued to give it to him?

Somewhere within my moments of bafflement, I began to go through the motions of getting ready. Rye Beddon cleaned me and dressed me, but I was too lost in my own mind to pay attention. A moment or two later the little woman scurried out of my room. I was soon to follow, though in a more casual manner.

I remember opening the door. I remember stepping outside of my room. I remember closing the door. I remember taking two, maybe three, steps outside my room. I remember feeling like something was off as I noticed that the usually busy halls of the palace were silent. I remember turning, feeling the urge to survey my surroundings, and seeing Rye Beddon with a cloth being held over her mouth while a guard kept her from squirming. I remember stopping for maybe a second, unable to contemplate such a scene. Then . . . I remember hearing someone run up beside me . . . I remember not having enough time to turn and see who it was. I remember a wet cloth being forced over my mouth. I remember struggling against whoever had held me still. I remember trying not to breath in the cloth, but its revolting gases overpowered me as I fought against its grasp. Everything suddenly went dark. That was the last thing I remembered . . .

* * *

I awoke with a very painful headache and the feeling of my stomach trying to force its way up and out of my body. Though whatever room I was in was dimly lit, what little light there was burned my eyes as I tried to open them. When I made the effort to stretch my limbs, I felt the constriction of the shackles I was o' so familiar with. My arms were chained above my head, and my legs were shackled to the wall a few inches off the ground. It didn't take me long to notice that most of my clothes were gone with the exception of my undergarments that covered my pelvis and my chest.

Once my eyes had finally adjusted, I could see that I was not in a cell I had ever been in before. It was nothing like *Ville Morte* or the dungeon Parthena was kept in. This place was different. From the shallow breathing and the soft, almost inaudible, rustling of metal near the corner I could tell there was a guard nearby. I was being watched.

* * *

I must have fallen asleep because I awoke to the sound of determined coverings clacking against the hard, cold stones of my cell. I waited until they had stopped directly in front of me to open my eyes. I was not surprised at who was standing before me.

"I apologize for such a dramatic capture." She smiled, removing her cloak. "I couldn't seem to help myself." The effect of the gases was not what had my stomach churning; the sickening stench of pounds of paint was what nearly took me over the edge. "Are you enjoying yourself?"

"Not as much as you are, Your Majesty," I hissed, clenching my fists.

She chuckled, handing her cloak to one of the several guards she had brought with her. "Chained to a wall and still you have your sense of humor. Such a trait is worthy of admiration."

"How accomplished I will be to have the admiration of a queen," I muttered, mentally ripping her to shreds. "Too bad the queen before me lacks the essentials of being great. You're merely . . . mediocre, if that."

Reining in her anger, she signaled to a guard. I knew what was coming but still didn't have enough time to brace myself for it.

The guard rammed the handle of his sword into my stomach repeatedly until I choked on every breath. "Is that all you got?" I spit a mouthful of blood at her feet. "It seems my hands aren't"—more coughing—"the only ones stained red."

"I do what I have to do to protect my kingdom." She shrugged, stepping closer to me.

"You destroy the majority of your people to protect the few who entertain this idea of a justifiable dystopian society." I forced a laugh. "Not only are you mediocre, you're downright stupid."

"Mind your tongue, vermin," a voice from deep within the shadows hissed. "I would love more than anything to cut it out myself." Completely at peace with the dark, he emerged from his hiding spot along the wall. A sudden rush of apprehension and embarrassment had me wanting to hide myself. The feeling increased as I watched him saunter over to the queen and tenderly kiss her cheek. Then he turned to look at me. "You are so predictable."

I tried to lunge at him, but my chains held me back. "I'll kill you!"

Calder chuckled sinisterly. "Temper, temper." I tried to lunge at him again.

"I have always had eyes on you, Arianna," the queen interjected. "You thought that I wouldn't find out about your secret meeting with my sister? This is *my* palace, this is *my* kingdom—everyone and everything belongs to me."

"You are not my queen!" I shouted, wanting desperately to break free and strangle her.

"O', and you believe my sister is your queen?" She laughed, shaking her head. "What has she provided for you? I have given you everything, yet you're such an ungrateful little whore that you denied yourself the right to see beyond your self-righteousness."

Snarling, I snapped, "She is everything you are not. You have brought shame upon the Acheros throne!"

The queen stepped forward and slapped me across the face. "You believe she can do any better? That brainless twat?"

"By choice I kneel to her. That is the least I can say for you," I barked.

"You are just like everyone else. I knew you would betray me. Everyone loved Parthena." Fuming, she began pacing in front of me. "Everyone thought she was perfect."

"Yeah, I know," I baited her. "Even your own father chose her over you."

Distress cracked her paint as I began to see the first sign of an honest emotion. "That was the easiest decision he ever made."

"If your father could love her so easily, how do you think a kingdom will take to her?" I inquired. "The fear and distrust you have implemented can easily be washed away by the purity of the true heir to the throne."

"I was always meant to be queen!"

"No, you were not," I shot back. "Your father knew what demons lurked inside you. That's why he tried so hard to be rid of you."

"My father loved me!"

"Then why would he send you away once Parthena's mother moved in? He wanted nothing to do with you! He wanted you out of his life!"

"That is not true!"

"It is true and you know it. You are the queen that no one wanted."

She couldn't control her breathing as anger spilled out of her. "To hell with you!"

"No, to hell with you, *Ophelia!*" The guards gasped as I used the queen's name out loud. She, herself, was dumbstruck by my blatant disrespect to the crown. The guards all went to reprimand me, but the queen held up her hand.

"Leave her be," she replied, composing herself. "You think you know the truth? All I wanted was to please my father, and nothing I did was ever right. I watched my mother fight for her crown and for my father's affection. Then *she* came along. My father never smiled at me! But the moment that bitch was born he couldn't stop. He shipped my mother and me away to his summer palace and forbade me from contacting him unless I agreed to disown my mother. I did so for a while and lived with my father and Parthena. But he tired of me and shipped me away again! Back at the palace that bastard child was living a life of luxury, and she wasn't even his firstborn. I thought it was an act of God when that whore's mother became infertile. My mother hoped he would want us back. Instead, he searched for more woman, and they birthed him more bastard children. I hated every single one of them. My father made me and my mother be present for the birth of all forty of those runts. And every time one was born he told me that they were next in line for the throne." Audibly grinding her teeth, she continued, "I was more than elated when those bastards died. Because now I was the heir to the throne. He had to accept me now! But my father was never one to disappoint. He damned my mother and condemned her to hell. All of the blame was thrown at my mother and me. He ordered his subjects to stone her whenever they saw her. Because of his proclamation my mother ordered me to never be with her. She didn't want me to get hurt."

"He must've not have been satisfied with that."

She shook her head. "He wasn't. A few weeks later he had my mother killed, publicly. Then to add salt to the injury he threw a celebratory party for her death. My father . . . made me mourn my mother in silence. Her head was the centerpiece at the table. Parthena thought it was hilarious. Everyone did."

"That's why you had Parthena's mother killed."

She chuckled. "The day my father died was the best day of my life. Because finally, after all the things he put me through, the throne was mine. As queen my first order of business was to have a traitor killed, publicly, then to sentence the other whore to life in prison."

"What about Parthena's baby?"

She must've been surprised that I knew so much about the secret she tried so desperately to cover up. Still, she continued, "That satanic beast would have taken my throne. I could not allow that to happen. I ordered my guards to beat her until she bled from between her legs. They said it didn't take very long. I would have had her killed too . . ."

"No, you would never kill Parthena. You're too proud for that. All your childhood your father locked you away and spoiled your sister. You're merely returning the favor."

"Yes!" she hissed. "Now she knows what it's like to have nothing."

"You never did grow up." Again she signaled to the guard, and he pummeled my stomach with the handle of his sword. It wasn't until I was sagging against the chains did he stop. Blood dripped from my nose and mouth as I tried to control my breathing.

"The throne has always been mine." She lifted my head as I fought to remain conscious. "And no one"—she jerked my chin so that I was looking right at her—"no one will take it away from me. No matter how many lives I will have to destroy." The room went hazy, and her voice echoed in my ears before everything, once again, went black.

With a sudden jolt I was snapped back to reality. I wasn't chained against a wall; this time I was sitting, my hands were tied in front me, and there was a dark hood covering my face. From the constant jostling I soon realized I was in a carriage. As if to emphasize my conclusion the wheel dipped into a hole, causing me to bounce against the side of the carriage. There was a soft chuckle beside me, and I knew exactly who it was. Even before he began talking.

"I was beginning to think you were dead," he snickered.

I groaned. "God doesn't favor you that much, Calder."

"Possibly so." Again the carriage was rattled by the rough road. "But who needs the acceptance of a God when you have the adoration of a queen?"

I scoffed, adjusting my position to make myself more comfortable. "Though I am the one with the hood over my head, you seem to be the only blind one. You follow a queen who wishes for nothing less than the destruction of her own kingdom?"

"Yes." He laughed, patting my shoulder. I flinched away from his touch, which only made him laugh more. "You see, Arianna, that is the only way to survive. Though you may not always agree with something, if it will ensure your survival then you must keep your mouth shut and do as you're told."

"You're telling me that you disagree with the will of the queen?"

He laughed aloud. "No, you incompetent fool. I was speaking more to you than I was to myself. I do not disagree with my queen." I felt him lean closer to me as he placed his hand around my ear to hold in the sound of his voice. He whispered, "Actually, I tell the queen what to do."

"Get off of me," I growled, bumping him with my shoulder.

"Temper, temper . . ." More laughter. "That is your problem. If you had not been so self-righteous this would not be happening to you. You would be invited to the queen's table and sipping wine with the most treasured lords and ladies of Islocia."

"Go to hell, Calder," I spit, turning my back to him just as the carriage began to slow. When it came to a complete stop I heard the side door, opposite me, begin to open. Then Calder sighed.

"Unfortunately my first-class ticket to hell isn't set for today. Yours, on the other hand, is." And with that I heard him slide out of the carriage. Less than a minute later the door I had been leaning against opened and I fell to the ground. Hands, several of them, roughly forced me to my feet. My bare toes scraped against the cold sand as the guards began dragging me to wherever I was going. Outside of the rattling of the guard's armor I could hear the overwhelmingly loud shouts and hollers produced by a large crowd that seemed as though it was surrounding me on all sides. Whoever they were, they were angry with me. Words like *whore, traitor, harlot,* and *slut* spilled from the mouths of those who once praised my name.

"Step lively," the guard behind me shouted over the roaring crowd. With a shove to my back I flew forward and clashed against wooden steps. "Hurry up now! We don't got all day! Move it!" Forcing myself to ignore the unbearable bite of pain, I somehow managed to stand upright even with my hands tied as they were. A cold wind hugged my limbs and sent an awful shiver down my whole body. "Come on, girl!" I heard a man from above shout down at me. When I had ascended a few steps I felt someone roughly grab my elbow before thrusting me on a wooden platform. A few more hands pushed and shoved me until finally they allowed me to stand still. My arms were still tied and that damned hood was still over my head. I could tell that the crowd was now in front of me. And though they were below me it did not diminish their sudden hatred of me.

Unwilling to stand, barred to the world, I made an effort to move from where I was. Unfortunately I hadn't realized that there was a large man standing directly behind me. He grabbed me by the top of my head and thrust me to the ground. Before I could even hold up my hands defensively he wailed on me. I was hacking and wheezing after only two of his punches. The crowd cheered as he wrapped his hands around my throat and, in one quick movement, forced me onto my feet. I would have fallen down again except the man behind me held me, through the hood, by my hair. In that same instance I felt the presence of someone standing in front of me.

"Remover her hood."

On command, the man released his hold on my hair and yanked the hood off of me. I was nearly blinded by the deathly rays of sun and almost fell backward. Once my eyes finally adjusted to the light I saw who was before me.

"Throw her next to him," the queen ordered, holding my gaze. He did as he was told and dragged me away from her. Grabbing me by my shoulders he shoved me toward the back of the platform, causing me to hit whoever was in the way. Looking out at the sea of people I saw that I was in the town square. It seemed as if every Royal in Islocia had gathered. And they were not happy. Standing off to the right toward the center of the platform was the queen, and behind her was not the gallows but rather the guillotine.

"Arianna?" a voice next to me whispered. I gasped at the sight of the man curled up on the platform. When I kneeled down to his level I could see the extent of his injuries. My heart hurt in the worst possible way.

"Your Majesty . . . ?" He had been beaten, badly so. There was a large gash above his eye; and his nose, mouth, and chin were stained in his blood. They had stripped him down to his undergarments, and I could see the purple fist impressions through his thin white clothing. He was shivering, trying to defend himself against the unrelenting cold. His usually playful brown eyes were clouded by fear and pain. The charm and enchanting poise he once exuberated was gone. The king was a tall, muscular man who, although weathered from running a kingdom, was sweet and a proud-standing dignitary. That man was long gone. He was covered in filth, and his usually well-kept beard and hair were cut off. His clothes were torn from the slashes of a blade across his skin. And his arms were shackled with rusty iron chains. It pained me to see him in this state . . . He was a king yet he did not resemble one. The queen did not only strip him of his crown but also of his dignity.

"She's going to kill us," he said solemnly.

"I will save us," I vowed, touching his knee. The crowd erupted into dismay, and the king jerked away from me, appeasing the crowd.

"There is nothing to be done. If she wills us dead, then dead we will be." His serenity was baffling. In the face of death the king remained calm, almost at ease with the situation.

"You're just going to give up and accept defeat?" I wanted to be angry with him, especially when he smiled. Just as he was to explain, the queen began talking.

"My lords, my ladies," she began and the crowd floated into silence, "I come before you with an unbearable truth that has cut me deeper than any wound a queen, your queen, should have to endure. A crime against the monarchy has been committed. A crime so vile, so sordid, that the only acceptable punishment is death." The crowd grumbled and she silenced them. "An insurrection has occurred in my own palace. My most trusted liaison has confessed to having an ongoing sexual affair with my husband, the King of Islocia." The crowd erupted into angry shouts and cries. "Bring forward the adulterous snake!"

One of the guards came over and yanked me to my feet, tied a cloth around my mouth to silence me, and tossed me to the foot of the queen. Almost immediately I was being pelted with stones and rotten food. Instinctively I covered my head with my hands.

"Arianna Korinthos!" The queen continued, "I hereby proclaim you an adulterer and a traitor to the crown." I could barely hear her over the roaring of the crowd and the multitude of stones being aimed at my head. "Bring the other criminal forward." The king joined me a moment later, and the queen stated the same proclamation she had said about me. "Such a crime is punishable by death!" I screamed at the queen and even attempted to attack her. King Araun held me back. He shook his head and placed his hand over mine. That only made the crowd angrier.

"Behead the king!"

"Kill them!"

"Death to those who defy the queen!"

"Behead the king!"

The king reached and pulled the cloth out of my mouth. Just as I was to argue our innocence he placed his finger over my mouth and shook his head.

"People of Islocia!" the queen continued, quieting the crowd. "You all know that I am a forgiving queen. And because I am in a forgiving mood I will spare the life of the adulterous whore. She will die in a cell, not by the guillotine." The crowd did not agree with her proclamation; frankly, neither did I.

"No!" I screamed, turning to the queen. "Your Majesty, you know we are innocent! No such crime has been committed."

"I have thousands of witnesses inside and outside the palace who will attest to you and the king spending intimate time together," she countered, and the crowd blindly accepted her evidence over the truth. "One witness is even willing to step forward and speak now." She turned to her guards. "Bring the informant forward."

My immediate assumption was that Calder would be speaking on behalf of the queen. I was sadly mistaken.

Walking toward the queen was a man I had never guessed I would see. And by the way the guard held the hidden knife to his back, I could tell the "informant" wasn't here voluntarily.

"Tell the kingdom what you saw," the queen demanded, stepping aside so the tiny, frail, thin man with pointy features could be seen by all.

Swallowing past his apprehension, the man, with his unmistakable accent, said, "It is true. I have witnessed Lady Korinthos . . . entering and exiting King Araun's apartment . . ." The guard behind him inched the knife closer to his back and whispered, "Keep going."

"When I saw . . . her . . . leave his apartment during ungodly hours, she was a mess. Her hair was all out of place, and her clothes were always halfway on . . . I let my curiosity get the better of me, so one day I entered the king's apartment and saw them"—he pointed at the king and me—"in bed with each other." The crowd gasped and then threw abhorrent, crude words at us.

"That's a lie! That never happened!" I shouted and soon regretted it. The guard nearest me grabbed me by my hair with one hand and punched me across the face with the other. The armor that covered his hands cut a long gash across my cheek.

The queen returned to her place, front and center. "Jepson, do you speak the truth?"

The guard behind Jepson dug the knife deep enough into his skin to create a few droplets of blood. When he turned to look at me, I could see that the queen had had him beaten as well. His eye was swollen shut, and dried blood was on the collar of his shirt. He mouthed the words "I'm sorry" before responding, "*Oui*. I speak of no farce."

"There you have it!" she spoke to the kingdom. "Proof of their crime!"

"Your Majesty, I beg of you, listen to me," I wheezed, shaking off the urge to pass out. "No such crime has been committed."

"My dear, the evidence against you is overwhelming." She gave me a sympathetic smile. "Yet I still let you live. When will you be satisfied?"

"If one must die today then kill me! Spare the king! I will die in his place," I pleaded.

She chuckled, kneeling to my level, and whispered, "How noble. Still, I will not kill you. That would make things too easy for you. I know you do not fear death, you welcome it. What sort of punishment would that be if I obliged you? Letting you rot away in a cell, knowing that you will blame yourself for the death of the king, is more satisfactory."

I lunged for her but the guards quickly pulled me back. "You are a monstrosity of evil!"

She shrugged and then turned to her guards. "Take him to the guillotine."

"No!" I freed myself from the grasp of the guard and grabbed the king. He was so in control of himself that he even tried to calm me.

"Arianna, Arianna!" He put his hands on both sides of my head to get my attention. "I need you to do something for me."

"Hurry up!" the queen barked. The guards tried to get me to let go of him, but I held on for dear life.

The king looked over his shoulder at the queen and then turned to look at me. He replied hurriedly, "Give Parthena my love, send her my apologies . . . we will not wed in this life, but possibly the next." It had taken three guards to pull us apart. One held onto me while the other two were trying to escort the king to the guillotine. Struggling against the hold of the guard, I reached for the king. He turned and grabbed both of my hands in his and smiled at me. "It will be all right, Arianna."

"Your Majesty, we are innocent!" I sobbed tearlessly.

He sighed and kissed my hands, once again igniting fury within the crowd. "When caught in the eye of a totalitarian, it is not a question of innocence or guilt—it is a matter of worth. My value to Her Majesty has dwindled to nothing. She doesn't need me for anything, and for that, she will have me killed." Without warning a guard came up and punched me in the stomach, causing me to release the king's hands. He tried holding on, but the other two guards had pulled him away. He shouted over his shoulder, "Tell Parthena I love her, and that I always will!" The two guards dragged him away from me and toward his death. The executioner stood by the lever as the king neared the guillotine. The skies suddenly darkened, and the storm clouds cast an eerie shadow upon the kingdom. A moment later it began to rain. The heavens were very angry. Frigid winds began to torment my barred flesh. There was no source of warmth anywhere near me. Lightning flashed across the sky, and the crackling whip of thunder shook the platform.

The queen's slaves were quick to shelter her beneath a veil as she shouted over the icy rain, "Any last words?"

The king stood, honorably, proudly. Even as the rain drenched him, causing his clothes to cling to his weakened body, he stood, for the last time, as a king. He spoke to the kingdom, shouting over the wind and rain. "The woman before you is not the manifested resemblance of the honest monarch we all wish her to be. She sits upon a throne while the blood of millions drips from her hands, yet you call her your queen? She smiles down on her kingdom built off the backs of commoners and slaves, yet you call her your queen? She fills her plate to the brim while thousands starve and millions die of disease, yet you call her your queen?" He thrust his dripping finger toward the queen. "Calling this demon your queen should be the only crime punishable by death. A foreigner is upon the throne!" He kneeled and laid his head on the base of the guillotine. The executioner checked to make sure he was aligned with the angled blade and then went back to the lever.

"This isn't right!" I screamed and tried to run for the king, but the guard who held me threw me to the ground. I felt no physical pain anymore. The numbness of the freezing rain and the emotional withdrawal had me feeling nothing . . . except dread.

"All hail the king!" King Araun shouted as the rain washed away the blood on his face. "All hail the king!" My voice broke as I pleaded for the king's life.

The executioner placed his hand on the lever as another deafening crack of thunder erupted.

The executioner released the lever as lightning scarred the sky.

The blade came down as the freezing rain soaked Islocia.

And then . . . even after the heavens cried for mercy . . . the king was no more . . .

A wave of grief suffocated me as I watched his head drop into the basket beneath the guillotine. My heart sunk to the pit of my stomach, and my eyes burned with the need to cry. The crowd applauded the executioner and sang praises to the queen for killing the "traitor."

In the distance I heard a bloodcurdling scream. My body was weighted with so much sorrow I didn't want to make the effort to turn and see who it was that was mourning the king so loudly. But I did turn. And I did see who it was. The beautiful fair-skinned woman with ocean-blue eyes and golden-white hair was being held by two guards off to the side of the platform, where no one could see her. She wept loudly for the loss of her friend, her king, her love . . .

I could no longer bear to look at the weeping widow; it hurt my heart too much. So I turned my attention to the queen who seemed pleased with herself. She sauntered over to me. "Like I said before"—she smiled, signaling the guards to take Parthena back to her dungeon—"no one will take my throne away from me. No matter how many lives I have to destroy." The smug look on her face, as she walked away, was the epitome of evil and the façade of invincibility.

CHAPTER 13

"GET UP!" THE VOICE GROWLED. Beaten senseless and broken beyond repair, I whimpered on the ground. Blood was my bed, pain my blanket. Hours and hours and hours I fought this devil! I fought. Begging for my own life! Begging for survival! "You worthless child! Get up! Fight back!" I could not. I could not rise. I could not win.

"Take my life if it pleases thee!" I cried, choking on my own blood. "I hand it over!"

"Death?" I heard the soft cry of a sword being drawn. "Death is too easy. Death is too merciful. I am not a merciful man."

"I cannot fight you anymore! I have failed you! Living, I shall not!" Tears, the last ones I'd ever cry, splashed onto the sand that clogged my windpipe.

He slid the sword across my back, not cutting me; its coolness was a relief to my sore limbs. Kneeling down beside me he laid the sword so that I saw only my reflection. The battered child who cried the pain away stared back at me.

"Is this who you want to see? Is this who you want to be?" he hissed, grabbing me by the hair and forcing me to look closer. "If so, take the sword from my hands and welcome death. But welcome it on your own terms."

I considered it. I considered ending it all. I considered a pain-free beginning.

"Only the strong can die honorably. The strongest never see an ending to their own life but to others. The weak are already dead. The weakest take their own life. Which are you?"

I grabbed the sword . . .

My body was numb. Chained only by my wrists, I curled up against the cold damp wall of my cell.

For seven days and seven nights the queen sent in her guards to further punish me. They were relentless as they tortured my mind and sometimes even my body. On the first day of my torture, they beat me until their knuckles were bruised and bloody. Every day after that my face throbbed from being swollen shut. I could no longer see out of my right eye, and my left would've soon followed had they continued their beatings for another day. Many times they held their knives to my throat and threatened me with death. The queen was right—I welcomed it. Once, on day six, I tried to lean into the knife, hoping to end it all. The physical pain was not what was unbearable; it was the emotional burden that weighted me and threw me over the edge. Unfortunately, the guards were too smart to allow my suffering to end so easily. I assume that the guards were given strict orders to keep me alive because when I passed out they made extraordinary efforts to wake me back up.

The queen was diligent in her punishment. Not only was my body beaten and battered, but she made an effort to cloud my mind with too many emotions for me to handle. Every day when the guards came in, they told me of Parthena and how she wept the hours away. One day, the fourth day, they had me believing that she took off her clothes and had hanged herself in her cell. That was the closest I ever came to crying . . . until they told me it wasn't true.

On day three the queen came and visited me. She joked that she ordered her slaves to tie the king's head to Parthena's cell. I soon became physically sick. She had continued talking, but it was all lost to me. I was lost in me. My mind betrayed me as it replayed the king's execution over and over all day every day. The evening hours were the worst. My solitude, how I longed for its death, was only interrupted when the guards came in. Other than that I was left to my own mind. After an hour or so it would travel into a deep, dark world full of hate and misery. It was my own personal hell. And I was burning with rage from the inside out.

The other days were unremarkable. Nothing other than the same everyday torture occurred. I was starved from dawn until dusk, and nightmares assaulted my sleep. Voices in my head provoked me and pain numbed me. Soaking in darkness, I felt my stoic walls rebuilding themselves. I knew I should have never allowed myself to become so vulnerable among the people I shouldn't have trusted. The second I became comfortable with the devil, she took all that I had away from me. My home . . . my freedom . . . my king.

My body was numb.

The loud creaky door somewhere along the wall deep within the cell opened. Three guards, each carrying a torch, entered my cell. I made no effort to prepare myself for the onslaught. Taking a deep breath and pulling my knees to my chest, I looked up at them. They were the same three guards as always.

"Wakey, wakey, girl," the guard out front cooed just as they reached me. "It's judgment day."

I didn't move. Wasn't entirely sure if I could.

That same guard sighed and said, "Russell, Tidous, help her up."

I winced away from the light they shined in my face and curled tighter into my ball. "Leave me be." They either ignored me or didn't hear me. Either way they pulled my legs from my chest and forced me to my feet. I was too weak to stand, so I crumbled back down to the ground. Frustrated Russell began dragging me by my armpits. I groaned from the soreness but made no efforts to break free.

"Wait," Tidous said, stopping Russell. Tidous was substantially younger than the other two guards. So young, in fact, that his whiskers had yet to fully grow. "I'll carry her for you." Without protest Russell dropped me and returned to the lead guard. At first I thought I was imagining the gentleness in which Tidous handled me. He lifted my head first then scooped me up with his other arm under my legs. It was clear that I wasn't heavy to him. I hadn't eaten in a little over five days. When they did allow me to eat it was no feast. My meal was merely a few scraps of food the guards decided they didn't want to eat.

"You two lovebirds off to the altar, aye?" The lead guard snickered. Tidous ignored them and we began exiting the cell. I hid my face in his breastplate once we were outside and I felt the wrath of the light. It wasn't necessarily bright out; it was rather dull and cloudy. I had become so accustomed to the dark, desolate cell that anything besides its comforts pained me. My iron chains hit against the guard's armor as he loaded me into a carriage. A moment later the other guards joined us in the carriage, and then we were off. They hadn't bothered to restrict my vision, so it was safe to assume that my next destination would be my last.

Wherever the queen had imprisoned me, it was out in the country in the middle of nowhere. There were no villages or any hint of human presence. The gray skies had blanketed the countryside, causing it to resemble the shell of a gravestone. All of the vegetation was lifeless and bare due to the winter season creeping in during the night. The limbs of the trees that raced alongside the carriage reminded me of the bones that protruded out of every child in the Bastille . . . The look of fear in their eyes was nearly larger than their stomachs . . .

The carriage plowed over a stone, which caused me to bump against Tidous who was sitting right next to me. I muttered an apology while returning to leaning against the door and continued looking at the bare landscape.

After a long while of traveling, we finally came to a place I recognized. Lárnach. The usually bustling streets were not filled with Royals, and seemingly all of the shops were closed. Lárnach too was stripped bare of its life. My stomach churned as we crossed the roundabout of the town square. I couldn't bear to look at the guillotine. The memory was too fresh in my mind . . . the memory of when I lost my king.

"I thought there was to be a hanging today?" Tidous asked as we exited the town square.

Frustrated, I muttered, "God, why do you continue to punish me?" I could have lived a thousand lives without ever hearing the mention of a public execution.

"There will be," Russell replied. "Her Majesty ordered for the gallows to be moved elsewhere for the time being."

It wasn't long after that that we left the town square and continued toward the palace. As we turned onto the road that would lead us directly to the driveway, I noticed that it felt like such a long time since I had been to the palace. All of the beautiful trees and bushes that decorated the path to the entrance of the palace were naked and dull.

"Where did Her Grace move the gallows?" What I would give to slit Tidous's throat myself. The more he mentioned the gallows, the more the sickening in my stomach increased.

Slowly the carriage came to a stop at the top of the driveway to the palace. Russell was the first to exit, and then the lead guard, and finally Tidous. The lead guard was the one who opened my door and caught me before I fell to the ground. They steadied me on my feet before releasing me. Steering me with my chains, as an owner would his dog, they led me to the front of the carriage. The lead guard pointed straight ahead at the palace and said, "Walk." He didn't wait for me to follow through with his command as one by one they filed back into the carriage. I watched them depart before turning back toward the palace.

"Well, that's one way to say welcome back." Those assholes didn't even have the decency to take these damned chains off. I assumed that another guard was supposed to be meeting me here to escort me to the palace; I was in fact a criminal. But I figured that because it was so cold that that duty was passed up by all.

Ignoring the frigid gnawing of winter's embrace, I began walking down the driveway. The row of trees, Angels' Teardrops as Lyrrad had called them, which were once lively and proud, were now barren and pitiful. The white petals that coated their limbs lay abandoned on the cold, hard ground. I knelt down and twirled one in my hand, remembering what Lyrrad had said about them. He claimed that they were the lives the Acheros family would and have destroyed. I was sorry to realize that when I finally understood the truth of his statement, it was already too late. These petals were the souls lost due to the monster upon the throne. I placed the petal back on the ground, o' so gently, and said a prayer I was taught when I was a child.

The sudden neighing of a horse shot me back to reality. Standing, I noticed that the sound came from the steps of the palace. I was fifty trees or so away from the palace, so I could see the horse and a few guards wandering about. Next to the guards was a large wooden frame of some sort. I wasn't entirely sure what it was, so I kept walking. As I got a little closer, not close enough to understand the structure, I noticed another guard on horseback coming into view from the side of the palace. At first I thought I imagined the steady rhythm of a drumbeat, but as I got a little closer the sound became louder and louder. I was still nearer to the edge of the driveway than I was the palace as another guard on horseback came into view.

My heart stopped; I froze where I was. Apparently the queen wasn't finished punishing me.

Trailing behind the guard on horseback was a line of . . . children . . .

I took off running toward the palace! Every tree passed by me in a blur! My legs were moving almost as fast as my heartbeat. Ignoring the pain and the soreness and the weight of my iron chains, I forced my body to carry me faster! As I got closer I could recognize the faces of the guards. In particular I recognized the shiny silver-haired guard leading the pack . . .

Lord Jamison, Sir Crichton, and the executioner stood near the gallows as the children lined themselves up with their nooses.

"No! Wait!" I screamed, hoping to buy myself some time. Lord Jamison saw me coming and signaled the children to ascend their stools! "Wait!" Sir Crichton then pointed to the other guards lingering about, and they too turned to see me. They began to charge.

The first guard that came at me was met with a swing of my chains. The heavy links caught him in the mouth, and he dropped to the ground immediately. Three more guards trailed behind him. The first of the three swung at me with his sword; I blocked it with my cuffs. Using my shoulder I plowed him into the second guard, and they both fell to the ground. I stumbled over them and ran head first into the final guard. He grabbed me by my hair and swung me around before throwing me to the ground. Rolling a few feet away from him, I somersaulted into a standing position and kicked him in the chest. He fell back a few feet, and I took the time to finish him off. Just before he got his balance, I jumped into the air, and with all my might I punched him across the face. While he was disoriented I wrapped my chains around his neck and squeezed until his face turned blue and his eyes bled.

I looked up as the nooses were being placed over the children's head. Just when I thought things couldn't get any worse I realized I recognized two of the faces up there. Teta, looking so fragile and scared, tried reaching for her brother, but he was nowhere near her. Going down the line I saw Zakai at the end of the row. He too was reaching for his sister. I saw him mouth the words "It'll be okay," but the fear in his eyes was prominent. Again Teta tried to reach him but Zakai was too far away from her. Then she turned and looked at me. It was just for a moment, but I saw a glimmer of hope flash across her eyes. I had to save her. Lord Jamison's eyes locked with mine as I forced my way to the gallows.

"*Aoife*!" Teta exclaimed, pointing at me! Hastily Lord Jamison shouted at the executioner to get into place. I thought that once I reached the platform I could retrieve Lord Jamison's sword and cut the ropes before the executioner pulled the lever . . . if only things were that simple.

As I came upon the platform, at unprecedented speed, I was able to get one foot up on it. Teta's arms were outstretched to me, and I reached to grab her. Unfortunately I hadn't seen that the guard to my left was charging toward me. Like the force of being trampled by a thousand bulls the guard tackled me to the ground. For a moment longer than I expected we wrestled until finally I was able to reach underneath his helmet and gouge his eyes.

Just then Lord Jamison hollered, "Ready the lever!" Taking the guard's sword, I hurled it at the executioner with all my might. He took too long to see what was happening, and it pierced through his leather tunic and straight to his heart. The sword went so deep into him that it protruded out of his back while blood spurted from his chest. He was down in less than a second. Taking several deep breaths, I almost let myself believe that the danger was gone . . . but I knew I would never be so lucky.

Drawing his sword, Lord Jamison ran full speed at me. Using my chains as a shield, I blocked his first swing only to be met with a very painful slash across my arm with his second. My blood covered the end of his sword as he came at me again. Ignoring the pain and gushing blood, I went on the attack. Swinging my chains I caught his sword on one of the links. Using him as a pole I twisted into the air and pulled the sword from his grasp. I underestimated his reaction time, for as soon as the sword left his hands he charged me. Again I was tackled to the ground; only this time Lord Jamison was on top of me. His wispy silver hair covered my face, blinding me as I went to punch him! Just as I was about to make contact he grabbed my chains and twisted them so that my arms couldn't move. Struggling beneath him he turned and yelled, "You! Pull the lever!" The children pleaded for their lives as a guard, somewhere off to the side, ran up to the platform. While Lord Jamison took his eyes off of me I was able to surprise him and buck my hips. He released his hold on my hands, and I cracked him across the face with the chains. His jaw broke before my very eyes. I pushed him off of me just as the guard reached the lever. Retrieving Lord Jamison's sword, I ran to the platform.

The guard grabbed the lever and pulled back as hard as he could just as I threw the sword. The platform fell from the children's feet, and for a moment they were free falling . . .

I had planned for the sword to cut through Teta's rope so that she would drop unto the ground but . . . "No!" The sword went a little too far to the left and missed her rope. "Teta!"

Every child, every single one of them, fell as the platform did. Every child, every single one of them, fell. A few cries and a couple of shrieks of terror escaped from them as they fell. Every single one of them fell. It was as if they would fall forever . . . that was until the rope caught. All of the little bodies suddenly stopped, and the unmistakable sound of necks snapping resonated throughout the palace grounds as their bodies jerked, causing them to bounce, lifeless, on their ropes.

Teta's eyes were on me as her life was slowly slipping away.

"Teta!" I unleashed a bloodcurdling scream as I watched her fight for her last breath. Her legs were kicking and her arms flailing as the noose tightened and tightened. She didn't weigh enough for the rope to end her suffering . . . her body had to exhaust all of her oxygen before she was to be released into the arms of death. Out of my peripherals I could see that some of the other children had stopped struggling. Zakai had died immediately . . . Teta was still hanging on . . . pleading for breath.

I went to attempt to rescue her, but it was to no avail. All of the fight had left me as three guards grabbed me by my arms. My eyes were riveted on Teta . . . o' how her little body fought.

"Cut her down! You have to let me cut her down!" I sobbed, "Please look at her—she's just a little girl! Cut her down! Please! You have to cut her down!" Seconds passed, and Teta's legs were slowing and she had stopped flailing. "Cut her down! She's just a little girl . . ." But it was too late. Death had wrapped its greedy hands around her neck and emptied every ounce of life right out of her. My heart drowned in sorrow and agony. It felt as though someone had taken me and rubbed me raw with sadness until I bled all over. The look on her face . . . the look on all of their faces . . . they were counting on me . . . and I let them down . . .

The guards put up no fight as I sank to the ground and buried my face in my hands.

Islocia slowly faded into a gray abyss as thunder rolled across the sky. It was as if the heavens were blanketing the hallow land with its own sorrow and agony. Eventually, as Islocia slipped effortlessly into its depression, the saddened skies began to cry for the children whose lives were cut short. They cried for the villages that burned at the hand of a tyrant, and they cried for me . . . for I could not cry for myself . . .

"Bravo!" I heard clapping and laughter descend the palace steps. "Bravo! What a remarkable display of passion. And so suspenseful!" The queen chided, "I thought when you threw that sword that you would save her. I really did. Such a pity that you missed." She stepped around a few fallen guards before coming to stand over me. Behind the queen I could hear the children dangling on their ropes; cold, shattered, lifeless. It was a massacre of innocence. She continued, "My God, Arianna, you look terrible. Has someone been hurting you?" I was so angry, so devastated, that I was frozen with fury as I felt her smile down upon me. "You can't help but think . . . if you had done something—anything—different would you have been able to save the lives of these eight children?" She paused as if she were expecting me to respond. "Pity." I heard her turn and head for the steps. Looking up I saw her nod to the guard nearest the platform. Understanding the silent command, he went and cut the ropes that held the children. I had to look away as their bodies fell to the ground. The queen looked down at the children, smiled, and then said to me, "Arianna, there seems to be a bit of a mess on my lawn. Would you mind disposing of the vermin for me?" She snickered and finished with, "Once you're done with that, clean yourself up and join me in my apartment for dinner."

Little Innocence

Little innocence, little innocence, please take my hand. I can lead you away from this pain and this suffering. I can fill your hearts with life again. Little innocence, little innocence, please take my hand. I cannot bear to see your stomachs so empty; I cannot bear to see your eyes so sad. Little innocence, little innocence, will you join me up here? Follow me into the kingdom of heaven and dance among the angels without fear. Little innocence, little innocence, my heart aches for you. I can feel the hunger that rips through your tiny frame; I can feel the difficulty in pushing through. Little innocence, little innocence, please watch your step. For the dead cannot carry themselves to rest, not while stuck in this mess. Little innocence, little innocence, I'm crying for you. I do not wish to witness such agony and to see you so blue. Little innocence, my dear sweet little innocence, I'm calling for you. Can you hear me? Little innocence, little innocence, please take my hand, and I will show you a life that you not only deserve but understand.

CHAPTER 14

THE QUEEN REALLY DID MAKE me clean up all of the bodies. She made sure that the guards supervised me as I loaded each child into the cart that would take them away. That was after they had me check to make sure every child was dead.

After I finished cleaning up the bodies, she had me escorted to my old room. Rye Beddon was waiting for me. She carefully removed all of my clothing, what little there was, and set them aside. I was so numb with agony and grief that I didn't feel anything she was doing. I only knew she was doing it. She had me bathed with those same scents she had when I first arrived. In the beginning I thought they had smelled divine; now they burned my nose. She cleaned the slash on my arm and wrapped it in a clean cloth to stop the bleeding. When I was all washed and clean, she dried me off and then had me stand in the middle of my room while she dressed me. The clothes the queen instructed me to wear were tight, unbearably tight, and gaudy all the same. I didn't have the strength in me to protest. My dress tightened around my chest and waist to the point where I could not breathe. The bottom of my dress fanned out enough to give my legs plenty of room. Following the dress, Rye Beddon went to paint my face. I grabbed her arm and shook my head. Wearily she turned and looked at the guards who stood only a few feet away. I heard one of them approach. He pulled Rye Beddon's hand free and then held my hands behind my back. Rye Beddon continued with the paint.

When I was finished the guard released my arms and proceeded to escort me. I caught a glimpse of my reflection in the mirror as we began to exit my room. Stopping, I looked at myself. For the first time since I arrived I looked exactly like the Royals, with the exception of my iron shackles. But everything else was the same. Bright, colorful gowns and porcelain faces. Rye Beddon had painted over my bruises and swollen eye so that it was hardly recognizable. Yet even though my imperfections were covered, never had I looked more disgusting.

I found the paint to be exceedingly ironic. Its purpose was to cover imperfections, yet, as my face began to burn and itch, it destroyed the very thing it sought to redeem.

As we walked down the halls of the palace, I couldn't look anyone in the eye. Hiding behind these looks had me feeling anything but confident. Besides, my mind was not here. It was with those children . . . It was with Teta and Zakai. I wanted to believe that their souls would be safe. And that no matter how painful their death was they'd be free. Finally free.

"Her Majesty has been expecting you," a guard said, standing outside the entrance of the queen's apartment. He opened the door and the guards and I walked in. As expected it was just as magnificent as any of the other rooms in the palace, but I was not in awe. I was numb to the world. Merely a corpse going through the motions instead of feeling . . . or living.

"Beautiful, isn't it?" Her Majesty said, coming out of one of the many rooms. "Come, let me give you a tour." The guards and I followed her as she led us into a hallway that then transported us into her bed chambers. "All of the monarchs that have blessed the throne have been born on that bed. It is here where I spend most of my time. Some of the Grand Royals will join me, but mainly they spend their time over here." She pointed to a door snuggled near the back of her bed chamber. "This door will lead you to a corridor where a dozen or so rooms can be found. My servants, the Grand Royals, and I spend a lot of time in this internal apartment." I was bored. I did not care to hear anymore of her rooms. Honestly there were too many to count. She led me into the Noble Salon, The Guard Room, and finally the antechamber of the Grand Couvert. "This is where we will be eating," She said cheerfully. A table was dressed in fine linen and slaves stood about. The guards who had been escorting me removed my chains and then pulled the chair out for me. I sat and he pushed the chair back into the table. The queen took her seat next. Folding a napkin over her lap, she signaled for a slave to fill her cup. When the queen's cup was full, the slave, a small withered boy, scurried over to me and filled my glass before returning to his spot against the wall. His chains matched mine.

"A toast." The queen smiled, raising her glass. She disgusted me. That smile, her cadence, it all angered me further. So much so that for a moment I considered taking my glass, breaking it across the table, and stabbing her in the neck. The guards would then have killed me, but I wouldn't have minded. On our way to hell I'd continue to kick her ass until Satan pulled us apart.

But I didn't. Sighing, I took my glass in hand, not bothering to raise it.

"To my dear, dear friend, Arianna Korinthos. Welcome home." Her smile widened as I snapped the neck of the glass. The contents spilled on the white cloth, and the slaves rushed to clean it. The queen casually took a sip of her own drink. "Well, I must say, Arianna, you clean up very nicely. Considering how unfavorable your day has been, you look nearly average."

"If only I could say the same for you," I replied, toying with a shard of glass.

Puzzled, she inquired, "What is it you mean by that?"

I had nothing to hold back. If she was to kill me, then fine, I will accept death graciously. I had absolutely no reason to bite my tongue any longer. "You are an ugly queen. The ugliest of them all."

Just as she was to reply, one of the slaves announced that dinner was to be served. A moment later more slaves entered the room, and they began filling our plates. It seemed odd that, although there was a famine, our plates were filled to the brim. Everything one could possibly hope to eat was on the plate.

The queen did not hesitate and began eating right away. I, on the other hand, didn't seem to have much of an appetite. Looking up from my plate, I glanced at the servants along the wall. They were so fragile, so malnourished. Even though some of them were adults they were hardly bigger than any of the children I had seen in the Bastille. Everyone, with the exception of the Royals, were starving. Yet I was the only one who could see it.

Too full of shame to stare at them any longer, I returned my eyes to the plate. The smell of the food was enticing, but I did not want it. I didn't want the steamed vegetables or juicy pieces of fruit. I didn't want the fresh rolls or sautéed onions mixed into my salad. I didn't want the cutlets of meat that still had steam fuming off of it. I didn't want any of it. I wanted those eight children back. I wanted to keep my promise to Teta and Zakai. I wanted to go home . . .

"Eat up, Arianna," the queen said around a mouthful of food. "You don't want your meat getting cold. It certainly doesn't taste as divine when it is room temperature."

Suddenly a thought struck me.

It had to have been day two or three during the time she had me locked away in a cell, when the guards came in grumbling about how hungry they were. They had mentioned that the famine had not only attacked the villages, it had begun to creep into the polished walls of Lárnach. Since the winter season had made its presence known, it was the worst possible time to be stuck in a famine. There was not going to be enough food stored to last the entire season, let alone enough food to fill one's plate. More importantly, there were no livestock. Many of them had become sick due to the poor water. Whatever livestock was left was too sick to feed to people and too skinny to get any food out of them. Yet here I am with a plateful of cutlets.

"I find it odd that in a time of famine you have plenty of food. Plenty of meat," I muttered, looking up at her.

She smiled with pieces of meat clinging to her teeth. "I am prepared for any and all situations. No matter what I have to put in my mouth, this famine will not defeat me. Eat up."

"Where'd you get the meat?" The smell, the tangy burnt smell of the meat was unfamiliar to me. It was not chicken, pig, venison, or cow. It was nothing I had smelled before.

She swallowed another mouthful of food. "I utilize my resources." Accepting another slab of meat, she began cutting it. "Consider it more like recycling."

Covering my hand over my mouth, I pushed my plate away from me as I heard the queen snickering. Forcing my stomach to settle, I quickly drank my glass of wine before asking for more.

"Arianna, you believe that survival can only take place when one is stranded in a desolate forest. But that is not true. I am surviving every day, because I know what it takes to live." She smiled, wiping her mouth.

"You survive by destroying others weaker than you," I replied. "How noble."

She chuckled, sipping her wine. "Yes, Arianna. I do what I have to do to ensure my rightful place on the throne. And if that means I have to kill, manipulate, or torture people to get what I want, then so be it. It's really not that hard to get away with. People these days are too trusting, it's pathetic." Stroking the stem of her glass, she giggled. "You were definitely the easiest to control. And the most fun."

"Excuse me?" I hated the way her eyes sparkled as I grew angrier and angrier. "I played no hand in the destruction of your own kingdom. You did that yourself."

"No, Arianna, you were the most helpful." She set down her glass. "Because of your ignorance I was able to get you to relieve your duty as protector over the villages near the coast. With you gone my soldiers had no problems capturing them." Her smile widened as realization settled across my face. She laughed sinisterly and said, "You douse my throne in blame yet you turn a blind eye to the truth. Yes, Arianna, I took advantage of you. I manipulated you." She sighed, leaning back in her chair before replying, "It wasn't difficult either. And it wasn't entirely my fault. You could have left. You could have went home. But you didn't want to. I allowed you to live a life of luxury, and not once did you ask to visit your village." She smiled, signaling the slave to pour her more wine. "Your poor, poor village. You left them helpless— for what exactly? A few fancy dresses and overpriced food? Lord Jamison didn't even break a sweat when he captured the Qingkowuats. O' and your dear friend . . . Meenoah was it?" She chuckled, covering her mouth with her hands as if to hide her crudeness. "She tried desperately to fight back. Really gave it her all." More chuckling. "Well, let's just say we left her there, rotting with the rest of those vermin people. I wonder if the rats have begun to pick at them yet."

Heavily breathing I clenched my fists in my lap. I wanted to hit something, kill something! No! I wanted to kill someone. And that someone was sitting right in front of me with that bloodstained smile plastered on her painted face. All the bad she had done battered my mind as it poured in all at once. The impossibly high quotas, the raids, that mother jumping off a cliff with her newborn, the queen throwing out all of the food at the party, Lyrrad's death, the Bastille, child hangings, Parthena, Parthena's baby, the king's death, Teta and Zakai's death. Everything she had done. Every awful terrible thing she had done drowned me! I couldn't take it anymore!

She rose from her seat and walked over to the window nearest the back of the room. "You should learn to fear, Arianna. With the snap of my fingers I can take a life away."

Panting with rage, I replied, "You may order for the death of another. But do not allow your mind to stray from the fact that I am the one to fulfill your command. Blood is on my sword, on my hands every time you wish for me to take a life. And let me just say, I am very good at it."

She turned and smirked. "Is that why you were so good at letting those children die today?"

Enough was enough. Taking the knife next to my plate I threw it across the room; it was aimed directly at her. She was too slow to understand what was going on as the knife spiraled and cut her across the cheek. A small amount of blood spurted as she screamed, covering it with her hand.

"Now everyone can see how ugly you really are," I hissed. The guards were on me in a second. But I was too determined to fail. Dodging the first guard's swing of his sword, I rolled to the floor. Using my chair as a weapon I swung, hitting him in the chest. He fell into the other guards, which bought me a few seconds. I took the sword from the fallen guard and slayed two more of them. Running as fast as I could I tried to exit the queen's apartment only to be met with five guards running my way! I took off in the opposite direction. Pushing, shoving, and dodging Royals, I managed to make it to the grand staircase; the only problem was that another batch of guards was waiting for me. The five guards trailing behind me were catching up quickly; the ones at the bottom of the stairs were now ascending them! I could not fight ten guards at once . . . I had to think . . .

Gripping the banister of the staircase, I hoisted myself on top of it and began sliding down. The guards on the staircase were getting closer, too close, so I jumped off the banister and plummeted to the ground. My ankles nearly snapped when they broke my fall. For a moment longer than I needed I wallowed in pain. But as I heard the rattling of the guards' armor I forced myself to ignore the pain and run. Run, run, run! I made a turn into an unfamiliar hallway. There was lots of doors, too many to count. The guards were out of sight for the moment, but I knew I only had seconds to think. So I opened one of the doors, and o' so quietly, I closed it and hid inside. In less than a second I heard the guards run right by me. I waited another second before I peered out the door. There were no guards in sight. Stealthily I exited and headed back toward the staircase. I had to figure out how to get out of the palace.

Right as I made it to the staircase, I heard someone yell, "There she is!" There had to have been twenty or so guards charging down the stairs. Again I began to run! Making a sharp left down a more familiar hallway, I trampled over a Royal. He hollered in protest but was quickly drowned out by the sound of armor and determination. The guards were coming for blood; I had in fact assaulted the queen.

Finally! I had made it to the entrance of the palace. Unfortunately, just as I opened the door, a guard greeted me with a punch to the face. The combined force of me running at full speed and the power of his punch had me flying off the ground. But I didn't fall. Absorbing his punch, I twisted in the air and landed on my feet. I charged him right when he drew his sword. He swung first, barely missing my neck. I sidestepped to the left and swung at his head. Although he wore a helmet I was able to scrape his neck. With a yelp he fell to the ground. The guards who had been chasing me had just caught up to me as I exited the palace. There were no other night guards on duty so everything was all clear. Dropping my sword, I quickly ran down the steps and untied the guard's horse.

"She's getting away!" I heard one of them shout. Mounting the horse I kicked the heel of my foot into its side, urging it to go. Stirring up a cloud of dust we left the guards behind us.

The horse was unbelievably fast. We were halfway down the rows of Angels' Teardrops by the time all of the guards filed out of the palace. When I turned back to look at them I saw that they had given up.

Triumphant, I steered the horse away from the palace and took off to the forest. Not wanting to test my luck, I didn't slow down until I was deep within the dense, dark forest.

Once my heart rate simmered and I got control of my breathing, I began to feel the effects of winter and the substantial amount of physical beatings I was forced to endure over the past couple days. My chest, back, legs, and face cried with soreness. A strong wind, strong enough to almost make me lose my balance on the horse, sliced through every stitch of clothing I wore, battering my body. Within seconds my teeth began to chatter and I was shivering uncontrollably.

But that was not the worst of it.

The worst part was realizing all that had happened to me and to the people I respected the most. The queen was right . . . I let those things happen. Blinded by wealth and titles I destroyed the lives I swore to protect . . . The Qingkowuats . . . Teta and Zakai . . . The king . . . everyone I had deemed important was dead. Everyone I vowed to honor and fight for was dead. Everyone who ever mattered to me was dead . . . Because I had failed them. I had failed . . .

Anger swelled in me all over again! I needed to kill something! I wanted to kill something! Anything to get my mind off the unbearable amount of loss that I am forced to live with for the rest of my life! Never, not once, had I failed anyone! Never had I risked losing all that mattered to me! Never had I been blinded by someone I should have never trusted!

Dismounting the horse, I stormed over to the nearest tree and began wailing on it! I had to do something to get my mind off of everything I had lost. Ignoring the chunks of skin that were left on the tree I continued to hit it over and over and over and over again and again! Teta's face was forever cemented in my mind! She called for me! She thought I'd be there to help her! But I failed her! The king, who I loved and trusted, was dead because of me! I had failed him! Parthena was now left alone in a cell with no more reason to live because of me! I had failed her! All of the children who died by the deadly grasp of a noose died because of me! I had failed them! I kept hitting the tree; I couldn't stop. Even when I began to process how painful it was I hit it even harder! Harder! Harder! Harder! Harder! I screamed the pain away! It was too much for me. This, these feelings, were too much for me . . .

It wasn't until I was out of breath and stiff from the arctic breeze did I stop. Leaning against the tree I sank to the ground, defeated, hoping my mind would turn itself off. It didn't. Every face of every person that I had failed burned into my brain. They were so deeply implanted that it was to the point where I could see nothing but their pain—the tear streaks on Teta's face and the king's head being cut from his body, Parthena as she wept for her love, the anger in Zakai's eyes when I went to visit him in the Bastille, and those children dangling from the gallows and the smirk upon the queen's face.

Knowing that everything she had given me was to manipulate me . . . hurt the most. My ignorance and stupidity led to the massacre of innocents.

Frustrated, I began clawing at my clothes. I hated them! I wanted nothing that the queen had given me! Recklessly I untied the dress and freed myself from its deathly grasp. I started scrubbing at my face, trying to remove the paint! The sickening stench rotted my stomach! I tore off the gem-studded coverings and threw them as far away from me as I could. Still I felt dirty, filthy! Then I remembered that I smelled like a vile Royal. I had to remove the smell! Digging my hands into the hard forest floor, I rubbed dirt all over my body. I grabbed the moss from the trees and did the same thing. If I could have I would've ripped my skin off! I even tried to! I wanted nothing to do with anything involving the queen, the Royals, or the palace. I hated everything and everyone. The world had proven to be a violent, relentless, unforgiving place controlled by the hands of the wealthy. Everyone was my enemy. Any person who raised a sword at me was my enemy. The world was my enemy, and I had to defend myself at all cost. No matter how many lives I must take. No matter how many souls I will send to hell. I will avenge my king. I will avenge Teta. I will avenge Zakai. I will avenge Meenoah. I will avenge the Qingkowuats. I will avenge all who fell to the poisonous grasp of Queen Ophelia. I am strong. Strong enough to kill the mighty, just as I had before . . .

He slid the sword across my back, not cutting me; its coolness was a relief to my sore limbs. Kneeling down beside me he laid the sword so that I saw only my reflection. The battered child who cried the pain away stared back at me.

"Is this who you want to see? Is this who you want to be?" the Conqueror hissed, grabbing me by the hair and forcing me to look closer. "If so, take the sword from my hands and welcome death! But welcome it on your own terms."

I considered it. I considered ending it all. I considered a pain-free beginning.

"Only the strong can die honorably. The strongest never see an ending to their own life but to others. The weak are already dead. The weakest take their own life. Which are you?"

I grabbed the sword. Forcing myself to stand, ignoring the pain and destitution he had caused. I grabbed the sword. On shaky legs I stood ready, ready to fight him. Ready to kill.

The Conqueror drew his sword too.

I did not see a man standing before me. I did not see a person standing before me. I saw all the agony, hate, sorrow, and torture he put me through. I saw my blood, my sweat, and my tears. I saw my empty childhood, and emptier stomach. I saw the people he had me kill and the scars of those who tried to kill me. I saw everything but a goddamn human being standing before me. Which is why when I killed him, when I stabbed my sword through his heart, I did not weep for the loss of my guardian. I did not weep for the loss of my Conqueror. For he was weak, too weak, to live. I was strong. Stronger than him, stronger than my pain, stronger than all who stand against me. . .

Rising to stand, I mounted the horse again. With a strong kick of my heels she soared through the forest as vengeance and determination fueled my rage.

Until my last breath, my last drop of blood, my last heartbeat, I will fight until the queen is dead. I will fight until Islocia is free. I will fight. I will fight. I will fight!

PART II

I will always be in pain. I will always be angry.
But what I do with that rage determines what my life can be.

CHAPTER 15

FRIGID WINDS WRAPPED THEIR GREEDY claws around me and embraced me as if we were close friends. Pulling the elk skin shawl tighter around my shoulders, I cuddled against the tree I was leaning against. I tried to quiet the clacking of my teeth, but I was to no avail.

In Islocia the winter season rarely, if ever, delivered the flurries of snow. Here, we are greeted with freezing winds and colder rains. Sometimes the raindrops froze, but never do they form the porcelain silhouettes that mimic the layers of flakes that top Mt. Grim Wall. The temperature is only deadly at nighttime, when the sun escapes the pain and the necessity of a fire is prevalent. The only issue with the fire is that when the rains come it soaks the branches and douses the fire. I am lucky to survive the night . . .

I cannot recall the amount of days I have spent wandering the Iclin Forest. Thirty? Forty? I lost count after the first seven. The deepest, darkest portion of my mind had consumed me the minute I decided to pursue my hatred of the world. Returning to my sadistic realm, I dwelled in gore and violence while rejecting mercy and loss. I was not happy unless something was dead. No matter the victim. This rage . . . this fury kept me burning through the night when my fire would not. I would not allow myself to die, not when breath still escaped the lungs of Islocia's oppressor. The cold may put a dagger through my heart and release its icy poison through my veins, but I will not die. I cannot.

The sun was beginning to peek over the horizon, its rays painting the gray sky pink. I had survived another night of the treacherous winter season.

Due to the cold, vegetation was scarce. The plants fought bravely against the harsh weather conditions during the day and following through into the night, only to lose their fight to the frost in the morning. It was a horrible time for crops and an even worse time for someone without a food storage. But I knew that I wasn't the only one to be suffering through the cold. All of the villages would be feeling the effects of hunger and the bone-chilling gnaw of the winter season. Only the queen's belly would be full. Only the queen's bed would be warm.

Surging to my feet, ignoring the uncomfortable stiffness from being balled up all night, I marched over to the nearest tree and hit it with all my might. My hand vibrated from the force. Thinking about the queen in her perfect world, while thousands of her people died, infuriated me. I wanted her dead! I wanted everyone dead! And once all who were slayed by my hand rested at my feet, I would then put the knife to my neck. It would be the only outcome that satisfied me.

Pulling my hand away, I inspected it. Careful as not to cause any more harm to it, I unwrapped the makeshift bandage. Pieces of my skin clung to the rotted fabric, but the sharpness of the pain was easy to ignore. My knuckles were purple, either from the trauma or the cold, and my bone was visible at the end of my pinky finger. Puss and decaying flesh were well-preserved on the cloth and on my hand. Most of the color had gone elsewhere, which made it seem as if no blood ran to my hand at all. Curiously, with my other hand, I began pulling back some dead flesh. When it began to feel uncomfortable I pulled harder, wanting to see if warm blood still continued to flow through me. I soon realized that when I twisted the skin it began to hurt a lot more, which means I must be getting close. Roughly I gave my hand a good yank, and finally fresh blood appeared very slowly, almost like it was coming out in intervals. For some reason or another, the sight entertained me. Especially when it began to harden, almost immediately, before my very eyes. Unfortunately, it didn't take long for me to get bored of that. So I licked up the rest of the blood and wrapped the same cloth around my hand. And with that, I continued on into the rest of my day.

My afternoons consisted of scavenging the immense Iclin Forest for anything of sustenance. Most of the forest critters had left months ago; only the adolescents who were too young to understand the changing of the seasons wandered about. The first few weeks were most favorable toward me. I was lucky to have caught a few rabbits and a sickly doe. The doe did not have enough meat for me to salvage, so I skinned her and wore her hide. The rabbits weren't as malnourished, though if given a few more weeks to live they would have soon followed the path of the doe. I had no problems preserving the meat, considering how cold it was. Keeping it clean was another issue, but that was the least of my concern.

I made an effort to use all parts of the animals I killed. The hide was used to keep me warm and to cover my feet. Some of the hide was used to make a belt, which would then carry all my daggers and a few other weapons in it. With their blood I painted my face and marked the trees, just in case any lingering, starving predators lurked about. Their bones were used as weapons. I found very creative ways to dismember a spine and construct a spear using the doe's femur. The doe's lower ribs were my daggers. I tied her vertebrae with a vine and wrapped it around a stick to make a club. Her larger rib was the shell of a bow, and I used a tightened, thin, sturdy vine as the string. It wasn't the most structurally sound weapon, so I ended up using her shoulder blade, sharpening it against some boulders, to carve a tree and make a wooden bow. The arrows were made out of her radii and ulna. Those too were sharpened with the boulders. The rabbit bones were too small to be used as weapons, so the more durable bones like its teeth and hind legs were of better use. I tied the teeth, using a vine, to the end of its femur and used that to skin the animals. The work was tedious and difficult, but I had to do it. I had to live.

Walking over to my horse, I untied her from the tree and mounted her. The rumbling deep within my stomach indicated that it was time to hunt. I urged her into a trot. Squeezing her shoulders with my knees and wrapping my fingers around her mane, I quickened our pace and soon we had begun to gallop. Gliding over the rough forest floor, we made our way to the semi-frozen creek near the center of the Iclin Forest. Some of the animals stayed near the creek. Possibly because that's where their mothers had left them and they're waiting for them to return, or because it is the only water source within a day's walk. Either way it was the best place to hunt.

Once we neared the creek, I slowed her to a stop and dismounted. Her deep-brown coat and midnight-colored mane blended in perfectly with the scenery of the naked forest. Leading her toward the creek, I released her and crouched into the cold grass, completely out of sight. Silencing my body, I heard my horse walk over to the creek and begin to drink. Any animal, predator or prey, would be drawn to the newcomer. I just had to be patient.

It was hardly a moment later when I heard another creature stir up the grass and make its way toward the creek. Mirroring the softness of the forest, I could distinguish the sounds of two heartbeats, one being my horse, strong and calm. The other was nearly unrecognizable. It wasn't a doe because a doe's heartbeat is quick, almost like a hummingbird flapping its wings. This animal's heartbeat was slow and steady. I knew it couldn't be a predator because my horse would've scattered by now. So what was it?

Braving a look over the prickly blades of grass, I was surprised to see that it was a buck. He was huge, nearly standing several inches taller than me. His large, deadly antlers parted the water as he took a leisurely sip. The brown, furious beast outweighed me by more than a thousand or so pounds! If I were to kill him, that meat would last me for days. My mouth watered at the thought of his rich, tender meat burning over a fire. His hide would last until the end of the season, and his strong bones would make for much sturdier weapons. How favorable I am to have such a luxury wander into my forest. I would be a fool to let such an opportunity go to waste.

Therefore, I began my attack.

Slowly creeping through the grass, remaining out of sight, I made my way toward my meal. I was about four yards away from him when a cold breeze lifted my scent into the air. The buck raised his head from the water and began to look around; he sensed me. Slowly, o' so slowly, I reached for my bow and then my arrows. The buck resumed drinking. Crawling over the rough, hard ground I placed myself in the perfect position and waited to take the perfect shot. He lifted his head again, and I felt him looking in my direction. My body was silent—o', was I still. Another breeze tousled the grass, and I knew that the buck was getting antsy. I had to make my move.

The moment I felt him turn away from me, I quietly, like a cat stalking a mouse, rose up onto my knees and readied my arrow. Getting a full view of the massive creature almost dented my appetite for him. Taking him down would be a challenge unlike any other, but it was a challenge I was willing to accept.

Pulling back the bow as far as it would go, I aimed it at his neck. But then reconsidered. The buck was coated in several thick layers of nearly impenetrable fur. Especially around his neck. I knew that a single shot with an arrow would not bring the creature down—I could only slow him down. Therefore, I decided to aim it at his hind leg. Even though I would then be fighting adrenaline and fear, I knew that it would slow him down just enough for me to have a chance.

Taking a slow, deep breath, controlling every muscle in my body, I released the arrow on an exhale. It zipped through the air like a fly fleeing from a bird. Tunneling through the frigid air, it targeted my prey.

That moment of impact consisted of a sharp yelp from the beast and then running. Running, running, running. The buck took off, away from the danger. He was too quick for me to fire another arrow.

Leaping from the grass, I began running after him. My horse, how clever she was, ran up along side me, matching my pace. Not wanting to lose any momentum, I continued my running as I grabbed onto her mane; she didn't slow. Wrapping my fingers in her mane, I quickly hoisted myself up and onto her back, and we were off! Soaring over fallen trees we ran down the elk. The arrow I had shot him with had dug deep into his leg, causing him to limp as he ran for his life!

"Come on, girl! Faster!" My horse did as she was told and sped up. We were right on his tail!

Readying another arrow, squeezing for dear life with my knees so I didn't fall, I aimed it at his other leg. Once again it zipped through the air and pierced his leg. He cried in pain as he slowed just a little. Digging my heels into my horse's belly, she sped up as he slowed down. Not wasting any time, I untied the rope, which was constructed out of three vines that had been braided together, and made a lasso.

My horse did her best to remain steady, but the forest floor was unforgiving as her hoof nicked a rock. I nearly flew off of her as she stumbled, but I kept my balance by gripping her mane.

The buck made a quick right turn around a tree, and we followed closely behind him. I swung the lasso over my head and prepared to capture him. Dipping below a low tree branch and brushing the dry leaves from my face, I waited until he was in the right position. The thunderous roar of hooves beating against the ground mirrored the intensity of my heart.

As we neared a clearing the density of the forest subsided, but it would only be for a moment. I knew this was my chance. Tightening my grip on her mane, I sent my lasso flying. My precision was perfect as the rope caught him around the neck. Unfortunately, the second the rope tightened around his neck, all hell broke loose!

I had underestimated the size and dexterity of the buck. He was much bigger and stronger than what I had originally thought. I was only holding onto my horse with my knees while both hands were on the rope when the buck tripped over his feet and crashed to the ground. My horse followed immediately after him, and I was thrown from her back! I flew through the air for a handful of seconds before colliding into a large, thorny bush. There wasn't enough time for me to register the pain before I realized I was still holding onto the rope. All of a sudden the buck started running again, with me dragging behind him. My first instinct was to let it go, as I was being mutilated by the forest debris as the buck stumbled about, but I knew that if I did I would not have another meal for weeks. Only a fool would give up such a prize.

Wrapping the rope around my wrist, I pulled out my dagger. The buck continued to drag me, but he could no longer run. I could see the blood dripping from his shaky hind legs as he tried to keep himself upright. He bleated to the heavens as the pain settled in. His eyes were nearly bursting from his skull as he fought for breath. The more and more he pulled me around, the more the lasso tightened.

When he had finally stopped running and was only stumbling in place, I pulled myself upright before cutting my wrist free from the rope. Once I was free I quickly rolled away from him. As I found my footing and turned to face him, he shot me a death glare and aimed his antlers at me. His nostrils flared as he dug his front hoof into the dirt. The buck roared his anger at me. With my dagger unsheathed, I took a few steps back and prepared for a very dangerous game of chicken.

The mighty beast dipped his head so that every pointy spike on his antler was aimed at me. I pulled out another dagger and took a deep breath. He began charging me. My heartbeat matched his pace.

With every passing second I felt the weight of his anger, his rage. He wanted me dead—I wanted him dead. Only one would be the victor.

It was going to be me.

Masterfully I dodged his charge, jumping off to the side, and quickly I began throwing all of the daggers I had! *One, two, three, four, five, six . . .* I alternated between my right and left hand as I pulled all of the daggers from my belt. Eight of them punctured his stomach while the other four nailed him in the face. He bleated in pain as he bled profusely onto the forest floor. Within seconds he toppled over. The ground shook violently as he fell, creating a cloud of dust that blanketed his defeat.

Without hesitation I ran over to him and climbed on top of his huge, writhing, fluffy body and picked up the rope that was still wrapped around his neck. As hard as I could, with all the strength left in me, I pulled and pulled and pulled. His massive head thrashed wildly! One of the small spikes on his antlers pierced my arm, causing my own blood to splatter onto him. I screamed in pain and continued to pull hard on the rope. Knowing that it would take him too long to die this way, I pulled out one of the daggers in his stomach and plunged it deep into his neck. Once wasn't enough, so I did it again and again and again and again! His blood coated my face and chest as his life seeped into the forest floor. No more than a minute later, the beast lied limp. Almost completely drained of blood.

I had won. The beast had been slayed.

Exhausted, as my own adrenaline started to wane, I stood from the fallen buck. His blood cascaded down my face as I went to retrieve my horse. Turning back to look at him, I noticed that I felt no mercy or sympathy toward taking his life. One of the few things the queen taught me was that all creatures were meant to die, innocent or not. If that's the way life is supposed to be, then there clearly is no reason to weep over any loss. No matter how brutal. No matter how righteous. No matter how deliberate. No matter how unjust. The lion never weeps for the death of the lamb.

Shivering, shivering, more shivering. I cuddled against my tree and fought bravely against the cold, although it was to no avail. The raging midnight winds battered me, clinging to my weakened frame. My top teeth cracked against the bottom ones, sending an unbearable bite of pain throughout my mouth. I detested the cold. Every night, every single night, it mocked me. The wind howled with laughter as it turned my body numb, leaving me vulnerable to every element of the night. I tried to keep a fire going, but winter would not oblige me with the luxury of warmth. It would only embrace me, giggling to my face as I tried and tried and tried and tried to pull free from its grasp. Squeezing my eyes shut, I prayed to the heavens that I would be relieved of the bitter hold that the winter season had on my body. I prayed that I would be relieved of the tumultuous brutality of the devilish winds.

Suddenly, like the calm after a storm, I felt everything cease. Still hidden behind my eyelids I no longer could feel the punches of the artic breeze. I could no longer feel the thrashing of the winter season. Everything stopped. I had no feeling. Numb. Completely. Nothing like the sore numbness caused by the icy winds. I was literally numb. No external feeling whatsoever.

Braving a look, I opened one eye. Slowly! Slowly! Slowly! Slowly! Slowly! I took my time. I took my time opening my eye. But before it was a fourth of the way open I closed it immediately, sinking back into the comforts of the dark. I tried my other eye. Slowly! Slowly! Slowly! Slowly! Slowly! I took my time. I took my time opening my other eye. But before it was only an eighth of the way open I closed it. Immediately. Immediately I closed my other eye and sank back into the comforts of the dark. I was numb. Numb. And slowly, slowly, slowly losing my mind.

"Aoife! Aoife!" A small, small, small voice called somewhere off in the distance. This voice did not share the same space as me. No. This voice was far beyond my eyelids. Far beyond my place of solitude. This voice was on the outside. *"Aoife! Aoife!"* I winced at the panic that was made more prominent in the tiny voice as my senses began to work. The air around me was impossibly dry, not hot, but dry. As if every inhale were the consistency of a pile of charred leaves; I coughed with every exhale. With my eyes still closed I started to feel the weight of the air around me. It was heavy. Very, very, very heavy. The more and more it pressed down on me, the more and more I needed to breathe. But with every breath I took, my throat burned from the dryness. It felt as though my throat was a scratching post for

feral cats. The pressure from the air continued to push down on me. Down, down, down, down. My lungs shriveled up into tiny raisins as the air around me wrapped its talons around my chest and squeezed. Squeezing, squeezing, squeezing! I was being constricted so tightly that I did not have enough air to scream. Only a whimper escaped. Only a whimper . . .

Suddenly, as my eyes were forced open from the buildup of pressure in my chest, everything stopped. Everything stilled. For a moment I thought I had died. The only thing I could see was white. There was no sky, no trees, no ground . . . just white. But then, I heard that voice again. *"Aoife! Aoife!"* It sounded so far away. So, so, so, so far away. I stood. On shaky legs I stood and tried to follow the voice. But I was quickly lost in the whiteness. There was nothing but white. White. White. White. White. White. White. White. White. White. White. White. White. White. White. White. White. White. White. White! It's all I could see! There was nothing but white! Even when I tried to hide in the comforts of darkness I was still consumed by all of the white! The inside of my eyelids were white! Everything was white! A vast expanse of white with that small, tiny, miniscule voice repeating *"Aoife"* over and over and over and over again. *"Aoife! Aoife!"* Then again, *"Aoife! Aoife!"* Then again, *"Aoife! Aoife!"* It didn't stop. Just like the whiteness it swallowed me until there was nothing left for me to hear or see. *"Aoife! Aoife!"* White. White.

"Stop it!" I covered my ears with my hands to block out the sound. "Please stop!" But the voice kept crying and the whiteness weighed on. "For the love of all that's holy, stop!" An hour passed, maybe a day, and nothing had changed. Somehow I had managed to find the ground and I fell to it. Curled up in the fetal position I screamed away my discomfort. But it only seemed as if the voice grew louder, and the whiteness shined brighter. *"Aoife! Aoife!"*

"Please stop! I beg of you! Have mercy on my soul!" In an attempt to silence this hellish environment, I had clawed at my ears until they were merely hanging on by one or two layers of skin. "Please stop!" The blood from my ear danced around my face and mocked me. Their sinister smiles cut me until I bled with disgrace. The blood droplets sang the same tune as the voice. *"Aoife! Aoife! Aoife! Aoife! Aoife! Aoife! Aoife! Aoife! Aoife! Aoife! Aoife! Aoife! Aoife! Aoife!"*

"Ahhhhhh!" I screamed with all my might. I screamed and screamed and screamed and screamed and screamed until the vessels busted in my eyes and my throat choked on its blood. I screamed!

Then everything stopped. Everything stopped. There was nothing. Everything stopped. The whiteness had gone and the chanting, the malicious, sadistic chanting had stopped. My eyes took a moment to refocus, and suddenly I was transported to the front of the Belle Palace. But I was not alone. In front of me were the gallows. Hanging from them were crows. Black, gawky, wretched crows. Dead. They hung from the gallows, dead. Dead. Dead. Dead. All of them dead. A murder of crows. A murder of crows.

Suddenly I heard a loud screech come from the sky, and I looked to see thousands and thousands of crows. They nearly blackened the gray sky as their wings resembled daggers slicing through the air.

Off to the side of me I heard a footstep. Then more footsteps. A twig snapped. The sound of armor rubbing against armor told me that there were guards by me. I turned and looked and confirmed that I was right. Now I was surrounded. None of them wore their helmets, yet all of them had no face. Only a mouth. Their mouths were laughing at me. They had no weapons. Neither did I. But they were laughing at me.

I went to take a step toward them, but then I heard that tiny voice again, that tiny, tiny, tiny voice say, *"Aoife! Aoife!"* I turned back toward the gallows, where the sound had originated, and was heartbroken at the sight.

Teta, Zakai, King Araun, Meenoah, Maille, and some of the members of the Qingkowuat village were there. They stood in front of the gallows. Their eyes were on me. Teta and Zakai were holding hands; they looked so thin and fragile. So lifeless. King Araun smiled down at the infant hidden beneath the blanket in his arms before returning his somber gaze to me. Maille, Teta and Zakai's mother, stood behind her children and stroked their hair. Meenoah and the other elders looked gravely at one another and then looked back up at me. They were all looking at me.

Another screech broke the stillness of the scene, and my attention was redirected to the fifty or so crows that suddenly landed on the gallows. Their yellow eyes looked scary against their midnight frame. They were fowl creatures who found comfort in death, and here they were staring at me. I took a step forward, and suddenly I felt something hit my shoulder. The liquid substance poisoned my nose while it began to burn my skin. As I went to look at it I felt something else hit my back. Immediately it started burning. Burning. Burning. Burning. After seconds it became unbearable, and I tried to wipe it off, but it wouldn't. The smell, the pain—my body revolted against the unknown arsenic. Yet more and more and more of it continued to hit me. It was painful, unbelievably so! I screamed as it seared into my skin! Within a matter of minutes patches of my flesh dropped from my bones and onto the ground. And the fire raged on. Burning! Burning! Burning! It felt as though I was bathing in hot coals!

Over the sizzling of my skin and my pointless screaming I heard the cackling of the malicious guards. Turning to look at them, as I held a large piece of skin on my arm together, I saw that they were throwing the burning substance. At first I didn't understand what it was, but as the crows, high above, released it bowels and the guards caught it deftly, I understood what it was. I understood why they were laughing.

Angry, fuming with rage, I went to lunge at them; but I heard a scream come from the gallows! Turning to see I saw that Teta, Zakai, Maille, King Araun and his child, Meenoah, and the other Qingkowuat villagers were no longer standing in front of the gallows. O' no. They had suddenly fallen into a pit filled with a thick, sticky, red, wet substance. And all of them, every single one of them, struggled to keep their heads above the surface.

Instinctively I charged toward them! I had to save them! I had to save them! I had to save them! I had to save them! I had already let them down once. I could not let it happen again! But as I ran faster and as I got closer to them, the guards threw more and more bird droppings at me. I had to force myself to ignore the searing, burning pain! I had to force myself to ignore the chunks of flesh that fell from my body. I was going to save them. I had to.

Diving head first into the pit. I quickly realized that the thick, sticky, red, wet substance was . . . blood. Fighting the urge to vomit every meal I had ever eaten, I tried and tried to swim through the pit and reach the people I had let down. Teta . . . o' how she fought for her life. Kicking, screaming, and clawing for that last breath. Zakai . . . o' how he did everything in his power to save his sister, never minding what he would have to do to save himself. King Araun . . . my king . . . he held the infant over his head and fought with everything he had to keep them afloat. Maille tried to swim over to her children, but she was too weak . . . she was too weak. She was the first to drown. Meenoah and the other members of the Qingkowuat village were soon to follow Maille's path. They sank deep below the crimson pit with no more than a whimper. No more than a whimper . . .

Teta, Zakai, and King Araun were still alive! I could save them! I could save them! I fought against the impenetrable density of the blood. My arms and legs cried as I pushed them to work harder and faster. I wasn't going to fail them again! I couldn't!

Suddenly, out of nowhere, crows started falling from the sky! First it was one, and then two, and then ten, and then thirty! After a second or two they all started to fall like rain during a thunderstorm! Several of them hit me, but it did not affect me. I kept fighting! I kept fighting. Dodging crows and pushing through the crimson pit, I fought to reach Teta, Zakai, and King Araun. I fought! I fought! I fought! I fought! I fought . . .

King Araun dipped below the surface and was going to come back up for air, but crows by the hundreds poured onto him from the sky and dragged him underneath . . . The infant . . . his child soon went under as well.

My heart sunk; tears swelled in my eyes. But I could not stop! I could still save Teta and Zakai. I could still rescue them! I had to save them! I had to save them! I had to save them! I had to save them . . .

Zakai put most of his efforts toward keeping his sister afloat and wasn't paying attention when four crows swooped in and raked their claws down his face. In an effort to rid himself of the crows he released Teta and shooed them away. But before he could grab Teta again, another crow came in and pulled Zakai by his hair. He shrieked in pain, but that only signaled more crows to come, and together they pulled him under.

"No!" I screamed but was silenced as I choked on a mouthful of blood. "Teta!" I fought to stay above the surface. "Swim to me, Teta! Swim to me!" The pain, the sorrow, the fear in her eyes tore me to shreds. "Please swim to me! I will save you!" Flailing her little arms, she tried to come to me. She tried. She tried. She tried. But the crows saw her, and they would not let her live. Together they flew to her and grabbed her by her arms and her hair. She let out a bloodcurdling scream and reached her arm out to me.

I was so close! So close to her! Just an inch, maybe two, and I would have her! I would save her! Reaching my hand out to hers, we touched fingers. Kicking with everything I had, I pushed myself forward and wrapped my whole hand around hers. For a second, relief flashed across her eyes. She thought she was safe. She wasn't . . .

The blood was slippery, and with one hard tug the crows pulled her from my grasp. I tried swimming after them, but they were too fast and too strong! "Teta!" I cried, forcing myself to not give up hope. I could still save her! I could still save her!

But I couldn't. I didn't.

The crows lifted her thin body out of the pit and held her in the air. She looked down at me as bloodstained tears dripped from her face. With the softest, smallest, quietest voice she whimpered, *"Aoife . . ."*

And with that, the crows plummeted back down to the pit at full speed. Taking Little Teta with them, they dove deep, deep, deep, deep down into the crimson pit . . . leaving nothing behind but a whimper. Only a whimper . . .

Defeated, destroyed, heartbroken, I cried to the heavens as the cackling laughter from the guards lifted me out of the pit and back onto solid ground. Dripping blood, panting with sorrow and rage, I heard the sound of another laugh. A laugh more evil than Satan himself. Looking up onto the steps I saw *her*. The destroyer. She had a child's dismembered arm in her red hand and slowly, o' so slowly, she took a long savoring bite out of it. The meat clung to her teeth as she smiled down at me. Then she and the guards continued their laughing. Laughing! Laughing! Laughing! Laughing! Laughing! Laughing! Laughing! Laughing!

The remaining crows swarmed overhead, screeching along with their laughter. Blood ran down my face as anger spilled out of every exhale. I had just enough rage to kill *her*. I had just enough rage to die knowing she was dead too.

I turned toward her. Her pale, pasty skin and matted auburn hair disgusted me. My hands ached with the need to have them around her neck!

But as I took that first step toward her, all of the crows suddenly raced down and sheathed my entire body. I fought to get them off, but more and more and more came until I could see nothing but black! Black! Black! I fought to break free but I couldn't. They had overpowered me. Death had overpowered me . . . A moment later I was swept off the ground by the crows. They flew me, shielded in darkness, until finally the vile creatures stopped. Except, I wasn't expecting them to let me go.

Falling, falling, falling, falling! There was nothing beneath me. There was nothing to break my fall. Only death. Only certain, inevitable death as the ground got closer and closer and closer and closer . . .

Gasping for breath I pulled myself from that nightmare! My mind ground to a screeching halt as my surroundings went back to normal. I was in the forest, wrapped in the buckskin, leaning against the tree by the fire. The freezing winds still brutalized me, and I felt that my legs were stiff from lack of movement. I was fine. Everything was fine. When my breathing slowed I wiped the sweat from my forehead and took several deep breaths.

It was just a dream. It was just a dream. I was just a dream.

Still, I didn't sleep much after that.

My mind had finally performed its final act. It had basked in applause and now it took its bow. Before all that is sane and just in the world, it took its bow with no more than a whimper . . . only a whimper of protest as darkness seeped in and destroyed my sanity.

The Feast

Am I a human? Am I sane? Is this a life that I live in vain?
Have I failed those who loved me? Have I
awarded those who shame me?
How precious life is, when it's not yours that is living.

Am I evil or am I just? Have I lost my chance to bask in lust?
Starving my soul and strengthening my rage,
I have only just acquired my plate.
Though trapped in this being, and suffering through
all, I dwell in solitude, hoping never to fall.

Am I ruthless? Am I merciful? I can only
imagine the insurmountable sorrow.
A spoonful of hate. A cup of blasphemy. How
hungry I am to rid myself of this agony.
A dash of wrath. A side of a fuming temper. How
famished I am to complete this supper.

Am I insane? Or am I lonely?
I must finish my meal before feasting on honesty.
A famine has been born, deep inside me it grows, and
it is I that has to suffer this most dreadful world.

CHAPTER 16

"SHH, SHH, SHH," I WHISPERED, stroking my finger down his sweaty cheek. "Do not be afraid, dear friend. It will be over soon. I promise you that." Whimpering, like a pup left out in the rain, the man trembled as his eyes pleaded for understanding. "Just tell me what you were doing in my forest. And then, only then, will I let you go."

The old man tried to speak. He screamed muffled words against the vine wrapped o' so tightly around his mouth. I had tied the vine so tight that the skin that connected his bottom lip to his upper lip bled as the vine dug deeper and deeper into him. With every incoherent word he tried to convey, blood drip, drip, drip, dripped from his mouth.

"Speak, you wrinkled beast!" I commanded, slapping him across the face. Big, fat, salty tears swelled in his eyes before plummeting to the unforgiving earth. I cackled at his dismay. Stalking away from the man, I went to lean against my tree and pulled out one of my daggers. "If you oblige me, filthy vermin, I will allow you leave. I promise you that." Again he tried communicating with his muffled words as he winced at the pain of doing so. Shaking my head, I went back to the man and knelt down to his level. I grimaced at his rotten stench and held my hand over my nose. He flinched away from my quick movements, fearful of the dagger in my hand. "Do not worry, old man, I will not harm you. I was actually hoping you were enjoying the week or so that we've been spending together. Are my accommodations not satisfactory? Am I so bad a host that you wish to leave so soon?"

He nodded his head as if his life depended on it. Which it did.

I suddenly became very angry. Surging to my feet, I thrust my dagger, releasing it from my grasp, into the hallow sky and watched it disappear. "You worthless life! You insolent fool! My kingdom you have entered yet you have not the ability to speak?" Searing with rage I stalked away from the man, only to return a minute later with another dagger in my hand. Again, I knelt to his level. Slowly, o' so slowly, I stroked my finger down his cheek again. He quivered at my touch; I smiled at his discomfort. "It's funny, withered soul, that I was lucky enough to find you. I can only imagine what would have happened to me if you have found me first." I grabbed his cheek and tapped the dagger on his chin. "Were you sent here to kill me?"

He quickly shook his head.

"No? Then were you sent here to spy on me?"

Again he shook his head. More tears slipped onto his pearly white and bloodstained beard.

"Then why were you here?"

Those watery gray eyes, o' how they pleaded before me. His famished, boney, shriveled-up frame trembled as I began to giggle at him. For days on end this man had been the source of my entertainment. I loved the way he screamed as I cut him along his arms and legs. I enjoyed his sorrow as I told him stories of the ways I want to kill him. He was my only house guest; it was my duty to treat him as such.

Unfortunately for him I was beginning to get bored. His weariness had brought me no more pleasure. Therefore, it was in fact time for him to die.

"Speak, desolate peasant!" I bellowed, spitting in his face. "Award me your last words, for I command it of you!"

Anger swelled up inside me again. I could see red—red, blasphemous fury! Taking my dagger I plunged it into the tree trunk, just behind the old man's head. He wept as though I had taken his life.

"Tell me! Why were you here?" I punched him in the stomach. "Tell me!" I hit him again. "Tell me!" I hit him again. "Worthless waste of space!" I hit him again and again and again and again! I couldn't stop until I had beaten him so bad that his body lay limp against the tree.

Grabbing his head I lifted it up and smacked him a few times until his eyes were able to look at me. As I looked into his eyes I noticed how lifeless they truly were. This man was nearly three times my age, and I had assisted in opening the door wider for life to exit and death to enter. Poor man. It is a pity that I had no empathy toward him. We are all meant to die—why ignore something so inevitable?

"Old man," I sighed, smiling as I held his battered head, "I think we have a bit of a communication barrier." Moving his head so that it was leaning on my arm, I reached for my dagger and cut the vine that tied his mouth. "Remember, if you try to scream again, I will cut your tongue out." He didn't even put up a fight. Once the vine released him and I pulled my arm away from his head he fell over to the ground, gasping and wheezing for air as he clung to the last bit of life in him—pathetic. Walking over to him I kicked him onto his back so that I could see his face. "Now that I have freed you, speak."

Raising his hands, as if to surrender, he mumbled something I did not understand. I went to slap him into talking but he recovered quickly. "P-p-peace. I b-beg of it." I groaned at his gurgled words.

Impatiently I waited for him to continue, and after he coughed up his lungs a few times he finally did. "Have . . . m-mercy . . ."

"I will award you that. I vow it," I promised. He wasn't convinced but he had no choice. Talk or die. Those were his options. "Now tell me why you were here."

He sighed in defeat and replied, "Her Majesty placed a bounty on you. If someone were to capture you alive or dead, she would pay the victor four thousand kerts."

I laughed, rising to my feet. "And you thought that *you* could defeat me? Stubborn old fool! I am invincible! Not even the cannons can suppress me!"

Still breathing heavily, he raised his hand to stop me. Once I was silent he continued, "No, I was just a scout. A group of soldiers hired me to wander the forest. They thought that an old man stumbling about would be less suspicious. How wrong they were."

"How wrong indeed!" I shouted, giving the forest a good once-over. "How many of you are there?"

He took a deep breath as he mustered up the energy to reply. "Maybe a dozen. They offered the scouts a handful of kerts. I could not resist it. I have a dying wife and four grandchildren to care for. The famine has taken everything from us. Please understand that this was my only chance to finally be able to provide for my family."

"At my expense!" I snapped, turning back to him.

He flinched away from my rage as he replied, "They said you were an outlaw who had dishonored the throne. She told us what to think."

"And you, faithful servant, followed her blindly! As if you had no mind of your own! I do not pity you!" I put the dagger to his throat. Again the trembling, again the tears, again the whimpering, again more fear. The routine was dull and I was bored, sufficiently so.

"Please, you promised to have mercy on me. Think of my grandchildren, think of my dying wife who wishes nothing more than to have her husband by her side. Think of them . . . please do not kill me," he sobbed, covering his eyes with his bruised hands.

I held the dagger there a moment longer, underscoring my intent, before pulling away from him. As he had done many times before, his bowels emptied onto the forest floor.

"You are dismissed. I have no more use for you. I promised you mercy, and because I am an honest woman I will oblige you. Go forth and leave," I hissed, standing up and turning away from him.

At first he didn't believe me, but he did not wait to ask me of my intentions. Instead he gathered himself, wiped his face, and slowly, o' so slowly, stumbled away from me.

I gave him a minute. Only a minute. I gave him a minute. I promised him mercy, so I gave him a minute.

After that minute, he had only managed to walk five or so feet away on his crippled legs. I walked up behind him. There was no time for him to turn and see me. There was no time for him to try and flee. There was only time to die.

Coming up behind the old man, I wrapped my arm around his head and pulled him to my chest. Just as he was about to slip and fall to the ground I took my dagger to his neck. Like slicing the core of an apple, I cut his throat to the bone. A small pitiful shriek escaped him before he began to choke on his own blood. With my dagger deep inside his esophagus, my hand completely submerged in his neck, I yanked as hard as I could until I heard the dagger slice through the bones of his neck. He was dead in less than a second.

Once I pulled my hand free from his throat, the body dropped loudly to the ground. His blood soaked my arm, but it did not bother me. I actually enjoyed it. Using that same hand I wiped the sweat from my forehead and walked away from the old man, leaving him behind.

I had enjoyed him; he was nice. That is the only reason as to why I gave him a merciful ending.

The old man's testimony made it clear that my vacation was over. Ophelia would not allow me to run loose throughout the forest forever. She wanted me dead. Hell, she needed me dead. As long as I was alive I would be a threat to the throne. Her throne. It was obvious now—she feared me. Apparently, I had given her good reason to.

I was no longer alone in the forest. People, her people, would sell their own souls for a fraction of the reward she was offering. Four thousand kerts. Even Royals would dirty their hands for that amount. Especially in a time of famine and despair.

I was being hunted. The hunter was being hunted. How marvelous. It had been so long since I was presented with a substantial challenge. An army of guards wanted my head. O' how deliciously marvelous.

Smiling, I signaled for my horse. A moment later she trotted up beside me. I grabbed onto her midnight mane and hoisted myself up onto her back and urged her into a running gait.

"Death . . ., accompany me on this ride."

"Blasphemous fools!" I chided, dancing around the mess I had o' so decisively created. It had taken me days to set up such an elaborate plan, and only seconds to execute it. "You are all incompetent idiots who couldn't lead a blind man straight!" I howled in laughter as I took in their weary faces. "No one is as incredulous as I. I, the clever gal who defeated your train and captured you all! I who threatens the throne and therefore threatens the stability of Islocia! I who holds all of your insolent lives in my bloody little hands! Yes, knights of the queen's pathetic guard, I am the one who can never taste the bitter substance of failure, and I am the one who has never had to beg for the mercy of death. I am the one who enjoys the plight of the dying and the sufferance of the mighty. It is my voice that will haunt you as I send your souls into hell. For you are mine, all mine. And I am going to have so much fun with every single one of you."

"You do not inspire fright. You're a woman," one of the guards to my left hissed. I turned toward him and smiled before walking over to where he was tied up to the base of a tree, just like the other nine were.

Kneeling to his level I replied, "I took out twelve of your fellow guardsmen. You are tied to a tree. Need I say more?"

He guffawed as if my statement was completely ludicrous. "You expect me to believe that a little lady, such as yourself, devised a plan so explicit that you killed nearly twelve men and incapacitated the remaining nine? Now that, just the thought, would make us blasphemous fools."

I smiled at the brave guard. He spoke valiantly. I admired his confidence and lack of discretion toward an immovable force such as myself. Unfortunately, his valor did not match his intellect. I shouldn't have been surprised that this waste of space couldn't believe that someone like myself could devise a plan as intricate as the one I had. It took me ages to set up and even longer to wait for them to cross my path. But once they had . . . it all happened beautifully.

Reaching my hand out to him, I stroked my fingers down his cheek, running my fingers through his inky black beard. He winced away from my touch, but I just leaned in closer and used my other hand to stroke the other side of his face. His radiant brown eyes searched my face for an understanding I was not willing to give.

"You are right," I said, tracing his cherry-red lips with the tip of my finger. "It would be entirely absurd to believe that I, the little lady I am, could defeat such strong and intrepid men." I leaned forward so that my mouth was at his ear while my hands returned to stroking his sideburns. "But I do believe that seeing is believing. Wouldn't you say so?" I took only a second to look into his eyes before I placed my left hand at his chin and my right hand at the back of his head. In one quick, deadly movement I yanked my hands clockwise until I heard his neck shatter beneath my grasp. Releasing his now lifeless head, it hung very loosely on his shoulders with his eyes wide open.

Even though I had sufficiently ended his life I wasn't satisfied. It was clear that these guards underestimated my carnal desire for pain and gore. Therefore, I must prove myself to them.

Untying the charming fellow, I dragged him into view for all of the guards to see. Horrified they watched as I stripped him from his tunic and cut him from his throat and all the way down to his navel. Once that was done I got a vine and tied his feet together before hoisting the end of the vine over a tree branch that just so happened to be hanging right over the center of their prison. When the vine made it over the branch I pulled as hard as I could until the guard's limp body began to rise and sway in the breeze. Blood drained freely as his intestines began to spill out of him. Once he was at the height I desired, I tied the vine down and inspected my work. Finally satisfied, I turned to the other guards and bowed to their silent applause. "Does anyone else doubt my abilities?" I asked, searching their faces for a response they were too frightened to give. "No? Good. Now let's get started, shall we?" Wiping the blood from my dagger I sauntered over to another guard. This guard had very long legs, indicating his height, and was strapping in stature. He had bright red hair that was tied back into a ponytail . . . just like . . .

Closing my eyes against the pain, I swallowed past the lump in my throat.

This guard was very handsome, so much so that the harlots of Lárnach would kill themselves for a go at this green-eyed Gaelic devil with his long locks of ruby hair and bulging muscles through his heavily armed armor. How lucky I am to enjoy such a delicious specimen.

"What is your name?" I asked seductively, playing with a loose strand of his hair.

Swallowing, his throat working, he replied, "Sir Daniel Jamison of Islocia."

I gasped, playfully covering my mouth with my hand, "Any relation to Lord Jamison?"

"Yes." He nodded. "He is my father's brother."

Disappointed, wishing I could have enjoyed him more, I cocked my head to the side and sighed. "What a shame. I really hate that man."

"He spoke very highly of you," he replied nervously as his eyes darted away from me.

I chuckled. "Do not kiss my ass because you believe it will spare your life. That man wants me dead just as much as I want his head." Placing my hands on both sides of his face, I moved my body so that I was straddling his lap. "Daniel, I need answers. Can you answer some questions for me? Please?"

Straining to contain his fear and arousal, he nodded.

"Good boy." I ran my hands down his clean-shaven face and then to his chest. "Now tell me, how many of you are out there looking for me?"

"A little over fifty guards," he replied quickly. "There are a few base camps scattered throughout the forest."

"Base camps for only fifty guards?" I inquired, moving my hands to his neck.

"N-n-no," he stammered, eyeing the dagger at my hip. "The base camps were set up to capture any remaining villagers in the forest."

Raising an eyebrow, I asked, "How many base camps are there? Where are they?"

"I don't know how many there are, and I don't know where they all are."

Forcing myself down a little harder on his hips, I reached my hand down to his package and squeezed lightly at first. "Daniel, it would be wise if you told me the truth." I squeezed a little harder, licking my lips at how uncomfortable he became. He wanted desperately to squirm free, so much so that he tensed at my touch.

"Okay, okay!" I loosened my grip on him. "I honestly don't know how many there are, but I do know that there is one very close to this location. Head east from here and you will find it. It's about a day's walk away."

"Good boy." I released him completely and watched as he sighed and leaned his head against the tree, breathing heavily. "Is there anything else you think I should know?"

He shook his head. "No, I swear."

"Promise?" I returned my hands to his face and leaned an inch or two away from his lips.

He nodded and I felt his muscles tighten beneath me. "You really are a good boy, aren't you?" Before he could respond I shoved my tongue down his mouth and suckled. For a second he didn't do anything. He remained idle, absorbing the situation. And then…as men often do…he indulged himself in the temptation and allowed himself to enjoy it.

I felt the eyes of the other guards on Daniel and me. Each of them wanted me; desire and lust spilled throughout our little prison. The forest was silent. Barely a sound escaped. Only the licking and suckling of Sir Daniel and I radiated throughout the forest.

Sir Daniel was so lost in me that he didn't feel me reach for my dagger. The bulge between his legs thickened as his lips and tongue kissed down my chin and neck before returning back to my mouth. His saliva began to drip down the corner of my mouth as he strained to deepen the kiss. His arms were tied behind his back; consequently he couldn't take control over the kiss. The only thing he could do was take it. Though the thickness in his pants was probably increasingly uncomfortable, he could do nothing about it. I was in charge.

Again he kissed down my chin and suckled on my neck. Rolling my head to the side I allowed myself to enjoy him. So much so that words of praise escaped from my lips. He continued to tease my neck and I continued to urge him on. It was almost too much. I should have asked him to stop but I didn't. I wanted it. I wanted him. He was so good. I wanted more. "Yes . . . ! *Calder*!" I gasped as I heard the words slip from my mouth.

He froze.

As did I.

Everything around me was still. Everything had stopped.

The words I had just said had me reeling. Disgusted I pulled away from the guard.

I could not, for the life of me, explain why I had just . . . why *his* name . . . why had it even been brought up! My mind was lost to me, once again. I had lost it entirely.

Angrily I thought of ways to take back my words! I wanted to destroy my tongue and burn it in a fire! But I couldn't cause myself harm! That would be ridiculous!

Wanting to rid myself of the memory of this very odd encounter I pulled out my dagger and put it to his mouth. Confused, while wasting precious seconds to defend himself, he made no moves to deter me. He only looked at me quizzically. But the sight of him riled me. I didn't want him anymore. He was revolting, increasingly so! Therefore, I took my free hand and forced it into his mouth and grabbed his tongue. As he awoke from his lust-filled dream he released an unearthly scream as I shoved my dagger into the back of his mouth. Thrashing his head he tried to get me to let him go. He even bit down on my fingers as hard as he could! Angered, as blood spilled from his bite marks on my finger, I removed the dagger from his mouth and punched him in the throat. Naturally he tried to heave out a breath as his jugular tickled the back of his neck. With his mouth wide open I grabbed his tongue again and put the dagger to the back of his mouth. This time I was much quicker with my assault. Like extracting the meat from a turtle I hacked off his tongue, ripping it from his mouth as blood and painful screams exploded. So overcome by pain he cracked his head against the tree, trying to subdue it.

Having a look at his bloody tongue in my hand, I suddenly felt better about the whole situation. It was as if my little slipup had never occurred. At least for him it hadn't. For he could no longer repeat the words I retorted.

Wailing as loud as a woman in labor, the wide-eyed and fearful Sir Daniel was nearly incoherent with pain. It was beautiful. Extremely so. The ruby locks of his hair were the same shade as the blood that now created a beard around his chin and down his neck. His wild brown eyes grew to the size of dinner plates as fear and agony consumed him. The handsome man Sir Daniel once was, was now gone . . . forever. It made me smile.

Rising from his lap, I stood and wiped his blood from my blade on my arm. With his tongue still in my hand, I wiggled it, listening to the slapping noise it made.

"The blame for the loss of your dignity should not be placed upon me. It should be placed upon your uncle. If he had killed me when he had the chance, this would have never happened," I chided, taking his tongue and tucking it away in Sir Daniel's breastplate. "For safekeeping." I winked.

The night was exceptionally cold. Even though I had the buck's hide to shelter me from the raging winds, I still shivered beneath it. Though that was nothing compared to what the guards must have been feeling. Many of them wore nothing but their tunics underneath their armor. Two unlucky souls died almost immediately from hypothermia. The remaining guards howled almost as loud as the wind as they lost some of their toes and fingers to frostbite. Lucky for me, the night was dry and I was able to find some wood and make a fire. The fire, blazing beautifully bright and warm, parted the inky black sky. I knew that the guards could see the soft glow of my fire from where I was a mile or so away. Constantly, like a child needing milk, they hollered and screamed for mercy. "Save us from these wretched winds!" They'd say, "Cursed be those who have not warmth! Mercy, mistress, mercy!" Their howling got so obnoxious that I decided to oblige them.

"God be praised!" they sang as I approached them with a burning branch. "Blessed mistress, thank you!" another guard cheered. Sir Daniel even chimed in too, mumbling incoherent words that no one understood.

"Quiet all! I beg for peace!" Their howling and wailing ceased as I stepped forward, dodging the swaying guard that still hung from the tree. "Forcing me from my comforts only to accommodate you has not made me feel gracious!" I growled, surveying the remaining six. "Your wish is for warmth, fine. I shall give you what you want but . . . not in the way in which you would think to want it." Stalking over to the closest guard near me, I cocked my head to the side and examined the gentleman. Though the forest was blanketed in darkness I could still see, due to the soft glow of the burning branch, his muscular build and aged facial features. He violently shivered before me as he eyed the burning branch, his eyes pleading for warmth. So I obliged him. "Burn in hell," I whispered to his shivering frame before returning my eyes to the rest of them. "All of you. Burn in hell." And with that, I forcefully shoved the burning branch down the guard's breastplate and watched his body light the world. His screams mirrored those of the innocent children imprisoned in the Bastille. His eyes, those pain-filled eyes, reflected that of Zakai as he watched his sister's life slip away. His body, his charred flaming body, underscored the hatred and fuming rage that will forever consume me for as long as I shall live.

The guards no longer complained for the duration of their stay.

CHAPTER 17

THE FOLLOWING MORNING I TOLD the remaining guards that if they ate their charred mate, they would be released. I told them that they each had to consume a major body part. Naturally, after expressing their disgust, they opted for an arm because it was the smallest. I would not allow them to eat just a finger or a hand. They had to consume, not just taste, a human being. They had to chew human flesh. They had to fill their stomachs with their mate's body. Then and only then would I be satisfied.

Two guards got an arm. The others wanted a leg. So the other two got a leg. There was one guard left. I decided to give him a choice. I told him, "If you would rather me kill you I shall oblige the request. It will be a slow and painful death. You will weep for mercy for hours, maybe even days, before death shall oblige you. However, if you want to live you must eat his cock. Then and only then will I be satisfied." After allowing him a minute or two to deliberate he chose to eat the cock and live another day. But there was another stipulation. Seeing as he had the smallest piece, I thought it would be fairer if I untied him and he would then feed the other guards their meats while I kept a dagger to his back.

Watching them being forced to eat their burnt comrade was beautiful. I enjoyed it more than anything else. Especially when they began to vomit from the vile taste. Especially when they ate all the way down to the brittle bone. Especially when I cut their mate's head off and force-fed them his eyeballs, tongue, throat, ears, and teeth. I especially loved watching the final guard put the tiny cock in his mouth and nibble at the flesh. I couldn't bear to feed it to him myself, so I left him untied and watched. He hurled more than the others before he even got the shriveled thing in his mouth! It was beautiful. I love how his whole body turned green as he swallowed the first bite. I couldn't have been happier.

But all good things must come to an end. Therefore, when I became increasingly bored with them I decided it was time for them to die. Before I killed them I made them all crowns of thorny vines and tied them very tightly around their heads until blood dripped from their temples.

Thinking it would be exceedingly unfair to just slit their throats or throw them off a cliff I thought it more creative to have them kill each other. Just to save me the energy.

I explained to them that their final task was to defeat each other in combat and then, the lone victor, would be released.

Of course they were excited that they were finally going to be untied after nearly a week of confinement. But there was another catch. They were allowed to be untied; however, their hands would remain tied and their ankles were tied to their trees. There were enough vines for them to be able to move freely but not too far. Although it took a little encouragement—me frightening them with ways I was going to kill them—they finally agreed to do it. I also let them know that if they tried to escape, I would be in the trees with a bow and arrow.

Their fight was brutal. It truly showcased the human desire for survival. Soldiers, all in the same rank, scratched, clawed, bit, gouged, and murdered their fellow brethren all in the name of survival. I watched from the trees as Sir Daniel was the first to die. One of the guards had shoved Sir Daniel into a tree and, using his fist, smashed his brains onto the trunk. Another guard then came up and attacked the guard that killed Sir Daniel. He knocked him to the ground, and the assaulting guard wrapped his legs around his comrade and strangled him with the strength of his knees. That guard then quickly dodged a kick from one of the remaining three guards. He then somersaulted to his feet and went to tackle one of the guards, but his vine caught and he fell to the ground. Stunned by his own ignorance he laid on the ground for a moment too long as another guard came up and stomped his skull in.

It wasn't long until there were only two guards left. I was enjoying the show so much that I came closer just to witness the grand finale!

The first guard charged just as the second one began to make his move. Metal on metal collided with so much force that sparks flew! The second guard, much smaller than the first, bounced backward and stumbled to the ground. The first guard would have continued forward, but his vine wasn't long enough. This then gave the second guard more time to regain himself. Panting and sweating he took a deep breath before following through with his attack. He charged again. Instead of clashing like they had before, the second guard dipped below the swing of the first and tripped him by pulling on his vine. Again the first guard fell to the ground. But this time, the second guard didn't hesitate. Instead he ran to the fallen guard and grabbed him by his neck and pushed as hard as he could on his throat. The first guard, the seasoned soldier, wheezed and gasped for mercy, but the second guard would not let up. His life depended on it.

The first guard took several very long minutes to die. His entire face went from bright pink, to red, to blue, and then to purple. And even as he watched his comrade die, the second guard held his grasp and emerged victorious.

The spectacle was so astounding that I applauded him. I even removed his thorny crown and kissed him on the cheek! "Bravo! Bravo! Bravo! The winner has been declared! Take your bow!" I sang, dancing around him and his now dead mates. "Bravo!"

Exhausted and battered, the guard did not delight in his victory with me. Instead he held out his hands and asked to be released.

I reluctantly obliged him.

He then asked if he could go.

Quizzically I asked, "You are not proud of your accomplishments? Nearly eight days of torture and confinement and you, lone survivor, you emerge as the victor yet I see no celebration in your eyes. Why is that?"

The broad-standing young fellow took a few much-needed deep breaths before replying. "You forced me to witness the desecration of honor. You forced me to murder men of the Queen's Guard. You forced me to murder my brother . . ." He turned to look at the guard he had just killed. "How is that a cause for celebration?"

I took a step closer to the guard. He was my height with a lean build and long blond hair. His age was that of a young man but no older than a gentleman. The soul of his irises mirrored that of a black hole as the comforts of death slowly settled in. I asked him, "Have you ever killed a man?"

He shook his head. "Not until today."

I sighed in understanding. "I see. Your hands were once clean, and now they are stained red for the rest of your days. But do not worry. You will get used to it. You may even come to enjoy it, just like the queen and I have. She kills for glory, I kill for redemption. If you truly explore the depths of reality you will come to the conclusion that glory and redemption are two horns on the same goat. The only difference being that redemption is justifiable and, well, glory is a farce."

He scoffed, "All this effort for the theory of justice." He shook his head. "Who's to say your reason is more justifiable than another? Dead is dead. Murder is murder. You define my queen as a vile beast who kills for the enjoyment, yet what is it that you do? No matter the reason, no matter the cause, *you* are the sword who slays innocence just as you say she does. You crucify people in order to fuel your insanity and create this subject of a retribution!"

Anger fumed inside me, so much so that I slapped him across the face. "It is not my insanity that has led to my retribution. It is my retribution that has led to my insanity!" He didn't show enough fear from my hit, so I punched him in the esophagus. He stumbled backward until he collapsed to the ground. Stalking over to where he had fallen, I grabbed him by his breastplate and shook him while he coughed for air! He reached to grab for me but I was too quick. I dropped his breastplate and grabbed his arm as it went to reach for me and twisted it until he hollered in pain. "Listen to me, boy, and listen well. You do not know of what you speak! I have killed my entire life. I have drank the blood of those I've gutted! I am the embodiment of fear, pain, desire, and misery! You, small pathetic piece of shit, could never comprehend the brutality of a life with a sword tied to your hand from the moment you were born! I have witnessed the desecration of innocence at the hand of a queen who is as real as the truth from a sinner's mouth. It is *her*, that cold-blooded bitch, that provides the tools to build my retribution. It is *her*, that impious slut, who drowns babies in their sleep and eats children for supper! She is the reason for my rage, my sorrow, and my cruelty. If that is not the making of a justified vengeful slaughter of those who follow her, then I do not know of one that is!"

The guard tried to pull his hand free again and groaned louder in pain, "You are insane!"

"Not by my own doing," I growled, rolling off of him. He fell silent, gazing up at me with those hollowed-out black irises. "What reason do you have to continue baiting me? I have allowed you leave. Now take advantage of it and go," I snapped as I began walking away from him.

I did not hear him rise and start to leave, so I turned and looked back at him. He replied, "You and I both know that you will kill me the moment I consider turning my back and running."

Smiling, I shrugged, pulling out my dagger. "What is the shame in dying for the theory of hope? I promised to release you. And that I have. How far you will go—well that's up to you now, isn't it? I gave you a head start. Take advantage of it."

* * *

It was midday when I decided to follow Sir Daniel's directions and search for the guards' camp. I remembered he had told me that the camp was a day's walk east. Therefore, I retrieved my weapons and mounted my horse, who I had now named Midnight due to her inky-black mane and tail. I guided her into a leisurely canter and then we were on our way.

The sun was high in the sky with a scatter of gray clouds accompanying it. The brisk morning breeze had subsided, and for the first time all winter I began to feel the warmth of the sun's rays. Some of the wounds I had encountered, from what seems like a millennia ago, were beginning to show signs of healing too. The gash from Lord Jamison's sword had finally scabbed over. Just as well as the slash from the antler of the buck I had killed. My eye, from the beating of the queen's minions, was numb enough for me to pick off the dead skin and dried puss that had leaked from it. The swelling had gone down enough for me to finally open it. Unfortunately, my hand was not beginning to heal. The skin surrounding my exposed bone was nearly black with infection. No matter how many layers of skin I peeled off, the infection would refuse to cease. Furthermore, my bones were out of place. My middle knuckle was an inch or two from where it should be, and my smallest finger was, probably, completely separated from its socket and only hanging on by a few ligaments. It ached constantly but I fought through it. The cold helped to numb it but only herbs could heal it. Herbs I did not have due to the fact that winter had destroyed all living vegetation. I knew I could not risk losing my hand, but it seemed all the more plausible as time went on and on and on and on . . .

As the day wore on and the sun began to sink behind the clouds, leaving behind streaks of orange and pink, I had yet to find any sign of the camp. For a moment I was beginning to believe that Sir Daniel had given me wrong directions. But as I ventured deeper and deeper into the Iclin Forest I noticed that there was a trail of gray smoke leaking up into the sky. It was about a mile or so away. It seems Sir Daniel hadn't let me down after all.

Slowing Midnight to walk, I allowed her time to cool before we continued to the camp. She had done so well, so much so that I led her off the trail we were on and found a little creek for her to drink from. Hopping off of her back I went to check her legs and chest for heat. Seeing as we had been going for hours on end with few breaks, she was covered in sweat and panting heavily. Cupping some of the cold water into my hands, I poured it onto her legs and splashed some onto her chest. I then did the same to myself. The cool water felt amazing over my bruises and cuts. I then took a large gulp of the water and relished in its taste as it soothed the insides of my body. I took another drink, moaning as I quenched my thirst.

Suddenly, I heard the grass to my left rustle. Instinctively I reached for the daggers at my waist and surveyed the area around me. I was surrounded by nothing but grass and eerie trees that cast horrifying shadows as night began to make its presence known. Looking around me again, while also noticing that Midnight had no reaction to the sound, I bent back down and took another drink. Then I heard that same sound again! This time I pulled a dagger out and quickly threw it in the direction of the sound. Still, I saw nothing. Feeling uneasy, especially knowing that light was limited, I went over to Midnight. Just as I was about to mount her I heard that same sound, only this time it didn't stop in the grass—a splash quickly accompanied it.

"Who's there?" I screamed, drawing the sword I stole from one of the guard's corpses. "Make your presence known now!" For a moment there was nothing. No sounds, no nothing. Only me and my very confused horse. Then as if to torture my mind even more, I saw, with my own eyes, the grass shudder as if hiding something behind it. Slowly, I stalked over to it. With my sword in front of me I went to poke at the grass. Just as I was about to peer inside, it moved again! "Who's there!" Stabbing my sword through the patch of grass, I swiftly hacked the prickly blades until they were nothing more than little stubs. Panting, I noticed that there was still nothing there.

Just as I was about to return to my horse, I heard that same damned sound! Only this time, when I turned back toward the noise, I did see something.

My heart dropped into the deepest pit of my belly. Terrified, utterly and irrevocably horrified, I took a step back and sank to my knees . . . Have my eyes deceived me? Why has my mind continued to play these tricks on me? This can't be real! This isn't real! Heavens help me! Lord, God, Almighty Father above, why do you continue to torture me? Have I wronged you so often that I deserve *this*?

Before my very eyes, my very own eyes that taunt me not only in my sleep but in reality as well, little, frail, withered, dying Teta stood before me. She was thin, an ounce shy of having the equivalent weight of a corpse. Her bones were so prominent that it pierced through her paper-thin skin. Her hair was matted in knots and filth. Little Teta's once young and beautiful face had now shriveled down to nothing but bruises, dirt, famine, and death . . . she resembled death. The small child who was once so full of life was now nothing. If the wind blew hard enough, it would carry her away with no hesitation and without difficulty.

"This isn't real . . . this can't be real . . .," I muttered, unable to take my eyes off the little girl.

Little, lifeless Teta slowly, as if the effort was too great, reached her hand out to me and pointed. The child, how I had fought so hard to save her, terrified me. She was so . . . withered down to absolutely nothing. It destroyed me. Just looking at her destroyed me . . .

"This can't be real," I whispered, quivering before her.

Cocking her head to the side, she continued to point at me. Then miraculously she replied, "You let me die. You let *her* kill me."

So overcome with misery I buried my hands in my head. "No, Teta, no. I tried to save you. I did everything I could to save you! Please believe me!"

"No, you let me die. You let me die," she replied in a lifeless, monotone voice. It was as if her words echoed throughout her hollow body.

"This isn't real! You're not real!" I sobbed, clawing at my ears.

"My death was real. I died because you couldn't save me. You killed me. You let the bad men kill me . . . you let them kill us all."

"I tried to save you!" I screamed at the little child. She didn't even flinch. Why should she fear me? She had faced the horrors of famine, misery, and inevitably death all at once. I was nothing to her.

"Why did you let them kill me? You were supposed to protect us."

I couldn't take it! The image of her body hanging from the noose filled my every thought. Her cold lifeless body swaying from gallows . . . "Teta, please! I tried, I did everything I could to save you! I wanted to save you!" Looking up from my hands I noticed that she had come closer to me.

Her black sunken eyes glared down at me as if she had no pity for me. She hated me. She despised me. She had every right to. "I wanted to go home. I wanted to see my brother. I wanted to hug my mommy. I wanted to grow up. I wanted to live . . . you took that away from me. You let me die. You let me die . . . you killed me."

"Teta, I wanted to save you!"

"No!" Her voice crackled like the whip of thunderous clouds, shaking the earth beneath me. "You chose them over us! You chose them! You killed me. You killed my brother. You killed my mommy. You killed your king. You killed us all. You did nothing to save us. All you wanted was to save yourself."

"I would have given my life to save you!" I wailed, throwing myself at her feet. Disgusted she took a step back. First it was only one, and then two, and then she turned and began walking away from me entirely. "Teta, wait!" But the child continued to keep walking away from me. "Teta, let me explain!" I tried to get up to follow her, but I tripped over my own feet!

"You killed us all! You killed us all!" Her voice continued to echo in my head as my little Teta walked out of my life just as easily as she walked in . . . it wasn't long until her frail body disappeared into nothing and she was, once again, lost to me . . . forever. Never for me to meet again until it is my time to share a space on the gallows or house the mighty swing of a sword in my heart.

Shattered. Defeated. Broken. I pulled myself into a tight ball and sobbed, tearlessly, for all of the people I swore to protect and ultimately let down in the end. The grief of their loss was so heavy that I felt crushed. My heart ached for them. It ached for Little Teta. It ached for Zakai. It ached for my king . . . it ached for *my* people. I missed not having Meenoah to guide me. I missed not having my king to talk to. I missed little Teta and Zakai. No matter how hard I tried to mask the pain with the pain of others, I missed them. I wanted them back. I wanted to tell them I was sorry! I wanted them to know I did everything I could! I wanted another chance to save them!

Screaming, screaming, screaming, and screaming! All I could do was scream! The pain was too much for me. I was never trained on how to deal with loss. I was never trained on how to mend my own shattered heart. I was never trained on how to accept a mistake I should have never made . . .

"I'm so sorry, Teta . . .," I sobbed into the ground. "I'm so sorry. I'm sorry I let you down. I'm so sorry I let you all down . . ." But just like little Teta was left alone with no one to comfort her as her body hanged from the gallows, I was left alone to wallow in the dirt.

* * *

Mounting Midnight, I urged her into a gallop. The sun had finally bowed to the moon as it unleashed its sprinkle of stars into the blackened sky. A cool breeze continuously swept through the bare branches of the trees, causing them to sing their unnerving tune. Shadows consumed the Iclin Forest and danced in the spotlight of the moon. In the distance wolves howled to its might while owls cried high above in the trees.

Everything suggested the deception of serenity. Everything, from the creaking trees to the earthy groans, it all suggested the presence of evil. It would be my loss to not take advantage of such a scene.

Although the sky had darkened and the trail of smoke leading to the sky had faded into it, I was close enough to make out the soft glow of torches off in the distance. As I came closer to the camp I could hear the soft murmur of voices.

When I was about a hundred yards or so away from the camp, I slowed Midnight to a halt. Jumping from her back I used my last vine to tie her to the tree. Considering the plan I had been constructing in my mind, I would definitely need an escape route.

Leaving her behind, I began my trek to the camp. I crossed, o' so quietly, over fallen tree trunks and frigid moss-covered boulders. Using the glow of the fire as my guide I pushed through the dense dark forest. The only weapon I could carry along with me was my sword. I figured, if I was meant to die I would die honorably and completely at a disadvantage.

The voices from the camp grew louder and louder as I got closer. It didn't take me long to figure out that most of the guards were drunk and nearly unarmed. As I made my way over one of the huts they had constructed, I peered around the corner very, very, very slowly. I looked for about a second and a half before I shrunk back into obliviousness. I had noted that there were two dozen guards lingering about. None of them were in their armor. They were so entirely unprepared that I no longer assumed my own death.

Suddenly, I heard several loud popping sounds. One after another. It wasn't like any sound I had ever heard before. It was loud, almost like an explosion, but the sound didn't seem like it could be producing something that could house something as large as a bombshell.

For a moment I thought I had been found, but then I heard laughter coming from the guards. Braving another look I peered around the corner and saw four guards, each of them holding a long metal tube of some sort. At one end of the tube was a knife; at the other was some kind of handle. The guard closest to me had the contraption on the ground with the knife facing up. He was sticking something in it. When he was done he lifted it up and held it in a similar manner someone would hold a bow and arrow. Except he didn't have a bow. Once he was ready I saw him pull something on the handle. And again I heard those loud mini explosions. The other guards did the same thing, and they too created that same sound.

I was so incredibly confused that it took me a while to realize that the guards were aiming at something. Slowly, quietly, I moved from behind the hut and went to one that was closer to where the guards were. Again I peered around the corner. Looking past the guards I saw that the guards had tied a doe to a post. It was dead, lying lifeless beneath the post in a pool of its own blood. Probably due to the holes that gutted its stomach. I could only assume that the tubes they were holding were the cause of the animal's death.

Not wanting to risk getting caught, I moved away from where the guards were and headed toward what I thought was an empty hut. The hut was rather large. Its wooden walls were thick and lengthy. There were no windows and only one opening. I didn't hear any voices coming from inside of it, which meant that the guards were passed out or it was empty. Either way I was going in.

Readying my sword I made my way around the hut and, without being noticed, went to open the door. When I noticed that the door hadn't budged I saw that it was locked from the outside with a chain bolt. Holding my sword above my head, with all the might I had in me, I brought it down on the bolt and freed the door.

Expecting the guards to awaken, I began my assault.

Then as I entered the darkened hut, a soft whimper grabbed my attention and yanked it toward the corner of the hut. Huddled tightly together was a group of frail, sickly children. There had to have been around eight little ones cowering away from me.

Immediately I put my sword away and knelt to their level. "Peace, friends. I'm not here to harm you." I couldn't bear to make eye contact with them. Especially the little girl that held on tightly to a little boy who held her protectively to himself. "Shh, shh, stay quiet." The children did as they were told, though they still continued to look at me with eyes full of terror. "Where did you all come from?" For a moment no one spoke. Knowing how terrified they were, I tried to smile for them. It didn't seem to help until a boy of about twelve years spoke.

"The guards raided our village. They took everything. Including us."

"Did they tell you where they were going to take you?"

He shook his head. "We have been here for a few days. They said we won't be leaving for another couple more. We haven't eaten since we were captured. Please, can you help us?" The boy was so frail yet so brave. He hadn't given up hope. He hadn't given up on me.

"I will help you. All of you." Looking around the hut I noticed that there were several large barrels in the corner opposite of the children. Walking over to them I slowly opened the top and saw that they were full of black powder. "What is this?"

"I don't know what it is, but I know that it is very dangerous. They filled their weapons with it and fire it like a canon. Except small balls come out and rip bodies to shred . . . that's how they captured our village," the boy replied.

"It explodes." It wasn't a question though the boy replied yes.

My initial plan was to set the camp on fire. But as I continued to dissect the mechanics of that idea, I knew that that would take too long. By the time I lit all of the huts on fire they would already be putting them out, and there would be no way for me to escape, let alone all these children.

However, now that I discovered this powder, I could cause a much more detrimental reaction.

"I will save all of you. That I promise," I vowed, looking at all of them, "but I'm going to need your help." The boy looked from me to the other children and then back to me before nodding.

In the end the children and I waited until most of the guards had either passed out or fallen asleep. As the night wore on there were only three guards that had the task of being lookout. Other than that the camp was deathly silent. If there weren't several lit torches on every hut, one would be able to walk right by the camp without ever noticing it, minus the continuous snoring of the drunken guards.

With the plan all in place, I signaled the children into their positions. The little children who were too young to understand what was going on and one of the older children were sent to run toward where I had tied down Midnight. I told them to wait for me there until it was over with. The remaining four children were to stay with me.

The plan was to roll the barrels out of the hut and space them between the other huts on the outside of the camp. Once they were spaced, relatively evenly, they would then tie a rope, which I had found in one of the other huts, to the barrels and connect all of them. The children would then take a burning branch and light the rope. In theory the rope will catch the flame and the flame would then follow the rope to the barrel. The barrel would, naturally, explode. There was enough length between the rope and the barrel that the children had plenty of time to escape before the actual explosion. I was very clear that the children had to run as soon as the rope caught fire. They told me they understood.

As everything settled into place I surveyed my surroundings, just to make sure that there were no lingering guards anywhere in sight. Lucky for us, all was clear. The three guards who were meant to keep watch over the camp were easy enough to get rid of—that was my main job. It was quick, clean, and silent. All three went down with nothing more than a whimper as they bled out.

Now that everything was in place, I lit the first burning branch. The boy, Christopher, lit his branch off of mine. The other children, Mary, Josiah, and Declan, lit their branches as well. I wished them all luck and reminded them to run in the direction that I sent the little ones. They all nodded and went to their positions.

The signal to light their ropes was to be initiated by me. I would throw my branch on the roof of the hut I was near. The roof was made of straw and twigs, so it would catch fire quickly, and all of the children would see it. I hoped that the smoke would put the guards into a deeper sleep, but of course that was all in theory.

The time had come. I threw my branch.

As if destined to burn, the roof of the hut exploded into the flames! Orange, yellow, and red flames licked their way into the dark night sky as it consumed the entire hut.

It wasn't long after that when I saw Mary begin to run. Josiah then followed, and shortly after that Declan ran to the rendezvous point. The only one I was missing was . . .

All of a sudden, the barrels exploded! One after another after another after another. Entire huts were obliterated within seconds. The noise was so earth-shatteringly loud that I had to cover my ears! In a matter of minutes the camp was enclosed in smoke and flames. Burning wood popped and crackled as huts clattered to the ground. Guards scrambled, doused in flames. Others died immediately. Body parts, arms, legs, heads rained from the sky! I would have been delighted by the sight, but I didn't see Christopher run. The hut where his barrel was to be placed hadn't exploded.

Hurriedly I rain toward his location. Dodging fallen guards and greedy flames, I raced to him. When I arrived there I noticed that his barrel was untouched and Christopher was nowhere in sight!

"Christopher!" I screamed over the roaring of the flames and cries of pain from the guards. "Christopher!"

For a while there was no response. Fearful of the worse, I ran through the burning camp and searched for him, screaming his name over and over and over again. "Christopher! Christopher!"

Out of nowhere a guard emerged from the flames and swung at me. I saw it coming so I dipped below his swing and punched him in the gut. He stumbled backward before tripping over his feet. I quickly climbed on top of him, ignoring the raging flames and searing heat. I punched him in the face to get his attention. "There was a boy! Where is he? Tell me now!" The guard didn't reply, so I brought his head to mine and head-butted him. Dazed, he tried to focus his eyes back on me. I slapped him to help him out. "There was a boy! Over by that hut!" I pointed to the untouched barrel. "Where is he?" He was too confused to speak, but his eyes told me everything. They darted to the left. I followed his gaze and saw a guard holding Christopher by his thin neck and unleashing an unnecessary amount of punches on the poor boy. From where they were, several yards away from me, I saw Christopher spit up blood as the guard continued to beat him.

Dropping the guard I had, I ran straight at the guard who had been beating Christopher. Without hesitation, I tackled the guard to the ground. Surprised, he released Christopher and gave me enough time to get my hands around his neck. It only took a second to snap it in half.

Releasing the guard's lifeless body, I rolled over to where Christopher was. Grabbing him by his shoulders, I lifted him into my arms. "Stay with me, Chris! Stay with me!" With all the strength I could muster, I threw him over my shoulder and ran to the outside of the camp. The blinding light from the raging flames hindered my escape, as did the wall of fire created by the burning huts. Sweat poured from my body as the heat and smoke wrapped their deadly claws around me and squeezed as hard as they could. "Stay with me, Chris! Stay with me!" He groaned in pain from being jostled just as I dodged a wall engulfed in flames that fell to the ground.

As I made my way to the outside of the camp, I sprinted toward the rendezvous point. Chris wasn't a very heavy boy, but he was tall, and carrying him was difficult. I could feel the blood from his mouth drip down my back as we made our way through the forest.

When we were about fifty yards from safety, I saw one of the children running toward us. Mary busted through a bush just as I caught sight of Midnight.

"What happened to him!" she screamed, horrified.

"Never mind that," I replied, setting Christopher down. Looking behind me I noticed that there was about half a dozen men on horseback storming through the flaming camp and heading in our direction. "Take Christopher and put him on my horse. I'll lead them away."

"I can't! I can't! Don't leave us, please! Don't leave us!" Mary cried, panicking. "Please don't leave us, please! I can't do this! I can't! I can't!"

Frustrated and running out of time, I grabbed her by the shoulders and said, "Mary! Shut up! Now is not the time for that! Take Christopher to my horse and get as far away from here as possible. I will come find you, I promise. I promise. But I need you take the children out of here or you all will die." I looked over my shoulder and saw that they were coming and gaining on me fast. "Go! Now!" Mary nodded and wrapped Christopher's arm over her shoulder and began helping him to Midnight.

Noting that the children were heading to safety, I quickly ran in the opposite direction. The men on horseback had seen me and were following close behind me. So close in fact that I could hear the pounding of their horses' hooves thundering behind me.

Diving over a boulder and hurriedly regaining my feet, I pushed myself to run as fast as humanly possible.

But it wasn't enough.

They had caught up to me.

I was surrounded.

"Whoa, whoa, whoa," one of them said as they circled me with their horses. "Look what we have here."

"Check this out, boys," another one from behind me said. It was too dark for me to see their faces. There was no light—only me, a sword, and six men on horseback. I tend to be accustomed to those odds.

I drew my sword.

One of their horses cried in fright. "Sword!" Immediately I heard them draw their swords too.

"Well, come on then!" I bellowed, egging them on. "What are you waiting for?"

One of them began to charge at me. He kicked his horse into high gear with his sword aimed right at my head!

I was ready! I was ready to die. I was prepared to die. I wanted to fight. I needed to fight!

I was so focused on the man charging at me that I didn't register the sound of footsteps walking briskly behind me. But before I could turn and see what it was, I felt something with that of the consistency of a rock hit me on the side of my head. Instantaneously my vision was cloudy before being absolutely consumed by nothing but darkness. I felt my body crash, hard, to the ground, and all feeling left me. I left me. Everything went black. Everything went away. As did I.

CHAPTER 18

My head was pounding. It was as if someone was taking a hammer and beating me across the head constantly for hours and hours and hours on end. The pain was so terrible that I didn't even want to open my eyes! The back of my head throbbed so loudly that my ears began to want to burst from all of the pressure inside my skull. I was in pain. Agonizing. Incredulous. Searing. Pain.

But that wasn't the worst of my troubles.

I had been captured. Naturally, I assumed that the guards had caught up to me. But why would they keep me alive? According to Ophelia I was worth more dead than I was alive. So why hadn't they killed me?

"Is she alive?" I heard the voice of a man who was standing a few feet away from me. My nerves quivered at the sound of his deep, raspy, and sensual voice.

"Yeah. She was murmuring things all night," another male voice said.

"What was she saying?"

"Something about Christopher and the children. It was hard to make out."

The first man sighed before saying, "Let me know when she wakes up. I want to talk to her."

"Yes, sir." And with that I heard them walk away.

An hour or so passed before anyone else came to visit me. Nothing had really changed. The pounding in my head continued, and I had yet to open my eyes. I tried to listen for any indignation as to where I was, but the only sounds I heard were murmurs coming from the outside.

"Still unconscious?" It was the second man's voice from before.

"Apparently so." I felt a one of them nudge my knee. "What do we do if she doesn't wake up?"

"No idea," the second man said. "Talk to him about it."

"We could throw her body out in the forest to attract predators so we can hunt—"

"Not going to happen." It was the man with a deep, raspy, sensual voice. I felt him come close to me. Slowly, o' so slowly, he moved a piece of my hair out of my face and tucked it behind my ear. My breath caught involuntarily and his hand quickly retreated. "Leave—both of you, now." With nothing more than that I heard the men exit. Unfortunately, I still felt the man very close to me. His body heat was radiating off of him and rudely wrapping itself around me. I wanted to lean away from him. I didn't like people this close to me. Especially people I didn't know. "I know you're awake." His voice, how it caressed every inch of me. My reaction to him made me want to kill him! I wanted him away from me! Feelings like these only led to heartbreak . . . "I'm just going to clean your wounds." I felt his hands—his rough, large, meaty hands—touch my arm, sending a shock of electricity shooting throughout my entire body! Instinctively I flinched away from him.

"Don't touch me," I spit, breaking my façade. He removed his hand from me a moment later, and then I heard him stand. I thought he was going to say something, but he didn't. The next thing I knew he was walking away and leaving me.

I thought that he was going to return shortly after that, but long minutes passed and no one came to see me. I was alone again. Lost in my own mind . . .

"Open your eyes," a small, adolescent voice commanded. "Open your eyes."

One moment I was consumed by darkness, the next, light flooded my eye sockets until I could see nothing but white. When my vision became focused I realized that I was sitting on the palace steps of the Belle. In front of me were the gallows with a murder of crows clumped together on one noose as if they were protecting something.

"Open your eyes," that same small voice said again. The voice was coming from beside me. I turned to see who it was, and my heart stopped and shattered into millions of pieces. I was so distraught that I felt my eyes sting from where tears should have fallen. Beside me was little, shriveled, nearly weightless Zakai.

He was sitting absentmindedly next to me on the palace steps with his arm on his boney knee and his chin resting on his hand. He wasn't looking at me. The small, dark-haired boy's hollow eyes were riveted on the noose surrounded by the crows. He didn't look at me once. "It's not fair that you have the option to open or close your eyes. Open your eyes."

"Zakai . . . I—" But my words fell off at the end. There was nothing I could tell this boy to make him feel any better about what happened. I had failed him. When he needed me most I had failed him. Not even words could heal those wounds.

"Fairies," he said, allowing the silence to settle in before he continued. "She used to believe in fairies. I don't know why, but she loved to believe in fairies. She was convinced that each person had their own fairy that followed them around and protected them. Do you know what she named her fairy?" I shook my head even though I knew he wasn't looking at me. "Aoife. I didn't understand it. But then she described what her fairy looked like. It looked like you. She was describing you. You were her hero. You were her protector."

"I would have given my life for her." I buried my face in my hands, too overcome with guilt to look up.

"Open your eyes!" Zakai snapped. I did as I was told. "You don't get to close your eyes! Open your eyes! My sister is dead. My entire family is gone. They don't get to choose life anymore! So open your eyes! Open your eyes and look at what you did! You took everything away from me. All I wanted was for you to save my sister. I wanted my sister to have a chance at life. But she's dead. You let her die. You watched her die. You hardly tried to save her."

"I did everything I could to save her!"

He chuckled sardonically. "Clearly that wasn't enough."

Frustrated I stood and towered over the boy. He didn't even flinch. "Your sister meant everything to me. I fought like hell for you and her. For all of those children! If I had known what was going on I would have saved you all. What is it you want me to do? I wanted, with all my heart, to save her. I'd give my life to trade places with her!"

He shook his head, continuing to stare ahead. "No, Arianna. I *did everything I could to save her. Who was the one who made sure she got food and water while we were locked away? Who was the one who kept her hidden from those vile guards that trolled the cells for vulnerable girls? Who was the one that cleaned her wounds every night? Who was the one that gave the shirt off their back so she would have something to lie on at night? Who was the one that fought the other children off of her so they wouldn't steal her scraps? Was it you? Was it you who gave their absolute all to protect her? Because the last time I checked, you were too busy dancing with kings and sipping tea from golden cups to recognize what was going on with your own people."*

I wanted to argue back with him. I wanted to tell him that I did try to protect them. I wanted to tell him that I would have done more if I had known how bad it was. But it was too late for that. It was too late for a lot of things . . .

"I miss my sister," he continued. "I miss my mother. I miss my home. I want to go home. More than anything in the world I want to go home. I want to play in the woods while mother makes supper and father tends to the fields with the other men. I want to watch the sun tuck itself in for bed. I want to attempt to count the stars that dazzled the sky. I want to see my friends and scare Teta with the spiders we found in the swamp. I want to live, Arianna. But that will never happen . . . will it? I'll never get to do any of those things ever again, will I?" He sighed, continuing to stare straight ahead. A tear slipped, o' so slowly, down his dirt-stained face.

"I'm so sorry, Zakai. I'm so sorry." I reached out to put my arm around him, but he scooted away from me.

"Don't feel sorry for me. I know I did everything I could to fight for my life and my sister's. You should feel sorry for yourself. You have yet to realize the importance of every drawn breath. I cherish the little moments now. You know why?" I shook my head even though I knew it wasn't entirely a question. "Because in the end, it's all I have to hold on to." The weight of my grief drowned me in formidable sorrow. Many people imagine hell as a fiery pit of chaos and destruction. They imagine thousand-degree weather and flames that rage on endlessly for all of eternity. But that's not hell to me. Not at all. This. Sitting here listening to this boy speak of a life he had barely begun to live was hell. Sitting here listening to him describe the pain he goes through because I failed him was hell. Sitting here listening to him yearn for his sister, mother, father, home, and people. This was hell. It was pure torture that tore me apart like two rabid dogs fighting over a bone. All I could say was, "I'm so sorry I failed you, Zakai. I'm so sorry."

"You didn't fail me," he said. "I never once thought you were coming to save us. I never considered you my protector." His words were like a knife straight through the heart. The emotional pain I felt was like my blood spilling from my chest and covering all of the steps to the palace. "You didn't fail me. You failed her." He pointed straight ahead at what he had been staring at during our whole conversation.

Following his finger, I looked over at the black, bulging bundle of crows cocooning around the noose. In a matter of seconds they dispersed and flew in every direction! Gawking and screeching the blasphemous beasts quickly left the gallows. The only thing they left behind was a small, lifeless little girl dangling from the noose by her scrawny neck. She wasn't facing us. But before the wind had blown and turned her toward us I already knew who it was . . .

"Hey, wake up." My eyes fluttered open slowly at the sound of an unfamiliar voice. My senses took a moment to come back to life as I was transported from one nightmare to the next. Only this one I couldn't wake up from.

In front of me stood three men. And they definitely weren't men of the Queen's Guard. These men were not draped in expensive armor or any sort of noteworthy fabric. They wore fur, homemade, and had small knives attached to their waistbands. Each of them were well-built men with short hair and battle scars caressing their toned muscles. They were all rugged and ruthless-looking men. Just one of these men could frighten anyone.

With my eyes open I realized I was inside some sort of tent. They had me tied to the center pole that kept the entire thing up. There was nothing else in the tent except me, this pole, and three very large and very intimidating men.

"Who are you?" My voice came out weaker than I had anticipated. The man closest to me kneeled forward. He was an attractive man with an unruly rust-colored beard covering the lower half of his face that matched the intensity in his brown eyes.

"We were just going to ask you the same thing. What were you doing near the guards' camp?"

I turned away from him, not wanting to reveal my identity. For all I knew these men were in relation to the queen. They could turn me in for the reward money.

"We have ways to make you talk, if you won't do it voluntarily," the man behind the one closest to me hissed, drawing his dagger.

I scoffed, "Death is a friend I have known a long time. You do not scare me."

"So you do speak," the man in front of me said, continuing to eye me.

"Not to you," I snapped. "Do what you want with me. I still will not tell you what you want."

"Stupid girl," the man with the dagger chuckled. "From the looks of you, I already knew that death is no stranger to you. But what about those children we found in the woods? Do you think they will respond to our threats as idly as you have?"

"You're so pathetic. Threatening children, how noble," I replied, shaking my head. "But if killing them is what you wish, then fine. Slay an adolescent. I still will not speak." Though I spoke confidently I prayed that they would not call my bluff.

"Suit yourself." The man kneeling shrugged before returning to his standing position. He turned to one of his comrades and said, "Bring me one. We'll do it here." The man who had said nothing the entire time nodded and left. "I'm not entirely sure what sort of people you have encountered in the forest. But I assure you that you have never before been in the presence of men like us. We do not falter at the death of a newborn. We do not weep for any loss of life. Not even the ones of our brethren. So killing a child wouldn't bother me, not one bit. Would it bother you?"

I chuckled, continuing my façade. "You assume that because I am a woman I will shed a tear for a child's blood spilled?" Not entirely lying, I replied, "I have killed dozens of children. Children from my own village. I did not care. Not one bit."

This time the man with the dagger spoke. "The older one of the children—what was his name? Christopher? He told us that you saved them from the guards' camp. He told us that you promised to protect them. Now my only question is why would someone, with a soul as black as night, save children? Especially when they seemed to have made a career out of killing them."

Damn it, Christopher. As if on cue the third man returned with Christopher by his side. But I was surprised. Aside from the bruises and gashes he received the night I saved him, he was well taken care of. His gashes had bandages around them, and he had on some new furs. Maybe I wasn't the only one bluffing.

"I don't know him," I replied nonchalantly. Christopher opened his mouth to protest, but I quickly shot him a look that shut him right up. The four men didn't seem to notice.

"Then you won't mind if we slaughtered him right here. Right now." The man holding Christopher stumbled a little. Christopher's eyes pleaded with me as he looked into mine. But I still said nothing to him.

"Not at all." I smiled.

The man with the dagger walked over to Christopher and held it to his neck. Christopher whimpered as he tried to pull the man's arm away. If the man was really going to kill him, he would've done it already. Meaning, he didn't want Christopher dead just as much as I didn't want to see him dead.

"Aren't you going to do it already?" I asked, refusing to look Christopher in the eye. "Come on!"

"What's a little blood spill, aye, chap?" he whispered sinisterly to Christopher. Completely terrified, Christopher tried to break free, but the man held him tightly. "I'll mount your head on the dinner table tonight as I pick my teeth with your bones."

"Sounds delicious." I continued baiting him.

"It will be." He inched the dagger closer to his neck, "I love the taste of human flesh."

I chuckled. "You must share the same plate as the queen." The man holding the knife to Christopher was a vile-looking man. He had a stern, evil face with ghastly, pale-gray eyes. He too had seen the shadows of death just as often I had. He too feared nothing. If it were just him and I all alone, he definitely would have had no problem killing Christopher and then me, all in the same swing. The scars that marred his neck and face told me that he had been in many fights that resulted in him as the victor.

Luckily, he wasn't the one calling the shots.

"Bacchus," the man with the beard snapped, "let the boy go." The man holding the dagger, Bacchus, waited a second or two before shoving Christopher down and storming out of the tent.

"What do you know of the queen?" the man with the beard asked.

"More than you," I replied, looking at Christopher. I wasn't sure if he understood my reason for not pleading for his life, but he didn't seem too upset about the situation. Christopher was a smart boy. "She's an impious whore who would sooner see the demise of all the pure innocents of Islocia before the demise of her kingdom."

"What relation do you have to her?" he inquired, showing more interest than I expected.

"What does it matter to you?"

Before he could reply, a skinny man wearing matching furs raced into the tent. The little man was buglike with his bulging pale eyes and lack of hair on his head. "Ezekiel, I need to speak with you. Now." The man with the beard, Ezekiel, nodded to the skinny man and exited the tent, leaving me with the last man.

"Bacchus and Ezekiel have introduced themselves. What about you?" This man was shorter than the others. And a little younger. He had dirty blond hair, also cut short. He didn't make eye contact with me. He just stood near me with his hand on his dagger. "You're not, nervous are you?" Still no response.

Now was as good a chance as any to make some sort of attempt at an escape.

Using the pole as leverage, I pushed up against it. With my legs I pushed on the ground and began lifting myself up to a standing position. Frightened, the man came over to me and pulled out his dagger. "Sit down!" he demanded. I ignored him. Quickly he put the dagger to my neck and shoved at my shoulder with his arm. I fell back to the ground with a thud. But I had gotten what I wanted. He was in the perfect position for me to strike.

His crotch was level with my head. Before he had time to move away, I head-butted him in his most sensitive place. Immediately he bent over. Now his head was level with mine. Using my legs I pushed myself up just high enough so that I could wrap my legs around his neck. This time we both crashed to the ground with my legs squeezing the air out of his esophagus. With all of the strength in my legs I squeezed as hard as I could. My legs were so tight around him that he could not even make a single sound to protest. Seconds passed and he still squirmed and fought for breath. Trying with all his might, he could not release the iron grip of my legs.

Fortunately for him, there wasn't enough time for me to finish the job. Ezekiel came back into the tent. Quickly assessing the situation, he sprinted over to me. With one quick jab to the face I released his mate. The world around me spun until I slipped, once again, into unconsciousness.

* * *

"Hey, hey, hey," I heard someone snapping by my ear. "Wake up." My eyes opened right when I wished they hadn't. Five men stood before me. Bacchus, Ezekiel, and three others I didn't know.

"Shit," I murmured, eyeing all of them. There were two men on either side one of the largest men, with the exception of Bacchus. The man in the middle was nearly a foot taller than I was standing up; he had muscles that put all of the allegories in the palace to shame. His hair was dark brown and cut short, a clear sign of rebellion against the Royals who all kept their hair long. His eyes, his magnificently sapphire-blue eyes, were sharp and impassive. He gave no emotions away in his stern, chiseled face with stubble growing along his chin. He was every bit as frightening as he was enchanting.

But I couldn't let my mind dwell on that. He was the enemy. They all were.

The man in the middle spoke first. "Are you all right?" His voice. That deliciously raspy, sensual voice had my brain reeling. I had heard that voice before. Somewhere in a distant past I remembered that voice. I felt it had a different effect on me back then.

Growling, as I felt for the first time in days how sore I actually was, I replied, "Who the hell are you?"

The other men looked at each other before the man in the middle responded, "You don't know?"

I chuckled. "Enough with the mind games. Just kill me and get it over with already." When no one said anything after a while, I asked, "That's your plan, isn't it? To kill me?"

The man in the middle shook his head. "No."

I didn't believe him. He was the enemy. They all were the enemy. I could trust no one. "Who are you!" I snapped, wishing I could attack them, but my arms were bound to a post behind my back. "You all think you're going to use me like some damned toy? Screw you! I'll kill every last one of you. Untie me and I will show you! I'll kill you all!" I was ready to fight. Adrenaline built up inside me like the ocean preparing for a tsunami. "Cowards!" I screamed, losing my composure. "Fight fair if you are to fight at all! I know you're working for the queen! She wishes me dead, fine, but I will not go down without a solid fight! Come on, you scum!"

"Arianna." My heart stammered as the man in the middle said my name. For a moment I thought I hadn't heard him right. He had said my name. How did he know my name? Who was he? What did he want with me? Breathing heavily, I eyed him skeptically. Kneeling down to my level, he peered into my soul with those dangerously captivating eyes. It took everything I had not to lean into him. He was riveting. He was dangerous. He was familiar. "Ari, it's me. It's me, Gabriel."

CHAPTER 19

I SPIT IN HIS FACE.

Immediately his puppets drew their knives. Bacchus moved so quickly that in a matter of seconds he had his dagger at my throat, his ghastly breath spilling onto my face.

"Stand down!" Gabriel ordered, wiping his face with the back of his hand. After a moment longer than needed, Bacchus moved away from me and returned to his former position alongside Gabriel—the name that had haunted me ever since that night . . . that awful, dreadful night of dismay. Gabriel. The man I had given my all to. The man I had worshipped. The man I had killed for. It was then that I remembered his voice. The slow, rhythmic sound of every word that poured out of his mouth seduced me. The command over his sculpted body and his ruthless followers enchanted me. Gabriel. The man who had saved me. The man who had fought for me, killed for me and, in the end, left me . . .

"Are you sure that's her, mate?" one of his men asked, eyeing me skeptically.

"With a reaction like that, no doubt this is her," Ezekiel snickered, tucking his dagger away. "Congratulations, Captain. You found your long-lost girlfriend."

I tensed at the word. Hatred. Pure, white, hot hatred cascaded through my body as the man I once wholeheartedly respected didn't even look me in the eye. He too must've had much distaste for that particular title too, because the next thing he said was, "Get out. All of you." When no one moved, he barked, "Now!"

"Come on, boys," Ezekiel said, gathering everyone's attention, his joking manner gone.

When everyone had left, I felt my heart racing in my chest. It was pounding so hard, I was sure he could hear it. But he didn't seem to notice. He just stood there. Magnificently constructed with slabs of taut muscle framing his body. He was mesmerizing. He was Gabriel. My Gabriel. The one who left me. Alone.

"Are you alright?" he asked. My toes curled at the sound of his voice. I hated the way my body reacted to him. How my breathing quickened and my nerves lit themselves on fire. I hated that he had this effect on me. I hated that he was here. I hated him.

"I'm peachy," I muttered, fumbling with my ties. "Never been better."

He nodded, obviously avoiding eye contact. "Do you need anything?"

"Besides the obvious?" I snapped, turning to look at my ties, which I had begun to loosen.

Again he nodded, but this time he didn't say anything.

"Are you going to let me go?" I asked him.

He shook his head. "One of our spies told us that you were a lady to the queen."

I shrugged. "So what if I was?"

Finally, he turned to look at me. His eyes, his piercing, dazzling, astonishing navy-blue eyes caressed my body before settling on my face. "So you understand our predicament? Here we have the personal fool of the queen in the palm of our hands."

"Whose hands?"

"Lucky you, Ari—"

"Don't call me that!" I hissed, wishing I could attack.

He continued, "You stumbled upon Sythos. The rebel camp."

Rebels. I should've known. Sighing, I asked, "What's going to happen now?"

He shrugged. "It all depends on what you have to offer us."

"Go to hell," I scoffed, turning my head away from him. "I'm not giving you anything. Not ever again. Besides, if your spy was any good at his job you would know that I got fired."

"She released you? Why?" he asked, showing as much interest as Ezekiel had when he had asked about the queen.

"Why do you want to know?" I countered.

"Why are you being so goddamned difficult!" he barked, suddenly fuming with rage.

"Go to hell, Gabriel!" I spit, lunging at him but was immediately pulled back by my ties. *Not yet.* "I don't owe you anything. You want to kill me? Fine. You want to turn me in? Even better. I can kill the witch myself."

Suddenly, his anger disappeared. He was calm and collected again. His muscles relaxed, and his eyes returned to a soft blue, which mirrored that of an ocean right after a hurricane. "Your allegiance doesn't lie with her anymore?"

"No," I replied, hating him. He thought for a moment, silence surrounding us.

"What do you know about the rebels?" he asked after a moment.

I shook my head. "Nothing, really. Just that you're all a bunch of unorganized savages that do nothing but chase their tails all day. You have no weapons and are small in numbers. All of the rebels—Sythos, Artis, Qualmi, and the Iraquin—were never even a concern for the Royal Army. You all spend too much time fighting each other instead of uniting. You're nothing but a band of misfits stomping your feet and throwing temper tantrums—" He slapped me. Hard. His hand leaving a sharp pain in my cheek. I smiled up at him. "Did I hit a nerve?"

"Well, what are you? You're nothing but the queen's personal bitch," he growled, narrowing his gaze at me. "Actually you're not even that. You're the former bitch. Tell me something. How does Ophelia's ass taste? I'm sure you would know since you spent all your time up it."

"Screw you!"

"Screw you!" he replied, mocking me. "Our spies told us everything about you. They told us why you're disgraced from the kingdom. You were too busy sleeping with the king instead of doing your damn job! My only question is why did she let you live?"

At the mention of my king a sudden wave of sadness crashed into me. I did everything I could not to think of him. I hated that he brought him up. "You don't know anything."

"I know enough," he replied, glaring down at me. "You're nothing but a whore and a traitor."

"Go to hell."

"You first." And with that, he stormed out of the tent. But that didn't stop me from screaming after him. "That's what you're good at, asshole! Leaving! You never cared about us! You never cared about anything but yourself!"

He wasn't gone very long. A moment later he stormed back in and got right in my face, stripping me with those eyes of his. "Now who doesn't know anything?" he hissed. Angrily he stood and paced the small area of the tent before continuing. "You know what? You're not mad because I left. You're mad because I didn't bring you with me. Well, here's something new for you to mull over—maybe I just didn't give two fucks about you. You were weighing me down. I didn't need the extra baggage. That's why I left your stubborn ass. Maybe you're right, Arianna. I didn't care about you. Not one goddamned bit. You were nothing but another girl in another village."

"You think you meant something to me?" I snapped, masking the pain of his statement. "I haven't given you one thought since that night. I didn't even know who you were. But you knew me."

Chuckling, he glared at me. "You couldn't remember me because you were too busy kneeling before the king every night," he replied sinisterly. "A whore never remembers the names of those she's serviced just so long as they pay, right?" That hurt the worst. This wasn't the Gabriel I remembered. That man was long gone. This man was cruel. Heartless. A blade through my chest would've been better than hearing him talk to me like that. The pain would be more bearable.

Luckily, I had just finished getting my arms out of my ties. Now it was time to attack.

Breaking free, I charged him head-on. Surprised, he didn't see me attack until I had already reached him. With my left hand I cocked back and cracked him on the jaw as hard as I could. He stumbled back a few steps, but I continued on. I hit him with a right hook right after the left. He fell backward, falling out of the tent. Quickly I climbed on top of him and continued to hit him. But I underestimated his strength.

After absorbing all of my punches, Gabriel caught my left fist and twisted my wrist. I screamed in pain, which gave him enough time to push me off of him. This time he was on top of me. I tried to wiggle free, but he was strong. Much stronger than I was. Grabbing my arms in one hand, he held them over my head as he wrapped his free hand around my neck and squeezed. Immediately black dots began blocking my vision. As air continued to escape me, I tried to break free. But he held on tight. Too tight. Looking up into his face I saw no emotion. Just the cruel heartless man that I never knew him to be. My hatred for him fueled my will to survive.

Using his hold on my arms as an anchor, I pulled myself so that my legs slid beneath him, moving my body forward. With his hand still suffocating me, I used all of the energy I had left and brought my legs to my chest before releasing them. With all my might I kicked him in the chest. He let go of my neck as he fell backward. I continued forward and climbed on top of his giant body. Stealing one of the daggers in his waistband, I put it to his neck. I thought this would be the end of it, but no, Gabriel was smart. With his right hand he went to reach for me. Taking the dagger off of his neck, I sliced his forearm. It retreated, but I didn't notice his left hand reaching for me. Painfully he twisted his fingers in my hair and yanked me backward. Again I hollered in pain. Throwing me off of him I rolled in the dirt, oblivious to everything that was around me. He quickly came at me again. Regaining my balance, I held the dagger, ready to fight.

He reached me in three strides.

I swung at him with my dagger in my right hand. He blocked it with his left and followed through with his right. He connected with my stomach. Unable to dwell on the pain, I tossed the dagger to my left hand and went to stab him. But he moved very fast for a man of his size and dodged the swing. But no matter, I still was able to cut him along his shoulder. He hardly winced at the pain. I backed away from him as blood trickled down his muscular arm. He continued to come to me. Only this time, he charged me. With the speed of an angry bull, he wrapped his arms around my waist and picked me up before slamming me to the ground. Once I hit the ground, the wind was knocked right out of me. Gasping, panting, begging for breath, I lay crippled with pain. I couldn't move. He had the advantage. Standing over me he grabbed the dagger out of my hand. Forcing myself to breathe, I tried to turn over, but he stopped me.

Closing my eyes, I willed myself to fight. Fight. Fight. Fight. Fight!

I surged upward. Sitting upright, I clasped my hands together and crashed them into his knees. Grunting, his leg buckled forward, giving me enough time to jump up using my whole body to knock him backward, hoping he would fall again. But he caught his footing and caught my punch. I tried to pull free but he was strong. Very strong. All I could use were my legs. So I went to kick him in the groin, but he caught my leg with his other hand. Throwing me completely off balance, he pushed me to the ground. But he didn't let me go far. Immediately after I hit the ground, he had me by my hair again. He forced me to my feet with one quick pull of his arm. I tried not to scream, but the pain was unreal. Emotionally and physically. I thought that he would never hurt me. Never betray me. Never leave. But he did. He did all those things.

Turning me to face him, his hand still clutching my hair, I looked into the depths of his eyes.

"Do it," I hissed, trying to free his hands from my hair. "Kill me. That's what you want, isn't it?" He continued to stare at me as if he was searching for something. Something he didn't seem to find. "Do it! Kill me! Kill me, Gabriel! Spill my blood onto your hands! Kill me! That's what you want, right? Do it!" I was so angry that I felt tears swell in my eyes. Tears, real tears. Closing my eyes, trying to stop them from falling, I continued to scream at him, "Do it! Coward! Kill me! I'm not worth anything to you anymore! Right? So kill me!" Removing my hand from his, I placed it on the dagger and pushed. But he wouldn't move it any closer to me. I tried to make it cut my throat, but he wouldn't move his hand. The muscles in his arm tightened as he refused me the right to die. He wouldn't kill me.

No.

He couldn't kill me.

"Captain!" a voice from behind me called. For a moment I thought he was going to ignore whoever was calling him. And I think he had planned on it. But suddenly, Ezekiel appeared beside me. "Captain, let her go."

"Kill the bitch!" I didn't have to turn and see who said that—Bacchus.

"Captain, you and I both know that you don't want to do this," Ezekiel told him, reaching for the dagger.

But Gabriel didn't move. He just glared into my eyes. The dagger didn't move toward me or away from me. He hadn't made up his mind as to what he wanted to do yet.

"Kill me," I whispered, staring back into his desolate blue eyes.

"Shut your mouth," Ezekiel barked. Turning back to Gabriel, he said, "Let her go. You don't want to do this. We need her."

Long seconds of silence followed before, finally, he sighed angrily and pushed me away from him. I stumbled backward and one of his men caught me. Gabriel had his back to me as he began walking away. But I wasn't done with him yet.

"Hey!" I screamed, pulling my arm free but having it snatched right back up again. "Don't you walk away from me!" He stopped but refused to face me. "You're a coward. You're nothing but a coward hiding away in the woods, masking the pain with this idea of a self-proclaimed mission to rid the world of discrepancies. You're nothing. You're no hero. You're no saint. All you do is run when things get tough. You run when you can't win. All you do is run and you run and run and run and run. The pattern is never ending! You ran away from me then just like you're running away from me now! Nothing's changed. You're a coward and you always will be!" Everything went silent. It was as if the whole forest—hell, the whole world—stopped to listen to us. "When you left that night . . . I thought I'd never see you again. And now, looking at what you've become, I wish I had never seen you again. Because then I wouldn't have to deal with the disappointment of you not being the man I always thought you were." I was gearing up for a fight. I was ready for his counterattack. But he didn't. He didn't turn to argue with me. He didn't scream or fight. He just continued to walk away from me. Leaving me, once again. Only this time I wasn't alone.

For some odd reason I had assumed that there were only a handful of rebels in his camp. I was shocked to see nearly thirty very strong men surrounding me. And all of them were staring at me.

"Why didn't you let him kill me?" I hissed, trying to yank free, to no avail. "You don't owe me anything."

Ezekiel turned to me with eyes as hard as stone. "I didn't do it for you. I don't even know you. But I know him. I know that he would tear himself apart if he had let himself kill you."

"What am I to him? I'm nothing but a whore, right?" I spit.

Ezekiel replied, "I don't know what you are to him. But I do know this. If he wanted you dead, he would've let us kill you the moment you opened your eyes." He turned away from me again, staring off to where Gabriel had disappeared into the forest. "You're not the first member of the Royal Guard that we've captured. But you are the first that we've kept alive."

CHAPTER 20

I DIDN'T SEE GABRIEL FOR DAYS after that. The rebels made me return to the tent I was originally in. Except this time they didn't tie me to the pole. They just tied my hands in front of me, as well as my ankles. I didn't complain too much. They spent quite a bit of time with me, constantly trying to decipher whether or not I was a friend or foe.

"What did you do for the queen?" one of the rebels, Gabel, asked around a mouthful of food. There were three rebels in the tent, Ezekiel, Gabel, and Hollis. Gabel and Hollis were twins with matching curly brown hair and beautiful green eyes. They were the younger of all the rebels, but just as strong. Their faces were youthful and lively, unlike the sinister Bacchus, who refused all contact with me.

"Nothing of much importance, seeing as I'm sitting before all of you now," I replied, finishing off the cold soup they had given me.

"Right, but you must've done something important, aye?" Hollis inquired. "I mean, Maddox, he's our spy, said that he saw you in fancy royal clothing coming out of the palace."

"He even said that he's seen you hand in hand with the king," Gabel added.

Every time His Majesty was brought up, all I could see was his battered body kneeling before the gallows. That memory haunted me. Consumed me. Destroyed me. "I was just one of her Ladies. Nothing more, nothing less."

"Did you really sleep with the king?"

"I heard you would have had his bastard, but the queen found out and had it cut out of you."

"Hollis! Gabel! That's enough," Ezekiel interjected. "You all need to return to your post now." Obediently the twins put down their bowls and left the tent. Ezekiel then turned to look at me. "Don't mind them."

"I didn't," I replied, setting my bowl down. After a moment or two of silence Ezekiel said, "If you want to get out of here, all you have to do is tell us what you were doing near the camp."

I chuckled. "You know damn well that he will never let me leave. No matter what I have to say."

"Maybe you could help us then," he suggested, making himself comfortable in the tent. It was apparent that I was to have a wet nurse at all times.

"Help you do what? Return me to the queen for the reward money?" I spit, leaning against the pole I was once tied to.

Ezekiel sat up, resting on one arm. Though he was not as finely sculpted as Gabriel, Ezekiel was an intimidating force in his own right. Even stripped from his battle attire and resting easy, he portrayed the dexterity of a soldier with an added edge to him. He was not clean shaven or properly pampered like the guards of the Royal Army. He was rugged looking. Like a man who had spent his life rummaging through the forest at night and slaying his enemies during the day. He was nowhere near the stature of Gabriel, but he is a man I would rather not take on alone. "What do you think it is we are doing out here?"

I shrugged. "I don't know. And I really don't care."

It was his turn to chuckle. "Such a young girl to be so bitter."

"Apologies for not smiling at my accommodations. You all have shown me the most welcomed hospitality, and it seems I must have forgotten my manners in the forest. Do forgive me for my crudeness." I rolled my eyes before closing them, wishing I could fall asleep.

"You learned to talk like that in the palace?" he countered.

"Among other things."

"Really? Like what?"

"How to kill."

His laugh vibrated the whole tent. "You're telling me a couple of posh pansies with their perfectly polished bums taught you how to kill? Blimey, I've been learning it all wrong since the beginning."

Rolling my eyes, I replied, "It's unbelievable how many lives I've taken. It's even more unbelievable that I've killed more people in my time at the palace than I ever did outside of it."

That shut him up for a second or two.

"Look, I have no desire to hinder your mission in any way, unless it affects me and mine," I said, looking up at him. "Just let me go. Please."

"What is your mission?"

"To kill the queen. And all who follow her."

He chuckled, rolling onto his back and staring up at the top of the tent. "We may have a lot more in common than you think, mate."

I highly doubted that.

* * *

My body jerked so hard that I awoke with a start. The nightmare I had been so deeply consumed in clung to my being until finally I forced my eyes open. It was the same dream I had been dreaming ever since I left the palace. Crows and death. Crows and death. It paralyzed my subconscious with fear. Sleeping was terrifying for me. Every time I closed my eyes, I saw nothing but the people I had failed. I could hear their cries for help, their pitiful screams for salvation, and their lives slipping away into nothing. Their souls taunted me, haunted me, tortured me, and ultimately destroyed me. And no matter what I did, no matter how hard I fought, I always lost. Every . . . single . . . time.

Taking a deep breath, I wiped the cold sweat from my forehead. I took a look around the tent. Ezekiel was happily sleeping a few feet away from me. There was no light in the tent. Only the soft glow of the dawn allowed for me to see things. Not that there was actually much to see. The tent was empty except for the snoring Ezekiel and me.

Testing my ties, I noticed that the rebels had had the brilliant idea of tying my hands in front of me. I literally couldn't have asked for a better scenario. With my hands tied in front of me, it allowed me to be able to reach the ties at my ankles. I figured that all I needed were my ankles to be free so that I could at least get up and run. In theory I would be able to sneak out of the tent and pass any lingering rebels. Once I got past them it would be a dead sprint away from here.

That was all in theory.

Of course, when all is silent and I am the only thing moving, every twitch is a booming echo in the small tent. I was so sure that every time I moved my hand, Ezekiel would wake up. But he didn't. It took me longer than I expected, but my ankles were soon free. Rolling onto my side, I used my upper body to push myself onto my feet. My joints and muscles creaked from being stiff for so long, but I was certainly glad to be up and nearly free.

Tiptoeing, as silent as a mouse scurrying across a bed of straw, I made my way around Ezekiel. I only moved in intervals that coincided with his snoring. Slow, slow, slow. Having as much control over my body as humanly possible, I made it slightly past his head without even hinting that I was up and moving. I was right in front of the opening. I was right in front of freedom. Taking a deep breath, I went over my plan again. I was just going to run as fast as I could out of there. I was going to run. Run. Run. I took another deep breath . . . I opened the opening of the tent.

Ahead of me was nothing but a beautifully painted purple, pink, and orange dawn sky that framed the leafy forest trees. Their shadows were shrinking as the sun began to rise higher and higher, casting its warm rays upon the chilled earth. It was beautiful. It was perfect.

But I was spending too much time looking up.

Before I had time to realize that the entire rebel camp was awake, I felt the presence of someone standing directly to the right of me. I had no time to prepare.

A large, burly-looking man glared down at me and grabbed me by my tied hands. He held me tightly to his chest, squeezing with all of his might. The man was so incredibly large that my feet were dangling off of the ground. His one arm was just as large as my entire stomach!

"Captain! She's trying to escape—" I cut off his words by head-butting him as hard as I could. I had hit him so hard the middle of his forehead split, causing blood to trickle down his nose and chin.

Returning back to the ground, I continued my assault. With my hands still tied, I cracked them against the back of his kneecaps. He fell forward just enough for me to hit him across the face once, twice, three times. I didn't stop hitting him until his nose was permanently crooked on his flabby face.

But I had wasted too much time on him.

All at once a handful of men grabbed me. I tried to wiggle free. I kicked, bit, spit, and clawed at them, but they wouldn't let me go.

"Keep her steady!"

"Grab her legs!"

I twisted as they each tried to grab me, causing them to sometimes lose their grip on me.

"Grab her!"

I wasn't going down without a fight. And they knew it.

Wham! With the force of a thousand boulders, one of the men punched me in the stomach. I thought I was going to cough up my lungs! But I couldn't dwell on that pain because a moment later I was hit again. *Wham!* Another man cracked me in the back of my head. The world around me spun so fast I nearly threw up the soup I had eaten last night. But I couldn't dwell on that either. Gleaming, rich, silky blood poured from my body. Another one of the rebels went to hit me. I held up my hands in defense.

"Stop, please!" I begged as he released his punch. "No more! No more! Help!" The pain was unreal. I was literally being torn apart. Even as I tried to block his punch I still felt the effects of it. "Stop! Please! No more!"

"Enough!" a booming voice snapped. Immediately the punches ceased. My body writhed uncontrollably in pain as they stood over me. One of them forced me to my feet. But I was too weak. My body couldn't take anymore. The man who held me had to hold my dead weight, for I could not support myself.

"She was trying to escape," the man holding me said. There was silence as I heard footsteps approaching.

"Bacchus, plant a pole somewhere deep in the forest. Tie her to it."

Bacchus replied, "Yes, sir."

"O', and Bacchus. Don't underestimate her again."

"Yes, Captain." And with that the world sunk into darkness. As did I.

"Give me your hand." I dared not look up. I had become used to the blackness that swallowed my body. I had become used to the despair that fed my soul. I dared not look up. I dared not speak. I dared not. "Open your eyes. Give me your hand." I couldn't comply even if I wanted to. My body was broken. My spirit shattered. I had used my last bit of strength when I defeated the Conqueror. I was empty. I was done. "Give me your hand. I will help you." The voice was persistent. The voice was warm. But I dared not look up. I dared not speak.

Suddenly, I felt something, something strong and warm, wrap itself around me. I had no other choice but to nuzzle into the sensation. I had never felt such a thing before. Warmth. What a strange thing it was. What a strange thing it did to me. I was being lifted off the ground, effortlessly. The voice continued to say, "It'll be okay. You're safe. You're safe. I've got you." Who's got me? Why are they helping me? Why do they care?

I don't know exactly how long we walked, but it certainly was a long time. But the voice, the warm voice that held me so tenderly, didn't falter in step. Didn't rest. It continued to carry me. My body, my small, withered body, swayed with the motion of this person's body. It was comforting. Ha! I had never been comforted before. Never, not once. The man who had raised me from a child to now had never once comforted me. But a stranger, a person I had never met, held me tightly. Cared for me. Comforted me.

"We're almost there," the voice said o' so softly. I still did not speak. I still kept my eyes closed. Even as we entered a place with more voices. Some were close; some were far. I heard animals bleating and carts passing by. Wherever we were, it was crowded and alive with activity. I felt the presence of people walking by me. Then all of a sudden, the voices simmered to murmurs, and I felt as though the sun had vanished. We had entered a tent.

"What is this?" another voice, a voice from a woman, asked.

"I found her in the woods," the warm voice, the voice that comforted me, replied as it set me down o' so gently on a pile of soft furs. A small fire blazed somewhere off to the side, chilling my brittle bones. I began to shiver and sweat involuntarily. "I couldn't leave her."

"You did fine, Gabriel. I'm glad you brought her," the woman said. I felt someone run their hand over my forehead. The skin was wrinkled but soft. Very soft. "She's caught a fever. Hand me that rag. I need to break the fever." A moment later a cold rag was placed over my head. "She should be fine upon the morrow. We'll let her rest for now."

I don't remember much after that. Just that I slipped into unconsciousness with Gabriel holding my hand.

When I awoke I was starving. My stomach snarled, pleading for substance. I became so uncomfortable that I opened my eyes, clutching at my stomach and trying to ease the pain. I groaned as another ripple of hunger crashed over me.

"Are you alright?" Gabriel asked. At first I thought I had imagined his hand stroking my shoulder. But then I felt him. I felt his warm, calloused hand glide over my rough skin. Rolling on my back I turned to look at him. My

breath caught at the sight of him. He was breathtaking. Never had I ever seen someone so remarkable. The alignment of his jaw, the craft of his chiseled body, the stubble that dotted his cheeks, and the way his skin poured like silk over his muscles amazed me. Those eyes, his deep, dark navy-blue eyes, melted me. His brown hair, his short brown hair, outlined the sternness in his face. He was squatting next to me. His position underscored the tones of his muscles on his sun-kissed skin. I had never felt a force so strong. "Can you hear me?"

All I could do was nod.

"Can you talk?"

I nodded again.

"What's your name?"

Swallowing past my apprehension, I replied, "A-Arianna . . ."

He smiled at my name. I was sure of it. Why that mattered, I don't know, but I know he smiled at me. "Where are you from?"

My voice came out stronger this time. "Nowhere in particular."

He nodded. "What village did you come from?"

I shook my head. "I didn't come from any village."

"What were you doing in the forest?" he asked as I began to sit up. My body was sore, unbearably so. I felt like an old door being forced open by rusty hinges.

"Nothing." I went to stand but he wouldn't let me.

"You need your rest, just relax," he said in that warm voice I liked so much. Just then a woman entered the tent. She was old, very much so, with skin the color of bark. She had four long gray braids that raced down her back and nearly touched her rear. The woman was round and colorfully decorated in a woven cloth with eccentric small wooden carvings hanging from her ears. Her face was small and kind. She smiled at me too.

"Good morning, dear," she said in her sweet, old-lady voice. "How are you feeling?"

"I'm hungry." As if on cue, my stomach growled viciously. Instinctively I clutched at it again.

She chuckled a hearty chuckle and replied, "That is good. It means you are feeling better. Your body is awakening. Gabriel, fetch her some soup, please."

"Yes, Meenoah," Gabriel replied before leaving the tent.

The old woman, Meenoah, came and sat cross-legged in front of me. A moment later Gabriel returned and handed the soup to the old woman. She stirred it as he remained standing at the entrance of the tent. "Tell me something," the woman began. "Where did you get those horrid scars on your arms?"

The Conqueror. He beat me. He tortured me. He forced me to kill. He forced me to suffer. Some were from him; others were from those I was forced to slaughter.

But I couldn't tell her that. I couldn't resurface a past I had just so recently begun to forget.

"I lived a former life I'd rather not acknowledge," I muttered, gratefully accepting the soup she offered me. I put a big spoonful in my mouth, ignoring the heat, and swallowed. My stomach's growl simmered to a whimper as I put another spoonful in my mouth.

"Did you hurt someone? Or did they hurt you?" Gabriel asked from the entrance of the tent.

I thought for a moment before answering. "A bit of both, honestly. I did what I had to do to survive. I always do."

I couldn't stop shivering. Though the winter season was beginning to fade into spring, the winds still battered my defeated body. Every muscle, every joint, everything burned in agony. All of the beatings. All of the pain I had ever endured exploded across my body. No matter how much I had wished I was numb, I felt everything.

Bacchus followed his orders to the T. In the forest, in the middle of nowhere, he planted a wooden pole into the cold, hard ground. He then tied me to the pole, with my hands behind my back, and left me. I was alone. Cold, broken, bleeding, and alone in the middle of the forest. My head was so heavy on my body that all I could do was let it hang. If not for the pole anchoring me to the ground, there would have been no way for me to hold my body upright. My legs had given out before I was even tied down. All I could do was sit and endure the elements and pain my body refused to allow me to ignore any longer.

It was so hard to keep my eyes open. Half the time I didn't want to, but I was in so much agonizing pain that I couldn't sleep it away. I had to take it. I had to suffer through it all.

A gush of wind barreled into me. All I could do was groan in discomfort. I was broken. Irrevocably shattered. Up above a hawk screeched, echoing throughout the forest. I longed to be free, just like the hawk. Just like I used to be.

Hours must've passed. Perhaps a day or two. And still I felt nothing but pain. The heavy weight of despair suffocated me, but I could do nothing. That was the worse feeling. I could do nothing.

Suddenly, I heard footsteps approaching. But I wasn't afraid. What else could they do to me? Kill me? Please, I welcomed death. I always have.

Using what energy I had left, I slowly lifted up my head to see who was coming. It was Gabriel, Bacchus, and Ezekiel. I didn't care; I put my head back down. I had no fight left in me. None at all. I had been defeated. I had lost. Again . . .

"She's had enough," Gabriel declared, standing gallantly over me. "Cut her loose."

Bacchus huffed in disappointment.

"Is there a problem, Bacchus?" Gabriel snapped.

Bacchus chuckled. "This whore is a traitor. She's tried to escape twice, yet you want me to cut her down?"

"Your point?" Gabriel snarled.

"My point, Captain, is that you're thinking with your cock and not your head," Bacchus countered. "How many chances does she get before you kill her? Or she kills you?"

"Mind yourself, mate," Gabriel growled. "I may mirror the sanctity of a saint, but do not forget that your blood on my hands would be no deterrent to me. I told you to cut her loose. Do as you're told."

Bacchus muttered something I did not understand before I felt him at my back. "You're one lucky bitch." he hissed in my ear as my hands became free.

That's funny. I didn't feel so lucky.

My body immediately fell to the side as I was released. I couldn't hold myself up. My body had had enough. Bacchus was disgusted as he roughly pulled me to my feet.

"You take her." He shoved me into Gabriel's arms. I didn't have the strength to pull free. I couldn't. "She's your problem. Not mine." He stormed off after that. Ezekiel looked after him but did not follow.

"W-why won't you just kill me already?" I asked, leaning against his hard, solid chest.

He sighed. I felt his chest rise and fall with the movement. "Not an hour goes by that I don't consider killing you."

I rolled my eyes. "So do it."

He shook his head, tossing me over his shoulder like a sack of potatoes. "Not yet. You don't get off that easy."

CHAPTER 21

HIS BODY MOVED WITH THE fluidity of a panther stalking his prey. He carried me so effortlessly, as if I was literally only a sack of potatoes. He had me over his shoulder, facing away from him. All I could see was his ass, his very nicely round ass, and the ground. Though I was glad he hadn't made me walk, I so wished I was being transported in a different position. All of the blood rushed to my head, making me feel as if it weighed a thousand pounds! I was uncomfortable. Unbelievably so.

Gabriel continued to carry me throughout the forest. Considering how long we were walking, I doubted that we were heading back to the camp.

"Do you remember when I found you in the woods?" he asked after a long moment of unbearable silence. I didn't have the strength to answer. But he didn't care; he continued anyways. "You looked just like you do now. Beaten . . . broken. I remember that. But you hadn't completely lost your spirit. Once Meenoah broke your fever and had you on your feet again you wanted to fight everybody. You were so mean and vile. I thought for sure we would have to kill you. It was like you were some sort of savage beast that had been awaken in the midst of charitable deeds. Your body was all marked up. You had fresh wounds and old wounds. After that first day anyone who tried to help you immediately became your enemy . . . including me."

I had no idea where he was going with this. But for some reason, the sound of his warm, raspy voice comforted me. It eased my pain just enough to keep me listening.

"It took ages for you to finally trust us. You had the whole village terrified. They thought you were going to slaughter them. But you didn't. You fought for them." His words fell off at the end. The silence stretched on as he continued hauling me off to nowhere. I didn't understand why he said those things. It all had happened so long ago; I'm surprised he remembered all those details.

Time scattered by as he continued to carry me. The sun had risen from its dormant state and had graciously made its presence known. Its rays poured down on my skin, soothing me. I welcomed the warmth . . . just like I had o' so many years ago.

Without notice, Gabriel suddenly took me off of his shoulders and dropped me to the ground. I groaned, loudly, in pain.

"What happened to you, Arianna?" he asked, standing over me.

I coughed as the dirt settled into my lungs before replying, "I don't know what you're talking about." Surveying my surroundings, I noticed that he had brought me to a cliff. A cliff I remember o' so well . . .

"Stop!" I shouted, watching the mother continue to run for the edge of the cliff.

"Jacob, hurry!" The boy's feet were hardly touching the ground as she dragged him faster and faster!

"Hey, stop!" I shouted again. She turned and saw me coming and dragged the boy harder. His foot slipped on a loose stone, and he fell from his mother's grasp!

"Mama!" he screamed, lying in the dirt as she continued running. Tears filled her eyes as she turned back to look at her son. "Mama, help me! Mama!" The infant began crying as she slowed and contemplated going back for her son. But I already had him. He didn't put up much of a fight; he only reached for his mother. "Mama . . ."

I pushed the memory out of my mind as fast as it had entered . . . I couldn't bear it. The mother, choosing to kill her family instead of being captured by the Royals—it pained me to think about it. It pained me to remember how awful things were for the village people. It pained me to realize that I wished—with all my heart—that Maille, Teta and Zakai's mother, had done the same thing and pushed them off the cliff. They could have avoided so much pain and suffering if they ended their lives like that. I didn't understand why the mother did it at the time, but after witnessing the desecration of innocence at the hand of the queen, I finally understood. I finally understood that in order to live, truly live a life without fear, they had to escape this world altogether.

"What happened to you? You used to protect these people. How could you betray them?" he asked, glaring down at me.

I shook my head, weighted with grief. "It wasn't my idea to have all of this happen. I'd give my life to undo what I've done."

"Bullshit," he spit, "you only cared about yourself."

"No." I shook my head again. "That's not true. I cared about everyone but myself."

"Is that why you went to work for the queen? Is that why you laid down every night for the king?"

Using everything I had, I went to attack him, but he kicked me down. Coughing, I urged the air to return to my lungs.

"What happened to you?"

Angrily I barked, "What happened to you? You left me! You're the one who abandoned us, all of us! What reason do you have for retreating like a damned coward?"

That really made him mad. Roughly he reached down and grabbed me by my shoulders and held me to his face. His eyes, his deep-blue eyes, froze over as he stared into the depths of my soul. "I am not a coward! I left to help all of the people of Islocia. Not just one village. Think about it, get this through that thick-ass skull of yours,—what good is it to spend all your time helping one village when you can help them all?"

"Why didn't you bring me with you?" I countered, trying to break free.

He rolled his eyes and let me fall back to the ground. "I wasn't going to leave the village unprotected. Meenoah couldn't do it all on her own. You were our best bet. I needed you to stay. I had to have someone protect them while we were away. But you couldn't do that, could you? You failed, miserably. You destroyed your own village!"

"I didn't know that was going to happen!" I screamed up at him.

"That's because you weren't thinking about the Qingkowuats, were you? You were thinking about yourself, and nobody else," he hissed, clenching his fists as he looked down at me.

I chuckled sardonically. "So you were thinking about the village when you left me?"

"Yes," he replied sternly.

"What about all those promises you made me, huh?" I had to fight back the tears as I resurrected old memories. "You promised that you would never leave me. You promised that you would always be there for me! You promised it would be me and you against the world, forever! You promised me a life together!"

He flinched at my words. The look on his face said it all. He had forgotten me. He had forgotten all that we were.

"You don't remember? Do you?" I was pissed. I was angry beyond belief! He had forgotten everything. He had forgotten me! Damn him! How could he forget! We were a team. He was my everything. I screamed at him. I couldn't help it. I wanted to hurt him! The things I did for him . . . everything I did was for him! I stayed with the Qingkowuats for him! I gave my life to protecting them for him! I would have died for him! Yet he forgets me! He never once came back for me! He never once sent anyone to come find me! He left me! Alone. He left me! "Burn in hell, you piece of shit!"

"Enough!" he shouted in his booming voice. "I did what I had to do for the betterment of Islocia."

"How noble," I snapped, turning away from him. "I wish I had killed you when I had the chance."

"But you didn't, did you?" His voice simmered to a hiss.

"What do you want with me?" I couldn't take it anymore. I was in too much pain, emotional and physical, to continue this. I needed to die; I needed to be free. Once and for all.

"What were you doing by the guards' camp when we found you?"

Defeated, I told him the truth. "I went to kill them. That was the plan." I told him what happened to Teta and Zakai. I told him how I escaped from the palace and had been living in the forest for months on end trying to form a plan to destroy Ophelia. I told him how I had captured all of those guards and tortured them until they told me where the nearest guards' camp was. He listened intently as I described how I saved Christopher and the other children from the camp. When I was done he was silent for a long while, mulling over all that I had told him. "Are you going to kill me now?" He didn't respond right away. "Can you do it quickly? I think I've earned that at least." Still he didn't say anything so I kept talking. "Don't let Bacchus do it. He'd enjoy it too much."

"Stop." Finally he spoke. "Just stop."

"Kill me, Gabriel, please," I begged. He couldn't look at me.

"I can't kill you," he muttered, staring down the dirt. "I just can't."

"Then what are you going to do with me?"

He sighed and turned to look at me. His eyes softened. "I'm going to give you a choice." He was silent before he continued. "I cannot kill you. I want to. But I can't. However, you can kill yourself. So you can choose. I will allow you to return to the rebel camp and you can join us. You can be a part of the rebellion to destroy the monarchy. You can be with me. If you don't want to do that, then the only way you leave this cliff is you must find your own way down."

I scoffed, shocked at what he was asking me to do. "You're making me chose between you and death."

He nodded.

"You're not going to let me just walk away from this?"

He shook his head. "No. You have to choose."

Turning away from him I stared ahead at the cliff. From where I was sitting I could hear the crackle of waves smashing into the boulders at the bottom. If I jumped, it would be imminent death. I would be no more. I would be free.

If I went back with Gabriel, the man I had once given my all to, how could I trust him? He had broken me so many times that I lost count. He had hurt me. Physically and emotionally, he had brutalized me like I was nothing to him. But it was Gabriel. The man I had been waiting for. The man I had longed for. The man who once longed for me . . .

"Why are you making me do this?"

He ignored me. "What are you choosing?"

I wanted him. My heart had been so empty without him. I wanted him. But he didn't want me. I could see it in his eyes. No matter what, he would never want me again . . .

I stood up slowly, my body groaning in discomfort as I stood for the first time in a while on my own. He reached his hand out to help me, but I shook my head. I had made up my mind.

"Good-bye, Gabriel." I turned away from him. Facing the cliff I made my walk to the edge. I didn't hear him follow me. He didn't protest. He let me continue walking. The waves grew louder and louder as I walked closer and closer to the edge. Still he didn't stop me. Maybe he was hoping I would turn around. Maybe he was hoping I would change my mind. Maybe he was hoping I would choose him. But I kept walking until I was at the edge. Peering down below, I saw the jagged rocks. I saw the rushing waters plummeting into the cliff. I would die on impact. No doubt about it.

One final time I turned to look at him just to see if he would stop me. His eyes were pleading with me, but he didn't say anything . . . he didn't move from where he was. He wasn't going to stop me.

Just then a large wave crashed into the cliff, erupting like a roll of thunder. I turned my attention back to the edge of the cliff . . . and gave myself what it wanted. I had made my choice.

I jumped.

The wind roared against my ears as my body plummeted down below. For a moment, as I accepted death and my body continued to fall, I thought I had heard Gabriel call me. I thought I heard his warm voice. But I would never know. I closed my eyes as I continued falling. The water was getting closer and closer. My life was ticking away by the second. And I was happy. O' so very happy.

Seconds before I hit the water, I let out a deep breath. The last breath I would ever take. Forever.

My body was swallowed by a wave . . . and everything left me. Everything. All of the pain. All of the sadness. Everything left me. I left me. Forever.

CHAPTER 22

"We have a new Qingkowuat," Gabriel said, coming into my tent. I was just waking up, cuddled underneath a pile of furs. He was looking good. Delectable, really, with his sun-warmed skin pulled tight over his taut slabs of muscles that hinted at his dangerous and wild side. He and some of the other men went out hunting this morning. Naturally he was covered in dried animal's blood when I saw him. But I liked it. It excited me in ways I couldn't believe.

"Do we? Who bred?"

He settled next to me, crawling underneath the furs and wrapping himself around me. I nuzzled into his chest and put my arms around his waist, happy he was back with me. Gabriel and I had fallen into a sort of routine. In the morning he would go out and hunt with the other men. When he was finished he would come and lie with me for an hour or so before we both had to get up. When we got up we would join Milo, another scout just like Gabriel and I, and we would run recon around the forest to make sure the Qingkowuats were safe. It happened every day. And I wouldn't change it for the world.

Holding me tighter he pushed his legs between mine and ran his fingers through my long, dark hair. "Maille, do you remember her? She owns the shop near the edge of the village. She gave birth to a baby girl last night. There's going to be a celebration tonight to welcome the newcomer."

"That's nice. Will we be attending it?" I asked, breathing in his familiar masculine scent.

"If all is clear tonight," he replied, continuing to play with my hair. "Shall I court you this evening?"

I giggled, tightening my grip around his solid frame. "Talk about a conflict of interest, eh?"

I felt his chest vibrate with laughter as well. "Maybe you're right." For long moments we cuddled each other. Tenderly he stroked my back, and I closed my eyes and rested against him. I loved having him like this. He was mine. No one else could have him. Just me.

"Gabriel?"

"Hm?"

"Never mind . . ." I shook my head, hiding from my own question.

"Ask me, Ari. Don't be shy." He always knew how to soothe me. He always knew how to make me feel safe, protected, secure, comforted. He coddled me so much that sometimes I nearly forgot about the haggard beast I was bred to be. He made me forget. He made me feel like a woman, his woman.

"Is this going to be our life forever?"

"What do you mean?" He pulled back from me and stared into my face. I couldn't help but smile at him. I had wanted someone for so long, and now I had him. He was mine.

"I vowed to protect the Qingkowuats in exchange for asylum. And I will honor that vow. But . . . I'm wondering . . . what about our future? What about our legacy?" I murmured, toying with the light dusting of hair on his chest.

His chest rose slightly, lifting me, as he sighed. "I don't know what the future holds. I made a promise to Meenoah that I would always protect her and her people." He was silent before he continued. "I never factored you into the equation. Touching you, like this, with your body so close against mine, makes me feel more alive than I have ever felt in all of my days. You are beautiful, Ari, and you are mine. I'd give us a life together. A small shack along the coast where no one can bother us, yet we are close enough to protect Meenoah and her people. We could have a life together, if you wanted to."

"I like that." I removed my hand from his waist and traced his lips with my finger. "All my life I had been subjected to nothing but pain and killing. I thought . . . the Conqueror . . ."—I said his name as if it tasted like poison—"had taken away my ability to feel like this. And perhaps he did, but you, Gabriel, you gave it back to me. I would die for a life of forever with you."

He leaned in slowly, o' so slowly. I felt the warmth of his body suffocate me. He moved his hands back to my hair as he urged me to lean into him too. I wanted him. Right then and there. I wanted him for all of my days. He was mine. I was his. He promised me it would always be like that. His lips were so close to mine. I had never kissed him before. I always wanted to. Now was my chance to finally become his, officially.

Just then, someone barged into my tent right before our lips could touch. Immediately we untangled ourselves from each other and turned to see the intruder.

"I'm sorry to . . . interrupt," Milo, the scout, panted. He was clearly shocked at how close we were. No one knew of our relationship, or potential for one. We had always tried so hard to keep it secret from them. "Gabe, there's been a breach. Three royal guards are riding in this direction."

The loving Gabriel and I had spent the morning with disappeared. He had transformed into his role as leader. "I'll be right there," he replied in his commanding voice. Milo left and Gabriel extracted himself from the furs. I too got up and began retrieving my weapons. He turned to look at me. "Stay here."

Shocked, I protested, "What? No."

"It's not a suggestion, Ari," he snapped, strapping his sword to his waist. "I need you to stay here and make sure that they don't come into the village. We will try to stop them, but we need someone here to hold things down. Gather the children and hide them in Meenoah's tent."

He was just about to leave, but I grabbed his arm. "I am nobody's wet nurse. I am a warrior. I was bred to fight."

"But you were ordered to stand down." He glared at me. I was going to continue arguing with him, but his eyes softened and he ran his thumb over my cheek. "Do as you're told. I'll be back soon." And then he was gone. He left me. Alone.

I did as I was told though. I gathered all of the children and hid them in Meenoah's tent, and we waited for them to return. We waited for hours. And hours. And hours. The sun had begun to kneel before the moon, and yet they still hadn't returned. Naturally, I thought the worst. They had been taken down. What they had thought was only three guards probably turned out to be thirty or a hundred! However many there were, they had lost. They were not coming back.

"Where are you going?" Meenoah asked, reaching for my arm. I turned to look back at her and all of the children. They needed someone to protect them. It was my job now.

"I'm going to make sure they haven't gotten into the village. I'll be right back," I promised before exiting the tent.

Nighttime was beginning to announce itself. The sun had fallen away, and the moon shone bright all throughout the village. Dusk had settled. All was quiet; nothing was scurrying about. The eerie silence worried me even more. Why hadn't they returned? Where were they? I only had a dagger as my weapon. The rest were in my tent. A dagger was all I needed. I was skilled, very much so, with any weapon. The Conqueror had taught me well. I was a weapon. Born and bred to be for all my days.

I crept silently throughout the village. I heard nothing for a while. Until suddenly the sound of whispered voices caught my attention. Had I not been so close to them I would have never heard them. They were talking so softly.

"Hurry, grab that! No, not that, the other one."

"Do we have food and water?"

"Take some weapons too."

"Hurry, before they realize."

"Come on, mate! Quickly now!"

Slowly, slowly, slowly, I peered around the tent that shielded them. My heart stopped once I caught sight of who they were.

"Gabriel, we've got everything we need. Let's go." Gabriel . . . my Gabriel. He and Milo were loading down their horses with supplies. They were planning on leaving. "Come on, mate! Before they come looking for us. Let's go."

"I'm coming, I'm coming." He was just about to hop on his horse, but he saw me. I had come around the tent completely. He had seen me. "Ari . . ."

"What are you doing?" I asked, stepping closer to him. I looked at the things he had packed—food, water, weapons, clothes. He really was leaving. He was packing to leave.

"Go back to the others." He didn't say it in his loving Gabriel voice. He was ordering me around again.

I shook my head, stunned. "You're leaving?"

He sighed and turned to the other scout. "Get a head start. I'll catch up." The scout nodded and left. "Ari, I need you to go back with the others. They need you."

"Where are you going?"

"I have to go, and I have to go now. I can't explain it to you. Go back to the others now, Ari!" he shouted at me. He had never done that before. "Now!"

"Are you coming back?"

"Probably not." He said it as if he didn't care. The man I had cuddled with this morning had left me. He was leaving me.

"You're leaving me?"

"Yes." He walked right by me and grabbed a sword leaning against the tent. He then returned to his horse.

"You can't leave." I went and grabbed him. But he pulled away from me.

"Get out of here, Ari!" he screamed at me again. But I was relentless. I wouldn't let him leave. Not without a fight.

"No!" I grabbed him again, but he knew I was coming. Quickly he grabbed my armed and pushed me to the ground. My body skidded across the dirt, but that pain was easy to ignore.

"Go now!" I went at him again. This time he grabbed me by my shoulders and threw me, hard, away from him. I crashed, face first, into the ground. "Get the hell out of here! That's an order!" I wiped the blood that dripped from my nose and got back up.

"Gabriel . . ." My heart hurt in the worst possible way as he climbed onto his horse. "Please . . . don't go. Gabriel!"

He didn't listen to me. He didn't look at me. He just left. He left me . . . alone. With no explanation. No reason. Nothing. He left me with nothing. He left me . . .

* * *

I had planned on being dead. When I jumped off that cliff I had planned on shattering into millions of pieces as I hit the boulders below. I had planned on finally being free.

But God did not favor me so.

I resurfaced. Choking on mouthfuls of salty seawater, my lungs burned for relief. I flailed helplessly, trying to control my body and mind. Waves, huge uncanny waves, battered me. Tossing me as effortlessly as a giant would a feather. I was being whipped around over and over and over again. The waves threw me into the boulders. My head split open on one of them. Blood seeped into the raging waters as I fought to stay afloat. Instinct took over. I couldn't let myself drown. I had to fight. It's what I had been doing my entire life. I fought for the queen. I fought for my people. I fought for my king. I fought for Teta. I fought for Zakai. I fought for Gabriel. It was finally time for me to fight for myself. It was time.

A raging wave rose above me; its whitecap casted a shadow over me as the wave continued to grow and grow and grow. It stood several dozen feet taller than me. Its power—insurmountable. Its target—me.

It crashed down on me. Hard. The force was so great that it pushed me right over a slick jagged boulder. I couldn't see anything. My eyes burned as the salt seeped in and clouded my vision. Water continued to pour into my lungs as the massive wave pushed me. I was spinning beneath the surface. Spinning, spinning, spinning, so much spinning! I didn't know which way was up! All I could do was hold what little breath I had and hope my body would float upward.

Luckily, I didn't have to wait long. With the help of an undercurrent, my body, my ravaged body, was swept away from the boulders and I surged upward, clawing my way to the surface. Gasping for breath I inhaled heavily, fighting to stay afloat.

When things settled, I noticed that the current had pushed me away from the boulders and toward land. I was about half a mile out from a beach.

Treading water, I turned and looked back up at the cliff incredulously. There was no way I should have survived that fall. Just like the mother who jumped with her infant, I should've died. I should've shattered into millions of pieces. My pain, my suffering, my life should have ended. Why do I keep surviving when those who deserve to live die so easily?

Taking more deep breaths, I began my swim back to shore.

If I was to live, then I must live for something other than that of the resurrection of innocence and justice. I must live for me.

CHAPTER 23

I BARED MYSELF TO THE WORLD. Stripped of everything I had fought so hard to maintain. I had been broken. Shattered. Brutalized. Reborn.

I don't know how I mustered the strength to crawl upon the beach. The ocean waves helped, pushing me slightly, allowing me to make my way to safety. I was exhausted, pleading for breath and strength to carry me. I don't know how I was able to gather myself to stand on two feet. But I did. Torn apart by forces uncontrolled by man, I still found the ability to stand. Then walk. My muscles burned with every step. My head was weightless. I stumbled about the forest, constantly losing my footing but never giving up. I forced myself to live. I forced myself to fight. My lungs fought for breath. My heart fought for strength. I pushed myself to prove everyone wrong. Even me. I was going to live.

My mind tried to betray me, clouding my vision and distorting the images of the forest. But I was not disarrayed. I fought through it. Trudging along, pushing myself, willing myself to live. It took everything I had. I wasn't going to give up; I was going to push myself until the end. Until my heart stopped and breath escaped me, I would keep going.

When I had jumped off the cliff, the sun had shone bright in the sky. As I made my way through the forest, it had begun to sink into its deep, luminous orange color that signified the oncoming sunset. The forest trees began to cast long shadows that seemed as if they wanted to reach out and grab me. Up above a hawk cried, circling overhead. Placating my imminent death for its own means.

It followed me for a while. Circling and circling. I didn't mind its company; it helped me keep the time. It gave me direction, literally leading me exactly where I needed to go.

All was silent as I trudged back into another hellhole of a different kind. The men, the tall, burly, rugged men, turned and stared at me. I knew how indecent I was looking. I was sure my clothes had torn off in the water, and what little remained did not shelter me entirely. But it was no deterrent to me. And neither were the men. No one made a move to stop me. They just watched as I shuffled into their camp. My eyes were forward; I did not stop to stare at anyone. I kept going.

I wasn't exactly sure where I was headed, but the hawk above seemed to know. It screeched and guided me in the direction of a hut. I stopped just outside of it, noting its weathered decor.

Panting. Exhausted. Standing on legs that wanted to give out, I waited. I don't know what I was waiting for, but I didn't make any move toward the entrance, which was covered with two doeskin sheets that parted in the middle.

A ravaged mess. That's how I felt. I couldn't stop shaking, I couldn't calm my breathing, and I couldn't take my eyes off of the hut. The clothes that had survived my ordeal clung to me only by the slickness of my skin, which consisted of perspiration and seawater.

I felt as if I had been standing for hours. A crowd began to assemble around me. Murmured voices toyed with my mind; I thought I could actually see each individual letter that made up the words people spoke.

Ezekiel appeared out of the hut after a moment. He surveyed the crowd before casting his eyes upon me. I didn't look him dead in the eye. I just kept staring at the entrance of the hut.

I felt someone grab my shoulder. "I'll take care of her," Bacchus hissed. I yanked my shoulder free from his grasp and kept my eyes on the tent.

He went to grab it again, but Ezekiel spoke. "Stop." He stared down at me. I felt the weight of his gaze as he dissected my motives. I had no weapons. I was clearly in no shape to fight. I was not a threat, not physically at least. "Captain!" Ezekiel called over his shoulder.

My heart started to thud painfully in my chest. My palms started to sweat, and I couldn't stand still. My weight shifted from one foot to the other, and my shivering refused to cease. He was coming.

The entrance to the hut burst open. Nearly standing a foot taller than I, Gabriel stood with tightly clenched fist. The veins in his arms pleaded for relief as they fought against the tightness of his skin over his massive muscles. His eyes were shadowed with fury as he stared down at me. His chest rose and fell as he breathed as heavily as I did. A large gust of wind rushed out of his flared nostrils. He was deliciously pissed and exceedingly unhappy to see me.

It was my chance to speak. I hadn't planned on doing it in front of an audience—hell, I hadn't planned anything. But I knew this was the only chance I would get. His deep dark-blue eyes tore into me as I stared intently back at him. For a moment words failed me. I didn't know what to say. He was staring at me so intently, so angrily. Clearly my decision to jump stoked the burning fire of his usually callous ego; it simmered into flames as the thought of my death weighed so heavily on him. Just like his decision to leave had forever suffocated me. It was only fair that he felt a fraction of the pain I went through.

"I . . ." My voice came out soft. Due to the large amounts of water I consumed, my throat was scratchy and raw. It was painful to speak, but I knew I had to. "I . . ." My entire body was shaking violently as I returned his glare. I was on the verge of collapsing. My body's fuel was weakening as I wasted time. It took all I had to finish what I had to say. "I . . . I . . . want to fight. I . . . want to fight for . . . Islocia and its people. I want to . . . do what's right. For the first time in my life, I want to fight for the right reasons."

He didn't say anything. He just continued to stare at me with those piercing navy-blue eyes. They cut me open and spilled my soul onto the ground for him to dissect. After the longest moment of my life he took several steps forward until he was only an inch away from me. His body heat was radiating off of him, wrapping itself around me and not letting go. I took an involuntary deep breath and breathed in his familiar masculine scent. My head got dizzy, and I had to close my eyes against the forces that had me entranced in him. The ripples of taut muscles . . . the severity in his look . . . how he could kill me with his bare hands . . . it all infatuated me. Blanketed me. Revived me. Gabriel could do things to me that no one else could. He was inhuman. He was unworldly. He was Gabriel.

My body gave out before he could answer. Slowly my eyes rolled to the back of my head, and my legs lost their strength. I wasn't sure if I fell forward or backward, but all I know was that someone caught me, and I sank, helplessly, into blackness. I lost all feeling. All sensations. Everything. I left me. Finally able to rest peacefully . . . for the time being.

When I awoke my body felt as if it weighed a thousand pounds. My limbs were sore, unbearably so. It felt as if they had been cramping the whole time I was asleep. Sweat misted my skin and my stomach howled for substance. My bones creaked from lying down for so long, and my throat burned, dry from the salt. If I had not the will to live, I would've slipped back into the world of the unconscious. Forcing myself to wake up was like treading water against a current. Everything was grounded. But I had to get up.

"Easy now," a female voice soothed. Turning to look at her, I was surprised to see that she was rather attractive. Even though she was kneeling down to my level I could tell that she was short. She had long black hair that she wove into a single braid that hung down her back. Her skin was the color of sand; her eyes were a nice cocoa brown. She looked like a nice girl, very skinny, but still attractive all the same. "I was told to not let you up."

"Did . . ." I cleared my throat, wincing against the fire that burned deep inside it. "Did they also tell you that I'm not one to follow any sort of rules?"

"Yes." She giggled, handing me a cup of water. I accepted it and drank deeply. My throat relished the coolness of the water. She then handed me a cloth to wipe my sweat away. "They also told me to always have a guard with me at all times when I deal with you." Looking over her shoulder I noticed Ezekiel leaning casually against a pole supporting the large tent they had me in.

"Damn . . .," I hissed, eyeing him. "He really wants you up my ass, doesn't he?"

He extracted himself from the pole and strolled over to me. "That's only because there isn't any room left for him anymore. According to him you've gotten pretty uptight lately, aye."

"What a charmer," I muttered, rolling my eyes. Sitting up I looked around the tent. It was rather larger, certainly bigger than the one they had me in before. This tent had several straw cots aligned next to each other. Most of the cots were empty except for a handful of them. There were women who tended to the people occupying the cots. They served them food and water and wrapped bandages. Three large wooden poles, evenly spaced, kept the tent up while the ends were anchored to the ground. Though the tent was large, it was rather cramped. The cot next to me was close enough for me to roll over onto it. Luckily it was empty.

"Abigail," Ezekiel called to the woman who handed me the water, "you let me know if she causes any problems. I'm going to tell the Captain she's awake."

"Will do," Abigail assured him as he exited the tent.

I sighed loudly. "Blessed almighty! Is he the air that fills your lungs or the sun that hangs high above the realm?"

She chuckled a soft chuckle and replied in her soft monotone voice, "Not to that extent. But the Captain is highly respected. He rescued most of us. He gave us shelter, food, and protection from the guards. We are indebted to him. At least I know I am."

"Why is that?"

By her silence it was clear that she too had a past she would rather forget. "I need to check your wounds." She stood and reached for my head. Quickly I grabbed her hand, ignoring the awful bite of soreness I felt in my arm. With my other hand I felt my head and noticed a bandaged wrapped around it. I was confused for only a moment because then I remembered hitting my head on the boulder when I jumped off the cliff.

"I can't leave for less than a second, and already you're trying to attack someone, eh?" Ezekiel snickered, entering the tent.

I released Abigail's arm and allowed her to redress my head wound. "Don't fret, dear friend. You're next."

He chuckled a throaty response. "I'm paralyzed with fear."

Ignoring him, I asked, "What'd he say?"

"He wants Abigail to make sure you're well taken care of. Then once you're able, he wants you to be introduced to the rest of us." He shrugged, handing Abigail another cloth to wrap my hand. Abigail peeled back the rotted cloth I had wrapped it with and observed it. It was worse than I thought. Three of my knuckles were yellow with infection and out of place. The skin around my little finger was black and rotted to the bone. Living outside in the cold had kept the pain down, but now I felt it ache and throb as she turned it over to look at it.

"We are going to need a lot of herbs for this," she noted to herself. Leaving me, she rose and walked to the opposite end of the tent. The small woman began rummaging through a wooden box.

Then I heard someone enter the tent. By the way my body reacted, chills shooting up my spine, I knew who it was. "What happened to your hand?" The sound of his deep raspy voice clawed at my senses. Turning to look at him, I braced myself for impact. As usual he was rugged and untamed. His muscles protruded out of his fur tunic, pleading for relief. The stubble that grew across his cheeks and chin underlined the ruthlessness in his wild look. His deep, dark, brown hair was recently cut to the root. He was decadent in a sort of animalistic and deadly way. He was dangerous, unbelievably so, and he was enticing.

I drew in a quick breath before replying, "I got in a fight with a tree not so long ago."

Ezekiel scoffed, "O', really? Eh, who won?"

Gabriel smirked and then knelt down to have a look at it. His large, callous hands tenderly, as if possible for a man so intimidating, touched my hand. "It's not broken. The infection is bad, but all you need is to peel off the dead skin and reset the bones."

"Thanks, I didn't realize you were an apothecary," I snorted, rolling my eyes at his analysis.

He stood then, towering over me like a mountain and a pebble. Turning to Ezekiel he said, "Give her a week to heal. Then send her to me."

"No!" I spit, surging to my feet, which was clearly a mistake as my whole body screamed in discomfort. "I'm fine. Get Abigail back over here and fix me up now." As if on cue Abigail returned with an armful of icky green and black substances in glass jars.

Gabriel chuckled sardonically. "You were unconscious for three days. Your mind may be well rested, but your *body*"—I shivered at the way he said that word—"still needs rest." The severity in his look was off-putting. He had grown so much since I had last seen him o' so many years ago. His hair that once touched his ears now rested very close to the skin upon his head. The wildness in his once-playful stare simmered into an icy deep blue that had little time for games. He had this set look on his face that did not mirror the man I had known. This man had seen many unpleasant things that he simply could not forget. No matter how hard he tried.

"There's nothing wrong with me besides my busted hand. I'm not going to lie around in this tent for another week! I am fine, and I'm the last thing you need to be worrying about," I snapped.

He stared at me for a moment longer before looking over at Ezekiel. Then suddenly he smiled, a fierce smile that was not a sign of joy or pleasure. "Fine then. Ezekiel, hand me your knife. Abigail, give her another cloth."

"What for?" I asked before she could.

"You're going to need something to stop you from screaming. Or biting your tongue off." He took Ezekiel's knife and handed me the cloth Abigail had set aside. "I'm going to fix your hand."

"Do you know how?" I scoffed, eyeing him suspiciously.

"Shut up, and put that cloth in your mouth. I don't have all day for this," he replied, waiting for me to stick the cloth in my mouth.

I shook my head. "I don't need it. Pain is momentary just like everything else in this world."

"Would you like me to give her a sedative, Captain?" Abigail asked quietly off to the side.

He shook his head. "She can handle it. Right?"

"Get on with it already," I shot, watching as he took my hand in his again. He smiled—a much nicer, gentler smile—as he placed his thumb on my middle knuckle and his other fingers underneath it. With one solid push of his thumb, my knuckle shot from its original position back into its rightful place with a loud popping sound that reverberated throughout the tent. "Ahhh!" I hollered at the top of my lungs as the pain registered! Ezekiel and Abigail covered their ears as my scream exploded out of my mouth. Tears stung at my eyes; my teeth ground painfully together as I tried to bite back my screams!

But it was to no avail! My whole body vibrated as sharp bites of unbearable, unimaginable, inconceivable screams stormed down the length of my body! I was breathless by the time the pain hummed beneath the line of uncomfortable and agonizing.

"Two more to go." He winked, watching as I panted with watery eyes, and put the cloth into my mouth. He turned to look at Abigail and said, "I think she would like something to numb the pain after I'm done." He turned back to me. "How does that sound?" I was too delirious with pain to object.

* * *

"Look alive!" Ezekiel boomed as we made our way deeper into the camp. The rebel camp was rather large. It was almost like its own realm. There was a small community area where the women and children did their routine duties: washing, cleaning, cooking, and assisting the wounded. There was also a brothel for the men to enjoy as well. The little communes were made up of small tents that could house up to four people. Next to the commune was another set of smaller tents that could only house around one to two people. Those tents were for the warriors. They made up most of the rebel camp. Ezekiel, Bacchus, Hollis, Gabel, and the other thirty or so rebels I had seen were all housed in this section of the small part of the forest they had cleared. Gabriel, as Captain, had a slightly larger tent that was tucked away deep into the forest. His tent was still in full view of the other rebels, but his section of the forest was not cleared—it was surrounded by trees. The hut he had come out of at first, after my journey from the cliff, was a meeting place for the rebels. Initially I thought it was his place to live, but that wasn't the case. He preferred solitude.

"Captain's on deck!" Ezekiel shouted as we walked into the small community of certified killers.

Immediately, before Ezekiel had even gotten his final words out, all of the rebel warriors rushed out of their tents and stood, stiff as a board, and gave their captain their full attention. I rolled my eyes at their obedience.

"Gentlemen," Gabriel said, nodding thanks to Ezekiel for the introduction, "we have a new rebel joining us. This is Arianna

Korinthos, former lady to Ophelia and the king. You will show her as much respect as she gives you. She is very knowledgeable of what transpires behinds palace walls. She could be of some use to us." Though I loathed his presence and his ideals, I was impressed with the control and admiration that he had from his people. I was also very impressed in the men he had assembled. Each and every one of them was strong, fierce, well-built individuals. They were all bred to kill . . . mercilessly. "Arianna, there are a few people you need to meet. The rest you will get to know later." The other men who knew their importance, or lack thereof, quickly returned to whatever it is they were doing. A few men stepped forward.

Ezekiel introduced them. "Arianna, this is Axel." The first contender was a short, mahogany-skinned fellow. He too was nicely built with taut ripples of muscle cascading over his dark complexion. His arms, though behind his back, I could see were covered in gruesome scars that hinted at a past doused in the terrors of a life most unthinkable. He was charming though, with a soft face and playful brown eyes underneath a sheath of inky-black, shortly cut hair. He smiled at me, eyeing me up and down as he went to shake my hand. "Axel is the sail that sends the ship forward. We could do nothing without him on any of our missions."

"Charmed," I said, accepting his hand but pulling it away when he tried to kiss it. "Why are you so important?"

He smiled a toothy grin. "I'm the ears in the trees, milady."

"On our stealth missions he hides out in the tops of trees with his bow and arrows. He keeps an eye out for obscurities. He and his mate, Ace," Ezekiel explained.

"Who's Ace?"

Just then a loud screech pierced through my ears. We all looked up and saw a hawk, the one that had led me here, plummet from the sky above before slowing to land. Axel stuck out his left arm, which I now saw was covered in two thick layers of fur. The hawk slowed his decent, flapping his impressive wings and aiming his talons at the fur. He landed perfectly.

"Ace helps me keep watch when the boys are scouting," Axel replied, showcasing the large bird.

"Beautiful animal," I said, observing the bird's razor-sharp talons and impressive intuitiveness. "How'd you get him to be so tame?"

"The same way the Captain got me to cooperate." The look on my face must've told him that he needed to explain. ""I learned to live in the forest, the hard way." He gestured at the scars that marred his forearms and shoulders. "My ma and pa, they didn't have much, but my life was happy. That was before Commodus had our village torn to shreds. My ma . . . she tried to save me so she grabbed me up and ran with me to the forest. She told me to hide in this bush until she came back for me. She then went to get my other siblings so she could hide them with me. I don't know what happened to my ma or my brothers and sisters. I just know that when things quieted in the village I found her body next to my two sisters. They were burnt real bad, along with my pa and my older brother." He cleared his throat before continuing. "After that I spent my time trying to survive in the forest. One day I was hunting quail, and I heard a baby bird crying for its mama. It was all alone. A fox or something had gotten the nest, but the little fella was small enough to hide under the fallen twigs."

"You saved the bird?"

"Yeah, his story mirrored mine. I couldn't leave him." He lovingly stroked the hawk's neck. "Ever since then, Ace and I have been inseparable."

"Lucky you." I smiled a forced smile.

"Moving on," Ezekiel said, motioning to the other gentlemen. "Starting from right to left, this is Guryon, Ajax, Aegeus, and Isaac. All four of these men were double the size of Gabriel. Thick meaty arms and legs spilled out of their fur tunics with veins coursing down their arms. Guryon had red hair, Ajax had black hair, Aegeus had brown hair, and Isaac also had black hair. They were impressive. Three times my size and meaner than Bacchus, or so that's how they appeared. "These fine gentlemen are the waves that push the ship. We were lucky to extract them from their other circumstances and have them join our team."

"Very nice to meet you," I said. Neither of them said a word.

Ezekiel leaned over and said, "They don't speak the common tongue very well." I nodded in understanding. He then motioned to another individual. "This here is Maddox." Maddox, a small, scrawny, pitiful excuse for a man, stood hunched over with stringy hair hanging off of his head. He was nearly my age, but age did not become him. "He is like the fog that sifts through the cracks in an old ship."

I snorted, "Enough with the pirate references! Just say he's a spy!"

Dismayed by my comment, Ezekiel took a moment to gather himself before replying, "As you wish." He turned back to Maddox. "Maddox is very valuable to us. He can take on many forms and disguises, which allows us to infiltrate enemy territory. He's the one that alerted us about you, in regards to the guards' camp."

"Impressive." I shook the sickly looking man's hand. "I'm usually quite observant. Were you a guard at the camp?"

He shook his head, disturbing his thin hairs. "No, ma'am. Do you remember the boy named Josiah?"

My brain took a moment to process before I remembered that that was one of the boys I helped save. He was found with Christopher and the others. "Yes, he was the boy that helped me light one of the barrels."

"Are you really so sure it was a boy?" He winked. Baffled by the idea of this man being able to mirror the appearance of a child, I looked at him incredulously. He scurried off away from me before I could ask him any more questions.

"Very impressive," I muttered, trying to wrap my brain around it.

"So what do you think?" Gabriel asked, stepping around Ezekiel to look at me.

I shrugged, watching the men go back to cleaning and sharpening their weapons. "If this is what you left me for, how can I compete with that?"

My sarcastic tone irked him. I could tell by the way his broad shoulders stiffened, but he didn't say anything about the comment. "Are you ready to see where you will be staying?"

"I'm radiating false excitement," I replied dryly as we began walking back toward the commune. As we passed a few tents with mothers nursing their children inside, I noted exactly what he was going to do. He was going to put me off again and have me cowering with the commoners. "I'm not going to be somebody's wet nurse. I don't want to live amongst women and children."

He stopped just outside of a larger tent, bigger than the one where I was resting, and turned to me. Music and women's cries of pleasure spilled from the small opening of the tent. From behind me, a man brushed my shoulder before walking into the tent and being greeted by nude harlots.

"The way I see it, you have two options," Gabriel said in his stern commanding voice. "You can care for the young and the dying in the clinic"—he gestured toward the tent Abigail was in charge of—"or you can spread your legs for my men to enjoy, here, in the brothel." I was aghast by his options. A part of me wanted to run a dagger through his heart. Which was probably very visible on my face because Ezekiel held his hand over the dagger at his waist. The other part of me wanted to be nowhere near Gabriel. I was disgusted by him. How dare he force me to do such horrid things! I was not bred to be nurturing or a whore! I was bred to fight and kill! He knew that!

"Bastard!" His body tensed as I rounded on him. "It is beyond me why you feel you have been awarded the opportunity to make decisions in my regard."

"Sheath your claws, Ari," he growled, searing me with his smoldering gaze. "Don't break the skin. Now is not the time."

I spit on the ground by his feet. "You may be their *captain,* but you are not mine."

"Then jump, Ari. Only this time, don't come back." His words sliced me open as painfully as a blade. "Do as you're told." He opened the tent wide enough for me to see two women servicing one of Gabriel's men. I turned away disgusted.

"I will not!" I closed my eyes as tight as I could until he finally closed that wretched tent. When I opened my eyes again I was facing the clinic. I couldn't imagine myself helping others in that way. I was too vile. Too cruel. Too untamed. I did not have the heart to assist those who deserved something a little more tender, comforting, and sweet.

"Fine," Gabriel huffed, drawing a dagger from his waistband.

I scoffed, shaking my head, "You can't kill me. Even you admitted to it."

He smiled. "You're right. I can't, but Ezekiel can." He tossed his dagger to Ezekiel and Ezekiel caught it deftly. Gabriel turned back to me. "It's your choice, again."

I was in no condition to fight. Especially with only one good hand. Gabriel had put all three of my knuckles back in place. I had thought that pain was excruciating, but I was wrong. Because after that he used a knife and carved off all of the rotted skin around my fingers. The sedatives Abigail had given me did nothing to numb the pain, and

Gabriel knew that. He knew a lot. He knew that I could not fight . . . he was trying to break me. I wouldn't let him.

"I won't fight Ezekiel," Gabriel gave a curt nod and began heading towards Abigail. But I stopped him, "I want to fight Bacchus." In a voice only he could hear I murmured, "Maybe then I'll be able to finally prove something to you."

Stunned, he asked, "What is it you think you have to prove?"

"That I'm worth it."

CHAPTER 24

IF BACCHUS HAD NOT BEEN standing only a few feet away from me, I don't believe Gabriel would have allowed me to continue on with this. However Bacchus *was* a few feet away from me, and he accepted the challenge gallantly.

Gabriel didn't say a word to me; he didn't even look at me. A man of his prestige did not take kindly to people disregarding his commands. And for that, he loathed me.

Standing before me was a man of infinite strength. Bacchus had shed his fur tunic, allowing his thick, meaty muscles to be showcased for all to see. He was nearly a foot and a half taller than me and nearly two hundred pounds heavier than I. He wasn't the most toned individual, but he was strong. I saw it in the way his body moved. Several deep scars marred his neck. One connected from his eye and traveled down his face to his chin. His large hands were sheathed in purple and blue veins. His pale-gray eyes sliced my confidence to shreds. There was no way I would be able to out power him. Even if I was in my best fighting condition I would not be able to defeat him. My entire body ached, my head throbbed painfully, my hand was sore, and my muscles were unbelievably tight. With every step I took, my legs tightened and cramped. My breathing was labored and my heart stammered every other beat. I wasn't in fighting condition. I needed rest. I needed medicine.

But as I looked at Gabriel, I knew I had to do this. His whole body was tense with anxiety. He refused to look me in the eye, but I knew he was thinking of me. A crowd formed around me and Bacchus; murmured voices filled the space between us. I shivered involuntarily as Bacchus circled around me. Gabriel knew I would not win; he knew that if Bacchus got his way I would be beaten dead. Maybe that's what he wanted, maybe not. My plan was a simple one—take as many punches as I could and hope for the best.

Ezekiel allowed me to have one weapon, a dagger. Bacchus refused one.

My body was so incredibly battered that the dagger shook violently in my hand. Bacchus smirked, believing that I was afraid. I was not. I tried to calm my breathing, taking deep breaths consistently.

The air stood still . . . the voices became silent.

A moment later . . . he charged.

I couldn't rely on my speed and agility, for I was too weak to move. All I could do was brace myself for the impact of the punch I was about to feel.

Thrusting my dagger outward, I attempted to slice him as he neared me. Unfortunately he caught my wrist and squeezed, trying to get me to release the blade. I held on as long as I could. Bacchus's ghastly breath spilled onto my face as he urged my fingers apart. I gritted my teeth, begging for all the strength I could muster. However, Bacchus was very smart. He reached for my other hand, the one that was o' so recently reset and skinned. Using his thumb and first finger, he squeezed one of my knuckles. I hollered in pain and released the dagger! The dagger fell to the ground as Bacchus pulled his arm back. His muscles bunched up as veins cut down his arms. The look in his eye told me he had no mercy for me. None at all.

His punch cracked against my chest, tossing me several feet away from him. I rolled across the ground, bathed in dust. My cry of agony frightened the birds, causing them to flee from the trees. I couldn't breathe. It felt as though someone had laid a boulder on top of me and then proceeded to sit on top of the boulder as I crashed to the ground. I couldn't contain my screaming and groans of discomfort. My entire body vibrated violently . . . all from one punch.

Over the blood roaring in my ears, I heard Bacchus approaching, coming to finish the job. I closed my eyes and prepared for another earth-shattering beating.

"Stop!" Gabriel's voice boomed. "Bacchus, that's enough." Though reluctant, Bacchus stopped his advance. "You've got what you wanted. Let that be it."

I heard Bacchus begin to walk away but not before saying, "Tell me what head you're thinking with now, Captain. You know I'd have killed her."

Gabriel then came over to me. He squatted down to my level and went to lift me off the ground, but I slapped him. He quickly recoiled. Using whatever strength I had left I tried to gather my footing but failed. All I could do was hold myself up with my arms, but not for long.

"Arianna, enough!" he barked, reaching for me again. But I screamed at him and threw my body toward him. I reached for his leg, but he kicked my arm away. "Stop, it's over!" I screamed at him again. Roughly he grabbed me up by my shoulders so that I was eye level with him.

"Get off of me!" I writhed violently. He shook me hard enough for my teeth to snap against each other. Tears stung at my eyes.

"Stop, it's over!" he growled, his eyes pleading.

"No!" I yanked my arm free, which then caused me to slip from his grasp. Before my feet touched the ground, I split my knuckle on his chin. He stumbled away as I crashed to the ground. The pain was unreal. Emotionally, I was carved raw. Gabriel, who once was my everything, stood before me. The man I loathed, the man I despised . . . was the only man I could ever imagine causing me this much pain. Tears burned at my eyes.

He came back to me, but again I tried to attack him. "Arianna, please!"

Out of the corner of my eye I saw something shift. When I turned to look, I choked on the very breath I had pleaded for. Teta, Zakai, and the king with an infant in his arms—they all stared down at me. Little withered Teta held on tightly to Zakai. Zakai glared down at me as he held hands with the king. My king. *My* king. Inside my chest my heart crumpled as a strong wind came and took them away from me.

I lost control of myself. Tears spilled down my face, splashing onto the forest floor. Blood dripped slowly from my nose. I couldn't contain my sobbing, which then turned into wailing. Every bit of unimaginable pain collided with my body and mind. My face fell to the ground as my arms gave out. All I could do was scream into the dirt, beat the dirt, and cry. The pain was so unbelievably unbearable that

I spilled all of the contents of my stomach. If I had had any strength I would've moved away from it, but I couldn't.

Gabriel grabbed me then. He rolled me away from my mess before lifting me and cradling me in his arms. I wanted to keep fighting. I even tried beating my fist against his chest, but they were weak attempts. He kept carrying me away toward the forest as I sobbed.

All my life all I had known was to fight. It was all I had ever known. But as he carried me away, as my body shut down and pain consumed my entire being, I realized that fighting was not enough. I had to break in order to rebuild myself. I had to be beaten down to nothing before I could finally grasp what is important. I had to lose everything—everything—before I could see what it is that is truly worth fighting for.

* * *

"This might hurt a little," Gabriel said, kneeling down to my level. He had some herbs mixed into a bowl and was covering my wounds with them. The substance was green and the awful smell filled his tent. I would have hurled again, but it turns out my stomach was quite empty.

I lay exhausted on his furs. I had no strength to even wince as he put the clumpy green mix on me. All I could do was lie on my back and stare at his ceiling. I couldn't bring myself to look at him; I had fallen apart in his arms. He had never seen me so raw. It unnerved me to be so . . . vulnerable.

"How are you feeling?" His voice was softer now, not as clipped and stern but still rugged and deep. Something had changed in both of us. "Do you need anything?"

I shook my head.

He finished with the green mixture before pulling out a long cloth. I heard it tear, and then he wrapped it around my hand. His strong hands kept mine from shaking too much as he attended to their needs.

After a dreadfully long period of silence, he finally spoke. "I wasn't . . ." He cleared his throat. "I wasn't going to let you choose the brothel. We may have our differences now, Ari, but I have too much respect for you to be used like that." I didn't say anything; I just lay silent and withdrawn. "When I saw you . . . when I had found you again. You looked so wild and volatile. So untamed. You looked every bit the beast you wanted to destroy, yet you didn't realize that it lived within you. I wanted you to work in the clinic because I thought that you needed time to be a human again. I saw the pain in your eyes, a pain I could never fathom, rest comfortably inside you. Turning you further and further away from this world. I didn't want to allow you to join us and fight . . . not so soon after your ordeal. Then when you told me what happened to you in the forest, I couldn't do it, Ari. I couldn't let you back into a world that tore you to shreds. I didn't have the heart to use you like a weapon. I didn't have the heart to lose you again, not so soon after I had finally found you."

A tear slipped down the side of my face as he stood. His words echoed inside me, wrapping themselves around me. I thought I had lost this man. I thought he had given up on me. I thought he had left me. He hadn't. He was here, with me, for me.

He was just about to leave the tent but I grabbed his hand. Another tear fell.

"Y-y-you . . ." I tried to ignore the pain as I attempted to speak. "Y-you left me. Why?"

He knelt back down to me, understanding. His eyes softened as he grabbed my hand and stroked his thumb gently over it. "I left to protect you. After Milo and I defeated those guards, we noticed another group of men off to the side. They were watching us. Naturally we thought they were enemies but they weren't. It was the first time I met Ezekiel and Bacchus. They told me what happened to their village and how they needed shelter. I would have brought them back to Meenoah, but then I thought of all the other villages that were going through what they were going through. So we decided to form a band of brothers and swear to protect all Islocians. The plan was to leave before you came looking for me. I knew you would fight to keep me. So I thought it would be best if you believed that I had died. I didn't want to take you with me, because I knew that if I left you with Meenoah that you would be safe. And I would always know where to find you. It wasn't easy leaving. It certainly wasn't easy staying away."

I swallowed past the lump in my throat and said, "I hate you."

He smiled at that. "I know you do." He stood, stretching. "Most of the rebels are out hunting right now, and I'm going to go join them."

I sat up, slowly, and asked, "What shall I be doing?"

Before he left, he stopped and said, "I'm sure you will find something to do." If I had been in a better condition, I would have argued, but I couldn't imagine doing any sort of strenuous physical activity. So instead I just sat there and enjoyed the silence. I decided to close my eyes and catch a moment of rest.

It wasn't long until I was awoken again.

A woman entered the tent. She was my height and heavier than I was. Her hair was the color of mud as it tangled roughly down her curvy frame. She had dark brown eyes that hinted at her no-nonsense attitude. "Cap'n told me to come find you when I wasn't busy." Her accent was thick, Gaelic really. Her words rushed out as she spoke them.

"Why would he do that?" I asked, barely opening my eyes. When I realized that she wasn't planning on leaving me alone, I readjusted myself so that my back was leaning against the side of the tent.

"Apparently, to him, I look like some sort of pansy. I'm supposed to show you 'round, give you a nice feel for the place." She shrugged.

"Do I have a choice?" I asked, flexing my hand to try and get rid of some of the numbness.

She shook her head, "Not if you want to stay on his good side. Come on, girl, let's get dis oiva wit."

I sighed and outstretched my hand. "Are you going to help me up?"

Chuckling, she replied, "Girl, you're going to have to earn it, ya?"

"Fair enough," I muttered, ignoring the tightening in my legs as I stood. I followed her out of the tent, and we began to make our way toward the commune. Like Gabriel had said, most of the men were gone. Only Guryon and Isaac, the two giant men I had met earlier, were left behind. They tipped their brow to me as we passed them and headed into the entrance to the commune.

"Dis here is Sythos," she began, pointing to specific places. "Oiva der is the clinic. Tat der is where many of the men get patched up. Abby is in charge of tat. Next to it is the brodel. Many of the women you going to meet work der. The smaller huts scattered about is where the refugees live. The rebels and the soivivers keep der space, you understand? We protect tem, they do the washing, right? Right." She continued talking as we headed toward the brothel. We stopped just outside of it. As if on cue, a woman moaned "yes" as loud as she possibly could. "Cap'n told me you ain't spending any time in dis place here. However, I thought I should tell you about it. Just so things is understood between us, ya hear?" I nodded. "The rebel boys here, they fight more than most. Dis here is a release for dem. They *all* take advantage of dis luxury of sorts, you understand?" I knew what she was trying to get me to understand, but for some reason her notion bothered me. I tightened my fists as I heard more women moaning. I stared back at her, relentless in my gaze. She had hit her mark.

"Is this the new recruit?" I turned to see another woman coming near us. She was tall and rather thin. Not deathly skinny but very thin. She had long blonde hair that she wove into two thick braids that ran down the back of her head like two horns on a goat. Her smile was razor sharp as she peered down at me with her fierce green eyes. She was older than I was; it showed in the lines around her eyes and mouth.

Immediately the woman I was with took a step away from the tent. "Yes, it is. The cap'n wanted me to show her 'round."

"I'll take it from here, Colleen," the woman replied, approaching us. Colleen nodded before walking off, clearly frustrated that she couldn't continue to bait me. "My name's Moira." She had an accent similar to Colleen's, but hers wasn't as defined. "The Captain never told me your name."

"Why would he need to?" I replied coldly.

She chuckled, eyeing me up and down. "Ezekiel told me you were going to be a tough one to crack. Lucky for the Captain, I love a challenge."

I sighed, clearly needing to improve upon my social skills. It seems my time in the woods had displaced my manners entirely. "My name is Arianna. Arianna Korinthos."

"Last names aren't required." She winked. "But it is nice to meet you, Arianna. The Captain has told me a lot about you."

"Anything good?"

She shook her head. "No."

That made me laugh. "That's good, I suppose."

She nodded this time, flashing her fierce smile. "It is! We need more bad around here. And according to the Captain, we need you."

"I just want to fight." I shrugged, following her as she began walking.

"That's good," she cooed, waving to a woman walking by with her babe in her arms. "But we will need that later. For now we need what's in your mind."

"I was never much of a scholar." Up above I heard Axel's hawk screech loudly. Moira stopped to look up at it too.

"They'll be returning soon. Come on," she replied, sidestepping someone's linen drying in the breeze. The deeper we walked into Sythos, the denser it became. It certainly was much larger than I anticipated. I tried not to look any of the people in the eye. A part of me, the naïve part that refused to end my suffering, kept searching for familiar faces. Meenoah . . . Maille . . . Teta . . . Zakai. To avoid disappointment I kept my eyes down until Moira stopped just outside a large hut. I heard young voices coming from the inside. Moira turned to look at me. "The Captain told me that you were a very skilled fighter. You hold nothing back, and when you feel it's necessary, you follow orders. We will need that. He also told us that you know what went on behind palace walls." I nodded. "The rebels are trying to build an army. And if you know anything about the rebels, it's not easy. Regardless of the horrid rumors that leak from Lárnach to the forest, people refuse to go against their queen. Due to this, there is much fighting between all of the rebel camps. The Captain has tried to be a mediator to quiet the ruckus, but his attempts are not answered."

"I can't make them listen to me. In the eyes of the monarchy I am a traitor," I replied, finally beginning to get the answers I sought after.

"But that's the thing! You are known. Every soul in every crevice of Islocia knows of your indiscretions. You are the proof we have long been searching for," she replied, her eyes searching for understanding.

"I don't understand how this helps." My mind was reeling.

She sighed, exasperated. "Stupid girl, if you were to speak with the other camps and share your stories of all that went on in the palace, we might be able to win over some more men who will join our cause."

"You want me to speak with other rebels in hopes that a herd of overstimulated men will want to join forces to revolt against the queen? A queen, mind you, with an army of thousands."

She nodded. "It is our only option. They want proof of our grievances. You can give them it." Understanding was like a rushing wave during high tide. It all made sense, all at once. They needed me, not for my dexterity with a sword but for the knowledge I acquired by living under the rule of Ophelia. She had given me plenty of examples to share.

Moira turned away from me then and lifted the opening of the hut we were standing next to. Suddenly, dozens of tiny eyes turned to look at us. Less than a second later, they charged from their seated position on the floor and greeted Moira. The children wrapped their scrawny arms around her and praised her name, kissing her hands.

"This is what we are fighting for." She smiled down at them; they only reached to her waist. "You and I will not live forever. Our innocence was taken from us years ago, and there is no hope of us getting it back. These little darlings, however, have a lifetime ahead of them. It shouldn't be taken away, especially for a reason that has nothing to do with them but everything to do with us. They shouldn't suffer for our mistakes."

A small girl extracted herself from the crowd around Moira. She was small; the top of her head hardly made it above my hip. Her short hair was the color of dawn as it shined in the sun. She had skin the same color of clay with beautiful big black eyes. There was a flower in her hair, and she pulled it out as she approached me. Something inside me forced me to kneel down to her level. Her toothless smile greeted me as she handed me the small yellow flower. She too kissed my hands before blushing and heading back over to Moira. My heart ached in the worse possible way. She reminded me of . . . another life that had suffered. Moira was right—they didn't deserve the hand they were dealt. Someone had to fight for them.

I stood up and looked her in the eye. "I will do everything I can to help."

She smiled her razor-sharp smile. "Good. I guess I don't have to kill you after all."

Moira continued to enlighten me on the methods of dealing with the other rebels. Sythos was clearly one of the most organized. Artis, Qualmi, and the Iraquin were the ones causing the most trouble. She told me that there was a long-standing rivalry between the Artis people and the Iraquin. Apparently, during a raid, the leader of the Iraquin people told the Royal Army where the Artis were stationed in hopes that they would stop the raid. Consequently, the next day, the Artis were stripped of nearly everything. The Iraquin deny it all, but the Artis say they have a source that corroborates their version of the story. Getting them to work together would be like me attempting to single-handedly redirect the currents in the ocean.

She then proceeded to tell me about the difficulties of the Artis people. They are less civilized than the other camps. They had one leader who was "elected" only by murdering the leader before him. Insurrections were common among the Artis people. They were never in one place at one time. Moving as the seasons changed, living amongst each other like wolves would in a den. It was survival of the fittest with those people. She also mentioned that the Artis people were mostly prisoners who had won their freedom fighting in the arena. Meaning, they weren't ordinary men. They were foul, vile, ruthless, and soulless men with no fear.

At first I didn't believe there was any way possible to get these people to cooperate. They hated each other, each demanding the right to size up the other's ego. Blood spilled between all three of them since the time of Commodus's reign. Yet she wanted me to forge a bond between them? Not to mention, the Artis people and the Iraquin had a similar distaste for the people of Sythos! It is said that they dislike the notion of Gabriel taking charge and throwing accusations at the queen. Besides Sythos, the other camps believed that the only injustice that the queen had committed was over-taxation and an unequal distribution of food for its people. But they attributed that to the bad harvest. The miscommunications between the truth and rumors were mind-boggling. They had no idea that children were sentenced to death and that their queen intentionally starved her people in order to feed her own greed. They knew nothing, and I was supposed to shatter their shelter of ignorance? I alone?

"The men are returning," Moira said just as she finished drawing out a map of the approximate location of the other camps. "They will need our help preparing the food for dinner. Portions are divided relatively equally. The women and children eat first, then the rebels fight over whatever's left."

"That's generous," I muttered, standing and exiting her hut. Just as we walked out I saw the men riding in from the forest on horseback. As I got closer to them I noticed that nearly all of them were caked in mud and animal blood; even their horses seemed to have bathed in it. The sight was familiar; a possible smile tugged at the corner of my mouth as I saw Gabriel dismount. He had shed the top of his fur tunic, letting his muscles ripple freely as the cool breeze dried the filth that covered him. His deep-blue eyes flashed my way as he went to untie the doe he had tied to the back of his horse. It had an arrow through its neck, a perfect shot. Once he was done with that he grabbed the doe with both hands and threw it over his shoulder. The animal wasn't small. The only indication of how heavy it actually was showed in how his biceps and abs tightened with every step he took as he carried it.

He walked past me, other men following with other kills. I followed them. They didn't go too far into the camp. Just far enough out of sight so that the children wouldn't see them skinning the animals before they were cut up and distributed.

"Want to give me hand?" he asked over his shoulder. It was directed toward me, so I obliged. Before I reached him he roughly threw the doe down. I knelt down to his level just as he was about to hand me a carving knife. He paused. "You're not going to try and kill me again, are you?"

I shrugged. "I might. We'll just have to see."

He smiled at that and handed me the knife. I started at the doe's hock and made my first cut. Gabriel started at its neck, yanking the arrow out with one quick tug. His strength caressed my insides. He was so brute and raw, it was mesmerizing. I missed that. I was beginning to feel at peace with him. His words from earlier in the tent comforted me, as did his presence. I could get used to this Gabriel.

As we began skinning the doe, I noticed some whispers behind us. I turned to see who it was, and I noticed a group of women, intentionally dressed lewdly, huddled together, staring at Gabriel and me. I didn't think anything of it so I went back to skinning the doe. As more time passed their whispers got louder. Words like "handsome" and "whore" got mingled together. Gabriel didn't seem to notice, but I did.

"It seems you've got some admirers," I said, trying not to sound too irritated.

He looked up at me first and then over his shoulder at the women huddled together. He smiled. "I suppose I do." The women burst into giggles as he turned back to his work. A moment later, one of the women extracted herself from the huddle and boldly made her way toward us. She was dressed in a long sheet of thin, colorful, and very much see-through material. To defend against the weakening winter season and the coming of spring, she wore a fur shawl around her shoulders. The woman was my height and slender. Her hair was black and flowed like water down her back. She clearly was a woman who did not dwell in labors such as skinning a doe. No, her job consisted of lying down for men who have had a long day. I could tell by the way the men gazed upon her, as if each of them knew a secret about her that they believed the others didn't already know.

"My Captain," she said in a seductive voice as she reached her hand down and stroked the hair on his nape. Gabriel turned and looked up at the woman. For a moment he was confused, and then he smiled at her. Not the cruel smile he presented to me but a real one. A smile I had not seen in a very long time.

"Fenella . . ." His voice thickened as he said her name.

She beamed as he called her by her name. Slowly, o' so slowly, she removed her hand from his neck and brushed a piece of her own hair behind her ear. "My Captain, I was wondering if you would come to me tonight. I have missed you." My heart thudded twice before stopping mid-beat in my chest. *Come to me tonight* . . . It seems Gabriel was not so lonely without me after all. He had this wench to keep him company during my absence.

Gabriel shrugged. "There is much work to be done this evening." He stood up then, completely towering over her. She looked up into his eyes as a starving child would look upon a basket of freshly baked bread. "Perhaps another time."

"Have you forgotten?" She touched his hand softly, stroking her thumb down his.

"Not at all." His smile widened. "How could I?"

She shot a sideways glance at me before replying, "You've been busy with other . . . arrangements."

It was only then that he looked at me. I kept my eyes down. "Yes, my duties can't always lie with you."

"They once did," she whispered loud enough for me to hear. "Quite often." Slowly, so he could see every enticement of her frame, she turned away from him and began walking away. But not before saying, "Don't keep me waiting too long, Captain."

He looked after her for a second before returning to the doe. That damned smile had yet to fade.

"That one of your whores?" I snapped, hating that the words came out as harsh as I meant.

He ignored me for a moment before shrugging. "Perhaps." Just then he sawed the doe's head off, completely decapitating it. He tossed it to the side. "You're not jealous, are you?"

That was it—that smug smile threw me over the edge. Anger boiled deep within me, an anger I had never felt before. I hated him all over again. Throwing down my carving knife and roughly ripping the hide off of the doe, I finished my job and stormed off. I had just begun to make my way around a tent, hoping to be out of sight, I heard footsteps following me. I half expected it to be Gabriel. I was too angry to talk to him. As I turned around, fuming with rage and prepared for another physical altercation, I realized it wasn't Gabriel.

"Easy, mate," Moira said, holding up her hands in surrender. I cooled a fraction of a degree.

"What do you want?" I spit, pacing in the dirt.

She started chuckling, but one fierce gaze from me silenced her. "Calm down, girl. Ain't nobody stole your goat." I didn't have time to dissect her foreign sayings. I was angry! Pissed! Gabriel had betrayed me! With her! That harlot! That whore! He had touched her. Kissed her. Laid with her! And he had the audacity to flaunt their affair in my face.

Affair? Good God, what had I become? Gabriel was no more mine than I was his. His decision to leave severed whatever we had before his departure. What did we have? I don't know! That's not the point! His presence angered me! He was not the man I thought he was. He was no better than any of the other rebels who took advantage of the brothel! He was a savage beast cowering in the forest with his men and lewd women. I was to be used just as they were.

"If I didn't know any better, which luckily I do, I'd say some man has done you wrong." She snickered, watching as I stirred up the dust around me.

"Shut up," I muttered, stopping only to give her another death stare. "I can only handle so much at a time. There aren't any words to describe the anger I feel!"

She sighed dramatically. "I believe the word is love. You're in love, stupid girl." If I had had a weapon of some sort I would have split her skull in two. Her brain would've been the centerpiece for this evening's meal, had I the chance to dismantle her. "Only a man can force a woman into this much rage."

"I do not love him!" That word. That pitifully dull word tasted like poison on my tongue. I spit to rid myself of it.

"Perhaps not now, but you did." She chuckled, shaking her head. "I can see it in the way you two look at each other. Your heart aches for him and his...*head* aches for you. The tension between you two is nearly visible. That's why Fenella felt so threatened."

I was just about to ask her to shut up again, but I stopped and began processing what she was saying. "Threatened?"

She nodded excitedly. "O' yes. Women only make such a scene when they feel they are in the midst of a formidable challenger."

I shook my head. "And how would you know so much about what women do? Are you not a woman?"

The smile that spilled across her face was tantalizing. She took a step closer to me and replied, "Like a man desires a woman, I too revel in their presence. I am satisfied by their touch just as a man is."

I cocked my head to side, confused. "But such a desire is forbidden." I gulped, mentally noting that I no longer had to see this woman as a contender. A contender for what? I don't know yet.

Shrugging, she replied, "Is there truly such a thing as a desire that isn't forbidden? Is there ever such a thing as any love not denounced?" She began walking away but not before she said, "My advice, show him what he's missing. Come now, we must serve supper."

I followed her back to where the meat was being served and found a place beside her. I began dividing the meat absentmindedly. Too lost in my own thoughts to focus. Do I love Gabriel? Is it possible for one's heart to desire a being whose presence makes you cringe? No! I could not love him—I hated him. He despised me.

I stole a quick glance in his direction; he was staring back at me. His navy-blue eyes were iced over as a familiar stern look set on his face. He had yet to wash the dried animals' blood from his hands and chest. So vile, so untamed . . . He mirrored me in that aspect. No one could control me; no one would ever dare attempt to control him. He was a force of his own, a beast riveted in laces of strength and power.

I looked away from him then and handed a bowl of food to a woman and her two children. She nodded thanks; I attempted to smile.

"Try not to behead your next customer," Moira muttered, smiling as Fenella approached. "Remember, ain't nobody stole your goat yet."

There was nothing I could do about the frown that marred my face as Fenella stretched out her hand for a bowl. Her brown eyes, the way she stood, told me she felt as if it were right for me to be serving her. Moira filled the bowl and passed it to me. I looked in it for a second before reaching it to her. She went to grab it, but I let it slip out of my hand. The food crashed and spilled onto the ground.

She gasped, covering her mouth. "Look what you've done!" I smirked unapologetically. "Clean this up!"

I shot a sideways glance at Gabriel, who was watching us. Every bone in my body ached to shatter her into millions of pieces. Unfortunately, that would only make things worse. "Apologies, but I cannot dispense seconds until all have been fed. It seems you must wait."

"How dare you suggest something so horrid?" she shrieked, pointing her scrawny finger at me. If I had not the patience I would have snapped it in two, but I didn't.

I smiled at her and suggested, "It truly was my fault that your food spilled. I shall make it up to you! I have yet to be served my food. How about you take my servings, and I will wait until all have finished to be fed?"

Mulling over it for a second she assumed herself the victor. "Yes! That is the rightful thing to do!" Moira made her another bowl of food, and she snatched it out of her hands. Before leaving she stepped closer to me and hissed menacingly, "You have yet to convince me that this was some accident. You better be mindful of how you treat me. I still have the Captain's favor. As easily as you dispense of this food is equivalent to how easy it would be to be rid of you." In that moment, at that very moment, she reminded me of Ophelia. The empty threats, the assumption of power, the façade of invincibility—it all mirrored the woman I swore to kill. And this is who Gabriel chose to associate with?

As if on cue, he approached us. "Ladies, what's the problem?" Fenella's entire persona changed back into the desirable harlot she was so proud to be.

I spoke before she had the chance. "I accidently spilled Fenella's food. In apology I offered her mine so that she didn't have to wait until all have eaten. It has left me without food but in Fenella's favor."

Gabriel contemplated this for a moment just as Moira handed him his food. He looked down at his bowl then. "You shall have mine, Ari."

"My Captain," Fenella gasped, finally understanding the game she had so easily lost. "You must eat. Here, take mine. I freely hand this over to you."

Confused, he replied, "Was it not you who caused a scene over the food in the first place?" He shot a look at me as she stammered over some words. "You have your food. Carry on now. Ari, come with me."

I shook my head. "Not all have been served. Leave me be. I'm going to finish this task. I'm sure you have other things to keep you occupied, *Captain*."

Not sure of what to do he replied, "Come to my tent afterwards."

"I'd hate to intrude." My heart quickened in my chest as he peered down at me.

"It would be my pleasure." His deep, sensual, raspy voice caressed me. Fenella heard every word, I was sure of it. Female triumph radiated across me as he gathered his food and walked away.

"Well done, mate." Moira snickered, nudging me with her elbow. "You do learn fast."

The sun had settled completely by the time all were served. What was left of the hunt were two deer carcasses and a handful of ducks and rabbits. I was baffled at the variety of food the rebels were able to acquire. How far did they venture out to feed a village of such size? It was admirable, the lengths Gabriel would go to sustain his camp.

"I figured I ought to start a fire, just so you wouldn't get lost," Gabriel said as I approached his tent. He was sitting on a log outside of it, blanketed in his fur tunic with a pot hanging over the small flame he had created. I joined him on the log directly across from where he was sitting. He chuckled at my choice.

"How clever you are to be so considerate," I scoffed, warming my hands by the flames. Though spring was soon arriving the night breeze still continued to chill the tips of my fingers. I wasn't dressed appropriately for winter. Moira had offered me a few of her outfits, considering mine were so badly worn. It felt nice to be covered, shielding my personal parts again. "I'm sure Fenella appreciates it."

"Ah." He smiled, coming over to me and placing his fur shawl over my shoulders. "I was wondering when you would bring her up."

"Intuitive too?" I gaped sardonically. "No wonder they chose to make you captain."

He chuckled at that and returned to his original seat. "Still as witty as ever, I see."

"I hate to disappoint," I muttered, pulling the shawl tighter around my shoulders, inhaling his masculine scent. I was dizzy with the smell of him. Peering over the fire. I looked at him. My heart thudded painfully in my chest. The soft glow of the fire softened his hardened appearance and enunciated every crevice of every muscle he had. My mouth watered as I watched his biceps flex with every twitch of his hand. Just as the flame's shadows licked up his body, I too acquired a similar thought.

How could it be that a man I hated could affect me so vividly? In that moment I understood Fenella's desire to trap him and claim him as her own. I craved him all the same. His power, his strength, his control, and lack thereof. It all consumed me, clouding my mind. I both welcomed and feared it.

But then a dark thought struck me.

Calder, the monster who had ravaged me both mentally and physically, wouldn't allow me to desire Gabriel as I should be able to. Those eyes—Calder's frigid glare was the polar opposite of Gabriel's deep blue gaze. Physically Calder would never measure up . . . charm and wit, however, Calder brought more to the table. But I despised Calder! Just as I despised Gabriel! Calder had held me, craved me, and wanted me. In the end I was hurt beyond repair. Gabriel would use me the same; he wanted my knowledge and nothing more. I saw it in the way he looked at Fenella and the way he looked at me. She gave him something he did not want from me. No, she gave him something he did not need from me. That was where she and I differed. I could not compete with her, not sexually at least.

"I kept your food warm for you." His voice, the voice that touched me, drew me out of my thoughts as the fire crackled between us.

"I'm not hungry," I said bitterly. In truth I was starving. My stomach ached for something to fill it, but I did not want *his* food.

"Shut up and eat it." He wasn't fooled. "I can hear your stomach from all the way over here." Like a cat stretching after a nap, he stood up and scooped the food into a bowl. He then walked it over to me and placed it in my hands. "Eat all of it. You're going to need your strength."

I rolled me eyes. "And to think I believed you had dismissed me for your whore. It seems I've moved up in the ranks?"

"Dismissed? Never." I looked up and our eyes connected. Something deep within me changed as he looked at—no, as he looked *in* me. "My mind has been scarred by you since I found you in the woods o' so many years ago. It is physically impossible to forget you. No matter how hard I use to try."

I swallowed hard, my throat working. "Is that so?" I was surprised my words were audible.

He stood and stretched, showing off his abs. "Besides, a whore is easier to dismiss than you are." My insides warmed at the compliment. "But a whore is much easier to come by and therefore more desirable in that aspect." He sat back down and then warmed his hands over the fire just as I had done. "There is nothing more satisfying than that of a sweet cunny after a long day of work." My heart froze over almost immediately.

And there you have it. Proof that all that my memory possessed was nothing more than a cunny to be used and then discarded.

Snatching up the bowl I threw it into the flames and began to storm off away from him.

"Where are you going?" His tone changed from friendly to firm.

"Away from you!" I threw off the shawl, hating his smell! "I do not wish to be in your presence any longer!"

"Come back!"

I turned quickly and snapped, "Do not sit here and unsex me as if I were a comrade out in the field! I am a woman too, and I do not desire to know what satisfies you, especially when it is of no relevance!" I continued, storming off, memorizing the dumbfounded look on his face.

"Arianna!"

"Go away, prick!" I threw over my shoulder as I headed away from him. He didn't come after me, which I was thankful for. As I went deeper into the sleepy camp, I realized I had nowhere to sleep. My anger had so easily swallowed me that I didn't even consider where my sleeping quarters would be.

Suddenly, an o' so familiar voice caught my ear.

"Trouble in paradise?" Moira chuckled, lounging outside of her tent.

I sighed, defeated. "Somebody stole my goat."

She laughed, a real deep one, and came over and slapped me on the back. "You can bunk with me, stupid girl." Smiling, I followed her into her tent. It was large for just one person. There was a straw cot off to the side and a rug on the ground. "You can sleep here"—she pointed at the rug—"until I can get you something better."

"Thank you." I meant it. Her razor-sharp smile signified our friendship as she tossed me a blanket and a handful of straw to use as a pillow.

"Get some sleep, silly girl." She yawned loudly. "We got loads to do upon the morrow. I don't take kindly to freeloaders."

"Duly noted."

"O', and another thing," she said just as I was about to settle comfortably into sleep, "you got to quit storming off whenever he hits a nerve. You're opening up the door for Fenella every time you do that."

I rolled me eyes, although she couldn't see it. "You speak as though this were some real competition with an actual victor in the end."

She laughed. "Love is like war, stupid girl. There are winners and losers. And when all the participants make that trip to heaven or hell, well, let's just say the winner always has a better story to tell the angels."

CHAPTER 25

THE FOLLOWING MORNING I EMERGED rejuvenated. My mind and body settled into its own bit of comfort. Moira had been right—I did need to stop storming off. It was petty and undesirable. Whether or not I wanted to be desired was a whole other matter in itself. However, I did have a mission. We all did.

The sun shone bright in the porcelain blue sky. A few gray clouds casted their shadows onto the camp as I made my way toward the rebels. Unlike the organized refugee camp, the rebels' camp was comparable to a village after a raid. Many of them didn't have the patience to make their own tents so they lay on the ground and slept. The tents that were standing looked just as ravaged as the men they sheltered.

Isaac and Guryon tipped their brow to me as I left the commune and marched through the rebels' camp. Most of the men were awake and preparing for the day. I was comforted by the fact that I recognized many of their faces and names.

"Good morning, Aurora." Axel smiled, coming up beside me. I rolled my eyes at his dig and greeted him accordingly. "I was surprised to see that you weren't sleepin' with us. But then again, Captain probably wouldn't have allowed it. He wants you all to himself."

"Is that so?" At that moment I saw Gabriel walking and talking with Ezekiel. As usual the sight of him captured me and warmed my insides. "I am no one's to keep. I favor the man that favors me."

Axel chuckled at that, eyeing me up and down. "You must have many . . . friends then. I have enjoyed a lot of time in the brothel, and never have I seen a woman more taunting. You are a forbidden fruit, Arianna."

"Why is that?"

"You are woman untouched, in a sense. A man cannot convince you into his bed. Not if he wishes to live."

"Very true."

"However, that won't stop them from trying. Especially when a prize, such as yourself, is so sweet."

"I've slaughtered many egos. It wouldn't be my first time crushing dreams. Though men aren't as easily broken, I believe myself capable of doing the job." Oddly I was enjoying myself with Axel. He was shorter than the other rebels. His dark skin tightened around a mound of muscles and did little to hide the scars on his arms. His playful brown eyes put a smile on my face as he eyed me.

"You want to truly break a man?" Axel said just as Gabriel and Ezekiel made their way over to us. "Show him something he can't have." He winked, eyeing me suggestively.

"Axel." Gabriel's commanding voice ended our conversation. "You and Ace need to join the scouts. Check the perimeter and report back at high noon."

"Yes, sir." Axel nodded. Using his two fingers, he whistled an unpleasantly high-pitched tone. A moment later Ace appeared in the sky, circling overhead. "I shall return." And then he was gone, heading toward the forest with Ace following up above.

"Did you rest well?" Ezekiel asked, scratching his rust-colored beard.

"Well enough." I nodded. "What is the plan for today?"

"An enemy camp was discovered a few miles west. The Captain and I were considering attack strategies."

"I attacked the camp at night."

"The camp you attacked was near a beach. Meaning that when they ran there was nowhere for them to go. This camp isn't located near any natural barriers. If we come at them, as you did, they would have ample opportunity to escape. If they are smart they've probably mapped out plenty of escape routes."

"So why not infiltrate and discover the escape routes and clog them with men when we attack?"

Both of them looked at me as if they had not expected me to be so wise. But the ever-pessimist Gabriel shot down my idea. "They've been stationed there for weeks. No new captures which means—"

"They know all who is present, and any new intruder would be noted, duly so."

Ezekiel chuckled and Gabriel replied, "Yes, that is correct."

"What are they surrounded by? Forest?" I asked, beginning to form a plan.

"We believe so. No rivers or bodies of water have been mapped nearby," Ezekiel replied. "What are you thinking?" My face must've given it away that I was deep in thought.

"Let's gather the others before we form this master plan of yours, Ari," Gabriel interjected, clearly annoyed that we had cut him out of the conversation. "The scouts will be returning in a few hours, and we will see what they have to say."

By the time the scouts returned, the sun had changed from a dull yellow to a sulky orange as it began its descent. Many of the refugees were doing their laundry while the rebels added clothes to the pile and sharpened their swords.

To occupy myself I helped Moira repair tents for some of the families. Once we finished with that we spent some time with the young ones. Although I would give anything to save the children of Islocia, I never quite had an interest in being in their presence. To me, children were bothersome when in close proximity. I understood their importance to societies and their lasting effects when my generation passes, but I did not necessarily desire them.

That was until I met Moira. She was a natural with the small, boney, gooey little people. Their eyes lit up like stars whenever Moira would grace them with her presence. They would clamor and reach just to hold her hand or wrap their frail arms around her own small waist. She loved them, and they loved her.

I, on the other hand, did my best to present a smile that was suitable for children. They didn't exactly flock to me as they did Moira. But they didn't fear me either. Especially one little girl. Her name was Karuli. She was the same little girl who had given me the flower out of her hair. Moira informed me that she was deaf and spoke very little. She communicated through frantic hand movements and grunting. A part of me, the very small and selfish part, liked that she couldn't hear. It means that although life could destroy her, she could just close her eyes and the pain would disappear. She could escape.

Little Karuli enjoyed being around me, and I began to enjoy her company as well. She didn't talk much but was demanding all the same. Making toys for the children was a pastime that the women refugees divulged in quite often. Therefore, when Moira and I were visiting the children some of their mothers taught me how to make the little straw dolls for the girls. When I was working on Karuli's, she made it clear, as she constantly looked over my shoulder to check my work, that I should finish it in a timely fashion. Whenever I did something wrong, she whined and pointed at the parts that I needed to correct.

"Patience, little girl," I cooed, tightening the tie around the doll's head. She responded by yanking on my arm and pointing at the doll's face. The doll had no face. "I don't know what it is you want me to do about it." The small girl with the coconut-shaped head went over to her mother, and her mother handed her some colored kernels. Peering at me with her dark eyes, she held up the kernels and picked out the eyes, nose, and mouth for the doll. "O', I see. You want your doll to see and smell and taste." She picked out two more pieces and pointed to the sides of the doll's head and then pointed to her ears. "You want her to have ears?" She nodded, her smile showcasing her missing front teeth. "You want her to be able to hear?" She did not look me in the eye when I spoke to her. Instead the clever girl read my lips and responded accordingly. This time she nodded again. But I shook my head. "She doesn't need to hear to be complete. She is beautiful just as she is." She didn't like that answer and adamantly shoved the kernels in my hand and pointed to the doll's head again. "Alright then, I guess I will put the ears in. Even though I think she doesn't need them." She beamed at me as I placed the kernels where she wanted. I chuckled at her excitement. "Go show your mom what you made." She quickly snatched the doll from my hands and scurried, as fast as her stubby legs would take her, back to her mother. I smiled after her. She reminded me so much of my little Teta. It tore me to shreds that I neglected to bond with Teta like I had with Karuli.

Behind me someone cleared their throat. Startled, I turned to see who it was who had found time to observe me during my moment of vulnerability. It was, of course, Gabriel gazing down at me. From his relaxed look, it seemed as though he had been there for a little while.

How much had he seen? Heard? "The scouts have returned. Would you like to join us?"

I nodded and stood, dusting my knees off. "Let's go." He gave me a curt nod before allowing me to lead the way back to the rebel camp. He was silent the whole walk back to their meeting hut. When we entered, it was a bit cramped. Isaac and Guryon glued themselves to the outer rim of the wooden hut, but their bodies still took up a lot of space. Other members of the rebels, who were all larger than the average man, squeezed tightly together with little space in between. Bacchus was near the center with Ezekiel, and Gabriel soon joined them. I put myself near the front, not daring to even come near Bacchus. I hadn't seen him since after our a little altercation the day before. I couldn't even meet his gaze, though occasionally I felt his burn through my face. Moira and Colleen joined us a moment later. They came to stand near me.

Ezekiel stood up to speak; the meeting had begun. "As you have all heard there has been another sighting of an enemy camp." The crowd grumbled. "Our scouts have told us that the enemy is located deep within the Iclin Forest. There are no natural boundaries or bodies of water surrounding them for miles. Unfortunately for us it means that there is no cornering them. Now what we could do is hit them when they leave for another raid."

"That's a lot of wasted man hours that could be going towards something more pressing," one of the rebels stated.

Ezekiel nodded. "It might be our best option."

Gabriel spoke then, dazzling me with his power and control over his "subjects." They revered him in a way that baffled me. I too fell victim when under his gaze. "So far it is our only option that will cause the least casualties. I want each of you to return home at the end of the day. That's the most important thing to me." They all murmured in agreement.

"This plan is shit," I muttered to Moira. Both she and Colleen turned to look at me.

"Well then, what you suggest then? Anythin' better?" Colleen questioned.

"Perhaps"—I thought plaintively to myself—"when I attacked a guards' camp I did it at night."

"So?" she inquired.

I mulled for a moment. "What if we did the same thing? Caught them by surprise?"

She scoffed doubtfully. "You heard the cap'n. They ain't got no borders surroudin' dem."

"Why not create one?"

"Arianna," Gabriel barked, turning my attention back to him. "Do you have something to add?"

Every eye in the room turned to look at me. For a moment my throat ran dry, but good ole Moira was there to nudge me back into reality. I cleared my throat. "I think I may have a plan."

"Go on," he replied, waiting.

I nodded. "When I attacked a guards' camp I did it at night. It was an impulse decision when I did it. I didn't take the time to observe the land or any barriers nearby. Nighttime was better for me because it was easier to move through the brush and not be seen. Plus, all of the guards were nearly asleep, with a few men on lookout. Getting rid of them was easy enough. The others were incoherent with drink and sleep.

"When I realized that there were children there I had the older ones help me. We went at the camp from the outside. I had the children circle the entire camp and light these barrels that would explode and catch their huts on fire."

"We can't infiltrate," Gabriel replied.

"I know, but in a sense we created a barrier that the guards couldn't pass through. We didn't need a mountain or a river to help us—we did it ourselves. Why not apply the same thing?"

"I see where she's going with this," Ezekiel added. "We can circle the camp entirely."

"Yes, but I think it should be done in layers. The first layer would be on the attack while the other layer wouldn't allow any of the escapees to flee," I concluded.

"That's a lot of men to be using at one time. We need some to stay here and guard our perimeter," Bacchus chimed pessimistically.

"The outer ring would just have to have wide spaces in between you guys," I corrected, shooting him a death glare. "The first ring would get as close to the camp as possible without being seen. The others would stay back far enough out of sight that if need be they can retreat or come save us. It's ingenious!"

The room was silent for a moment until soft murmurs allowed realization to settle in. Gabriel himself looked thoughtful as he considered it. "What if we wanted to go in on horseback instead of on foot?"

I thought for a moment. "We could have three layers." Bacchus scoffed loudly. Clearly he wasn't as impressed with my plan as I was. "At most we will need thirty men."

"Thirty of our fifty!" Bacchus argued.

"That leaves twenty to protect the camp!" I countered. "That is plenty. In fact, knowing that the number that will be remaining idle will be that big, why not make it forty!"

"Unlike you, princess, I do not condone the loss of brethren," Bacchus replied between clenched teeth.

The room fell silent for a moment before anyone interjected. Then Ezekiel turned to Gabriel. "It's your call, Captain."

Gabriel thought for a moment, clearly conflicted. He did not want to appear weak by taking the advice of a lesser sex. However, he didn't want the guards' camp existing as much as I did. My plan would work. If everyone was on board.

"I believe this plan may work." My insides tightened and released with renewed respect for this man. His gaze held me as he stared into me. I didn't want him to let me go.

"Bullshit," Bacchus cussed, slamming his fist. "Captain, thirty men to take down one camp? It's unheard of! We've done it with eight!"

"Yes, but we also lost three good men doing it that way. And those camps were much smaller, mind you," Ezekiel pointed out. "I recall you nearly losing your life as well."

"Perhaps we should do it with less men. Bacchus is right. Thirty is too many. We shall do it with . . . ten."

"Ten!" I began to argue, but Moira grabbed my arm, and I reined in my temper. "Gabriel, at least allow me fifteen men. No more, no less."

He turned to Axel and asked, "How many men did you observe at this camp?"

"Around fifty," Axel replied. "That's not counting their captures."

"Fifteen to fifty seems like pretty good odds to me," I muttered loud enough for them to hear. "If you put some men on horseback, it will heighten our chances. Plus the human barrier keeps them contained."

Gabriel continued to think as Bacchus remained doubtful. "Do you believe they will leave their camp unguarded?"

"At night it will certainly be easier to weaken their defenses," I retorted.

He laughed sardonically. "Not only are we using most of our men—"

"It's not even half!"

"Yet you want us to attack at night? Blimey!" He threw up his hands. "Would you rather us do it blindfolded with our hands tied behind our backs too?"

I rolled my eyes. "I'll be sure to find a torch just for you. I'd hate for you to take fright."

"Kiss my ass," he growled.

"Enough, both of you." The hut radiated with Gabriel's deep, sturdy voice. "I've made my decision. We will attack with fifteen men an hour after the sun has set completely. However, the outer layer won't be seven men just standing around with a sword while fifty men come at them. Instead we will have seven archers in the trees. The archers will be very close by, not a hundred yards out. Once the attack has begun they may be able to join us. The other four will be on horseback. The four that are on foot will partner with a rider. One will be a rider while the other is a passenger. Once the four on foot breach the camp, the men on horseback will come in to help. The archers will be in the trees assisting as well. The plan will be to condense the guards into the center of the camp while we move in and slaughter them from the outside in!"

"Brilliant!" Ezekiel stated excitedly. "That may actually work!"

"It will work," I assured them. "I know it."

"What do you say, boys? Are you ready for this ride?" Ezekiel shouted, thrusting his fist in the air. The rebels exclaimed and joined him in shouting their allegiance. Moira patted me on the shoulder—job well done. Ezekiel winked at me, and Gabriel and I shared a little smile of triumph. He reached his hand out to me then, and I confidently went to him. He pulled me close, his hands resting on my hip, and spoke in my ear over the yelling. He said, "Ride with me tonight."

I pulled back far enough to look up into his eyes. "Are you sure that I'm not going to kill you?"

He shrugged playfully. "I guess we will just have to wait and see."

* * *

Crouched deep on the forest floor, sheltered by the midnight sky, the roots that covered the ground edged themselves into my side as I lay still. Forest critters scurried all around us, creating their own rhythm of movement and sound. The trees above and around us sang their earthly tune as the archers took their places among them.

We had been camouflaged much longer than originally planned. It seems that the guards were oddly more celebratory. The wine hadn't stopped until well after the sun had disappeared and the moon hung high in the sky. One of the scouts overheard the guards talking and reported that the queen, the selfish witch she is, had captured a rebel camp and hanged all of its villagers. The children went first . . .

Sucking in my breath, I pushed the thought out of my mind. I had a mission to focus on.

Suddenly an arrow soared overhead and pierced the remaining guard that had been on lookout. That was our signal to advance.

On foot it was I, Guryon, and the twins, Hollis and Gabel. The riders were Ezekiel, Isaac, Bacchus, and Gabriel. Their job was to advance once we began the fight. Until then they stayed back with the archers, guarding our border. My team was crouched on the ground, waiting for the signal Axel had presented to us. It was time to advance.

Mimicking the whistle of a bird, I called to my team. We were all evenly spaced out around the camp on all sides. The guards had constructed their camp into a circle. During the day it made sense—it was easy to see an attack. However, for us, it was perfect. The plan would work astonishingly.

Raising my head I was able to see that we weren't very far from their huts. Whistling again, we began crawling forward. Our bodies were controlled, our sounds unremarkable. The closest to me was Guryon. Against my wishes Gabriel had made him my own personal guard, in a sense. He was meant to watch over me when Gabriel could not. Looking over at Guryon, I didn't quite mind his presence.

Having someone of his size fighting beside me drastically increased my odds for survival.

Continuing to crawl, we finally reached the huts. I crouched down; plastering myself to the wall. I waited until I heard the sounds of their snoring before I caught the reflection of the moon on my dagger, signaling to the archers that all was clear. Once Axel received my signal, he mimicked my whistle and the archers got their arrows ready. The riders would be moving in soon as well.

Calming my breathing, I took several deep breaths, gripping my daggers tightly. Looking to my left I saw Guryon staring at me. His nod told me that we were all in place and everything was ready. I was ready.

Soaring to my feet I charged into their camp. One guard who was sleepily wandering about spotted me. "Hey!" he shouted, coming at me. Quickly I tore a dagger from my waistband and silenced him. Before he hit the ground, another guard appeared from him his hut. "Intruder!" I silenced him as well, but unfortunately his comrades were already aware of my presence. It had begun.

Funneling out their huts in their drunken stupor, swords waving, they charged me. The first one that reached me swung high; I dipped below his swing and shoved a dagger into his throat. A guard I hadn't seen came up behind me and wrapped his hands around my throat, causing me to drop my dagger. I gasped for breath, noting that the other guards were nearing. Acting fast, I took my elbow and plowed it into his gut. He released me and gave me enough time to turn and crack him across the face. He was down in less than a second. Looking over into the trees, I screamed, "Now!"

Just as the guards came to swarm around me, all hell broke loose. Arrows began zipping through the air, causing the guards to fall. My team charged out of the darkness and began storming the huts.

Another guard tried to grab me, but I caught his hand, twisted, and shattered his wrist with a quick snap of my hands. His cry of pain was drowned out as I drew my dagger and plunged it into his eye. His blood squirted onto my body as I kicked his body to the ground.

Turning, I saw Hollis and Gabel tag teaming a guard. They ripped him to shreds in a matter of seconds. Unfortunately they hadn't seen the two guards coming up directly behind them. I ran over to them, flipping over a fallen guard. I pulled two daggers from my band and threw them at the guards. Quickly, within a blink of an eye, the guards had fallen. The daggers had drilled into their backs, shredding their lungs. Triumphant, I went to turn around and begin looking for the captures, but I was met with a fierce punch to the face. My world spun as I crashed to the ground, hard. Coughing, I tried to stand but he kicked me down. I heard the cry of a sword as the guard stood over me.

"Ready to meet your maker, sweetheart?" the ghastly guard hissed as he held his sword, execution style. As I rolled over to look up at him, a sudden wave of shadows surrounded the guard. I cracked a smile. Confused, he paused for a minute.

"No, I'm not ready yet, but I hope you are," I taunted as the guard turned to see Guryon's massiveness standing behind him. The guard shook in fright as Guryon reached down, grabbed the guard by his throat, and squeezed until he was no more. Not satisfied with that, he picked the guard up, turned, and threw his limp body at four guards heading our direction. They too fell to the ground.

"Thanks," I said as he reached his hand down to help me to my feet. He nodded, and both of us went to help out the others.

Dodging fallen guards and the archers' arrows, we made our way to the rest of our team. It took us a moment longer than expected to find them. Apparently the guards were smarter than I gave them credit for. To avoid the arrows of the archers they lit the roofs of their huts on fire. Thick, heavy black smoke suffocated us, clouding our vision and the sky, as we fought our way through the frenzy. Guryon watched my rear as I kept my eyes forward.

Suddenly, an earsplitting cry of pain pierced the sky. The sound was so horrendous that even Guryon took notice. We recognized the voice.

Charging through the curtain of smoke, we found Hollis and Gabel cornered near a hut. Six guards surrounded them, the smoke sheltering them from the archers. Taking in the situation, I saw where the sound had come from. Hollis lay wounded on the ground with his brother cradling his head. A sword was plunged deep into Hollis's left shoulder, blood spewing. Gabel held a dagger out in defense as the guards advanced.

All of a sudden, Guryon grunted loudly, stumbling forward. When I looked to see what had happened, I saw three guards coming up at us. One had cut Guryon along his back, blood draping his rear. As if Guryon hadn't totally processed the pain, he stepped forward just as that same guard began to swing. With his bare hands he caught the sword! The force of the blade cut deep into his hands as he began to squeeze it, tearing into the guard with his fierce gaze. The guard tried to follow through with his attack, but Guryon was strong, stronger than any man I had ever seen! His muscles bunched tightly in his arms, mirroring a mountain during a harsh winter storm. Gritting his teeth, Guryon pulled the sword out of the guard's hand and tipped it to me. I deftly caught the handle and began my assault. The first guard was easy enough; he fell with a single swipe. But the others came quick and with no hesitation. I did my best to hold them off, but there were too many! More men came! The archers were blinded by the smoke, so much so that they were little assistance as Guryon and I fought the guards.

Then . . .

As the earth began to rumble beneath our feet and trumpets sounded in the heavens, our salvation came.

The cavalry had arrived!

Charging through the dense smoke, sweat glistening off his body, Gabriel appeared on a white horse, his sword in one hand while he held onto the mane with the other. His eyes, hollow black spheres, were searing as he took control of the situation. "Attack!" he cried, and the others followed.

Ecstatic, I drove my sword into a guard's chest. Choking on blood, he sank to the ground as I yanked the sword from his chest. "Guryon! Go get Hollis and Gabel." Guryon nodded and plowed through three guards that attempted to stop him. He crushed them to the ground in one quick movement.

"Hop on!" The neighing of a horse turned my attention back to Gabriel after he was done slaughtering the remaining guards that had surrounded us. Reaching his hand down to me, he pulled me up onto his horse. Gripping the horse with my knees and wrapping my arms around his muscular body, I held on tight as he kicked it into gear. "What's happened?"

"Hollis and Guryon are injured. I sent him to retrieve Hollis and Gabel. The last I saw of them they were cornered. We need you guys," I replied just as a guard popped out of the smoke and attempted to knock us down. But Gabriel was one step ahead of him. Pulling tightly on the horse's mane, Gabriel commanded the horse to stop. The guard was coming too fast to realize we were no longer in his path; however, he was now in clear view of another archer.

"You guys held them off long enough for us to find their captures. Now that they're safe we're trying to file the guards into the middle of the camp," he replied, urging his horse to run again.

"How can you get them to the middle of the camp with all this smoke?" Looking ahead I watched as Ezekiel rode by with a handful of guards following behind him. He led them out of the smoke and in clear view of archers. They dropped like flies as arrows rained from the sky. "We need to get them to follow us out into the open." Ezekiel joined us then, galloping beside us.

"Hollis and Gabel need help—go find them," Gabriel ordered.

Just as Ezekiel was about to run off, I shouted, "No, wait!" Two guards came at us head-on. Ezekiel and Gabriel saw them coming and drew their swords. Running at them at full speed they swung hard, colliding messily with their bodies. The combination of speed and strength made it easy for the swords to slice the guards completely in half! Their blood splattered onto my arms and face. I was dripping with it by the time their bodies folded to the ground.

Ezekiel and Gabriel circled their horses so that they were side by side again.

"Ezekiel!" I shouted as they continued slaughtering more guards. "When you get Hollis and Gabel, tell Guryon to get out of sight. You need to be the distraction and get the guards to follow you."

"Follow where?" he asked, pulling back on the horse's mane as we neared the end of the camp. Looking at all of the burning huts, as smoke filed into the air, I thought for a moment as Gabriel pulled up beside him. No guards had made it far enough to come this far out. They all were fighting in the smoke.

"Is there a hut they didn't burn? Where does the smoke break?" I asked, eyeing all of the burning huts.

"Where we found the captures—at the opposite side of the camp. No one had burned it," Gabriel replied, looking in that direction.

"Captain"—Bacchus trotted up beside us, wearing his own display of kills with the blood of fallen guards—"we're too heavily outnumbered. The archers can't help us with all the smoke!" He coughed soot onto his arm.

"I have an idea," I said, looking at all of them. "But it's going to take all of us."

"Hurry up and spit it out! I don't want my men dying tonight!" Bacchus barked, wiping blood from his forehead.

"We each were paired with a rider, right? Isaac with Guryon, Ezekiel with Hollis, Bacchus with Gabel, and me with Gabriel. We need to retrieve them, yank them up from whatever they're in, and ride out towards the opposite end of the camp. The guards are sure to follow us. By the time they clear the smoke, the archers will be able to see them." They all seemed to understand, but I had to wait for Gabriel's okay.

He nodded. "Do it, now!" Ezekiel and Bacchus raced to find Isaac and inform him of the plan. Gabriel and I surged forward to implement the plan. His horse soared over dozens of dead guards without ever checking its stride. Flames raged around us, fighting to capture and consume us. Sweat poured from my body as I did my best to hold onto Gabriel. His tough skin was slick with perspiration as he steered his steed gallantly.

"Over there!" I shouted, pointing to where Hollis and Gabel were. All of a sudden, a loud explosion erupted around us, tossing us from the horse. The frightened horse panicked, bucking and kicking around us. I plummeted to the ground, my nose landing on a stone. I rolled a few feet before the dust settled. I was too dazed to see where Gabriel had gone, but over the ringing in my ears, I heard the guards coming our way. Rolling to my stomach, I prepared to push myself up off the ground when suddenly I was thrust onto my feet. "I've got you," Gabriel assured me as he pushed me up onto the now-quieted horse. He followed after me, returning to his original position, and kicked the horse, causing her to surge forward.

When I looked to see whether Hollis had made it, I noticed Ezekiel, Bacchus, and Isaac fighting off a huddle of guards that had begun to surround them. Hollis was loaded up on Ezekiel's horse, Guryon had climbed upon Isaac's monstrous horse, and Gabel too had found his ride with Bacchus. The smoke shielded them from the archers' view as the remaining guards surrounded them. Thick numbers cornered them, their horses frantic.

"They're outnumbered!" I cried, trying to see if the archers were in sight. "We have to distract them."

"Way ahead of you!" Gabriel charged head on into the thick smoke right in our team's direction. Sword swinging, he struck a guard in the back. Hollering in pain the guard fell to the ground just as the others began to realize what was going on. As the huddle's attention wavered to us, Ezekiel, Isaac, and Bacchus made their escape. Once they were clear we soon followed.

Repositioning myself on the horse, I was able to see directly behind us. Gabriel was close on everyone's tail, but the guards weren't following behind us fast enough. They would figure out our plan and stay hidden in the smoke! Or worse, they would begin their own attack.

My nightmares came true. Bursting through the smoke a line of guards holding a new type of weapon aimed them at the trees. Several loud pops originated from the metal tubes. I heard cries of terror coming from the trees as branches and people crashed down to the forest floor.

We were running out of time . . .

"We're not going to make it!" I shouted to Gabriel.

"We don't have any other choice!" he replied, continuing to follow behind the others.

He was wrong. We did have another choice. We needed another diversion.

"I've got this," I said, scooting to the far end of the horse, balancing myself by squeezing tightly with my knees.

"Ari, don't do anything stupid!" he warned just as we too cleared the smoke and began to see the forest. Looking back I saw the guards refilling the tubes and aiming them again. We only had seven archers—we needed them. We couldn't lose any more.

"I have to do this. It's the only way we make it out alive," I replied, preparing myself for what was about to happen. Taking several deep breaths I closed my eyes and held a dagger in my hand. "Just promise you'll come back for me this time."

I decided not to allow him to answer. I knew he would only divert me from my plan, a plan that would save all of our lives.

I jumped from the horse.

Flying through the dense black smoke, I tucked the dagger into my chest and bowed my head forward. When I hit the ground I didn't want to waste any time surging to my feet. I would need every millisecond to pull this off.

As my body made contact with the ground, I somersaulted several times, preparing to time my move perfectly.

Using my momentum as I rolled, I pushed off of my feet, causing me to go back into the air. High above the closest guard, with the dagger pointed at him, gravity took over.

My dagger . . . his face.

I crashed into him, knocking him to the ground. Not wasting any time, I dug the dagger into his eye socket, blood squirting all over me. As the other guards registered what was happening I began my assault. First I took out the guards with the metal tubes. Their reload time took too long, giving me ample time finish them off.

On all sides I was quickly surrounded. All of the guards began reaching for me, but I wouldn't let them defeat me. I was too skilled, too determined. It was not my night to die.

My limbs moved quickly as I took out as many guards as I could. It was all happening so fast, it was unbelievable. They were no match for me.

From behind me a guard was able to punch me across the back of the head. As I went to finish him I noticed a beautiful sight in front of me. I could see Axel in the trees.

Using the back of my head, I head-butted the guard behind me, dropping him to the ground, and then I ran toward the tree. The smoke hadn't reached this part of the camp yet. There was finally a clearing.

"Axel!" I screamed, thrusting my fist into the air. The guards had taken advantage of my moment of weakness and wrestled me to the ground. I clawed, bit, scratched, and spit at them. One by one they piled on top of me. "Ahhh!" The weight was almost too much. My lungs felt crushed; my body felt as though it would pop. I gasped for breath, struggling to force the guards off of me. Using all of the strength I had I held their weight as one guard lay completely over me. He tried to strangle me, but I urged his hands away from me. I will not be defeated. I will not be defeated. Screaming at the top of my lungs I shoved the guard off of me. The weightlessness was nearly intoxicating. My arms and legs were free.

He rolled a couple feet away from me before stopping himself. The determination in his eyes was prominent as he rose to his feet. He too didn't want to be defeated; he too would not go down without a fight. Luckily, I was not alone.

Just as he was about to come at me again, a swift arrow pierced straight through his neck. Thick red blood clogged his windpipe as he struggled for breath before falling to the ground.

All around me I heard the sounds of arrows charging through the sky and killing the remaining guards, one by one. I stood stock-still. Arrows swarmed around me, death embraced me, but I did not fall. Covered in blood and sweat I stood tall. Not to be defeated. I had won.

I had won.

The air around me grew silent as the last guard had finally fallen. Gasping. Pleading. Stretching for breath. A wave of his own blood silenced him, his eyes rolling to the back of his head. What a glorious sight. What a beautiful end.

Moments later Gabriel, Bacchus, Ezekiel, and Isaac rode up to me. Gabriel immediately jumped off of his horse and came to me. No, he rushed to me. Using both of his hands he grabbed my face; a smile, a real genuine smile, stretched across his face. "You crazy girl! You crazy stupid girl! You did it!"

Giggling, I wrapped my hands around his wrists. Looking up into his eyes I saw the old Gabriel. He was there, underneath his iron façade. He was waiting for me. "You came back for me."

"Always," he vowed, stroking his thumbs over my cheekbones. "I'm not letting you go again. No matter how many times you keep trying to run away from me."

I shrugged nonchalantly. "You know I like to keep things interesting."

At that he chuckled a hearty laugh, tossing his head back while pulling me into his chest.

Slowly, o' so very slowly, I melted into him. At that moment he captured me, surrounded me, owned me. I had given my life to him, and finally, after so many years, he was returning the favor.

Wine seemed to pour from the heavens as the rebels danced about. Victory was among us. A large feast was prepared for us when we returned. The refugees lined the entrance of the camp and praised us as we walked by, victorious! Gabriel carried the head of one of the guards and placed it prominently for all to see.

Amazingly the rebels had no casualties. Hollis, Guryon, and an archer named Tobias were the only ones to be seriously injured. Abigail was swift in tending to them so they would be able to join in the night's festivities.

Besides a wonderful meal, a large bonfire was presented to us. Women, the beautiful women of Sythos, danced for their heroes. The men were consumed in it, the sensual movement of their bodies. The curves of their breasts. I was positive nearly all of them would be flocking to the brothel soon after the party concluded. I was so overjoyed that I didn't care. I had finally won them over. They considered me a warrior now. I was theirs and they were mine. My courage on the battlefield had allowed them to be able to trust me. If I was willing to put my life on the line for them then they would do the same for me.

As the women concluded their dance, the children decided they wanted to show their gratitude. The small children pulled their favorite adults from the crowd and encouraged them to dance in front of the fire. It was comical to watch as some of the most uncoordinated warriors, such as Ezekiel, attempt to flow with the rhythm of the music. Beside me, Gabriel seemed to have found it funny as well.

All of a sudden little Karuli was scampering over to me. She reached her hand out impatiently, waiting for me to follow her. Nervously I shook my head, but it was too late. Moira had already seen me.

"Get on up there, stupid girl," she chided, winking at me. The crowd began to focus on me a little too much, so I did as I was told. Completely avoiding eye contact with Gabriel I made my way to the sky-high fire. Twirling Karuli, I laughed as she presented us all with dance moves of her own. The small child was beautiful in her movements, even as she guided me into the steps with the bet of the drums. I didn't know many dances; in fact I only knew the ones I was taught in the palace. Luckily I was a fast learner. I did not want Karuli getting upset with me.

As the drummers beat the bass and I felt the warmth of the colossal fire, I began to move fluidly with the music. Karuli was happy with my moves because then she added some more and continued to encourage me to follow. I did as I was told, wrapping my arms around myself and moving my hips to the beat. Tossing my hair back, I sank into the warmth of the fire and the festiveness of everyone's mood. For a moment, a small innocent moment in time, I was at peace. With these people, with this child, and with myself.

That was until I saw Fenella trotting over to Gabriel. Dressed in her most promiscuous outfit, a thin low-cut dress with a long slit that raced up to her hip, she began giving Gabriel his own little show. She gyrated her hips as seductively as she could, running her hands down her body, promising that she was available only to him.

I decided to stop trying to end their little shag. If Gabriel wanted her then so be it. I will respect that. He had finally accepted me into this camp; I would be stupid to ruin it over something so juvenile.

Turning away from him, I continued my dance. The flames licked greedily around me as I flowed, like water, with the music. Closing my eyes I spun around, weightless, smiling my joy. Applause erupted around me. I would have stopped dancing, but my feet wouldn't let me—I was at one with the dance. Besides, Karuli wouldn't have let me stop anyways. Lucky for her I didn't want to.

Suddenly, just as I was about to step into the beat, I felt a warm pair of arms reach around my waist. At first I was startled, but then I realized I was not in danger. I was with my people, people who would sell their souls for me. I was safe with them.

Opening my eyes, I was surprised to see Gabriel standing over me. His arms tightened around my waist as he pulled me closer into him. I took a deep breath, inhaling his masculine scent. His presence crushed me to him, causing me to reach out and stroke my hands down his back. The muscles in his back quivered at my touch. I chuckled softly as he held me close.

"Finished with your dance?" I muttered loud enough for only him to hear.

"No, I'm just simply starting a new one." His voice flowed down the length of my body, leaving a trail of flames behind. He spoke into my ear, his large body unbelievably close to mine. Looking over his shoulder I saw the sour face of Fenella sitting off to the side. Clearly, Gabriel had chosen a new partner. I couldn't help but smile at that.

As the night wore on and Gabriel continued to hold me in his arms, I finally realized what it was that made all the bullshit worth it. It's that moment, that one moment, when you can finally let everything go and just be yourself. When the world spins so fast that you stop taking the time to note its flaws. That was that night. The wine flowed freely, the people sang loudly, and my family slept safely for another night.

I was home, finally home at last.

CHAPTER 26

DAYS SWARMED BY, LEAVING BEHIND memories I swore to never forget. I settled nicely into Sythos. No longer feeling like an outsider, I began to make connections with the people, so much so that I started calling some of the refugees by their first names.

When I lived with the Qingkowuats I never truly took the time to get to know many of the villagers. They believed it was because I was some heartless monster whose only purpose was killing. And for a while I believed that to be true. But thinking back I realized it was because I was afraid of losing the ones I promised myself to. I was scared of defeat. When I guarded them I was all alone; no one was there to help me. If I failed them . . . when I failed them . . . it was my fault. I could blame no one but myself. I figured I'd be avoiding a world of hurt if I didn't even bother to remember their names. I've never regretted anything more.

Moira and I made daily visits to see the children. The more I went to see them, the more they began to like me. Whenever I went to see them they greet me as they do Moira, their boney little arms wrapped tightly around me, begging me never to leave them. Never to fail them. I promised I wouldn't.

Gabriel and I spent a lot of time with each other. Ever since that night at the bonfire he seemed to have gravitated towards me. Most often I found him watching me, his eyes soft. He no longer paid Fenella any attention, which she wasn't too fond of. Her temper tantrums were common nowadays. The refugees and the rebels were becoming tiresome of her. The woman who once had the Captain's favor was definitively downgraded to nothing more than a common whore.

Because Gabriel had been giving me so much attention lately, the rebels felt compelled to treat me as their own. I spent more time with them than I did with the refugees most days. I enjoyed their company; I enjoyed learning about their pasts, however shattered. It was apparent that we were all the same. All from broken homes, all from gory pasts. I saw what made their bond with each other so strong. There were no individuals in this camp—they were all one.

One evening we were all sitting around a fire, sharing our pasts. Some of the refugees joined us, but mainly it was the rebels—Moira, Colleen, Abigail, and myself. We were comfortable with each other. Bacchus, of course, had yet to warm up to me, but he wasn't as callously hostile either. His story, his upbringing, allowed me the chance to understand why he was so uncomfortable with outsiders.

"I never knew my parents, but that didn't bother me none," he began, staring intensely into the fire. "My village used to settle near Mt. Grim Wall before the monarchs overtook it. My leaders were prestigious men who dabbled in the affairs of the wealthy. They lived in the palace, while we mined the mountains for precious minerals. In return they would be rewarded by the monarchs with kerts never presented to us. Many of the other Royals were jealous of my village and the minerals we guarded. Because of this we were attacked constantly. Our men fell every day. I was but a boy when I watched my friends bleed out before my very eyes.

"Our numbers were weakening. Had we been attacked a few more times someone else would have taken our whole village. That was when our leaders decided to train our men to fight. They took us at our youngest ages. I was drafted, due to my size.

"The training was brutal. They would beat us from sun up to sun down. There were no moments of peace for us, not even at the age of seven. The older men would attack us at random. Many of us died. Those who survived were forced to continue fighting. No mercy.

"In a matter of years, once I reached my age of maturity, I was molded into a being far beyond that of any emotion besides death and killing. So I thought." He took a sip from his cup. "Around the time Commodus took the throne, our village was nearly impenetrable. No one could defeat us.

"Then one day, a woman came staggering into the camp. It looked as though she had been attacked. Her clothes were torn. Her face was bruised and bloody. At the time I was in command, so I ordered my men to take her and get her cleaned up. The next day I went to see her, and she was beautiful. Her hair was the color of the sun, and her pale skin reminded me of the moon. I was entranced by her. She told me her name was Sheila. She was so small and seemed so fragile. I tried to get her to tell me where she was from, but her past haunted her. I didn't want to force her." Hissing, he crushed his wooden cup and threw it into the fire. "I allowed myself to trust her. I allowed her to enter my camp. She became my purpose, my main focus in life. I gave her my heart, and she gave herself to me. I believe I might've loved her. If there was ever such a thing." A long moment of silence followed as he continued staring into the fire. We all waited silently for him to continue. "One evening I awoke to the sound of rumbling. But before I could even open my eyes I felt a knife at my throat. I was well-trained. All I had to do was snap the wrist of whoever wanted to attack me. But as I opened my eyes I saw Sheila on top of me, smiling down at me. It was a trap. Apparently she had snuck off in the night and led some guards to our camp. She knew I wouldn't be able to kill her." He shot a look at Gabriel and then me. "She gave me this scar." He pointed to the one that raced down his face. "She left me bleeding as she and her guards slaughtered my entire village and took everything of value."

"That's when I found him," Ezekiel chimed in, noting Bacchus's unwillingness to finish his story. "My village was close by and heard the ruckus. He was the only survivor. Everyone else had perished. We took him in for a while until our own village was attacked. The queen stripped us of everything once she took the throne. She was a fire so destructive that her blaze has still left the earth smoldering."

"It wasn't long after that when I found them. A scout and I had just defeated some guards who were coming to destroy my village," Gabriel added. He looked over at me. My face must've told him that I didn't wish to discuss the events that caused him to leave me. "Soon after that we made Sythos. Finding anyone we could in the forest. Refugees, rebels. We needed numbers if we were ever going to have a chance at survival."

"I was lucky when the Captain found me," Abigail replied, toying with her hair. "My village was a peaceful one. I was happy with a husband and four children. We were simple farmers, with nothing much to offer anyone in this world. But we were happy. That was until the Royal Army stormed our village, claiming that we hadn't met a quota that had been doubled the week before." A tear slid down her face as she said, "They killed all the men the first time they came through. My husband was the first to go. I was broken. He was my everything. The next month they came back, and we barely reached the original quota. But apparently it had been doubled again." She wiped fiercely at her tears. "They killed our children. They didn't take them like they do now, no—they executed them one by one with a single swipe of a sword. My youngest, Arkia, was the last one . . . she cried for me and I could do nothing. I had failed my children. Blessed to be that of a woman . . . I had one job in this world. It was to raise to my children so that they would contribute to this world. I couldn't do it . . ."

Moira leaned over and wrapped her arms around Abigail. Then, Moira began to speak. "My village was destroyed early into Ophelia's reign. Me and a few survivors were stumbling about the forest for weeks on end until finally we found another village that would accept us. We lived amongst them quite happily. I was especially happy with *her*. Her name was Giana and she was perfect. Not as rugged and quick-tempered as I am. She was sweet and kind. Never had she said a bad word about anything. I loved her tenderly. And she loved me. It always pained me that I was not equipped enough to give her something she so truly desired. My Giana loved and wanted children, but she loved me more.

"Our village was sort of a refuge for children. Many villages understood that their children would be taken if their quotas weren't met, so they sent them to us. We were hidden deep within the Iclin Forest, so deep, in fact, that it was nearly impossible for us to be found. They thought their children would be safe with us . . ." Once Abigail had gained control of herself Moira released her. "Giana and I took care of the children. I too began to fall in love with them. They were like Giana, sweet and innocent. Pure." Moira continued, clearing her throat. "That was before the guards found us. We were caught totally by surprise. They stormed our village, destroying everything in its path. That was the first time I saw the queen. She was pale like snow with deep, blood-colored hair. Her smile was toxic as she watched her guards desecrate her own people!" I understood her rage. The queen was a vile woman who only thought about herself. She believed the world revolved around her. She believed she owned us all. "They killed my Giana for trying to protect the children. It was as if she wasn't human at all. They took a knife and cut her throat. They walked right over her body, like she was nothing. I could do nothing. They had me pinned to the ground with a knife to my back." She sighed, shaking her head. "In a matter of seconds I lost everything." Silence followed. "The queen is an interesting woman. Some may call her a murderer who slaughters everything in her path. But that's not true. She lets some people live, as if to implement fear in us all. They let me live. They let me live with nothing." The fire crackled loudly as we all realized our pasts weren't as different as we thought. We were all the same.

We all had a mission of our own.

* * *

"Are you alright?" Gabriel asked as I settled onto his furs. He was sitting across from me, eyeing me. After the bonfire, Gabriel had invited me back to his tent. I was not in the mood to argue so I obliged him. I said good night to the others and found myself comforted by Gabriel's presence.

"Why wouldn't I be?" I asked, sitting cross-legged.

"You didn't say much tonight," he said, absentmindedly toying with a loose thread on his pants. "I thought perhaps that the discussion would be comforting."

I shrugged. "I had nothing to say."

He shook his head and stood. Walking over to me, he took a seat right next to me. Involuntarily I scooted an inch or two away from him. He chuckled. "You're always so guarded, Ari." He sighed, melting me with his gaze. "Have you ever considered that that may be where your fault lies?"

"Are you suggesting I'm flawed?"

"Aren't we all?"

I chuckled. "You may be able to accept your limits. However, that will never be me."

He tilted his head back in a deep chuckle. "That ego of yours will kill us both, had it not yet."

Again I shrugged. "I always dreamed of a peaceful ending."

He laughed again. "Death by stupidity?"

"Is it so stupid to have faith in one's capabilities? Wouldn't it be admirable?"

He shook his head, smiling. "I'll admire you from here while you find your way through hell. It's not always admirable to be dead, especially when the fault lies with you, eh?" Stretching his massive arms he yawned before running his fingers through his short brown hair. Gabriel was tantalizing to say the least. His body was sculpted by gods, topped off with an impenetrable face that showcased his control and might. The deep blue of his irises seared me with every flicker in my direction. He had grown so much since the last I had seen him. Before, his body was leaner and thinner. Now he was perfect. Every crevice of his muscles was sharp in the shadows that played on his features. He had grown nicely into this body.

"Why must you continue assuming that I am so imperfect?" I asked, trying not to stare.

He shrugged. "Maybe because I want you to understand that imperfection, though it has its limitations, is okay. It leaves you room to grow."

"I was not born to accept defeat," I replied stoically. "It is not in my being."

"What were you born for then?" he asked, leaning forward. The muscles in his stomach tightened with the movement. Try as I might I didn't want to stare, but it was damn near impossible. He was riveting. And he knew it. "Like what you see?" Quickly, my face burning red, I turned away from him. He laughed at my childish response. "I am used to provoking women, but you, Ari, a woman such as you is a whole new accomplishment in itself."

Trying to hide a smile I asked, "And why is that?" It took everything I had not to become engulfed in his presence. His body was like rapids over boulders. Rough, dangerous, hypnotizing.

"Capturing the attention of a woman, with all her purities, is an astonishing reward." He was so close that our skin was touching. I was nearly burned from the sensation. His masculine musk saturated me. I was losing myself in him, yet I remained forever guarded.

Swallowing, my throat working, I replied, "Do not assume me so pure." I was surprised the words were audible. He was so close. My body wanted to lean into him, to be touched by him. I couldn't control my desire. A large part of me wanted to give in.

Sighing, he leaned away from me. I instantly felt cold without him so close to me. I turned to look at him and noticed his eyes were closed in thought. "I was wrong to believe you had been untouched."

Anger replaced my arousal. "I am not one of your whores, Gabriel! Do not assume anything near that misguided farce!" Just when I was about to get up and storm out, he grabbed my wrist. His crushing grip kept me anchored to my seat.

"Were you not the king's whore?" he snapped, crushing me with his grip. It seems I wasn't the only one who was angered by the subject of conversation.

"Were you not Fenella's?" I spit, trying to yank my wrist free from his grasp. He didn't let go. I was humbled by the idea that I was not his alone, but I was angered that he toyed with a double-edged sword yet he remained unscathed. Was I the only one meant to bleed or would he as well?

"She was an exercise I grew tired of. Had you not been disgraced you would have remained the king's for the rest of your days," he growled, opening his eyes. Ice had frozen over his earlier playful mood. "Understand the difference?"

"I am no one's to claim," I hissed, matching his fierce gaze. "Unhand me!"

He didn't let go.

I hated that he had mentioned my king. Memories of him flooded my mind, suffocating me. My heart ached for him. He was the first honest man I had ever had the pleasure of accompanying, but he was crudely taken away from me.

"Had he not died . . ." I swallowed past the lump in my throat. "I would indeed be by his side."

Frustrated, Gabriel released my wrist as if it had burned him. "I'd have killed the bastard myself had I known of you two."

Surging to my feet, fueled by rage, I cracked him across the face. Surprised, he stared at me for a moment before reaching to grab me, but I kicked him in his stomach. I would have kicked him again, but he caught my leg and pulled it to his chest. I lost my footing and fell to the ground.

Quickly he climbed on top of me and pinned me by my wrist. He laid his entire body on top of me, crushing me with his weight. I couldn't even wiggle free!

"Sorry, did I insult your master? The man whose cock found its home in you every night?" he growled, anger dripping off of his tense frame.

"You don't know of what you speak, Gabriel!" I screamed, trying to wiggle free.

"You were his whore!" he yelled back at me. "Admit it! Say it! You were his whore!"

As loud as I could, I screamed "No!" into his face. I couldn't understand how someone so enticing could ignite so much rage in such a small amount of time. One moment I craved him, the next I wished him dead. It was that barrier that kept us so haggardly divided.

"Then what were you to him? If not his harlot he could tend to at any time, eh?" Roughly he pulled my arms higher above my head. I was at his mercy.

"You know nothing!"

"I know what I've seen!"

"Seen?" I laughed hysterically. "Were you some mouse scurrying around in the palace? No? Then you've seen nothing! You know nothing!"

"I was there!"

"Where? Up my ass? Because that's where you seem to be lately." Not entirely true but I was angry. How dare he accuse me of something he had no knowledge of.

"Gods be damned, you stubborn girl!" he said behind clenched teeth. "I was there when the king was executed! Hidden deep within the crowd of your ever-so-loyal subjects. I saw how you reached for him. How you pleaded for his life. I saw how you looked at him when he held your hands. It was then that I knew you were his."

"How could you know such a thing?" I hissed mere inches away from his face. Breathing heavily he stared down at me. I could feel his heart pounding against my breasts. I could feel his breath gusting over my face. I felt every inch of him. Had it been my option I would have never allowed him to get so close. I knew of such dangers . . . Calder had taught me well. But Gabriel was a skilled hunter. When he was locked on his prey, he was not one to be easily deterred.

"You used to look at me like that." He broke eye contact with me, turning his head to look the other way. Rolling off of me, he stood and walked to the opposite side of his tent. "Many nights I longed for you to look at me like that again. When I saw you looking at the king like that, I thought I had lost you."

"Gabriel . . ."

He held up his hand. "Enough." Releasing a loud sigh, he turned back to me. "The past is the past. I will not fault you for a time that holds no relevance."

"I was not his whore," I whispered, staring at his dirt floor. Braving a look in his direction I saw how he softened when his anger diminished. "There was not an evening in which I lay in the same bed as the king. He was not mine to have. And that was not how I wanted him."

"Then why such devotion to a man with nothing to offer? Was it his wealth? His prestige?" he asked.

I shook my head. "No. It was nothing like that."

"Then what?"

Raking my fingers through my hair, I looked up at Gabriel and replied, my heart stuck in my throat, "All my life I had known no father, and never had I thought he would be in the form of a king."

A long stretch of silence coddled us as we looked across at each other. To me, it was a relief that he finally knew the truth about me and the king's relationship. It was another burden I had finally shed.

He cleared his throat to end the silence. "So if not the king, then who?" My confusion was evident because he clarified. "The king was not your lover, then who was?"

My first instinct was to ask him why it was any of his concern. But I knew why it was. Gabriel desired me, and I was beginning to desire him. No matter how hard I tried not to. The idea of another man claiming something he believed he owned was poison on the tongue to him. Just the thought burned him from the inside out. I could see it in the way he avoided eye contact with me whenever he mentioned another man lying in my bed.

I decided to give Gabriel a partial truth. "My Conqueror enjoyed me in the beginning. I had no control over myself . . . I was quite young. He made it clear that I was never mine to own, you know?" I watched Gabriel intently as I unraveled my past. I could see the anger beginning to boil inside him again.

"Who was this man?" he hissed, clenching his fist.

"He was the Conqueror," I replied, forcing myself not to remember his face. "I never knew his given name, and I do not know anything of my parents. All I know is that the Conqueror bought me when I was just a babe. There were child auctions quite frequently during the time of my birth. Men would buy or sell their sons and daughters into servitude for a high price. Apparently my parents took part in such a trade."

Trying to rein in his temper, he asked, "What did he . . . buy . . . you for?"

"At first I was just his to use when the mood struck him. He was sick with drink most nights and would often force me to drink as well. I don't remember much. The memories have turned into hazy, misplaced recollections I don't mind to forget. When he was not using me for his pleasure I was used as his weapon. He began molding me when I was eight." I thought for a moment. "After my flower bloomed he no longer desired me in that fashion and I was strictly used otherwise. You see, the Conqueror was quite wealthy, but he had made many enemies. He needed someone to guard his wealth, so he trained me. The training was . . . unimaginable." Clearing my throat I added, "I am not one to complain. I endure all that I can with as much composure as I can muster. So when I say that the Conqueror's training was unimaginable, believe that I was lucky I survived. But I did survive. And I was very good at what I did."

"Where is this man? No, he is not even a man! Having a child fight his battles!" Angrily he beat his own hand with his fist. "I'll kill him!"

Standing, I walked over to Gabriel. I understood that my past was difficult to comprehend, but it made me into who I am. And who I will forever be.

Ignoring my apprehension, I stepped close to him and cradled his face in my hands. His breathing quickened at my touch. "It seems I am not the only one with a temper." He glared at my casualness in which I relayed my past. I had learned to accept it years ago; I know that it was all new to him. "Do not fret over something that was out of your hands."

"You didn't even have a chance." He closed his eyes against the realization of my lost childhood. "I'll kill him. Tell me where he is. I will ride out tonight and return with his head upon the morrow!"

I smiled at his determination. It was comforting to know how deeply Gabriel truly cared for me. "I put a sword through his chest a little while before you had found me in the forest o' so long ago. He is forever gone, rotting in the deepest depths of hell."

The way Gabriel held me in his gaze, it moved something inside of me. His porcelain navy-blue eyes blanketed me. The feel of his stubble under my fingertips aroused me. The way his lips parted with every breath coated me. Everything inside me screamed to have more of him. My desire radiated off of me as my breathing quickened and my palms began to sweat. My throat ran dry, and I could not force myself to look away from him.

"I am sorry I hadn't found you sooner," he whispered, reaching his hand up to my face and stroking his thumb down my cheek. My entire body ignited into flames as he touched me. I wanted him to never stop. I wanted him to touch me in other places.

Involuntarily I licked my dry lips.

The corner of his mouth twitched as he watched my tongue slide over my lips. A slow hiss seeped from his throat. He wanted me. I wanted him.

At first I thought that I was imagining him leaning closer to me. But as his lips neared mine, I felt the heat sear between us. My heart thudded painfully in my chest as my body responded to him. Everything heated as he moved closer . . . closer . . . closer . . .

"Captain?"

Immediately I jerked away from him and turned to see who had interrupted us. It was, of course, a very naked Fenella. She had made her dark hair fall lengthily over her shoulder, covering one plump breast but leaving the other one completely exposed. Her sex was unguarded, bared for all to see. It was clear what her intentions were.

Incredibly annoyed, I sighed and turned back to Gabriel, who was clearly not impressed with what he was looking at. In fact he had only looked at her for a second before turning back to me. However, I had had enough.

"I'll leave you to it," I whispered before removing my hands from his face. He tried to reach for my arm, but I sidestepped him and headed toward where Fenella was guarding the entrance. "Excuse me." She moved a fraction of an inch so I could squeeze by.

I was not in the mood to play this game with her. In fact I was partially glad she had showed up. I had lost my head for a moment. I wouldn't let it happen again . . . like it had with Calder. Gabriel and I had a mission to rescue the people of Islocia. And no matter how good it felt to have his body so close to mine, I knew that it would only lead to trouble if I had followed through with my intentions. I craved Gabriel like a bee seeks honey, but I could not give myself to him. It would be all that I could ever offer, and once he tired of me like he had Fenella, I would be nothing.

And that duty, I will leave to Fenella. She will forever remain the discarded whore while I remained his truest friend.

CHAPTER 27

"THE CAP'N WANTS TO SPEAK wit you," Colleen said as she came into me and Moira's tent. The sun had barely begun to peek over the horizon; consequently Moira and I had yet to stir.

"I have only just managed an hour of rest." I yawned, turning away from her. "Tell him I am asleep."

"Not me job." She sighed. "Go tell him yourself." She didn't wait for me to reply.

I lay still for a moment, reveling in the peacefulness of sleep, before Moira decided to comment. "Might as well get it over with." Frustrated, I kicked my covers off of me and stood. Stretching, my body sore from lying on the ground, I adjusted my clothing so I looked presentable. "Give him a big smacker on the cheek for me, aye?" I threw my blanket at her as I left the tent.

Though it was only morning the camp was alive with activity. Mothers were washing their clothes and preparing breakfast for their children. It was humbling to watch the sleepy children stumble out of their tents to assist their mothers in chores.

As I headed toward the rebels' camp I noticed that many, if not all of them, were awake. Most were sharpening their weapons while some were even returning from the forest. Whether it was late in the night or early in the morning the rebels were always awake, actively protecting the camp at all costs.

Gabriel was standing in the middle of the camp, talking with Ezekiel. He had yet to put on his fur vest, his muscles bared for all to see. His abdominals flexed as he spoke quickly with Ezekiel. As I approached them I prepared myself for the onslaught of emotions I would soon be forced to deal with. The mere image of him had me weak in the knees! Had I really sworn him my friend when I desired him so feverishly? My blood boiled for him; my heart ached for him. My skin ran cold, needing his touch to heat me. I had officially lost my mind in him.

"You summoned me?" I said casually as I neared him.

I was nearly breathless as he looked down at me, his gaze searing with heated desire. "Ari"—he swallowed deeply, his throat working—"I wanted to speak with you before I rode out this morning."

I shrugged, acting as if I were cool as a breeze even though I felt as restless as a leaf in a hurricane. "What is it?"

Turning to Ezekiel, he nodded curtly. Ezekiel must've understood the silent command because he walked away. Gabriel came up to me and placed his arm around my waist and began leading me away from all of the rebels' commotion. He was silent for a little while; worry marred my brow. He was too serious, too focused.

"Is everything alright?" I feared the worst. Fenella had asked him not to see me anymore. She was, however, his true desire. I could not compete with that. She gave him what every man craves, and she did it valiantly.

"What?" He was so deep in thought that he had hardly registered that I had spoken. "Yes, yes, everything is fine." Finally we stopped walking and he turned me to face him. My breath caught as I absorbed the impact of his perfectly chiseled, rugged, defiant face. "Ari, I need you to know that nothing happened between me and Fenella last night. I sent her back to her tent." Confused, I stood silent. Why had he felt the need to tell me this? It was none of my business. "I didn't touch her, I swear." Still I didn't say anything. I was too lost in my own thoughts to reply. It was not his responsibility nor did he owe me anything. He had no reason to come to me and assure me of his celibacy. Just a week or so ago he had no issues explaining his sexual preferences with whores, and now he feels the need to assure me? "Gods be damned, Ari. I hardly looked at the wench!"

Chuckling, I placed my finger over his lips. His tension released in a rush as I smiled up at him. "I would not fault you for divulging in your *needs*. You crave a touch much softer than." He furrowed his brow at that remark. "I will not stand in the way of your satisfaction."

He reached up and gripped my hand ferociously. "Do not deny me this," he warned, his anger rising.

I smiled, wishing to ease his selfishness. "How can I deny you of something you never had?" That was a lie. And from the look he gave me he knew it. "Enjoy yourself, my friend. For that is the only sentiment that I can offer." And with that I peeled his fingers off of my hand and headed back toward the camp.

* * *

It had been ages since I had last had a hearty full-body cleansing. Dried blood and mud formed a thin layer over my skin. And after constant pestering from Moira, I was directed toward a waterfall where I would finally be able to be clean. Moira offered to go with me, but I decided to go on my own. I wanted time to myself. Although I thoroughly enjoyed accepting my new family, at times the camp could get a little . . . crowded. Time alone was sacred, even though I knew Karuli would be looking for me soon.

As the afternoon reached its peak, I lazily made my way through the forest and headed toward the waterfall. Moira had told me that it was a mile or so west. I didn't mind. I needed to stretch my legs and fill my lungs. I allowed my mind to calm itself, and I let my legs take over.

Minutes faded into an hour as I finally heard the first sign of the waterfall. Following a barely visible path, I caught sight of its majesty. The waterfall was beautiful. The sun's rays spilled onto the crystal-clear water. Diamonds danced along the boulders surrounding the serenity of the place. Soft, luscious grass carpeted the entrance of the waterfall. It was amazing. A little luxury tucked away in the Iclin Forest.

Stripping from my clothes, I walked slowly into the small pond capturing the waterfall. The water was cold yet soothing. As my waist sunk deeper, chills broke out along my arms. I could feel the dirt and grime washing away. When my breast brushed against the surface of the water, my nipples tightened. I smiled at the sensation before completely submerging myself. Water rushed overhead, swirling wildly around me before settling. I held my breath, stretching my lungs, before returning to the surface. It felt so good. I was at peace. I was happy.

I cannot remember how long I swam around, but I knew it was time to return back to the camp when my fingers began to wrinkle. I had enjoyed my time and was sad to see it end. But I knew that I was to be needed back at the camp. Gabriel would be returning, and I'm sure another mission would be forming. I assumed it would be time to meet with the other rebel camps. I was to be prepped by the next moon change.

As the wind blew me dry I began putting my clothes back on when, suddenly, I heard the snapping of a twig somewhere off in the distance. My first thought was that someone from Sythos had come looking for me, but as the sound disappeared and no one made themselves known, I knew something wasn't right.

"What a sweet surprise, aye, mate?" a gruff voice replied from behind me. Turning around, I saw a large, fat man appear from the forest. He wore a moose hide that did nothing to hide his paunch stomach that was nearly saturated in hair.

"Sure is." To my left another grotesque voice appeared. I quickly went to look at him and noticed he hardly looked any different than the first man.

"I'd like to show her my thanks of appreciation for the show." Another man appeared from the forest. He was much taller and muscular than the other two. He was also more . . . terrifying. It was nearly impossible not to see his intentions as his hand roughly gripped his crotch. These men weren't from Sythos nor were they members of the Queen's Guard. Their attire suggested a life consumed by the forest and the pain of others. Just my luck that they stumbled upon me . . .

"I wonder what her blood tastes like." A fourth man, tall and strong, appeared! He smelled the air. "She smells nearly as good as she must taste. I want her."

"She's mine first," the fattest man said. "You can have what I'm done with, understand?"

"Hurry up then! I'm starving," the muscular one hissed. They began to circle me, like vultures spotting their prey.

I had no weapons with me. And although I was healing nicely, there was no way I would be able to fight them off. The only thing I could rely on was that the camp was a mile or so away. I had to make it there.

"Where do you think she came from, aye?" the other fat one asked, squeezing his crotch even harder.

"Too far away to be from the palace. Besides, her clothes are that of a villager."

"Sythos?"

"Perhaps. Doesn't matter now, does it?"

They all chuckled as they began closing in on me.

"Let me have her!" the muscular one growled restlessly. His hands twitched frantically at his sides; his sharpened teeth were bared. Had it been their way . . . I was not meant to walk away alive.

"You'll get your turn," the fat one hissed. "I saw her first." He reached and freed himself from his pants. "She's mine." He lunged at me. His thick, pudgy arm reached for my neck, but he was too slow. I was able to catch his hand. But before I had time to fully attack, the muscular man came up and grabbed my other hand and chucked me to the ground. My forehead cracked against a boulder as the fat man mounted me.

"I like when they put up a fight." He smiled, spreading my legs with his fat thighs. "It makes me want it all the more." His ghastly breath washed over me, suffocating me. He was so unearthly large that he was literally crushing me to death. I couldn't breathe!

"Please, no!" I screamed, struggling beneath his hold. "Please!" He positioned himself at my entrance. I could feel the heat from him. As I looked up into his eyes I saw nothing but black holes where his irises should be. This man was without a soul . . . and would sooner see me dead before he ever released me. Exhaling onto my face, he laughed as he understood my fear.

"Take all of me." He chuckled, nudging himself closer. Before he started, he looked up at his comrades. "A little privacy, aye? You wouldn't want me peeking if it were your turn, eh?"

"Just hurry up," the muscular one growled.

The fat one laughed before returning back to me. "This is going to feel good. Just what I need before I pick my teeth with your bones. But not before my friends got them a turn, eh?"

"I'll give you anything you want." I was consumed by fear. There was nothing I could do. He was too heavy for me to push off of me. My heart beat painfully in my chest as I tried moving away from him. "Please, don't! I'm begging you."

"I like when you beg." He smiled. "Tell me to stop—that'll really get me going."

"Please!"

"Yes, louder!"

I feared the worst. There was nothing I could do. This man, this vile beast of a man was about to steal something away from me that was not his to have. Yet here he had the power. I was to be violated and then killed. Would this really be my end? Was this how I was meant to be taken? All my efforts, everything I had been through, would bring me to this? A death so unfathomable that I couldn't have imagined it if I had tried. Yet there I lay, at the mercy of a beast with no intentions except to see to my death.

A tear slid down my cheek, which only excited him more. "Please . . ." Another tear slipped from my composure.

"It'll be over soon." I closed my eyes against the shame . . . "Open up." His mouth was at my ear.

Suddenly, exactly when I had thought the heavens had closed on me forever, I heard the sound of a sword being drawn.

Before the fat man could register what was happening, I watched as his eyes went from dark, soulless holes to lifeless beads as a sword pierced through his back.

"Ari!"

Gabriel!

Crawling free from the now-dead fat man, I was able to see Gabriel holding a dagger in each hand as the remaining three men began closing in on him. The muscular one attacked first. Gabriel stabbed the dagger in his stomach. He cut him just under his chest, but the man ignored the pain and tackled Gabriel to the ground. They wrestled in the dirt for a moment until I saw a splatter of blood shoot into the sky. At first I thought it was Gabriel who had been stabbed, but from underneath the once-muscular man Gabriel appeared. Coated in blood but unharmed.

Every bone in my body wanted to run to him. He could not fight them alone. He would be killed . . . because of me . . .

"Gabriel!"

He didn't turn to me. He kept his eyes on the remaining two men. "Get out of here, Ari!"

"I'm not leaving you!"

"Now!"

"No!"

All of a sudden a pair of strong arms grabbed me from behind. Instinctively I tried to break free, but he held me tight. I screamed, but Gabriel didn't look over at me. The other muscular man was beginning his attack.

"Let me go!"

"Shut up, Arianna!" Ezekiel . . . it was Ezekiel. "Come on!" Throwing me over his shoulder, he took off, running away from the waterfall!

Beating his back with my fist, I screamed at him. "Let me go! What are you doing! You have to help him, please! You can't leave him!"

He ignored me as he sprinted back to the camp.

"Don't leave him!" I continued to scream. "How could you leave him? Go back for him! He needs you!"

Ezekiel didn't drag me back into the camp. Instead he brought me into Gabriel's tent and dropped me on his furs.

"What are you doing!" I yelled. I would've gotten up, but Ezekiel pushed me back down. "You have to go help him! How could you leave him?"

"The captain gave me an order, and that was to get you. I did as I was told." He was angry with me. Not for screaming at him or beating on his back. He was angry that I had put his captain in danger. He could get killed over me. "He'll be fine."

"You have to go help him, please, Ezekiel," I pleaded. "He's all I have too."

Ezekiel avoided eye contact with me and began to walk out of the tent. "Don't leave this tent. Guryon is standing guard. Don't leave this tent!" He left me then. Alone, afraid. Where was Gabriel . . . was he alive? Was he hurt? This was all my fault. I shouldn't have gone to the waterfall alone. I should've paid more attention to my surroundings. And now . . . now I had endangered Gabriel . . . I had risked his life . . .

Curling up into a ball, I sobbed silently as I realized what I had done to the man I cared so deeply for. There's a chance he wouldn't return to me . . . and it would be my fault. I could lose him . . .

It was that pain that struck me so intensely. I was frozen in agony; my heart ached for his return. I needed him. I wanted him. Gabriel . . .

The sun had disappeared completely as darkness swallowed Islocia. The hunters had returned an hour ago with tonight's supper. But I was in no mood to eat. I hadn't moved from my spot on Gabriel's furs since

Ezekiel dumped me off there. I was terrified. Worried. And alone. That was the worst part—being alone with my thoughts. All I could think about was how I could've done something different. Instead of standing like a fool, I should've jumped in and helped him! Why hadn't I helped him! He would've at least had a better chance of surviving. But I denied him that . . . like I had denied him other things . . .

Suddenly, as I sank deeper into my depression, Gabriel came bursting through his tent. He was covered in blood. Some of it was his and the rest was of those he slaughtered. A bruise grazed his brow, and several fresh cuts lay along his shoulders and one dripped from below his navel. He was ferociously tense as his dark irises burned down at me.

Immediately I surged to my feet, but he held his hand up and walked to the opposite side of his tent. His whole body shook with fury as he turned his back to me. More bleeding cuts seeped from his back as he breathed heavily. He pulled out a bottle from behind his weapons and drank deeply. He drained the entire bottle in a matter of seconds.

"Gabriel . . ."

He held up his hand again. "Stop. Just stop." Throwing the empty bottle, he took several more deep breaths, but they did nothing to calm him. His fists were clenched so tight his knuckles were white against his skin. All of a sudden he turned and kicked some of his weapons, causing them to clash to the ground. "You were supposed to stay there! You weren't supposed to come here!"

Confusion took the place of my concern. "What are you talking about?"

"The Qingkowuats! You were supposed to stay there! You were never meant to come here! Ever! Now look what you've done!" he yelled, shooting me with his fierce gaze.

Anger began to fume inside me! How dare he! Was it not him who stated that the past was the past? "An army came for me, Gabriel! What was I supposed to do? Had it been my doing I would've given my life for them!"

"Yet here you stand," he spit, pacing around the tent like a caged panther. "You should've never come here!"

For the life of me I couldn't understand this man! One minute he wanted me, the next he pushed me away! What did he want from me!

Clearly it was something I was unable to give, for he refused me! No matter my efforts to patch up the past and accept his faults, he pushed me away! I hated him!

"What would you have had me do then, huh?" I hissed back at him. "Would you rather have me wander around the Iclin Forest and die? Would that death be more acceptable to you?"

"Watch your tone, Ari," he growled, nearing me.

"Or what?" I challenged, clenching my fist as well. "You will throw me out of the camp? You will have someone kill me?" He said nothing. "No, you'd never do that. Would you?" He turned away from me, breaking eye contact. "I have been sitting here, worried to death about you! Yet when you come back to me you preach to me about my duty to protect the poor! And what is it of your duty to me? What is it of your duty to your people, the ones *you* left behind? I fought for them when no one else would. Do not stand there and desecrate all I had done for them." He said nothing. But I wasn't done. "What would you have had me do? Huh? You tell me! What would you have had me do?"

"You led that army to your village. They were bleeding, and you struck the final blow." His words hit me harder than any punch he could ever deliver. "You know what I would've told you to do? I would've told you to leave them. You knew they were dying. You should've moved on and found another village instead of wasting your life away wandering around the forest."

"I was not going to leave them, Gabriel. I'm not you," I hissed, returning his angered gaze.

He chuckled sinisterly. "You know, Ari, for someone who portrays a merciless soul you seem to lack the conviction."

"Go to hell!" I bellowed just as I was about to storm out of his hut, but he ran up and grabbed my arm. Using his body he pushed me to the wall of his tent, pressing up against me. His body was crushed to mine as he peered down at me. "Let me go! I hate you!"

He gripped me tighter. "Why . . . !" His voice remained harsh though his eyes pleaded for understanding. He gripped my arms tighter, pinning them to my sides, making it uncomfortable. "Do you have any idea what you mean to me?"

I froze. My brain couldn't work that fast or strain itself to understand what he was saying.

"Every day since I left I hoped . . ." He struggled for words. "Damn it! Why couldn't you just stay away! None of this would've happened if you had stayed away!"

"Why is it so hard for you to accept the fact that I am here!" I yelled, struggling against his grasp. "You left me! With nothing!"

"I left you with a chance!"

"A chance for what? Life?"

"Yes!" he screamed, shaking me. "I've lived this life, a life on the run. A life that calls for my survival only when I take away the breath of others! I didn't want that for you!"

Trying to pull free, I held back tears that pleaded for relief. "I died every day since you were gone!" I screamed as loud as I could. He fell silent for a while. I said nothing. I waited until my breathing subsided and I could speak without sounding like I had choked on sorrow. "I would've rather died a million deaths than lose you. You put the knife through my heart when you walked out of my life. You shattered me into millions of tiny, helpless, pathetic pieces when you left me. You left me! You left me with no chance of survival because there is no world I would want to live in if you were not in it." Looking up at him I saw that his gaze had softened, but he still held onto me, tight. I had to look away from him. I was feeling too vulnerable . . . too raw. "When you left . . . I—"

He kissed me. With no hesitation. No second-guessing. He took his hand, releasing my arm, and tilted my head up, and he kissed me. Long and hard. His breath washed over me, saturating me in his masculine scent. My mouth opened up to him as he took over the kiss. Roughly suckling my tongue, he deepened the kiss. His grip was painful on me but I did nothing about it. I did nothing to stop it.

When he pulled away from me I was breathless. His chest heaved just as much as mine did. My mind was racing. Had he just . . . did he . . . did I . . . ? "Ari?"

I kneed him in the gut as hard as I could and pulled free from him. With a loud "oof" he fell to the ground, grasping his stomach. "What the hell?"

"Stay away from me!" I snapped defensively. "Stay the hell away from me! I've played this game, damn it! Gabriel, I've played this game and every time I lose! I lost you! I lost my dignity! I lost everything! I will not allow you to take your turn just as others have done so in the past! Enough!" My entire body was racing with adrenaline. "I will not be hurt again! Never again!"

He stood to his feet and approached me, slowly, tauntingly. His tense frame had changed entirely. Hunger replaced his earlier mood. His eyes narrowed in on me. Nothing could break his focus.

"Get back!" I warned.

He didn't stop. I didn't move.

"I thought the angels had abandoned me when I heard of the Qingkowuats' demise. But when I saw you that day you took down the guards' camp, I realized then that they had never left me. You were so angry and raw. Although it pained me deeply to hurt you, I did what I had to do to get you under control. But not even that stopped you."

"You hit me?" I remembered a pain in the back of my head when the rebels had chased me away from the camp I had burned down.

"Yes, Ari. I punched you." He came up to me and gently—as if the word were anywhere in his vocabulary—held my face in his warm calloused hands. "I, with my fist of synthetic fury, knocked you right on that taut little ass of yours. I guess that proves you're not as invincible as you thought." He chuckled playfully.

"Gabriel . . ." I sighed, exasperated. He was surrounding me. He was too much . . . I couldn't handle it! "You are too much . . ." My voice was barely above a whisper. "I can't—"

"Shut up!" His words were harsh, but he remained softened. "Shut that damned mouth of yours! I don't care how much you think you don't need anyone. I don't care that you've had to take care of yourself since the day you were born. I don't care! You're with *me* now." The wave of emotion that plowed into me released the tears I tried to hide. I sobbed as he held my face and blanketed me with the severity of his stare. "Everything in my being tells—no, commands—me to protect you! And I will. No matter if death is inevitable. No matter if I shall never see another light of day. I will fight like hell for you. Through all the catastrophic travesties of nature and man, I will be there for you . . . I give myself to you just as you will give yourself to me. Do you understand? Your fight is over, Arianna . . . you are mine now."

We stared into each other's eyes for long moments, absorbing everything we had to offer the other. Try as I might not to be taken by him, I wanted to! This man, this horrible, dreadful, enormous man had given himself to me. Willfully. Eagerly. Through all the bullshit and horrors we endured, we had found our way back to each other. He had finally . . . found me.

"Gabriel . . ." I sighed, releasing the rest of my resistance. He kissed me again and removed his hands from my face. His tongue, with its velvety lust, surged into my mouth. Captivating me. I moaned against the sensation. My head fell back as his mouth worked its way from my lips to my neck. I reached for his muscular shoulders, wanting the feel of his taut skin beneath my hands. "Gabriel." I said his name again. He hooked one of my legs around his waist and filled the empty space between us. My arousal heightened as his hands, o' his amazingly strong hands, ripped at my clothes. In seconds he undressed me, tearing the thin fabric. My senses were razor sharp, the feel of him against me spurring me on.

I gasped as his hands dipped between my legs and unearthed my longing to have him. Raking my nails down his back, he groaned erotically, the muscles in his neck beading through his skin and begging for relief.

A moment later he reached down for my other leg and lifted me off of the ground. He held me effortlessly. I continued licking my way down his neck as he reveled in capturing me. I was losing myself in him. And there was no turning back.

"So beautiful," he muttered, brushing my hair out of my face. "You're mine."

I ran my nails down his back again and looked lustfully into his deep blue eyes. "Prove it."

Gabriel always loved a challenge.

He brought me down to his furs, climbing over me in a rush and claiming my mouth once again. I was wrapped in the presence of him as he shed his last bit of clothing. His warm body engulfed me, swallowing my last ounce of control.

I expected him to take me, right then and there. No questions asked. I was so hot for him and he was hot for me. But he made no further advances, as if he were waiting for something. And then it hit me. As I looked up into his warm, hooded gaze, I realized he was waiting for permission. My heart ached for him in that moment. I was his. My body immediately craved his touch as if it were starved for him. Weak whimpers escaped through my parted lips as he grinded softly against me. I inhaled deeply, his scent intoxicating. "Take me, Gabriel." I couldn't wait any longer. Not when I needed him so passionately. "I'm yours."

He bent down and bit my neck as he surged into me. I cried out blissfully as the pain and ecstasy of the moment took me over the edge.

The entire act was rough, to say the least. No matter how our feelings may have been, it was a raw and a damn near animalistic performance. I refused to allow him to be totally dominant over me, and he refused to accept that. He wanted me completely submissive; I wanted to be seen as equal. We fought each other, through passion and lust, for dominance. But I wouldn't have had it any other way. It was perfect . . . beautiful. Just how it always should've been. I was his and he was finally mine. We were two beings morphed into one. My heart and my soul were his to keep for the rest of his days, and his heart, though he tried to guard it, was mine forever.

And no one would take that away from me ever again.

CHAPTER 28

A SOFT BREEZE SIFTED THROUGH GABRIEL'S tent and found its way underneath the furs. I pulled my feet in, refusing the chill but being immediately warmed by Gabriel's arms wrapped around me. Lately his masculine scent had clung to my being as fervently as a bee seeks a rose. Many evenings we found our way to each other, our passion fueling our haste. He would take me wherever privacy presented itself. Most afternoons, when he returned from hunting, he would take me into the forest and ravish me against a tree. When we tired of that we found a cave near the ocean. He particularly enjoyed how my cries of pleasure echoed throughout the stone walls. The waterfall was my favorite place to go. He chased away my demons as his hands caressed every inch of my body. His lips would find their way down my torso, heightening my arousal to a fever pitch. He did everything in his power to ensure my satisfaction. And I did the same to him. We were happy, finally happy, with each other. Everything, from lovemaking to coexisting, came easy to us. Whenever we had to work with the other rebels, Gabriel was cordial, but it was in those hours we remained untouched. But once the sun set and all was calm, he took me with a ferocious growl, marking me as his with a searing kiss that consumed my entire body.

"Are you cold?" he asked with one arm tucked under my head and the other wrapped around my waist. We were nude under the furs. I felt every hard inch of his muscular body sculpted against me. My arousal had simmered below boiling just long enough for us both to sleep and catch our breath.

Toying with his fingers I drew circles on his palms and replied, "How can I be cold when my sun and stars are finally in-line and shining down solely on me?"

His chest vibrated against me as he chuckled at the compliment. "Selfish girl, unwilling to share me with the world. I'm held prisoner to your lust and cunny, someone please melt the keys. I refuse to be rescued." He leaned over and turned my head so that I was facing him. Slowly, o' so tauntingly slow, he bent down and brushed his lips against mine. The little touch did nothing to stoke the burning fire of my desire, so I offered my lips up to him. He took them, sweetly at first, and then rough, wild, and wet. His tongue was like flames inside my mouth. Sweet, delicious torment. My toes curled as he tugged on my hair to take over my mouth and the kiss. I moaned involuntarily, pleading for more.

When he pulled free I was breathless and completely aroused. Gabriel grew to have that effect on me. Just the simple flick of his stare or sparkle in his eyes called me to him. My body always responded the same way to him. I became increasingly sensitive, and I was restless with the need to touch him. I had a similar effect on him. Whenever I caught him staring at me his gaze would burst into flames with just the twitch of my mouth.

"You're mine," I whispered, kissing down his neck and leaving a beautiful purple mark right next to the one I left him the previous evening. I had marked up his body with my nails and teeth. Our lovemaking was always so rough and raw that I could hardly stem a cry! He thoroughly enjoyed when I added the enticement of pain to the act. I too craved his mouth in a way that left marks on my skin. He always obliged me. Thoroughly so.

"All yours." His deep, raspy voice pulled me to stare into his eyes. His beautiful navy-blue irises—which could lead me into hell had he the chance—cradled me. I was engulfed in him with no hint of release when suddenly an irking thought struck me, which caused me to roll my eyes at his comment. "Did you tell Fenella the same exact thing you preach to me?" Throughout me and Gabriel's coming together, Fenella had made several attempts to attract his attention. One night she came to his tent, naked—again—but was shocked to see Gabriel deep inside me, pledging to never stop as I screamed against the sensation. Not even the irrelevant Fenella could've broken his concentration. He literally paid her no mind and continued to service me while I looked her dead in her eyes, smiling.

Exasperated he let me go and rolled onto his back. "Damn it, Ari. Would not the soul of the Gods satisfy this raging demon you suppress?" I followed him over and placed my arm across his torso, resting my head on his chest. "Do you not understand that all that I can offer you is yours to have? Had I have more, I would give it to you. You. And no one else."

"She does not believe it so," I muttered, remembering all the times she touched him and curved her lean body into his so that he held her. I despised her! I wanted her dead. "What drew you to her?"

"I'm not talking about her with you," he replied in his clipped stern voice.

"You asked me about my past. Now it's my turn," I replied, lightly touching the slight dusting of hair on his chest.

Sighing, defeated, he replied, "She was available. The rebels and I had been working long hours to establish Sythos and protect the refugees. Some evenings I would come in exhausted and needing relief. She was there and willing."

"Why *her* though?" I asked, irked that she made herself so available. "Why not the other girls in the brothel? Was she the prettiest?"

Quickly he pulled my face to his and kissed me. When he pulled away he smiled at me. "Enough with the questions, Ari. It is over and done with. I found her no more attractive than the other women in the brothel."

I thought for a moment then said, "And what of me?" He didn't know how to reply so I clarified. "You had to have found her somewhat noteworthy. Am I in comparison to her?"

He chuckled at my insecurities and slowly stroked his finger down my cheek. "Ari . . . my Ari. You stupid, stubborn girl." He kissed the tip of my nose. "It is not in my being to stumble at the sight of beauty. Though whenever I happen to lay my eyes upon you, I can't seem to find my step."

My heart melted as I registered his words. "Never had I heard words so sweet." I ran my finger over his lips. "I'm surprised they came from you."

He laughed out loud, kissing my finger. "Cheeky girl." Biting my lip, my hunger growing, I climbed on top of him and allowed him to take me. He sat up and shoved the furs off of us, wrapping his arms around my waist and burying his face in my chest. Running my hands through his short hair, I prepared myself for the wave of emotions and pleasures he would soon unleash on me.

"Look alive! The Captain is on deck," Ezekiel announced as Gabriel and I made our way into the rebel camp. The rebels stood as Gabriel approached. It was midafternoon, and the sun was warming the earth, preparing for spring.

"What do we got?" Gabriel asked Ezekiel as he made his way over to the fire bit. He grabbed a soaking cloth from the boiling water and wrung it out over the poached fire before scrubbing his face with it.

"We may have a problem," Ezekiel began. "Those men you killed near the waterfall a week ago, well, they weren't just wanderers. They were Artis. It seems they had travelled across the river and onto our side."

"Shit," Gabriel hissed, tension gripping his frame. "How long do we have until they realize what happened?"

"Our scouts told us that they figured out their members were missing a few days ago. They've been tearing apart the forest in search of the culprit." Ezekiel passed a quick glance my way. "They'll be heading in this direction soon."

"Damn it," he growled. "This isn't how I wanted to confront them. Damn!"

"What happens if they find us first?" I asked, trying not to stare at the way Gabriel's muscles tightened with tension.

"They'll slaughter us . . . all," Ezekiel replied.

"So what do we do?" I asked, trying to understand. From what Moira had told me, the Artis people were ruthless, cruel, and very dangerous. We needed them as allies, not as enemies.

"We have to find them first." He turned to me. "It's showtime, Ari. Saddle up."

"What?" I didn't have time to ask because he had walked away from me entirely. "What did he mean?" I asked Ezekiel.

Ezekiel replied, "We need you now, Arianna. If Gabriel is able to convince them to listen, you're going to have to explain things to them. Tell them about the queen and everything else that went on in the palace. It's all up to you now."

"*If* we get them to listen," I said, worry replacing my earlier mood.

"Yes…if they listen," Ezekiel agreed.

We didn't have to travel far to find the Artis people. I remember being told that they migrated with the seasons. Now that the river was no longer frozen, they must've crossed it to see if any vegetation or woodland creatures had found their way to the riverbank. They were no more than a stone's throw away from us. Hardly five miles. Clearly too close for comfort.

We were not warmly welcomed to say the least. When their scouts had caught sight of us they glided down from the trees, swords waving. They shouted obscene things at us, startling the horses. I didn't understand their words; they spoke in a different tongue. Gabriel instructed us to do as they said, so we dismounted and were all held at knife point.

As they brought us into their camp, it was apparent that they relied solely on their skills rather companionship. Their camp was a wreck. Clothes, food, weapons lay scattered about. Their women wore nothing but tattered clothes and were chained to their makeshift huts. The men were all unearthly large and terrifying. The emptiness in their eyes told me that they cared for nothing other than their own survival.

"Gabriel!" A booming voice erupted from the edge of the camp. The Artis people began to circle around us as our capturers shoved us into view. There were definitely more of them than there were of us. We had left half of our regiment behind to guard the camp. That left us with twenty-five men against nearly sixty of them! Each of them looked as if they were starved for the taste of our blood. "Welcome to Artis!"

"Diatomin," Gabriel replied gruffly as a shorter, pudgy man appeared from the circle. He was dressed in worn-out leather that did little to hide his stomach. "Not the warmest of welcomes, I see. We come as no threat."

Diatomin, who I assumed was the leader, took a sip out of the rusty cup he was holding and wiped his mouth before replying. "Not a threat? Was it not you who killed me men?"

"They crossed the line long before I took their lives," Gabriel replied. Before the last word fell out of his mouth, all of the Artis people surrounding us drew their weapons and took a step closer to us.

"So it was you!" Diatomin exclaimed. "Pity, I thought you as an honest, upstanding fella." He shook his head in mock disapproval. "It seems now I must see to your death, ya? An eye for an eye and all that other horseshit you live by."

"Diatomin, hear me out," Gabriel said, raising his hands in surrender. "I come as a friend, on my life I vow that. Set this fault aside and hear me out."

"Hear you out?" Diatomin nearly laughed. It was then that I became nervous. We were severely outnumbered, and we had now given these people a reason to have a vendetta against us. "You killed me men! For no reason!"

A few of the Artis men snarled as they approached us.

"No, Diatomin! It was not without reason, I swear to you!" Gabriel said as the closest man stood over him with his axe held high above his head, execution style. "They had come onto my land and were threatening the life of one of my villagers. I could not allow it. Let me speak to Crion. Allow me the opportunity to explain things to him. Face to face, man to man." Crion? Perhaps Diatomin was merely the middle man and this Crion fellow was the real leader.

"An outsider can only speak to Van Crion if they prove themselves worthy," Diatomin replied, almost offended. "You, dear friend, have proven to be nothing but a coward."

"Award me the opportunity to prove you wrong then," Gabriel offered, eyeing the man with the axe over his head. "If I am dead then so be it. Either way you get what you want, right?" Diatomin deliberated for a long moment, shooting glances between us and his men until finally he made his decision.

"Alright then, Gabriel," Diatomin replied. "I will allow you this opportunity. But you only get one. Here are the rules. Two of the men you killed were insignificant to us in every way. We will disregard their death as gift to us from you." I assume he was speaking of the two fat ones. "However, you did kill two valuable warriors and that we cannot ignore. You will be allowed one partner. The two of you will fight, to the death, against two of our strongest men. Death determines the victor. Care to play, *Captain?*"

"He can't be serious," I muttered to Ezekiel, who had been standing beside me. "Just to speak to this Crion man?"

Ezekiel leaned over and whispered, "It's how the Artis people work. Worth is based on your ability to survive. If Gabriel is able to win then his worth has become significant enough to Van Crion to get his attention. We need Gabriel to win." Ezekiel and the others wanted him to win to help our chances for survival. I wanted him to win so that he could return to Sythos with me. I needed him to win too. "No one has ever survived this game. That is why Gabriel waited so long to approach them. They're ruthless beyond belief."

"You're worried." It wasn't a question.

He nodded. "You should be too."

Gabriel turned away from the man with the axe and shed his fur vest, his muscles illuminated by the sun, warming his tanned skin.

"Bacchus, do you care to join on this one, my friend?" Gabriel said, turning to Bacchus.

Smiling his vicious smile, Bacchus stepped forward and replied, "I thought you'd never ask, boss. I've been waiting to stretch my legs a bit."

I was too overcome with worry to move from my spot. A large part of me wanted to run over to Gabriel and beg him not to do it. I couldn't bear the thought of losing him; I couldn't imagine it. He was my everything now, and so soon after I had finally had him he could be taken from me. I couldn't bear it!

Stealing a glance in my direction, he must've noticed my discomfort with the situation, for he came over to me. Reaching down to stroke my cheek, he peered into my eyes. I was terrified, and he could see it.

"Don't you have faith in me?" he tried to joke.

I had to swallow past several lumps in my throat before I could reply. "Just come back to me, okay?" My voice was hardly above a whisper. "Promise me that."

"Of course I will return to you. It is not my time, Ari." He smiled brushing a strand of hair out of my face. "I certainly haven't had nearly enough time with you." Softly, he leaned forward and kissed my forehead before leaving my side to stand by Bacchus in the middle of the makeshift arena.

The two warriors that Diatomin had chosen were massive, though that was entirely an understatement. They stood a foot taller than Gabriel, who happened to be a foot taller than me! The two men nearly outweighed Isaac and Guryon, which I assumed impossible before I had met them. The deep woven scars that laced their entire bodies were almost as intimidating as the unruly look in their eyes. Their irises were black and hollow; they felt no emotion and held no mercy. Purple veins bulged from their arms. Even Bacchus looked small compared to them! They were so inconceivably monstrous I thought for sure that I would lose Gabriel. But when he turned and winked at me I knew everything would be okay. Bacchus had love for Gabriel and would ensure his safety. And Gabriel . . . well, Gabriel was strong. And he would prove that, finally, for all to see.

* * *

"Am I supposed to be impressed?" Van Crion asked, sitting upon his iron throne. Two more of his unearthly men stood beside him as he looked down at us. Just like Ophelia, he had his throne raised over his subjects. If he could not get us to kneel then he would have to resort to other tactics. One being his throne.

Van Crion was an intimidating force in a category entirely of his own. He was tall, stretching two feet clear over my head. His body was lean and rippled with muscles. He had long, pale blond hair that ran down his back. His arms were coated in markings that he had carved into his skin. Ezekiel had informed me that whenever a new leader took the throne he must prove to the village that pain was simply an idea. One way they did it was by carving designs into their skin, with no sedatives, with the sharpest knife, and for all to see. His markings were healed and seemed old.

"You can feel however you want. I've done my deed. Now it's time for you to honor your word," Gabriel replied, panting heavily. Blood stained his chest and back. Some of it was his, and some of it was the two men he and Bacchus had slain. Bacchus stood beside Gabriel, mirroring his appearance. The only difference being that Bacchus had a long gash along his back while Gabriel had one bleeding from his forearm.

Bacchus and Gabriel had fought admirably. It was the most beautiful thing to watch as they destroyed the two Artis warriors. It was over in a matter of minutes. I was wrong to ever question any of their strengths. At one point during the fight, Bacchus had charged one of them head-on. Getting lower than him he wrapped his arms around his waist and hoisted him off the ground. Gabriel dislodged himself from the vice grip of the other warrior and charged the one Bacchus had in his arms. Leaping through the air Gabriel grabbed the man by his neck and cracked it over his shoulder. All three of them crashed to the ground. It was beautiful. Amazing. My hunger for Gabriel grew to a fever pitch as I watched him.

At the end of the fight he came to me, never checking his stride, and wrapped me in his arms. Grabbing my rear, he lifted me off the ground so that my face was level with his. He kissed me, roughly and passionately, for all to see. I was breathless when he extracted himself from me and went to find Van Crion.

"Fair words." Van Crion nodded, looking at all of us. "However, I know why you came here. And I will not help you."

Gabriel chuckled without humor. "Your loyalty is appalling."

Van Crion shrugged. "Perhaps. But the monarchy has been indifferent to us. They have caused us no problems, and I will not intermingle in your vendetta to destroy them."

"It is a justifiable insurrection by all means," Gabriel growled, clenching his fist. "Had you the ability to comprehend something beyond what you see, perhaps you'd learn a thing or two." At that, the Artis men drew their swords. Van Crion glared down at Gabriel; Gabriel glared back. The tension was thick between the two men, both inserting their dominance where it doesn't belong.

I stepped forward, assuming this was my cue. "What would it take to convince you otherwise? I mean wasn't it your village that was once raided by the Royal Army?"

Van Crion glanced at me for a second before releasing a breath and leaning back on his throne. "It would be wise for you to remind your whore to keep her tongue out of discussions too far ahead for her mind to reach."

My hand twitched toward the daggers at my belt. Gabriel felt the anger that was growing inside me and replied, "Mind yourself, Crion."

Van Crion shrugged and signaled for his slave woman to retrieve his drink. Once acquired, he drank deeply for a while before finally replying. "Mind myself? Have you forgotten that you are far from Sythos? You hold no advantage here."

Gabriel had to rein in his anger. Hating being at a disadvantage, he took a deep breath. "She does ask an interesting question. What would it take to convince you?"

Van Crion chuckled, taking another drink. "Proof. A witness, anything. You offer me nothing yet you want my loyalty?" He laughed again. "I am not giving my life for you, Gabriel. The Artis have minded their own business for years, and for that we are untouched by the queen you so despise. As long as everyone, especially those bloody Iraquin, stay out of our business that's how it will remain."

"What would you say if I happen to have captured this witness?" Gabriel asked. "Would you listen?"

Van Crion shrugged. "Show me the witness first."

Gabriel turned to look at me. I went to stand beside him.

"Van Crion, I would like to introduce Arianna. Formally known as Lady Korinthos, personal friend to Queen Ophelia."

Van Crion immediately soared to his feet, crushing his cup with his bare hands! "How dare you mock me?" He hissed, cutting me with his stare. "You claim to have the queen's fool before me! You are no better than those cunt lickers, the Iraquin! Leave! Out of my sight, now!"

"Crion!" Gabriel barked in his authoritative voice.

Van Crion stormed down the tiny steps to his throne and towered over Gabriel. Both men wanted nothing more than to demolish the other. Tension and strength radiated throughout their entire beings. Van Crion was taller and leaner than Gabriel. But height would not be the advantage if they attacked each other. Speed, dexterity, strength. That would determine the victor. The Artis people wouldn't intervene, o' no. They would only attack if Gabriel's men attacked as well. If Van Crion got into it with someone, he would have to prove himself worthy. Just like everyone else. Perhaps that was why he didn't attack Gabriel outright. Gabriel had proven to be a formidable opponent after all.

Suddenly, a small sticklike man appeared at Van Crion's side and whispered something in his ear. I was close enough to hear the words, but they were spoken in a different tongue. Nevertheless, whatever was said momentarily eased some of the tension. As the man continued to talk, Van Crion began looking at me.

When the man was done, he left Van Crion to think intently with his glare burning a hole into me.

"Gabriel." Van Crion's tone had simmered just below harsh as he spoke Gabriel's name. "My scout has informed me that there is a chance you may have been telling the truth."

Gabriel said nothing as Van Crion released a breath and began turning toward me. Up close, it was apparent that I was a mere pebble in the face of a mountain. His strength far exceeded anything I could muster. With every breath he took, I could see his muscles tense and release. Had he wanted to kill me, he would need nothing more than the slight exertion of his clenched fist. His lack of civility showed in the way he maintained himself and his camp. Formalities were set aside entirely when in the presence of this man.

"Who are you?" he asked, his thick breath spilling onto my face.

Maintaining my composure I took a deep breath and replied, "I was born Arianna Korinthos. When I was in the presence of the queen I was given the title Lady Korinthos. Former friend to the queen."

Van Crion chuckled, giving me a once-over. "Lady Korinthos," he muttered before looking up at the rest of his congregation. "The infamous whore of King Araun has come among us!" There was an uproar of laughter and applause from the Artis people. Shame washed over me like a cold bath after a war. I couldn't bear to turn and look at Gabriel. Although he knew the truth about me and the king, I'm sure it wasn't pleasing to the ear to hear vile things about your mate. "Tell me, girl, what did the king taste like? What were his preferences when he came in you? Did he prefer your bum? I always figured him for flame. Am I right?"

Boiling with anger, I allowed my rage to control me. Had I been in control of myself I wouldn't have cracked him across the jaw with all the force I could gather. But I wasn't in control. And I did hit him. Hard.

Everything went silent. No one laughed. No one clapped. Everyone had settled into shock as the realization of what I had just done settled.

"You little bitch—"

"I am no whore, and I am no bitch," I snapped just as he was about to raise his hand to me. "The women you have chained to your ego may never speak as openly to you as I have, but never mind them. I am a being all of my own. You have spoken to me in a regard that makes me want your head! You know not of me or where I am from. Death is my friend, and I love a challenge. Continue to talk down to me as though I am no more than rubbish beneath your feet, and I promise I will not follow through with a threat as hollow as your head!"

Behind me I heard Ezekiel and the others prepare themselves for an onslaught. The Artis people had drawn their weapons as well. Van Crion was glaring down at me in utter disbelief. He was clearly aghast at my outspokenness. His fists were clenched tightly at his sides, and his breathing came out ragged and rough.

"Who do you think you are?" he hissed between clenched teeth.

I took a step closer to him. "I am Arianna Korinthos. And I have something to say."

For a moment Van Crion said nothing. He only glared down at me. It was as if he didn't know what to say. Like he was debating whether or not to let me live . . .

"Speak then," he replied. Turning away from me, he went back to his throne and sat down. "Convince me to join your little war."

I looked at Gabriel, and he nodded for me to begin. Taking a deep breath I took one more look around me. This was my time. This was my chance. To prove to Gabriel, all the rebels, Van Crion, and myself that I was worth more than a good lay.

I began with the story of the Qingkowuats. I told them how we used to live. How we were poor but happy. I told them about Meenoah and the other elders. I explained how it was my job to protect them from the Royal Army. "One day I was out practicing my aim, in a clearing not too far from the village, when the Royal Army surrounded me. I tried to escape, and I killed as many as I could. In the end they captured me and threw me into a cell." I described in great detail what it was like to see the queen at the arena. The closest thing I had ever come to luxury was what the Conqueror kept from me, and that was nothing like what I had seen when I saw the queen. "After I had proven myself to her, she invited me to dinner. And not too soon after that she gave me the title of Lady Korinthos." Memories of the palace flooded my brain. The porcelain walls. The glistening chandeliers. The thousands of Royals that wandered about. I even began to remember the king . . . and our game of chess. "I was not the king's whore. I was his friend, seemingly his only friend. That was until I learned about his true love . . . Parthena." From what I could see, I had the attention of everyone in the entire camp. I don't know whether or not they believed me, but I had to keep going. "I met Parthena. And she told me the truth about Ophelia. The queen has her locked away in a dungeon. She is your true queen. She is nice and pure. She loves deeply and passionately. The queen had the king killed because the king told me about Parthena." Thinking about Parthena had my heart aching. But that pain only continued as I told them of Teta, Zakai, and the other children I couldn't save. "I had witnessed dozens of hangings. I had seen many children die for a reason I cannot fathom. Two children from my village were killed right before my eyes. And I could do nothing but watch."

Turning to my audience, I spoke up. "This queen you so blindly follow wishes for nothing more than the destruction of all those who cannot pour her tea! You mean nothing to her! You have nothing she wants except for the land beneath your feet! She will kill your children and take everything away from you because she knows she can. No one has ever dared to fight against such a formidable foe! Until today. Sythos is prepared to fight for our right to life! Are you?"

Van Crion spoke first. "How do I know what you're saying is true? How do I know that this isn't just a woman's sick act of jealousy?"

"I can only offer my words. But travel south, towards the coast, and you will find the Qingkowuat village destroyed with no living souls wandering about. While you're there check out the Tyi village merely a stone's throw to the west. If that is not enough for you, travel farther west from here for thirty or so miles and you will find the ruins of the Naïf village. And if that still does not satisfy you, then travel to Lárnach and watch a child hanging. They occur often. Perhaps even every day."

He stopped looking at me and looked at Gabriel. "Do you trust what she says?"

Gabriel stepped forward and rested his hand on my shoulder. "I do. I have witnessed some of the things she has spoken of. My scouts have also brought me back facts that validate her entirely."

Van Crion thought for a moment, scratching the stubble on his chin. "I will make no declaration until I receive facts of my own. In regards to what she has said, I will take it into account. But my scouts will do their own reconnaissance." Van Crion sighed, relaxing into his throne. "I will send you word of my decision within the week."

"Fair words," Gabriel replied.

"Now, be gone. I have other matters to tend to." Just then a sultry woman appeared. She was dressed in nearly nothing, with her attributes bared for all to see. She dropped to her knees in front of Van Crion, a practiced act.

* * *

Sythos was exuberant with joy as nighttime fell upon us. The refugees had prepared a feast for us and the camp was beautifully decorated. A bonfire was burning bright in the night sky as men, women, and children danced around it, singing their praises.

It had only taken Van Crion three days to make his decision. And he decided to stand with us in our fight. Gabriel was very grateful and even invited some of the Artis people to visit. A few of their women and men showed up, but Diatomin and Van Crion did not make the trek. Nevertheless, their acceptance was definitely appreciated.

The entire camp praised Gabriel for his outstanding leadership skills. The children had made him many beaded necklaces to show their gratitude. His men were ever so faithful to him, and I too had become even more engrossed in him. He was beyond words. He was my Gabriel.

"Would you care for something to eat?" a woman refugee asked as I stood and watched the festivities. "I could get you more wine, if it would please you."

"No, thank you, ma'am," I replied, trying my best to show a kind smile. "Please, enjoy yourself."

It seems I too was being thanked for my efforts in our rebellion. The rebels saw me as more than Gabriel's bedmate, and the refugees spoke and looked at me as if I were royalty.

It felt indescribable to be held to such a high standard. Never had I felt more accomplished in my entire life. Bacchus, evil and hateful Bacchus, had even come over to me and patted me on the shoulder.

It was a start to a relationship that would never pass the threshold of acquaintances. But that was good enough for me.

"Come to me, Ari." I heard Gabriel's deep voice coming from near the bonfire. He was sitting on a wooden chair; the refugees called it a throne, but Gabriel refused to call it that. He was surrounded by some of the rebels. Ezekiel and Bacchus sat by his side, drinking and eating, happily content. Isaac and Guryon stood behind them, showing an emotion that I assumed was contentment.

The entire camp was alive with happiness. Just like we all deserved to be.

I took my time walking over to Gabriel. Although our relationship was well-known to everyone with eyes and the ability to think for themselves, I still didn't want to be seen as some cock-hungry harlot.

As I approached their little spread, both Ezekiel and Bacchus raised their glasses to me. I smiled at them and went into Gabriel's outstretched arms. As gently as this man could muster, he pulled me into him and placed me on his lap. In front of us, people were dancing by the bonfire, thoroughly enjoying their evening. I clapped along with the beat of the music as Gabriel placed his hand on my waist and drank wine from his wooden cup.

"Did you see how this little lady stood up to old Crion? Cracked him right in the kisser!" Ezekiel chided, turning to face me. "Plus, that little speech of hers gave me the chills! He didn't want to admit it right then and there, but that fucker knew you were right."

I laughed at his drunkenness but was also humbled by his kind words. He was right, Van Crion knew I spoke nothing but truth. I saw it in the way his hollow eyes simmered beneath rage as I spoke of things he knew to be true. All I had done was validate rumors.

"Most beautiful thing I had ever seen," Gabriel purred in my ear. His grip on me tightened as he brought his cup to his lips. "Sythos!" he barked, gathering everyone's attention. For a moment the music stopped and everyone turned to look at Gabriel. He raised his cup and said, "A toast to our newest member who has laid her life on the line for us in times we so desperately needed her to. She is fearless, powerful, graceful, and beyond words. To Arianna!"

"To Arianna!" Everyone repeated cheerfully. I nodded my thanks, and everyone went back to the festivities.

The noise was so incredibly loud that I had to lean in close to Gabriel to say, "You just love putting me in the spotlight, huh?"

I felt him smile as he replied, "I like to make you squirm." The devilish gleam in his eyes as I pulled away from him sent a warm rush of anticipation down my entire body. Slowly he pulled my face in and kissed me, in front of everyone who wanted to watch, long and hard. I was shameless as I stroked my tongue deep in his mouth, battling with him for dominance over the moment. He smiled when we pulled away from each other and stroked his thumb down my cheek. "So beautiful."

I chuckled. "You're drunk."

"Not yet," he said just as he drank from his cup again. "But I may just let you get me there." Gabriel's body was a work of art. Even as he sat relaxed and at ease, he was still a magnificent force all on his own. His body was saturated in thick taut muscles that glistened with the sweat of his exertion. His fur tunic did nothing to hide his strength. His deep navy-blue irises captivated all who neared him, drawing them into him like the ocean to the shore during high tide. His ruggedness was handsomely shown in the short buzz of his dark brown hair. There was hardly anything for me to hold onto when he took me to his bed. This man was delectable. Astonishing. Gravitating. And mine. All mine.

"Come to me tonight," I whispered seductively.

Running his hand up my back and tangling his fingers in my hair, he replied, "I wouldn't want to be anywhere else." I kissed him, smiling the entire time.

"He doesn't want to speak with you right now," I heard a voice off to the side say. Pulling my attention away from Gabriel's ravishing face, I turned to see Moira blocking a visibly drunk and flustered Fenella. "Go sleep it off!"

"Unhand me!" Fenella whined, trying to get past Moira. "I need to speak to him."

"Go back to your tent," Moira commanded. Annoyed, Fenella turned to Moira, gurgled something in her throat, and spit it onto Moira's face.

"Slurp that, cunt licker," Fenella hissed, shoving by her.

Immediately I surged from Gabriel's lap and was about to storm over to Fenella, but she had already stumbled over to us.

She looked horrible. Even with her voluptuous hips and breasts, her body looked disheveled and wrecked. Her hair was thin and filthy, and her clothes were tearing and stained. Normally, women in the brothel took better care of themselves. Clearly, Fenella didn't want to make the effort. Not even as she came over to seduce Gabriel.

"Captain, my Captain . . ." She slurred her words as she struggled to remain standing. "I have . . . missed . . . you . . . you . . . terribly."

Gabriel sighed loudly, obviously annoyed. He was just about to reply, but I stopped him and took a step toward Fenella.

"What is it you want?" I asked, eyeing her from the top of her head to her bare feet.

Her demeanor took on an entirely different tone as she straightened her shoulders and pointed at me. "I-I don't want . . . to talk . . . to you!" She stifled a burp while swaying on her unsteady feet. "You are n-n-nothing to him."

I smiled a smile so sharp she winced at it. Leaning forward, I replied, "You are just a used-up whore who has yet to understand that her duties no longer lie with him. You're embarrassing yourself."

Fuming with rage, she reached down to her leg and pulled out a hidden blade. She went to stab me with it, but I grabbed her wrist with one hand and cracked her across the face with the other. Roughly she crashed to the ground, rolling a few feet away from me. She screamed at the top of her lungs, holding her bleeding lip.

The music stopped.

Everyone turned to look at us.

"Let me make something clear, you mindless twat," I snarled, walking over to her. "You are only here to spread your legs for men. You're a whore, a used one, and it's high time you know your place! I am here to help save Islocia. Now you tell me, which is more valuable? Which is more admirable?"

She chuckled humorlessly and turned to look up at me, blood oozing from her mouth. "Well, isn't that the sea calling the ocean blue? You were the king's discarded whore. And now you come to Sythos to what? Bend over for ours?"

Ignoring the anger I wanted so desperately to express, I smiled at her. "You lack the capacity for anything beyond a superficial rumor. No matter, I will ignore it. But be mindful of what you speak, my dear friend, because I would love nothing more than to cut off your breasts and force-feed them to you. I am a merciless soul, and all I can see is your death by my hands."

Frightened, she shot a look a Gabriel, hoping he would save her. "My Captain! How can you let her talk to me like that? I was your lover for many nights. I allowed you my vanity!"

"As whores often do," I muttered.

"Surely I am worth more than of what she speaks!" she exclaimed.

Rolling his eyes, Gabriel took a large gulp from his cup. "There isn't enough wine in the world to deal with these women." he murmured to Bacchus, who acted as if he was oblivious to the entire conversation. "What do you want, Fenella?"

On unstable legs she stood, stumbled for a second, and then finally gained control of herself. To her the world must've been sitting on its side, for she could hardly keep from swaying.

Raking her fingers through her hair and pushing up her breast, she replied, "Captain, I want . . . y-you to make a ch-choice. I am your lover, and this . . . intruder should mean nothing to you! I have been yours to do as you please with for far longer than I can even remember!" Her words were jumbled and slurring together as she spoke. "We r-rescued each other the day you found me. Return the favor. Discard her just as she is used to. I am your woman, enough of this girl." Gabriel didn't say anything. "Come to me tonight, and I promise I can make you forget all about her." Still he said nothing. "Have you nothing to say?"

Finally Gabriel stood and walked over to her. I thought he was going to stop and whisper something to her, but instead he turned just as he approached her and went to me. Without even checking his stride, his powerful muscles tensing with the movement of his body, he grabbed my face and sealed his mouth over mine. It wasn't long until his tongue dove deep into me, igniting my lust for him. I was needy and breathless when he pulled away. As the blood roaring in my ear simmered, I could hear the applause erupting around us. Gabriel had made his decision. And so had Sythos.

"You just tried to kill Sythos's most precious gem. You're lucky I don't kill you. I have no desire to ever want to lay my eyes upon you ever again," he growled, turning to Fenella. "I want nothing more than for you to leave my sight. Forever." Shattered beyond belief, Fenella nearly fell under the weight of his declaration. Her thin hands trembled as she covered her mouth against the anguish. "Moira! Pack Fenella's things and give her some food to go. She is no longer welcome here."

"Yes, sir," Moira replied gleefully.

"Everyone else!" Gabriel shouted, grabbing my hand and leading me back to his chair. "Enjoy yourselves. Eat, drink, and laugh. The night is ours. To Sythos! To family! To victory!"

CHAPTER 29

I HAD NEVER REALLY NOTICED THE sunrise. I knew it accompanied the dawn and it cast wondrous colors, but I never noticed it. To me, the sunrise was merely a signal for me to wake and begin the day. It was rudimentary. Normal. Unremarkable.

With my new life, everything changed. I awoke, but not in the same way. I dressed, but not as I used to. Things, whether simple or complex, took on an entirely new meaning. The sun was more than my light or beginning to the day. It was a sense of hope and redemption. Though shadowed by the night and force to succumb, it always found a way to rise again. Beautiful. Holy. Reborn.

Sythos's size had grown immensely ever since we began our endeavors to unite the remaining villages. Hundreds of new refugees caught wind of our plan as the weeks flew by. Joining us were the people of Rhine, Qualmi, Eikcaj, Ynafit, Herec, Kion, and the remaining members from Naïf. On average each new village brought with them a hundred or so people. Some even more.

Within this time we had also destroyed three more guards' camps. From what the spies were telling us there weren't that many left.

The Artis people, though I didn't completely accept their presence, made good on their word to assist us. Every day more men came over to pledge their loyalties; they even brought us supplies. However, the men from Artis were unruly, to say the least. Therefore, they had their own separate section of Sythos to reside in. Van Crion only visited a handful of times. He rarely spoke to me, but Ezekiel told me it was because he was uncomfortable around me. Not afraid, but more so because he didn't know what to make of me. In their camp the women didn't even know their own language. They were bred to be slaves to the men of their camp. So to Van Crion, I was an entirely new species. He also made a note to tell Gabriel that I wasn't to be invited back to the Artis camp. Ever.

Gabriel had declared to the camp that we would attack the queen within the next two moon changes. We wanted the element of surprise on our side, but the weather in Islocia was unpredictable. Though the winter season was making its leave, it wasn't definitive that it would remain as calm as it has been. The spring months would certainly be more forgiving.

As our camp grew, our roles changed as well. Moira, Colleen, and Abigail were in charge of the refugees. They made sure the majority of their needs were met. The refugees were obligated to help make weapons for the rebels. Ezekiel, Bacchus, and Gabriel were in charge of training the new recruits. Axel helped with training new archers too. My main task was to give as much information about the Royal Army as I could remember. I was also in charge of telling my story. No matter how many times; I had to. It was time the people of Islocia knew the truth.

The only people we couldn't get to cooperate were the Iraquin. They refused us entirely because of our association with the Artis. Even as I told my story, they only shook their heads and sent us on our way. Their leader, Aldous, wouldn't even come out to see us. Unlike the Artis people, he had his woman, Aphrodi, do all of his bidding. Unfortunately she had lost one of her sons during one of the many battles between the Artis and the Iraquin people. She would not budge. No matter what.

We especially wanted the Iraquin people on our side because their numbers were far beyond what we could comprehend. Even the Royal Army did not tread on the Iraquin. It is rumored that Aldous receives a pension from the palace to remain neutral in conflicts. If the Royal Army was to raid a neighboring village to the Iraquin then the Iraquin would have to remain silent. In exchange the palace pays them a handsome sum for their cooperation. It is possible to believe that perhaps maybe the Iraquin people did sell out the Artis people.

Our main concern with the Iraquin was that they would join the Royal Army. That would definitely ensure our defeat. The Iraquin cooperated on the pretense of a dictator. Due to the pension Aldous got from the palace he could afford the latest weapons to defend his camp. It would be a definite loss to lose them as allies. Therefore, Gabriel and I continued to try to persuade them to join us.

"Captain." Bacchus approached me and Gabriel as we were discussing how we would need to expand our camp to accommodate the new arrivals. The sun was hanging high in the sky, beautifully, shining down on us all. It was as if the heavens were approving our endeavor to destroy the queen. "The Artis men are threatening to start eating the children."

Sighing, Gabriel rubbed his brow and replied, "Take them hunting with you. We can't skip meals two days in a row."

Bacchus nodded. "Are you riding with us?"

Gabriel shook his head. "I need to put up more tents. Our scouts got word that some scattered villages are making their way towards us." Gabriel, Bacchus, and I began walking toward a pile of freshly made cloth and logs for tents. "Take as many men as you want. In fact, take most of them. They need to be kept busy for a little while. The herds should be returning soon. It should be plentiful."

"I'll leave Isaac and Guryon behind while we are gone," Bacchus said as we both watched Gabriel lift the long wooden logs and hold them on his shoulder. The muscles in his arms tensed tightly, begging for relief through his taut skin.

"No need, we will be fine, I assure you. Take at least one of them with you. I'm sure they would enjoy some time out." He grunted loudly as he moved the logs from their pile to an area off to the side of the camp. "How about here, Ari?"

"It's a little close to the forest. We might have to cut down some of these trees," I replied, looking up at the tall trees that towered over Sythos.

He shrugged. "That shouldn't take long." He turned back to Bacchus. "Fine, take Guryon and leave Isaac. He can help me with these trees."

Bacchus nodded and walked away. I had yet to take my eyes off of Gabriel. The sun complemented him so well—how could I not stare?

"You're staring." He snickered, grabbing me by my waist and pulling me into him. His body was warm against me. I couldn't help but respond sexually to him. My breast grew heavy, and my nipples hardened as I felt his skin through my thin layer of clothing. My sex grew hot and needy, and my eyes hung low with lust. Gabriel was a man who could torment my body with ruthless pleasure yet act so tender to the watchful eye. It was only in private that his ravishing lust was showcased. I felt it when he took me as his. I felt it as his nails dug into my skin and his teeth nibbled at my flesh. Purple bruises were left on my neck, arms, and breasts every morning after we were done. He was rough with me in a way that made the pleasure that much more . . . exciting.

"I think you were mistaken." I smiled, reaching my hands out to rest on his hips. O' how tough his skin was beneath the palms of my hands.

"That must be it." He smiled back at me, his navy-blue eyes warming me even more. Beneath us I felt the ground rumble slightly. Turning, I saw our men ride by—some on horseback, some walking—and head toward the forest. We waved them off as they went loudly into the Iclin Forest. Gabriel grabbed my attention again by putting his lips to my ear. "What do you say we take a break?"

Biting my lip, holding back a smile that would fill my entire face, I replied by taking his hand and leading him toward a vacated tent. It was one we had put together yesterday, and lucky for us, no one had claimed it yet.

Gabriel was patient until we were completely alone. Once inside the tent he grabbed my waist and turned me away from him. Immediately his hands were all over me. Sensation flooded throughout my body, and a slight moan escaped me as one of his curious fingers slid beneath my garment. "So beautiful," he repeated as I backed into him.

As his lust grew he became rougher. I loved it. But it wasn't nighttime, and people were around. We had to be quiet. "Don't tear my clothes too much. We have work to do after this."

Growling, he pulled my top over my head, and my bottoms soon fell to my feet. He turned me so I was facing him again, and he kissed me, bruising my lips with his teeth sinking in deep. I whimpered, but it did not stop him. A moment later he took me to the floor, covering me with his body.

My excitement was controlling me. I wanted him so very badly. Reaching for his pants I tried to push them down, but he stayed my hands and did it himself. In a matter of moments we were both nude and rolling all over the small tent. When he started thrusting, I had to stifle my screams by biting his shoulder. That didn't deter him;

in fact, it made him more excited. His groans of delight grew more feverish as he noticed how good he was making me feel. Linking my fingers in his hair, I pulled at the short ends as we reached our end. My body took over, writhing uncontrollably, taking his pleasure as it pummeled into me. Sometimes it was excruciating, but I loved it. I loved how my body shook with every hard spurt of his pleasure. I loved how my voice grew raw from acknowledging my delight. Our sweat mingled in with our kisses as he held me tight. The thick smell of sex permeated the small tent, coating us. Gabriel took me with a force so great I couldn't bring myself to rise so soon after we had finished. My body would be sore for days after; it was difficult at times to accommodate his size. But I took what he gave me; I took it graciously.

In the end we always ended up in each other's arms. Sweaty, exhausted, and happy. No matter how many times Gabriel took me, I couldn't stop touching him. His body felt . . . amazing against mine. He was so rugged yet soft. Smooth yet thick with muscles. At times I would trace the planes and crevices of his impeccable body. I couldn't help it. He felt so good to me.

"Good Gods." He sighed, tucking me into him. "You, little lady, will be the death of me."

Basking in female triumph, I stroked my hand up and down his torso. "We will be the death of each other."

I felt his body vibrate with laughter beneath my cheek as he replied, "I wouldn't mind going that way. With you."

"You don't mean that." I rolled my eyes, sitting up. He remained lying down, looking up at me with his magnificent blue eyes. The curve of his lips told me he had meant what he said. "You and I are different in ways that affect us entirely. People are counting on you to lead them to victory. And when all is said and done, they will still be counting on you. My job will be done, but yours will be just beginning."

He thought for a moment, running his hand up and down my back. "What will you do when this is all over?"

I shrugged. "Return to the coast, maybe."

"You would leave me?" he asked. I heard the catch in his voice though he tried to hide it.

I shrugged. Leaning back down so my lips were at his mouth, I kissed him lightly and replied, "Your hunger for war will simmer once all this is over, just as your hunger for me will, overtime. I do not plan to stick around for that." I kissed him again.

Reaching up he grabbed the back of my head and forced me to take his kiss. His tongue licked deeply into my mouth, claiming me as his own. In one swift movement he had sat up and I was beneath him again. He spread my legs with his own and settled between me. "I hate when I allow you the option to speak. You never end up saying the right things."

I laughed at his distress, running my hands all over his chest, and said, "It's a gift to speak as eloquently as I do."

He bent down to my neck and bit me. At first it was soft, but it grew harder as he grabbed my leg and forced it to his side. I released a breathless cry as the pain quickly registered. With his tongue he licked the shell of my ear, leaving a trail of fire. When he looked back up at me, I saw the ferocity of his lust and wanting. It crippled me to see the effect I had on him. I felt the same toward him, if not stronger.

With his other hand he went between my legs and found my sex. Slowly he touched me. He was nice at first, but right when that first little whimper escaped me, he became more and more rough. He never took his eyes off me as he continued. I, on the other hand, couldn't control my body. He knew just how to make me lose myself. The little growls that vibrated in his throat made it all the more intoxicating. I grew louder and louder as he pushed me closer to my limit. My entire body quivered with pleasure. I was sure by now someone had heard us. For the life of me I couldn't keep quiet. His eyes, his growls, his attentiveness—it stirred me.

"You like that?" he asked with sweat dotting his brow. I couldn't control myself enough to reply yes, but he knew I did. It felt amazing. No, more than amazing! It was incredible! "You think you're going to leave?" He was growling even more now. "You're sadly mistaken, Ari." He pushed deeper, causing me to nearly scream at the stop of my lungs. "You're mine." Those two simple words took me over the edge. Gasping and screaming, writhing uncontrollably, my body was pummeled by shocks and waves of insurmountable ecstasy. I was so lost in the moment that Gabriel had to hold my body down so I didn't buck and kick him. His eyes never left me. I felt them on me as he watched how easily he had made me unravel before his very eyes.

Gabriel and I had eventually fallen asleep in each other's arms. When I had suggested we get back to work he had refused to let me go. He wanted that connection we always had with each other once we had shared ourselves so openly. It was still midafternoon as we napped in the tent. For only a few hours we wanted to shut out the rest of the world. Nothing was supposed to happen. We had only closed our eyes for a few moments when suddenly, outside of the tent, we heard a bloodcurdling scream. It jolted us awake. A second or two later we felt the ground rumbling with the sound of horse hooves accompanying it. At first, as we looked at each other, we thought it was only the men returning from their hunt. But more screams came about as the rumbling grew louder and louder.

Hurriedly Gabriel went to put on his clothes. I did the same, nearly falling over myself, trying to get my bottoms on. A sudden continuous crashing sound reverberated throughout the camp. Outside the tent we saw the shadows of people running in every direction!

Gabriel and I were just about to come out of the tent when suddenly two armed guards charged in! For a second I was blinded by their shiny metal and crimson capes. The tent was too small for us to fully attack, which meant that the guards had the advantage. They tackled Gabriel head-on, all three of them falling to the ground. Gabriel was quick to respond; he quickly grabbed the guard by his helmet and smashed it into the second guard. Assisting Gabriel, I pulled one of the guards off of him. That guard went to grab me and pull me down, but I kicked at his helmet. Just as Gabriel and I were about to take the advantage, two more guards charged in!

"Ari!" Gabriel yelled as the guards picked me up and slammed me to the ground. All of the wind was knocked out of me as they held me down by my wrists. Gasping for breath, I tried to fight back, but they had me pinned. One of the guards forced me onto my stomach; the other held my arms behind my back with his foot holding my face down. My eye was forced shut from the weight of his body on my head, but out of my other one I could see that they had Gabriel pinned too, beating him. At first he took the punches as if he hardly felt them, but as time went on, seconds feeling like hours, they battered him. He couldn't do anything to stop them. They beat him so hard tears clouded my vision as I tried to wiggle free.

Just as I thought things were circling down the drain, Gabriel showed his true strength. I watched as his entire body tensed, his muscles contracting as they pelted him with punches. I knew what was coming. These guards would soon be sorry.

With a loud snarl, Gabriel uncoiled. His strong arms flew out to his sides, knocking the knees of the guards on either side of him. Without missing a beat he surged to his feet in one powerful push. One of the guards who had been holding me left and went over to try to contain Gabriel, but I saw the look in Gabriel's eyes. It was that of a hunter protecting his kill. The guard that had left me went to pull out a dagger and stab Gabriel, but Gabriel caught his wrist, snapped it, and pulled the guard in and broke his neck. Another guard appeared behind Gabriel, but Gabriel already knew he was there. He turned quickly and grabbed the guard by his helmet and threw him to the ground, but he didn't let him go until he had completely torn out the guard's throat. Blood squirted everywhere, covering Gabriel and the tent.

The guard holding me didn't know what to do. Two against one wouldn't be in his best interest, but Gabriel was coming over to us, quickly. Gabriel's body was sheathed in sweat and crimson blood, his abdomen tensing tightly with every breath. Several bruises were growing along his chest and under his eye. The beautiful navy-blue eyes I had seen earlier had vanished completely. Gabriel was in the mood to kill.

Just then four more guards entered the tent and grabbed Gabriel. I screamed as they too began beating him . . . again. The guard on top of me held me tighter as the other guards forced Gabriel to the ground. Protecting his head, he curled into a ball as more kicks and punches came. One guard even pulled out a knife and sliced Gabriel along his back. Gabriel bellowed in agony as his blood spilled.

"Gabriel!" My screams were muffled from my face being forced to the ground.

It was only a couple of hours ago that we were cuddling in each other's arms. It was only an hour ago where the outside world had yet to exist. It was only a couple hours ago when we were happy . . .

and when things were the way they were supposed to be. It had only been a couple hours . . .

"Gabriel!" I cried, wishing there was more I could do! "Gabriel!"

Over the sound of my own screaming and the screams coming from outside, I heard someone else enter the tent. He only spoke a few words, and my world froze. My heart stopped.

"Bring them out here."

Immediately I was forced to my feet and shoved out of the tent. Blinded by the sun, I stumbled for a few steps. I was just about to turn around and begin to attack when I noticed the army of men surrounding me, their swords pointing at me. From behind me I heard them push Gabriel to the ground. Exhausted, Gabriel couldn't bring himself to his feet. I ran over to him, holding my hands over the wound at his back in an attempt to stop the bleeding. Thick, dark blood oozed out of the deep gash at an alarming rate. My hands were quickly coated in his blood, and he was growing weaker.

"So this is who you left me for?" That voice . . . I remembered that voice. It brought chills to my skin and burned my ears like acid. I wanted to vomit at the sound of it. His thick, odious charm sickened me. He spoke as though he could taunt you into hell with only the twitch of his finger. The world was at his command. Unfortunately, at the moment, so was I. "It seems you two were too busy rolling in the sheets instead of protecting your own people." The more he spoke, the worse the situation got. I wanted nothing more than to get up and kill him . . . I should've killed him when I had the chance o' so many months ago. If I had, none of this would be happening. "Bring one of them forward," he ordered. A moment later his guard appeared with a frightened woman refugee. I didn't know her personally, but I knew she had come from the Rhine village. She was new . . . and she had traveled very far in hopes that we would be able to keep her safe. I think she had a little boy with her when she had come. He was counting on us too. "You know, we had many people searching this godforsaken forest for months on end. So many precious man hours were wasted on *you*! I myself even attempted to aid in the search, but we were to no avail. That wasn't until a little gift had been sent to us . . . from you."

"Kill yourself!" I spit, still holding my hands over Gabriel's back.

"Temper, temper." He chuckled, looking down at me from his black steed. His icy-blue eyes sliced me open and left me bleeding as he stared at me. "Isn't that what got you in trouble in the first place? Your temper, Lady Korinthos?"

I tensed at my old false title. "On my life, I will slaughter you. I vow it. Your days are numbered, *Calder*." There, on the blackest horse imaginable, Calder sat with all his false righteousness. His pale, lean, wispy body with his irises the color of ice stared down at me. His clothes mirrored his horse, black as night and undoubtedly unforgiving. It had been ages since I had seen him. Nothing had changed. That charismatic smile that could lure you into depths unknown was still plastered on his porcelain-white face.

"I don't know why you are so angry with me." He shrugged in mock dismay. "I am merely doing what I've been told. You see, my queen isn't very happy with you. In fact, she told me to kill you when I found you. And I plan to follow through . . . thoroughly."

"Fight me then, Calder. Just me and you . . . one on one. You really think you could win?" I challenged, pressing deeper on Gabriel's wound. "Fight me! You coward!"

"Enough with the theatrics, Arianna." He smiled, shaking his head. "I am not going to dirty my hands with the likes of you. I have these wonderful people to do it for me." He gestured toward the guards surrounding me. "But I will get to that later. Right now I need to speak to your herd of degenerates."

Turning his horse he walked a few feet away from me. Following him with my gaze, I watched as he walked over to another huddle of guards. In the middle of that huddle were the remaining refugees. They were helpless . . . they were only women and children. They couldn't defend themselves.

"Sad, pathetic wastes of space," Calder began. "I am Adok Calder, a Royal from the palace sent under the authority of your queen. She asks of you to return to your villages and continue life as it was. Your focus should be on your quotas and nothing more. As I do recall, many of you have lost your children due to the inability to please your queen. Luckily, she is a forgiving queen and will return your children to you as soon as possible, as long as you return back to your villages. If you decide not to leave now, then your children will be slaughtered immediately upon my arrival back to the palace." He paused as he looked at all of them. "Let me remind all of you. Any act of rebellion against the monarchy is considered treason. And all of you will be punished. Do not let these"—he gestured toward me and Gabriel—"idiots cloud your mind! Nothing of what they speak of is true. The only person you should every listen to is the one who has been divinely put here by God, or whatever gods you believe in, to lead you. Go back to your villages! And life will resume as it should."

Turning back to us, he trotted over. His horse was merely inches from me as he looked down at me. "I'm going to kill one of your followers. Is that okay with you?"

"Calder, don't! This is between me and you! Leave them out of this!" I screamed, still trying to contain the bleeding. Calder pulled his horse away from me and signaled for the guards to bring the woman refugee forward. "Calder, don't!"

"This is the only end to this little . . . insurrection," Calder said to the other villagers. Speaking to one of the guards, he said, "Kill her."

"Calder!"

Without hesitation the guard pulled a knife out and brought it to the woman's neck. I didn't know what to do! I could try to save her, but then Gabriel might bleed out. If I kept my hands in place then this innocent woman would die . . . all because of me!

Unfortunately the guard didn't give me enough time to weigh my options. With a quick plunge of the knife he ended the woman's life. Her eyes rolled to the back of her head as blood shot from her throat. The guard dropped her to the ground, her mouth and nose spilling with blood that now painted the ground.

"It is not my intention to threaten the lives of your people," Calder continued, walking his horse right over the fallen woman. "Personally, I don't like threats. They're too *empty,* if you will. In fact, that is why I always follow through with a simple promise. All of you will die, just as she had, if you do not do as I have told you. I will not give you and your family another opportunity to escape the wrath of your queen. Now go home. Live peacefully, and life will continue as it should. Do not trust what she says to you!" He said pointing at me. "She claims the queen was the one who called for the death of children. That's not entirely true. Ask this traitor what her job was at the palace. You will soon understand that she too played a part in the death of *your* children. Isn't that true Arianna?"

I could feel my heart pound painfully in my chest as images of child hangings filled my mind. What he had said was true. I had a hand in the death of children.

All was quiet in Sythos. No one knew what to say; they were all crippled with fear. I too was unable to speak. It was all happening too fast. I could feel the villagers growing angry with me and losing faith in our mission.

"Guards!" Calder shouted. "Bring forth the children."

My heart stopped as three guards came forward. They were holding knives to the neck of three small little children of Sythos, one of them being my favorite, Karuli. Her little coconut-shaped head was messy from the struggle she had put up. The black of her irises were huge with fright as she reached her hands out to me. Karuli's mother wailed in anguish as two guards held her back. They had hit her, her eye purple and bleeding.

"No!" I screamed, my voice breaking as the muscly guard held Karuli's life in his grimy hands. "Calder, you're a piece of shit! If you kill these kids, you will leave these people with no faith in the monarchy. You will give them a reason to rebel!" I was saying anything to keep his mind away from the children; I had to save Karuli. She was counting on me.

Calder laughed, throwing his head back as if I had spoken a funny line. "You were always the clever one, Arianna. But you continue to doubt me." He turned back to the villagers. "I will not kill these precious little angels. They will be in the custody of the queen until you all have returned back to your original villages. Until then, this will be the last time you will ever see these three children."

"Don't listen to him!" I screamed, trying to keep the villagers' attention. "I used to live at the palace! I know what they do with these kids! You will never see them again! Don't listen to him!" I wanted nothing more than to run over to Calder and strangle him! But Gabriel had yet to stop bleeding. He wasn't moving and his breaths were shallow. Just then Calder dismounted and walked right over to me. Before I knew it he had raised his hand and slapped me across the face. It stung for a moment, but it didn't move me.

He knelt down to me and whispered as Karuli's mother continued to scream, "You were given everything you could've ever asked for—kerts, dresses, bountiful treasures—yet you threw it all away for what? Him? Your inglorious bastard?" He chuckled humorlessly. "I am disappointed in what you have become. And I am even more disgusted with what you will be. Or shall I say, what you would've been. For now I must kill you. Because unlike you, Arianna, I am going to do what I am told. And you're right. The minute I return back to the palace, those children will be dead." He turned and looked at the kids. "A friend of yours told me that she"—he pointed to Karuli—"is your favorite. Is that true?" I was spilling with rage; it showed in every haggard exhale I was able to manage. "I shall see to it that the same thing that happened to your little village girl will happen to her as well."

From beneath me I heard the sound of Gabriel's weak voice. "I . . . will . . . destroy you." He was trembling, consumed by pain and lack of blood.

Calder looked down at Gabriel, laughter filling his sharp eyes. He said, "Unfortunately, friend, you will not get that opportunity. At least not in this lifetime. I have orders to kill."

Gasping, forcing out every breath, he weakly replied, "You better . . . hurry up . . . and do it then."

All of a sudden, the heavens opened up to us, and we felt the rumblings of horse hooves coming from the forest. Turning away from Calder, I looked toward where the sound was coming from, and I saw the most glorious sight. Our men were returning. And from the short distance they were at, they could see everything that was happening.

Charging from the forest, at a speed unprecedented, the warriors of Sythos raced toward us. Calder was shocked; he hadn't guessed that there were more to our camp than just women and children. Our men were strapping and vile. Ruthless and unforgiving. They didn't take kindly to being treaded on. We outnumbered them, and Calder knew it.

"Retreat!" Panicked, Calder scampered back over to his horse and mounted quickly. "Take those children with you! We need to leave!" Without waiting for their response, Calder kicked his horse into gear and raced away from the camp. The guards holding the children quickly tossed them onto waiting horses and mounted as well. Karuli was screaming at the top of her lungs, stretching her arms toward her mother. Her mother, after being dropped by the guards, did everything she could to try to reach her daughter, but there was too much chaos. Our men had made it to the camp, and one by one they were slaughtering the straggling guards.

Bacchus and Ezekiel were riding point. Following behind them were herds of our men. Some of the guards didn't have enough time to escape; consequently, they dropped like flies as our men who were on foot brutally cut them down. Blood poured everywhere! The cries of dying men were beyond words. It was a sound heard all throughout Islocia.

All the while I could only sit and watch. Gabriel was still bleeding and was too weak to rise, no matter how hard he tried. "Let me up, Ari!" he growled, trying to push himself up. I had to lay my entire body on him just to keep him down. Had he been at full strength he would've easily been able to overthrow me. But he wasn't. And whatever little weight I had held him down.

Just then, I felt the presence of a mammoth-sized man standing over me. I looked up, and it was Isaac. He was staring down at me with his dark eyes, a scowl on his usually indifferent face. Slowly, he bent down to us and shoved my hands aside. It wasn't my intention to let him move me, but he was definitely far stronger than I was.

Turning Gabriel over, Isaac cradled him and lifted Gabriel off the ground with little to no effort. Isaac left me then and carried Gabriel off somewhere. I would've followed, but then I heard the sound of Karuli's mother again. Except this time, it was a cry of pure sorrow. The man who had captured Karuli had disappeared into the forest.

My heart sunk . . .

Not again . . . Not again . . . How is it possible that I kept losing everyone I try so desperately to keep? How is it possible that I am never as strong as I need to be? "Not again!" I beat the ground! Dust flew into the air as I punched the earth with all my might! "No, not again! How could you?" I cursed the heavens, angry tears spilling from my face. "Not again!" Karuli would be dead within a few days. It wouldn't take long for them to return to the palace. And that's if Calder even decided to wait to get to the palace to kill them. "No!" My throat grew raw from screaming! Dirt now covered my hands. But the pain was obsolete. I couldn't feel it anymore.

"H-help . . . me . . ." Next to me I heard the weak voice of someone. I turned to see who it was and was disgusted to see one of the guards bleeding on the ground. His helmet had been removed, and thick blood seeped out of his mouth and nose. Someone had stabbed him in the stomach, for he was clutching it while more blood covered him. "P-p-please." He was so close to choking on his blood that a part of me wanted to just sit there and watch him die. It would've brought me so much pleasure to do that.

But I didn't. Instead, I needed him.

Getting up, I stood over the fallen guard and felt nothing as he cried in agony. He was pathetic. Crying? He didn't have the right to. He was young, yes, but he felt as though it was his time to hold a sword. All mercy left me.

Looking around I saw Guryon walking by as the rest of our men finished off some of the guards that hadn't escaped. Calling him over, I waited until he was near. "Pick him up for me." Guryon nodded and did as he was told. He held him so the guard was face level with me.

Even upright the guard looked worthless. He was groaning in discomfort as more blood leaked from his lower stomach.

"I'm going to ask you something. And you're going to answer," I told him calmly. "If you don't answer I will save your life." Confusion marred his face, so I continued. "You do not want to live once I've gotten a hold on you." Looking at Guryon, I said, "Do you have a blade on you?" He nodded. I went to his waist and pulled it out of his waistband and toyed with it in front of the guard. "Would you like me to show you what I mean?" Without waiting for his reply, I grabbed his hand and separated his fingers. He tried to pull it free, but my grip was iron tight. With his middle finger in my hand I took the small blade in my other hand and aimed in under his fingernail. Trembling, the guard tried to plead with me to stop, but I was beyond compromise. Taking the blade I pushed it under his nail until I could see the shape of the blade beneath the skin in his middle finger. The sound he let out was unlike anything I had ever heard. It was worse than that of the sound of a mother having a breech birth. "Now I'm going to ask you my question." Around me everything in Sythos had flown into chaos. Mothers were wailing and everything was nearly torn down. But my world was focused on this guard. He had my full attention. "How did Calder find us?"

Gritting his teeth against the insurmountable pain, he tried to speak but couldn't get the words out.

"I take it you want me to do this to your other fingers then? Huh?" I slowly—so he felt every inch of the blade—pulled it out. His hand shook uncontrollably as thick purple blood covered what was left of his middle finger. I then aimed the blade at his ring finger. "You married?" I asked, noticing the gold band on it. He nodded quickly. "I might cut this one off entirely." More tears fell from his face. I ignored them. "Answer my question or I will shove this down your wife's throat too."

Weeping like a woman, he replied over jumbled words, "S-s-someone c-came to the palace . . . s-s-someone from . . . from . . . the v-v-villages."

"Who was it?" I asked, rubbing the blade over his ring finger.

He shook his head. "I d-d-don't know. S-s-she didn't give her name."

"Where is he taking those kids?"

Sobbing, he said, "To the Bastille. The . . ." He coughed up blood and saliva. I waited patiently until he continued. "The queen . . . wanted to gather . . . all of the children there. We had orders to burn it once we returned. The kids were to be locked inside."

Angered, I dropped the blade and cracked the guard across the face. His nose shattered and a tooth fell from his mouth.

"Shit!" I cursed. "Follow me." Guryon obediently did as he was told, dragging the limp guard behind him. We walked over to where all of the villagers were crowded around one of the huts. They were arguing and screaming about something. I heard things like "Respect the monarchy" and "We need to leave." Ezekiel was trying to mediate the situation, but the villagers weren't listening.

However, I had exactly what they needed.

Pushing past them, sidestepping a weeping mother, I went to Ezekiel. The roaring of the villagers grew louder as I became the center focus.

"Everyone! Listen to me!" They didn't quiet down. "Listen to me!" I said a little louder. A moment later I was being cursed for bringing this on them. "Shut the hell up!" I roared. And finally things settled. "I know you are all angry! And you have every right to be, but you are angry at the wrong person! The queen will not allow you to live on her land! She wants nothing more than for your death and the death of your children." I nodded at Guryon and he brought the guard forward. "This man has just told me that the queen ordered her soldiers to gather all of the village children into the Bastille. Once they are all there, they're going to burn it down with your little boy or little girl still inside." Grabbing the guard's face, I whispered to him, "Say it."

With what little strength he had left, he nodded his head and said, "It's . . . It's . . . true."

One man stepped forward and asked, "So what are we supposed to do? Wage war against a monarch beyond that of which anything we can comprehend. She has shown the control she has over us! All you've proven to be was a liar and a traitor! Maybe we should fight you!"

Frustrated, I replied, "You may want to give up on your children. But I know there are mothers out here who are willing to defy this false queen in hopes of saving their child!" I looked every woman in the eye until it landed on Karuli's mother. "You lost your baby girl. And for that I am sorry." I turned my attention back to everyone else. "No matter if I ride alone, or with company, I am going to the queen. And with everything that God or the gods have given me, I am going to kill her and mount her head on my wall. I am not going to be a prisoner to fear, and neither should you. What I did during my time at the palace is unforgivable. And I will have to live with that for the rest of my days. But that is the past and this is now! We need to fight!" I paused as my voice grew more and more passionate. "I cannot give you courage. That is something you have to have for yourself. It is something you must dig for. It is something that you must find for yourself! The only thing I can give you is the promise that I will not stop until Islocia is free from tyranny. The warriors of Sythos and I are willing to lay our lives down for *your* children. What are *you* willing to do?" Going over to Guryon, I pulled another dagger out of his waistband. Looking at the guard and then looking back at the dagger, I tossed it over to Karuli's mom. "He's yours to do with as you please."

At that Guryon dropped the guard on the ground, and Karuli's mom picked up the dagger. I left them then and entered the hut they were all crowded around. Inside, Moira and Abigail were tending to Gabriel. They had a thick bandage that wrapped around his entire back. Gabriel was sitting up on the table, holding the bandage in place while Abigail put some herbs on it. He winced in pain as Abigail patted the bandage in place. I looked away; I couldn't watch him be in pain. He hadn't made eye contact with me either, which shows he didn't want me to see him that way either.

"I heard what you said to them," he said in a thick voice to hide the pain. "They won't follow us anymore, Ari. We've lost all their faith in us."

Sighing, I replied, "I know. They still want to trust her. They still think she's going to make good on her word."

"You know she won't," he said, nodding thanks to Abigail.

"I know . . ." Memories of Teta and Zakai assaulted my brain. I had to fight back tears as I remembered what Teta's little body looked like hanging from a noose. "That's how I lost Teta."

"Give us a minute," Gabriel said to the others. Moira and Abigail nodded and left the hut.

"Do you know what her last words were when she died?" I didn't give him time to answer. "She said *Aoife*. Do you know what that means?" He shook his head. "It's a name derived from ancient times. Meenoah used to tell the children tales of a woman named *Aoife*. She was said to be the greatest female warrior of all time. She was a hero. I was Teta's *Aoife*. I was supposed to save her."

"Ari, come here."

"No," I snapped. "Don't, Gabriel. I know I shouldn't let them affect me so much. I know I shouldn't be so controlled by my retribution. But you don't know what it's like . . . You have no idea what it's like to watch the desecration of innocence. You have no idea what it does to your soul to watch young terrified bodies fight for their last breath . . ."

"Ari . . ."

I held up my hand, suppressing a sob. "There is no way for you to understand the rage you must suppress when you watch a child you've witnessed grow up lie limp way before her time! You don't know what it's like . . .," I sobbed tearlessly, "to be a part of the death of millions. I do." Looking into his navy-blue eyes I felt the tears that wanted to fall, but I held them back. "I am the one who must live with this pain, this fury, this sadness for the rest of my days! Because, at the time, I was too tamed to stop it. This is my fault! And now it is up to me to make this right!" Clearing my throat, I said, "I'm riding out against the queen. War has been declared."

Standing, ignoring his own pain, he came over to me. He saw that I was too tense to touch, so he just stood there and looked down at me. "I will ride with you, but we need a plan."

"I have one." He smiled at that. He knew just as much as I did that the queen had declared war on her own people. It was time we retaliated. For once, we will be heard. Not with a cry for peace or a scroll written in the name of justice. No. She will hear our hearts! She will feel our rage! Not through speeches of the majorities or by the petition of minorities. No. She will see our blood. She will see our iron. And even more so, she will feel our wrath.

OPHELIA

Queen

I am Queen. Placed before God's feet and beckoned to divine prosperity. I am Queen. Held to the highest standard, gifted with infinite power. I am Queen. My subjects beneath me, I standing on their backs. I am Queen. To do with as I please, my Kingdom. I am Queen. Resistant to the fires of hell and forever graciously welcomed into heaven. I am Queen. I am Queen. I am Queen.

—Queen Ophelia Valkiria Asphodel Acheros of Islocia

CHAPTER 30

THE WORLD IS MINE TO do with as I please. Everything was made or created to aid in my prosperity. Gold trimmings, diamond jewels, and many priceless bounties of artwork are merely not enough to show the appreciation I deserve.

"My queen." Adok was kneeling before me. He was devilishly handsome, porcelain and clean. My heart was his and his was mine. At the moment, however, he was not in my favor. Not unless he delivered the news I had been so patiently waiting for.

"Have you found her?" I asked, staring down at his perfectly combed brown hair. Many nights I ran my hands through those silk strands. I wonder if he would join me again this evening.

"Yes, my queen." He had yet to show me his beautiful eyes; he kept them to the floor. It concerned me.

"Is she dead?" My voice echoed through *Le salon de la Paix*. It was my most beautiful room. But in this hollow palace were many beautiful rooms with many beautiful things that always found a way to bore me.

"Our informant did not make it clear that there were hundreds of those rebel savages. We were caught off guard and were chased out of Sythos. I am sorry, my queen," Finally, the impeccable blue of his eyes were shown. They really were magnificent. However, at the moment, he had failed me. Miserably. "We were able to capture some of their . . . offspring."

"That's something." I sighed, exhausted from this. Months and months I had my men searching tirelessly for that little wench. Yet here we have found her and again she had escaped. "Arianna Korinthos is like an oiled fish that is flopping around in an attempt to find the sea. And apparently, no one can catch her." The gown I had chosen to wear was stiff, and the layers were itchy. I wanted desperately to be undressed. However, I had many matters to tend to today. There were many documents for me to read. There was always someone somewhere complaining or begging me to change a law or circumstance. Frankly, I didn't have the time for it. "Bring me the informant," I said to Joseph, the guard standing by the entryway. "Rise, my love." Calder did as he was told and came to me. I stretched out my hand to him and he kissed it tenderly.

A moment passed and finally Joseph had returned with the woman I had requested. She was tall and slender with big round breasts that poked through every outfit I put her in. Her long brown hair sank to her waist, and the sensual spark in her brown eyes had my men falling over themselves just to be near her. However, what she made up for in beauty, she lacked in intelligence, dirtying her appearance all the more.

"My queen." Even her voice was lusty with temptation as she bowed low before me. I eyed Calder quickly and was happy to see his face was indifferent. Joseph, on the other hand, was itching to adjust the waistband of his crimson leather tunic. Disgusting. The old gimp couldn't get a rise from his manhood had the wench been on her knees before him.

I shook my head at that thought. For they weren't queenly thoughts. My mother, God rest her soul, would be very disappointed.

"Rise, my dear." I was forced to accept her presence in the name of the monarchy. As she stood, her body unfolded in waves of toxic paramour. "It seems we have a bit of a problem. Adok took you on your word and went and found the camp from which you came. He went on the pretense that you had given him all the information you had possessed. However, you failed to mention the simple fact that there were hundreds of men, fighting men, there."

The woman looked startled at my response to the situation. What she should be startled about is that she had failed her queen. She bowed again, kissing the floor. "I am sorry, Your Majesty. Truly I am. When I had left the camp it was only a few dozen men that had joined us . . . I mean *them*. Please, forgive me."

My mind was distracted. I couldn't care less about this woman; in fact, I did. She was so simple and repulsive. In a moment I wanted to march to the chapel and ask God why he had created such a mindless being. What purpose, besides that of what is between her legs, did she hold? Even her name escapes the capacity of my memory!

"I understand, my dear." I sighed, completely exasperated. "I do not fault you for being inadequate. Because if I faulted you, I would then have to fault my entire kingdom. Only God and I remain intact while everyone else lies around in pieces." She didn't appreciate my comment. I figured it was quite fair. "Is there anything else you wish to tell us?"

She thought deeply for a moment, really putting her all into it until finally she said, "There is nothing else."

I was not surprised. She had the mental capacity of a dead horse, maybe even less than that. I waved her off. "Very well, I'm done with you." I turned to Joseph. "Take her back to her room."

Joseph nodded and motioned for the woman to follow. Before the woman left she bowed her head, something I assume she is very skilled at, and left.

"She's a whole lot of nothing," Adok muttered, turning his attention back to me.

I replied, "Many people are."

"What do you want to do with her? We can't let her go, and the Grand Royals would never allow her to stay in Lárnach. The people of Yenyun and Kreni might house her but only for a sizeable fee," Adok said in his usual charming voice. He was so unlike the other Royals I surrounded myself with. I was deeply drawn to his intellect and wit. He, on the other hand, was drawn to my power. Together, we were an impenetrable force that even God himself could not destroy.

"I will not pay for that insufferable wench," My money will only be spent on things with a purpose. "Feed her to the lions for all I care. My main concern is Arianna and her band of misfits. What are we going to do about them?"

"I wouldn't be too entirely concerned. I gave a pretty little speech to her frightened herd. They're returning back to their villages as we speak." Adok was so confident, so sure of himself. I saw it in the way his mouth curved in a slight smile and the way his composure relaxed. He is exactly what I needed. Unfortunately it wasn't enough.

"She has already planted the seed for insurrection in their worthless minds." Just the thought of Arianna churned my stomach. How could something so mindless be such a credible threat to my throne? She was nothing but a weapon when she was here; now she's a martyr. "We may have suppressed it for now, but what about a few years down the road? Am I going to have to worry about this every time there's a bad harvest? I need them gone." My worthless peasants... they cause me so much trouble. Trouble a queen should never have to deal with. "Killing their children only stops their bloodlines. But that's not enough. I want them gone, entirely."

"That would destroy your working class. We need them to grow our food, breed livestock. We need them to do the work we were never meant to do." Of course Adok was thinking logically.

"So what do you propose we do? Succumb to every threat they make against my crown?" I was not in the mood to be angry, but in fact, I was getting there!

"No, a queen should never live in fear of her subjects," Adok replied, acknowledging my angst. "Therefore, I believe you should impose a tax on the middle class."

"What would that solve?" I was never one to denounce more money, but I didn't see how that would help my situation.

"Tax them so high that it forces them into poverty. Unfortunately, it would cut Lárnach's population in half, but Yenyun, Kreni, and Hellec would more than compensate for the loss," he replied nonchalantly.

I chewed over it for a moment. "Wouldn't that make them despise me just as my peasants do?"

"Give all of the credit to the Master of Treasury." He shrugged matter-of-factly. "Say you had nothing to do with it."

"They would then just ask me to fire him." This was getting nowhere, fast.

He thought for a moment. "All right, then say that the reason the tax had to be so high was because of the rebellious villages in the forest. It cost money to be rid of them, does it not?"

I nodded thoughtfully, catching onto what he was saying. "Those who fall into the poverty line would have to blame the rebels. Not me."

"Exactly, you were merely doing what any monarch would do. Suppressing treason." Adok was smiling from ear to ear. "March your troops through the forest and demolish all of those pagan villages. In the end your crown is protected and you maintain a loyal working class."

I couldn't hide my own satisfaction with this plan. It was brilliant! "Adok, my love"—I stretched my hands out to him and he came to me, grasping them tightly—"you just might have insured the survival of my legacy. You are my most prized possession." I kissed his hands. "Raise my army, and end this as quickly as possible."

"It would be my honor, my queen."

* * *

I have not the slightest idea as to why mirrors were ever considered a luxury. Yet here I am, sitting before the very thing I hate. One might ask themselves why a queen would be so disturbed by a mirror. Well, I am not disturbed by the mirror itself, but I am repulsed by the honesty of which it captures.

Grabbing the warm cloth I had brought to my room, I rubbed it on my face. The harder I rubbed, the more of my paint came off. Had it been my choice, I wouldn't use the mirror. It was a beautiful mirror. Gold metals were intricately designed around the frame of it, and ruby hearts were pinned to the base. Its beauty was remarkable; however, its purpose was dreadful.

I did not particularly like what I saw when I looked into my mirror. Especially when the paint was chipped away. I hated the paint. I hated how it smelled. I hate how it burned and irked my face. But I had to wear it. Mother always said a queen is only as powerful as her beauty.

When I was little, I used to watch my mother paint her face. She used the palest of colors for her base and red for her blush and lips. She thought that if she could mirror perfection, then she would somehow become perfect. Overtime, however, the paint began to eat at her face. Consequently, she would wear more of it. And more. And more. Until finally, my mother disappeared altogether. I never understood why she would put herself through that. I believed her to be the most beautiful woman in the world, yet she did not see herself that way.

Now as I looked upon my red and blotchy skin, I knew why she did it. Wrinkles were creasing my brow, and my face was succumbing to the downward pull of the earth. My once-luscious auburn hair was stiff and turning gray at the roots. My lips, how pink they used to be, were now pruned and thin. I was wasting away, and only the paint could keep me preserved.

From behind me, I heard a knock at my door.

"Who is it?" I asked as one of my handmaidens began brushing my hair. My handmaiden was young; I believe her name to be Margret.

"Lord Calder, Your Majesty," another one of my handmaidens replied from the door.

"Let him in," I said to her. A moment later Adok was strolling in. Taking a peek out of my massive floor-to-ceiling windows I noted how dark it had suddenly gotten. It was possibly the middle of the night. Adok must be here to wish me a good night. My handmaidens would soon be dismissed, and my candles, a hundred or so of them, would be put out. Finally, it was almost time for me to retire to my bed.

"Your Grace"—Adok kneeled and then rose to kiss my hand—"I have come to bid you good night."

I gave him a halfhearted smile and nodded. "Good night."

He kissed my hand again. "Good night."

Suddenly, there was a rapid banging at the bedchamber door. I looked at Adok; the look on his face told me he did not know who it could be. He had his hand on the dagger at his waistband.

"Who is it?" I asked.

"It is Sir Crichton, Your Majesty," my handmaiden replied.

"Send him in." I relaxed immediately. So did Adok. Always my protector.

Sir Crichton came charging into the room a second later. The determination in his step told me that something was aloof. "Your Majesty." He kneeled and then quickly stood. "We have a problem." Sir Crichton was a strapping fellow. He had a finely trimmed beard and a luscious head of golden hair that flowed down his back. Eyeing my handmaidens, I saw as they all straightened as he walked in.

"What is it?" I asked, noting how heavily he was breathing. He must've come directly from the Bastille after he had heard whatever news that was troubling him.

"We got word that the rebels are still gathering. Their numbers have tripled, if not quadrupled, in the last few days. They're coming this way," he replied.

I was appalled by this information! "How do you know?"

"Another one of our camps was taken over by them. We didn't stand a chance." He didn't keep eye contact. Instead, the pathetic oaf stared at his feet.

Enraged, I stood and paced the space of my room. "You told me they were returning to their villages!" I pointed at Adok. "Now they're heading towards my kingdom with an army of wild beasts!"

Adok maintained his composure and replied, "When I had left they were leaving. Apparently, Arianna's powers of persuasion are a lot stronger than I had thought."

"Your trust in that callous attitude of yours is about to cost me my kingdom!" I screamed, throwing things off of my nightstand.

Everyone was quiet. They didn't know what to say or what to do! How much more worthless could they be?

"Get out!" My handmaidens bowed quickly and then scurried out of the room. Sir Crichton was quick to follow. Only Adok stayed. "How could you let this happen?"

He shrugged. "They're smarter than I thought."

"O' good, I'm glad we've got that understood," I hissed. "Now what are you going to do to fix it?"

"They're not stupid enough to attack you with their offspring still in the Bastille, which means you have two options. Kill all of their children now and send a few men out to spread the word of what happened."

"That sounds ideal." Mother would hate that I couldn't control my temper. But she never foresaw me dealing with problems like these! I deserved some leeway.

"Perhaps, but it might also give them what they need in order to fully go against their queen. By killing their offspring, you're giving them nothing to live for. So consequently, they have nothing to lose," he clarified.

"What's option two?"

He thought for a moment. "My guess is that they are going to try to get their offspring back before they attack the Royal Army. They're going to storm the Bastille."

The Bastille was a fortress of my collection of degenerate little beasts. Had I the money I would keep them locked away forever, but that to me seemed too lenient. I wanted to kill all of the little bastards, and sometimes I got most of them, only to refill it again. But that wasn't enough. I wanted them all gone. Child or adult. None of them deserved to live on my land. I would end this brawl. I would end this little rebellion, once and for all.

"Send the Royal Army to the outskirts of the Bastille as soon as possible. We will meet them there and finally end this revolt against the monarchy," I proclaimed, walking over to the window, staring out at my kingdom.

Adok shook his head, his hands clasped behind his back. "No, Your Majesty, this isn't a revolt." He followed me over to the window and stood beside me. "This is their chance for a revolution."

CHAPTER 31

THE REBELS AND I MANAGED to gather the true patrons of Islocia. There were ten thousand of us, an impressive number by all means. It was merely a fortnight ago that we had all stormed an enemy camp. It was so simple, all of us working together to demolish our foes. We stripped them of their dignity and their resources. Consequently, we had armed every last one of our warriors. Whoever was of the age of eighteen or older, whether male or female, was given a sword and taught to swing. If we were to die, she would have to kill us all.

Gabriel mounted his horse as our army aligned themselves into a collective group of ragged, savage-like beasts with a dire thirst for revolution. Ezekiel, Bacchus, and I were already mounted as Gabriel trotted up and down the line. An army of ten thousand against an army of nearly fifty thousand. The only thing that gave us advantage was that we were fighting for more than gold—we were fighting for our lives and the lives of our children and their children's children.

As Gabriel made his way back over to us, all eyes on him, he turned his horse so that he was facing them. The sun was nearly setting, casting an orange blanket over all of us. The sky was clear, and the forest was silent. It was nearly time.

Gabriel spoke, "Brave people of Artis, Qualmi, Rhine, Eikcaj, Ynafit, Sythos, and many others, the lives we have been living before have withered down into this very moment. I cannot promise a safe return home. I cannot promise a victorious end." He paused as his words settled. "I can only promise that from this day forward everything will change! When we march through the depths of the Iclin Forest we will see the villages destroyed by the mighty! We will see the lives lost due to the hand of an unjust queen! Let those images absorb in your mind. Let them settle so that you may never forget all that we have lost and all that we have the potential to gain!" He held the attention of everyone in his presence. They all looked up to this man, this man who had fought so long and hard for them. They trusted him, they needed him, and they loved him. "Her Majesty, the vile whore, will take notice of our *great pilgrimage* to her gates!" Cheers and applause erupted. "We will flood Lárnach like a wave charging the shore!" Gabriel continued over the cheering. "Royal blood will coat our arms, our swords, our fury, and our rage! It will not be doused by their pitiful cries for mercy! A deaf ear we shall turn! For they have always turned forever away from us!"

"Kill the queen!" Scattered cries for justice rang throughout the camp.

"Gather your courage and follow me! Make this march to the Bastille with me! We will charge it together. We will tear it down brick by brick until every child is free!" Mothers cried in delight at Gabriel's words. "We will then make our way to Lárnach and slay the dragon who has been burning us to a crisp! Like the phoenix reborn we have risen from the ashes and are ready to fight! Ride with me, my brothers, my sisters! Our thirst for blood will never be quenched unless all are free and those who have wronged us are dead!" The entire camp erupted in cheers and applause. We were ready.

Gabriel turned to look at me, our gazes held. He could see the suppressed rage burning through my irises. But in his eyes, I could see his worry. Our time together was dwindling. Though we hoped to win the war, there was a chance that both of us could lose the battle and others would have to lead our followers to victory.

"It'll be to the death," I said loud enough so only he could hear.

"It'll be to our death," he replied. Turning back to everyone else, he said, "To the Bastille!" And before long our trek began to the Bastille, leaving behind the desolated guards' camp that hadn't stood a chance.

REBELS

CHAPTER 32

NIGHTTIME SETTLED ALONG THE SHOULDERS of the rebels. Hours and hours they marched through the dense Iclin Forest. Through marshes, swamps, fields, and rivers, they clothed their bodies with the tatters of the forest. Every man and woman ached with the cry of sore limbs and heavy hearts. They had not realized how painful the trek would be. They had not realized all that they had to give in order to receive all that they had lost.

Was the pain, however momentary, worth the reward?

The rebels answered that question as they continued on toward the Bastille. They would not let their weakened bodies postpone their victory. No! They would only stop when they had won.

Their pilgrimage to the Bastille was a dauntingly unforgiving march. When they were forced to walk through the mud, they nearly sank to their knees as the thick goop swallowed their bare feet. Bugs swarmed around them, igniting a high level of irritation. Many of the rebels' efforts were expended on swatting the invasive creatures, although they were to no avail.

Water was scarce and food nearly nonexistent. Their leader, Gabriel, had promised them salvation if they accepted that their journey would challenge every fiber of their beings. The rebels had no choice but to push through their discomfort.

Ten thousand savages marched through the forest, shaking the earth with their pounding feet and determination. Swords swayed at their hips as their legs continued to carry them to the battlefield.

Hours and hours they marched. And with each passing hour their will grew to heights beyond conceivability! They saw nothing of which they left behind—no, they saw all that stood waiting before them. The lives of their children hung in the balance. The lives of future generations were counting on the success of these uncivilized beings.

As their march continued, it was often that they passed the remains of other villages. Dark ashes mingled with the wind as the rebels took notice. Some villages had been raided long ago; however, some raids were rather recent. So recent, in fact, that the bodies of the victims had yet to rot into the ground. The thick stench of death clung to air, embracing every rebel as though it were welcomed. Huts were torn to pieces. People, the queen's own people, were hanged by their necks from the trees, swaying eerily with their eyes forced opened.

Gabriel told some of the rebels to cut down those people and lay them gently in the earth so that they may finally rest. Mothers couldn't help but cry as they saw little innocent children tied up on the branches by their necks. It sickened every last rebel while also strengthening their determination.

"Do you see what she does? How she treats those who defy her?" Arianna spoke, pointing toward the desecrated village. "She has disgraced her people. Therefore, she has damned her own kingdom! Innocence, in its purest form, was lost . . . for what? A couple carts of grain?" She spit on the ground. "She will not get away with this."

The rebels murmured in agreement and continued their march to salvation.

As the time slowly crawled by, Gabriel noticed the exhaustion that had begun to suffocate his army. He turned to look at his people and saw how haggardly their trek had beaten them. Their rags hung loosely on their bodies, caked in filth. Due to the famine, his army was already withered to bones, but this journey had taken pieces of them away as well. They needed rest.

"Halt!" He held his fist up, and everyone stopped their procession. Looking around he decided that where they were was as good a place as any to rest for a few hours. They had settled upon a small clearing. Trees were scattered about but nothing as dense as it had been during the day. The grass would be soft enough for them to sleep on but hard enough for them to groan when they wake. "We will rest here for a little while. Unload your bearings and stay in sight of everyone. A few scouts will search for water. In the meantime, rest."

Everyone sighed in relief as they plopped down on the ground. To them, as their bodies spread out on the damp, prickly grass, it felt as though they were lying on straw mattresses surrounded by feathered pillows. Their bodies were tired and battered, and that was before they had even taken a single step onto the battlefield. They were still a few days' walk away from the Bastille, and time was certainly the enemy.

"Gabriel . . ." Arianna said his name as though she were starved for the taste of him. Together, Arianna and Gabriel were a force unchecked. Their impeccable strength and determination showed in the way they carried themselves. Gabriel, a being carved by gods, stood tall with a scowl painted forever on his chiseled face. Arianna, with all her ragged beauty, was sensual in a way that hinted at lust with danger lurking subtly beneath the façade. Like the tide to the shore, Gabriel and Arianna were constantly gravitating toward each other. Both dominant in their own right, they were anything but independent of each other's attraction.

Dismounting from his horse, Gabriel walked over to Arianna, absorbing the breathtaking effect she had always had on him. He was itching to claim her, but he had to suppress his desires for the moment.

"Time isn't on our side." Her voice crawled across his skin as if she had touched him tenderly. Before he could reply, he had to clear his throat.

"I know." He sighed, restraining himself from reaching out and touching her. "But we can't keep going and risk losing most of our people."

She nodded, her dark hair pouring over her shoulder. Stepping closer to him, she replied, "He's going to kill those kids. He's going to kill them all."

Gabriel stiffened at the reminder of the man who had gotten the better of him. *Calder*. The pasty Royal who had charged their camp in an attempt to scatter the rebels. Those icy-blue eyes of his could not hide the underlying attraction he had for Arianna. It lit Gabriel's blood on fire like a spark to firewood. Though Arianna had not said it, he knew that man had had her. He could see it in the way he looked at her, spoke to her. Calder's words dripped with cynicism and lust for the woman who had claimed Gabriel from the beginning.

"His blood will soon fertilize the ground," he promised, staring intently into her misty eyes. "It would bring me nothing but pleasure to see him dead."

"I want to be the one to do it," she said, staring just as intently into his eyes.

Gabriel shook his head. "You get the queen, Calder is mine."

She chuckled at his domineering statement. "We'll see."

Gabriel smiled inwardly at his stubborn mate. She had always had a way of challenging every decision he made. It stirred him when she tried to take control and he was forced to restrain her.

"Get some rest," he demanded, wanting desperately to sneak off with her somewhere and wrap up in her. But he knew it was not the time.

"You first." She winked, a surprising sign of affection that he was not used to. "I'm going to help look for water." Turning away from Gabriel, she walked away from him, leaving him breathless. Her hips swayed tauntingly, seductively, and she did it effortlessly. Every man in the camp turned to watch her walk away, each of them aching to have her. But she was his. And his alone. That's why he had to destroy Calder.

The night wore on, coating them in the chilling blanket of dawn. Torches were lit to allow for better vision in the dense night. Stars, bright and high in the sky, sparkled over the sleeping rebels.

Ezekiel and Bacchus were constantly on the lookout for any potential dangers lurking in the forest. Gabriel too hadn't rested as he should have. Not to be outdone, Arianna refused to lie down and sleep also.

"Couldn't have asked for a more peaceful night," Bacchus said in his thick, throaty voice. His pale eyes were surveying the forest as he sharpened his sword. "Hopefully, the weather will stay constant and even the playing field for us."

"Don't count on that, mate," Ezekiel chided, sitting next to Bacchus. They had managed to find some loose branches in the forest and had created a little bonfire for the rebels and a smaller one for themselves. The crackling of wood was the only sound loud enough to cause a disturbance besides their own voices. "The queen has God by the balls. The world is at her disposal, as it has been since the dawn of time. We just happen to be the only idiots to defy it." Although he was joking, it was a concern. It is believed among many that the reigning monarch was divinely put upon the throne by God. By defying the queen, would they be defying the true king above? Those who were religious enough to ponder such a thought believed so. Others didn't mind shoving the question aside.

Bacchus thought for a moment. "I suppose you're right." Roughly, Bacchus shoved the stone he used to sharpen his sword down the steely blade. Spitting on it to finish it off, he looked at it. The moonlight caught the shine of the sword. "A foolish thought to fuel a foolish dream."

"What the hell do you mean by that?" Ezekiel asked, turning to look at the large man sitting near him. Bacchus was a force all on his own. Not only in his size but his appearance as a whole. Scars, trophies from previous battles and wars, were nearly as intimidating as his unforgiving demeanor.

Bacchus shrugged his heavily muscled shoulders. "You and I both know there is no end to this trek in which we all survive."

Ezekiel thought for a moment, stroking his rust-colored beard. "That's rather optimistic of you. Thank you for sharing."

"I have been prepared for death since I was able to understand what it meant." Bacchus shrugged, continuing to stare off in the distance. "It doesn't bother me much."

"That's unfortunate," Ezekiel replied cautiously, eyeing Bacchus's mood. "So you don't fear death?"

Bacchus shook his head. "No." He paused for a moment. "And neither does she." Ezekiel followed Bacchus's gaze and saw what he had been staring at. Arianna and Gabriel were speaking discreetly with each other. The attraction between the two was as palpable as if they were reaching out and embracing. "The Captain will kill himself trying to protect her. And she will kill herself trying to satisfy her retribution."

"I would give her more credit than that," Ezekiel replied, watching the two interact. Everyone understood why Gabriel was so overwhelmed by this woman. She was beautiful and confident. She was dangerous in a way that lured men to her instead of frightening them. Gabriel was not immune. No matter how many times he had tried to assure his men that *she* would not affect him as easily as she had, no one believed him. "She loves him."

Bacchus disagreed. "She loves the idea of him and the martyrdom that comes from leading a voyage such as the one we are on. She loves his resources and perhaps even the past they shared. But I'm not convinced she loves him." He stood then, gripping his sword with white-knuckled force. "Look alive, we've got company."

Before Ezekiel could reply he heard the soft muffle of horse hooves coming from the forest. Surging to his feet in one powerful push, he brought his fingers to his lips and whistled loud enough to jerk everyone awake.

"Archers to the trees!" he shouted, shedding his relaxed manner. "Weapons ready!" Gabriel and Arianna broke their conversation and ran over to Bacchus and Ezekiel. "Captain, we heard horses in the distance. But have yet to gather a visual."

Taking on his commanding role, Gabriel replied, "Find Axel and see if perhaps the archers would be able to spot them." He turned away from Ezekiel and to everyone else. "Ready yourselves! Form a circle, everyone facing out!"

The rebels stood on sleepy legs; crust stuck around their eyes with their swords out and ready. Their position allowed for them to see any oncoming enemy no matter where they came from the forest.

Moments passed slowly as the sound of determined hooves grew louder and louder. The soft rustle of armor had the rebels on edge. Perhaps the queen had decided to bring the fight to them.

The intruders appearing from the forest, covered in armor, were not the queen's men. In fact, they weren't Royals at all. The queen's men always wore their standard crimson capes. These people had no capes and certainly didn't have the quality of armor the queen's men had. Their armor was rusted and heavily worn.

The intruders surrounded the rebels on all sides. All of them mounted on horses with swords tucked at their sides. It soon became apparent that they weren't here to fight. The rebels were the only ones with their swords drawn.

Gabriel stepped forward, extracting himself from the fortress of rebels. He began walking over to one of the intruders who had walked his horse forward. Arianna was close on Gabriel's heels.

"Aldous." Gabriel said his name cautiously.

The man who had stepped forward dismounted his horse and reached a hand out to Gabriel.

"Good evening, Gabriel," the man said in a voice that clearly hadn't been tainted by filth or famine. He spoke as though he were a Royal. "Do you mind telling your people . . . to put down their weapons? You clearly outnumber us, tenfold. We are no threat, just friends among friends." Aldous looked over Gabriel's shoulder and noticed Arianna. "Arianna, isn't it?"

"So many times I have traveled to your camp and you have to guess at who I am?" she hissed, eyeing him skeptically. Arianna had grown increasingly distrusting of the Iraquin, especially Aldous and his mate, Aphrodi. They had sworn many times that they would never accept anything Sythos had to offer. And yet, here they are calling them friends.

"My apologies," Aldous replied quickly. "It wasn't my intention to insult you."

"I believe that was the entire purpose of our little interaction," Arianna snapped. Unlike Van Crion, Aldous was used to women taking the reins. He was an expert in defusing bombs before they were able to explode.

"Then you must forgive me. The fault was certainly mine." He bowed slightly. "I hope we can move forward?"

"We'll see." Arianna released a fraction of her tension.

It was Gabriel's turn to speak. "What do you want, Aldous? You're not exactly welcomed among us."

Aldous nodded. "I see that. For you have not told them to lower their weapons."

"Traitors don't deserve leniency!" Gabriel didn't have to turn around to know that one of the Artis men had spoken. "I'd cut your head off had I not the respect for the man you're talking to. So tread lightly. I will only stay calm for so long."

Aldous smiled a humorless smile at the outspoken rebel. "It seems civility is always lacking in the Artis ranks. I am, however, impressed that you were able to form so many coherent words."

"That does it!" The Artis rebel went to charge Aldous but was stopped when Gabriel raised his hand.

"What he has to say determines if I will let you have him," Gabriel said, not breaking eye contact with Aldous. The Artis rebel grumbled as he settled back into his place.

"You've tamed them." Aldous chuckled sinisterly. "Impressive."

More Artis rebels growled like wolves starved for a buffalo. "I only have so much leverage with them. I'd stop while you're ahead."

Aldous shrugged. "Whatever you say."

"What do you want, Aldous?" Gabriel was growing increasingly impatient with the charade. Aldous was a man of stature and prestige, so it seemed, but it was rather telling that the Royals kept his income so low that he would never have enough to be able to join Ophelia's court. He was merely a high-ranked peasant.

"It seems your little rebellion has frightened the queen." Aldous replied with his hands clasped behind his back. Aldous was a tall, thin man who could not physically compete with any of the men under Gabriel's command. He was average, with average features and a stocky stature. His arrogance made up for what he lacked physically, and his money surely put him above the other rebels. "Apparently she has decided to raise a tax on the lower-ranking Royals in Lárnach. Consequently, she sent her goons to my village and raided us. They stripped us of our weapons and required us to accept an indenture servitude status once the former Royals began buying plots of land. It appears the queen has decided to wipe out her working force and replace it with people who can remain loyal to her."

"Dumb wench," Arianna muttered. She didn't particularly care that the Iraquin had been raided; it was more so the actions of the queen that had her thinking out loud. "Does she not realize that that's going to turn her own people against her?"

"You don't give Her Majesty enough credit." He chuckled, masking his own rage. "You and your band of misfits are being blamed for the tax increase. She claimed that due to the overwhelming opposition to the throne, she has to expend more kerts towards suppressing you heathens."

"They believed that?" Arianna asked quizzically.

Aldous nodded, his long dark hair shaking with the motion. "Within the few days her popularity amongst her lower middle class has tripled. They are applauding her and thirsting for your destruction all in the same breath."

Arianna shook her head in disbelief. "They're all brainwashed!"

Gabriel ignored her and said, "You came all this way to find us and tell us this? What is it you want from us?"

"Do you always believe I have some sort of agenda?" Aldous asked sardonically. Gabriel waited for him to finally state his purpose. "The guards believed that they had taken all of our weapons. However, I always knew that the queen's trust was hollow. Therefore, I hid some resources in a place I knew they would never search."

"Do you want us to pat you on the back?" Arianna barked, clearly annoyed with Aldous's presence.

He continued, "Due to Her Majesty's tax increase, it seems my status has dwindled to nothing. In fact, she wants all of us gone so that her new working class can breed a new generation of obedient Islocians."

Bacchus snickered, catching everyone's attention. "Captain, he's saying that the odds stand better for him to join our team when his has abandoned him."

"That's what I'm hearing too," Arianna chimed.

"I can offer you weapons and horses for more of your men to ride on. Also, I bring with me fifteen hundred men who are willing to lay down their lives for your cause," Aldous added.

"What does your whore have to say about all of this?" Arianna spit. Gabriel eyed her, the warning clear in his eyes. Arianna didn't care.

"Her opinion means little to me." Aldous shrugged.

Arianna chuckled. "She left you for a Royal, didn't she?"

"No!" Aldous was always quick to deny. He composed himself and said, "Her Majesty offered her a house in Yenyun as long as I was not to come with her. My Aphrodi didn't even hesitate."

"Pity," Arianna spit. "I'm sorry for your loss."

"Don't be." Aldous smiled his sinister smile. "She was pregnant with my child when she left. It will always be a constant reminder to her of what she whored herself out for. Regardless, Gabriel, do we have a deal?"

Gabriel thought for a moment. He wasn't entirely sure if he could trust Aldous. It was obvious that he was only willing to join the rebels to save his own hide. Yet the rebels needed his supplies and his men. It would benefit them greatly.

"How can I ensure your loyalty?" Gabriel asked.

Aldous shrugged. "My men will dismount right now and hand over the reins of their horses."

"I'd rather they hand over their weapons until it's actually time to use them," Gabriel negotiated, crossing his muscular arms across his chest. It took every muscle in Arianna's body not to grab his face and smother him in a rough, passionate kiss. She loved when he turned into an alpha male.

"How do I know your men won't kill mine?" Aldous looked directly at the Artis rebels.

Gabriel followed Aldous's gaze and chuckled before turning back to him. "I'd fear for your own life more so than the lives of your men. Besides, we would gain nothing by killing your men. It would be a waste of time and energy. We need the numbers, and you need our protection."

"I wouldn't say it necessarily like that," Aldous scoffed, placing his hands on his hips. "It's a mutual partnership at the least."

"Take it or leave it," Gabriel replied in his authoritative voice. "I don't have all night."

Aldous thought for half a minute before he turned to his men and nodded. A second later they dismounted from their horses and dropped their swords on the ground. Gabriel signaled for some of the rebels to pick up the fallen swords and grab the reins of the horses.

"Ezekiel will fill you in on our mission. For now just try to keep up." Gabriel turned and spoke to his army. "Pack up! We're leaving now."

Ezekiel fell into step with Aldous and began laying out the details of the plan. Gabriel and Arianna mounted their horses while the others did the same. When all were ready, they continued their journey to the Bastille where the queen would be waiting for them.

Many of the rebels had never been given the opportunity to lay their eyes upon the wonders of life outside of their villages. They had never seen the intricate designs of buildings or royal structures. It was a sight unlike anything they could have comprehended. It was as if a sinner had been awarded a glimpse of heaven's gates as they saw the giant structure of what was the Bastille. They all felt small, unworthy. But that didn't stop them. They lined themselves horizontally, spread out along the wide stretch of the open field before them. Their weapons were drawn, many of them mounted on impatient horses, their hooves digging into the unforgiving ground.

Gabriel trotted in front of their line, making eye contact with every single one of them. Their hearts pounded painfully in their chests. He could see the fear in their eyes, but it was overshadowed by the possibility of revolution. They knew all that they had to lose. Their homes. Their lives. Their children. Gabriel's chest tightened as he realized that these people trusted him to lead them to victory. He would not let them down.

"It seems the day *is* bright," Ezekiel said to Bacchus, who was mounted next to him. The possibility of a smile tugged at Bacchus's mouth as he too noticed the cloudless blue sky. "Perhaps *His* favor has wavered."

"Today we don't stand as individuals!" Gabriel shouted, cantering his horse up and down the line of rebels. "No longer will you identify as being from separate villages! Today, on this very day, we are one! We stand together! We fight together! We will die together! For our families! For our homes! For . . . our . . . freedom!" The rebels hollered in agreement, banging their swords on their shields. "Mercy will be left at the gates! Blood will be shed and victory will be ours! Gather your courage. Gather your strength. Our march to salvation has led us to our final task." He turned and pointed his sword. "On my life, I will fight until every last drop of blood has spilled from my being. Today, on this very day, we will all be free! Every slave chained to the throne will break free. Every child imprisoned in the Bastille will be free! You will be free! On this day!" The enthusiasm that spilled from the rebels was intoxicating. It ignited their courage, strength, and their will.

Across the field, directly in front of the Bastille and nestled on a hill, was the Royal Army—all fifty thousand of them draped in their shiny armor with crimson capes flowing behind them. The size of the queen's army was impeccable. It looked as if not even God himself could penetrate the human fortress they had created. For every eleven rebels there would be fifty guards to suppress them. The odds were heavily against them. Undeniably, the rebels should be demolished into dust. However, they would not accept those odds. The passion they had for their cause outnumbered the kerts the queen used to raise her army.

The queen, not wanting to miss all of the excitement, brought her and her posse to witness the massacre she had arranged. She was sitting in her royal carriage, dressed in a deep crimson gown with a heart-shaped headdress. Her auburn hair was plaited into a mound upon her head with her crown placed firmly on top. The royal standard waved excitedly in the breeze as she smiled plaintively down at her rebellious subjects. In front of her carriage, directly behind the army, was a large band eager to play. There were four hundred trumpet players and two hundred drummers. The queen, the ever so flauntingly ostentatious woman, spent a small fortune to have them there, playing for her during the entire battle.

"Your Majesty," Lady Dynia, a Grand Royal, whispered, "are you not afraid?"

The queen turned to her dear friend and shook her head. "Why should I be afraid when I have God on my side? I've demanded a victory, and therefore I shall receive it. Why do you ask?"

Lady Dynia shrugged, fanning herself. "I wasn't expecting so much opposition. Their numbers are great."

"Mine are greater," the queen snapped. Turning to Calder, who had shed his black attire for battle armor, she said, "Let's get this over with. I do not wish to be here past the dawn. I hear the chef is preparing quite a feast back at the palace. I do not want to be late." Calder nodded, taking the queen's hand and kissing it softly.

"As you wish, Your Majesty." With that he exited the carriage and mounted his horse. "Men! Ready your swords!" he shouted, trotting over to Lord Jamison. "Her Majesty wishes to end this as quickly as possible." Due to an injury sustained by the former Lady Korinthos, Lord Jamison could only nod.

"We will wait for them to come to us. Our canons will slaughter them as they climb the hill," Sir Crichton suggested and Lord Jamison nodded in agreement. But Calder shook his head. "Her Majesty wants this over quickly. We will charge first."

Sir Crichton, though he disagreed, nodded. "Another thing . . . the rebels have armed their women."

Annoyed, Calder snapped, "And? As many raids as you have been a part of, you shouldn't blink an eye at that. And neither should your men!"

"Yes, Your Grace. However, many of the hired men you imported from Yenyun, Kreni, and Hellec aren't used to slaying women. They make up a large portion of our army," Sir Crichton replied cautiously.

He too knew that Lord Calder was prone to rages that resulted in many injuries and deaths.

Smiling his sinister smile, Calder cut through Sir Crichton's armor with his icy stare. "They have been paid a handsome fee. This should not be an issue." Slightly concerned, though he didn't show it, Calder spoke to the rest of the men. "Those who have chosen to fight alongside Her Majesty and suppress this rise of treason should be mindful to remember the generosity that the queen has bestowed upon every single one of you. Your job is to kill, not think. Or feel. Leave that to us civilized folk. Remember your duties! And never forget them."

Back across the field, Gabriel and Arianna were side by side. With what little armor was passed out, they managed to acquire some. Their horses were restless with the need to run.

"Are you ready?" Arianna asked Gabriel, staring deeply into his navy-blue eyes.

Gabriel nodded. "More than ready."

A small moment of silence whirled around the space that separated the Royal Army from the rebel army. No one knew who was going to make the first move. Because the Royal Army was on a hill, it would be more suitable to the rebels if the Royal Army charged first. An uphill battle would only add to the Rebels difficulties.

Suddenly, there was a sound coming from the Royal Army. A loud horn pierced the sky, signaling the beginning of the battle. Following the horn, the queen's band began its concert while the Royal Army released their first wave of soldiers.

Beneath the rebels' feet, the earth rumbled loudly as the soldiers approached. Pouring down the hill like a glass of wine filled past the brim, they charged toward the rebels.

Arianna looked at Gabriel, and Gabriel looked back at Arianna.

"To the death," she said so quietly Gabriel could hardly hear her.

"To the death," he agreed.

"Archers! Ready your arrows!" Ezekiel called, raising his hand. When his hand dropped the archers would release their arrows, and soon after that the rebels would charge. Ezekiel looked at Gabriel to give the signal. As the soldiers neared, edging closer and closer to them, Gabriel counted the steps until they were close enough to fire. *One . . . two . . . three . . .* He looked over at Ezekiel and nodded. The archers stepped forward, none of them on horseback, and aimed their arrows to the clouds. Ezekiel dropped his hand and the arrows zipped into the sky. For a few seconds they disappeared into the bright baby blue above them, but surely enough, a second later, they rained down dramatically on the incoming soldiers. Like flies on their last breath, many of the soldiers dropped dead to the ground. The archers reloaded as the soldiers kept coming and did the same thing. By the hundreds the soldiers fell.

"For freedom!" Gabriel yelled, pointing his sword toward the oncoming soldiers. "Charge!"

Like bulls released from their pen, the rebels flooded the battlefield. Some on horseback, others on foot. Gabriel, Arianna, Ezekiel, and Bacchus led the pack with their swords pointed forward. Within a few strides they collided with the oncoming soldiers. With a few quick swipes of their swords, the rebels cut down many of the soldiers who had led the charge. Blood splattered onto Arianna's face as she decapitated a soldier who had tried to throw her from her horse. Arrows zipped through the air, penetrating through the soldiers' armor.

The rebels who weren't on horseback did a phenomenal job throwing many of the soldiers off of their horses and finished the job as they hit the ground. The first wave of the Royal Army was surprised to see how vicious the women were when a sword was put in their hands. They were relentless as they cut throats and gouged eyeballs. Astonishingly, inch by inch, the rebels were pushing the Royal Army back toward the Bastille.

From her carriage the queen watched as many of her men were so easily slayed by the rebels. Though she tried to hide it, she was beginning to get concerned. She held her composure like any monarch would, but as an arrow soared through the air and landed directly in front of her carriage, she couldn't help but gasp. Angered, she summoned Lord Calder. He appeared a moment later.

"What the hell is going on?" she shouted over the noise of the band, irritation spilling from her perfectly painted face.

In attempt to remain calm, Calder replied, "We still have more men to send out. We didn't want to send them all out at once, Your Majesty."

"Send more," she snarled, shaking his confidence.

He nodded once. "Yes, Your Majesty." Exiting the carriage, Calder signaled to Sir Crichton to release the second wave. A moment later they too began charging down the hill.

On the battlefield the rebels were beginning to feel more confident as they continued to push closer and closer to the Bastille. Unfortunately, their moment of triumph simmered as the Royal Army introduced a few new weapons.

Up on the hill, a loud explosion erupted from a cannon. As the cannonball plummeted to the ground, it exploded right in the middle of the rebel army. Bodies disintegrated as the blast spread its flames across the rebels' ranks. Thick black smoke momentarily suffocated the rebels, giving the Royal Army a slight advantage. Even more devastating, the second wave had made contact.

Arianna circled her horse as she saw a soldier tackle a woman to the ground. Holding her sword out, she shoved it into the soldier's back. He hollered in pain, which gave the woman enough time to scramble to her feet and pierce the soldier's throat.

Another cannon fired, erupting dangerously close to the brim of the rebels' front lines. More black smoke clouded the rebels' vision. Gabriel went to signal the archers, but he did not see the soldier running directly at him. Swinging his sword wide, the soldier went for Gabriel's head! If Gabriel had waited a second longer, he would've been killed at that very moment. Instead he ducked beneath the swing and uppercut the soldier. The man fell from his horse and was soon trampled by one of the rebels.

"Archers! Aim for the cannons!" Gabriel shouted over all of the commotion. Just then a loud popping sound went off near Gabriel's head. Instinctively, he hunched his shoulders to brace himself against the sound. Gabriel turned and noticed that the soldiers were carrying what Aldous had informed him of earlier. He had called them muskets. It was some sort of handheld cannon that could end a man's life with a single shot. Gabriel had asked Aldous if he had any, but Aldous shook his head and said that the queen had stripped him of all of them. They were so new that he hadn't even had time to hide them in his village.

Noticing the musket, Gabriel charged the soldier who had it. The soldier saw Gabriel coming and quickly attempted to reload his gun, but he took too long, and Gabriel was able to behead the slow soldier. Picking up the musket, Gabriel quickly climbed back on his horse and went to find Axel. Axel was near the back of the army with the other archers. Gabriel galloped up to him and tossed him the musket.

"Figure out how to use it!" There was only enough time for those words, for a loud scream that Gabriel knew all too well, struck his heart. Turning away from Axel, he watched in horror as several guards surrounded Arianna. Each of them holding a musket at her.

Forcing his horse to run, he charged in Arianna's direction, praying that he would get there in time. Gabriel's horse soared over many dead bodies, some royals and others rebels. He hardly noticed them. He could only see Arianna.

As he reached them, he jumped from his horse, flying through the air, and tackled one of the soldiers. They wrestled to the ground for a moment, dust flying up! Arianna took advantage of the distraction and went to attack the other soldiers. She slayed two of them just as Gabriel cracked the soldier in the mouth and ripped the musket from his hand. Holding it like he had seen the other soldiers do, he pulled the little metal piece near his finger and the musket fired. The soldier's face, where it was aimed at, exploded messily.

"What the hell is that?" Arianna asked excitedly.

Gabriel shrugged. "I don't know. But I like it."

Up on the hill many of the soldiers were becoming uneasy as they watched what was happening below them. Although the rebels were gaining the advantage, the Royal Army was slaughtering them. From their position on the hill the soldiers could watch, painfully, as the Royal Army decapitated women. Young and old.

"What the hell did we agree to?" one of the soldiers from Yenyun muttered to his comrade. "They're slaughtering women!"

"I didn't sign up for this," the other guard replied, shaking his head. Disgusted, he broke his rank and marched over to Sir Crichton. Getting right in his face, he hissed, "Have you and your queen gone mad? Look at what you're doing to your own people! There are women down there!"

Calder, overhearing the commotion, came over. "What seems to be the problem?"

The soldier looked away from Sir Crichton and looked Calder up and down, wondering why this man was in charge. "You're allowing for the slaughter of your own people?"

Calder scoffed, irritated. "They're traitors. They must be abolished."

"The men maybe, but the women? Have you all gone mad?" the soldier shouted, getting the attention of the other soldiers standing around. "I'm not going to be a part of this!"

Angered, Calder cocked back and split his knuckle on the soldier's chin, dropping him to ground. Standing over him, Calder screamed, "You will do what you're paid to do! I don't need you bitching over a few irrelevant savage whores!"

"Hey, get off of him!" Another soldier came over and pulled Calder away.

Wiping the blood from his face, the soldier who Calder had hit replied, "I'm not going to do this." Untying his sword from his waist, he dropped it on the ground and pushed past the other soldiers.

"Stop that man!" Calder shouted. But no one moved. "Didn't you hear me?" On the contrary, another soldier stepped forward and put down his sword as well and followed behind the one who had left. Frustrated, Calder went and picked up the sword and signaled for his horse to be brought over. "Fine, if you will not fight for your queen. Then I will." No one was inspired; instead more soldiers dropped their swords.

"Now is a time to be concerned, Your Majesty," Lady Dynia whispered after overhearing the commotion that had gone on outside. The queen said nothing and continued to stare ahead.

"Captain!" Ezekiel called, galloping over to Gabriel and Arianna. A little out of breath, Ezekiel gasped, "Captain, look on the hill! Her men are deserting her."

Gabriel followed Ezekiel's gaze and smiled inwardly. The rebels were gaining the advantage. Kicking his horse into gear, Gabriel shouted over his shoulder, "Tell everyone to charge forward! We're going for the Bastille!"

Although a large portion of the rebels had been cut down by the soldiers, there were still enough to even out the odds.

"Charge the Bastille!" Ezekiel shouted. "Charge the Bastille!" The rebels, though beaten down, enthusiastically charged forward at full speed.

From inside the carriage the queen watched as a wave of rebellious savages began heading right for her. They were easily slaying her men, cutting them down to nothing but body parts. Her heart pounded painfully in her chest. The sweat that started to dot her brow was causing her makeup to run down her face in dark, ugly streaks.

"Where is Calder?" she asked quietly, too full of fear to speak aloud. Her band was still playing, not noticing the herd of vengeful rebels heading right toward them.

Her personal guard, Joseph, replied, "He rode into the battlefield, Your Majesty."

She thought idly for a moment. "Protect me at all costs, Joseph."

He nodded, standing outside the carriage. "To the best of my abilities."

On the battlefield, the rebels were coming dangerously close to the hill. Sir Crichton tried to signal archers to fire on them as they began their climb, but he was losing control. More and more soldiers were deserting their queen! For a moment he thought it would be safest for him to do the same thing.

"To the Bastille!" At the base of the hill, the soldiers heard the rebels cry. Men and women alike began to surge up the hill.

Calder, followed by a handful of loyal soldiers, were coming down the hill, facing the rebels head-on. Although Calder had never shown his skills, it was soon obvious that he was a very skilled fighter. One by one he slayed many of the rebels who neared the hill.

"Protect the base of this hill! They mustn't reach the queen!" Calder shouted. In front of him he saw the heard of rebels coming for him. They were savage and angry. Fueled by hate. "Don't let them get to the queen!" he shouted again.

The hundred or so soldiers who had followed him nodded with their swords and muskets faced outward.

Gabriel led the wave of rebels to the base of the hill. His angst increased as he noticed who was down there, waiting for him. *Calder.*

The soldiers and the rebels clashed painfully into each other. Muskets rang out and swords sparked against each other. Gabriel dismounted his horse and began his assault. With one strong punch, he shattered a soldier's jaw. Gabriel had hit the man so hard that pieces of the man's tooth dug into his knuckles. He easily ignored the pain and continued his hunt.

Calder was soon within sight.

Fear coursed down Calder's frame as he watched the ravaged leader of the rebels approach him. Thick, meaty muscles tightened with the need to rip Calder apart. Calder only had a sword. He never took the time to learn how to use the musket. One sword against one giant. One very pissed-off giant . . .

Like a bull recently cut, Gabriel charged forward. Calder did the same, holding his sword with two hands. They crashed. Calder swung for Gabriel's head, but Gabriel was prepared for that and spun away from the swing. Quickly reacting, Calder swung again and connected with Gabriel's forearm. Gabriel didn't even flinch at the pain. Instead Gabriel went at Calder again. Calder tried to strike Gabriel, but this time Gabriel kicked Calder's wrist, causing Calder to drop the sword. Now Calder was really scared. Maliciously, Gabriel walked closer and closer to Calder.

"You should have killed me when you had the chance," Gabriel growled, clenching his fist. Calder kept backing up and didn't realize there was a slight incline behind him. He tripped over his own feet and fell back onto his rear. Gabriel towered over him, dripping in sweat and the blood of those he had slain.

"Mercy?" Calder pleaded, his chest expanding painfully with every breath. "Have mercy."

Gabriel silenced his pleas.

Back on the hill, the queen sat fearfully in her carriage. Her ladies around her were just as nervous. Constantly they asked if they could leave and return to the comforts of the palace. But the queen simply ignored them. She was too consumed by fear.

"Majesty!" Joseph shouted from outside the carriage. He appeared a moment later, worry wrinkling his jaw. "Calder is dead and the rebels are climbing the hill!"

"Send the third wave," she replied, nearly soundless.

"We've tried! They won't budge!"

The queen hadn't noticed she was shaking until Lady Dynia had put her hand on hers. Her mouth ran dry, and her mind was scattered. "This can't be happening." In a moment, the queen would lose everything. Her kingdom. Her dignity. Her life.

"Your Majesty! What do you want us to do?" Joseph prodded.

The queen shook her head, unable to think. "This can't be happening."

"Your Majesty!"

"This can't be happening." All of sudden, the once-cheerful and excited band had stopped their playing. Their tunes were now replaced with frightful cries as they too deserted the queen and ran for safety.

"Your Majesty!"

Lady Dynia leaned forward and spoke to Joseph. "It is time to yield, Joseph." Lady Dynia's eyes fell from Joseph to the small slave child the queen had brought along to serve them. He was cowering in the corner of the carriage, draped in rags with chains on his wrists and ankles. The boy was frightened, fear prominent in his eyes, but there was something else glimmering subtely in his irises. "It's time."

"Captain!" From behind Gabriel, he heard Ezekiel's voice. Turning away from the mangled body that was once Calder, he saw Ezekiel coming. "Captain, look!" Ezekiel pointed to the top of the hill.

Gabriel looked at where Ezekiel was pointing and was shocked into silence. For a moment he couldn't believe what he was seeing.

"Gabriel! Gabriel, look!" Arianna called, trotting over to them. "They're surrendering!"

"Halt, everyone!" Ezekiel waved his hands in the air to stop the remaining rebels. "Halt!" One by one the rebels slowed from a run to a walk and finally stood still. Their adrenaline had wavered, causing them to be exhausted. "Look!" Ezekiel pointed to the top of the hill.

All of the rebels followed where he was pointing to. As they looked up, a small child with chains around his ankles and wrists stepped forward. The royal carriage was pulling slowly away while the remaining soldiers threw off their armor and put down their swords. Even the soldiers at the base of the hill threw down their swords in surrender.

On the hill there was a small slave boy dragging something behind him. Judging by the effort he had to exert, it was much bigger than he was, and much heavier. But surprisingly, the little boy was smiling as he lifted the heavy white flag. Using every muscle in his body, the little boy swung the flag back and forth. Back and forth. Back and forth!

"To the Bastille!" Gabriel yelled. Erupting into cheers of delight, the rebels shot up the hill and quickly ran the rest of the way to the Bastille.

When they got there, there weren't any guards to hinder their journey any further. Mothers shoved roughly past the men and tore down the door to the Bastille. Arianna too rushed inside. For moments on end, more women disappeared inside of it. The men waited patiently, expectantly. Gabriel, Ezekiel, and Bacchus nervously watched the entrance of the Bastille, hoping for the best. It was certainly a possibility that the queen had decided to kill the children beforehand.

Silence filled the space between the Bastille and the rebels. Gabriel thought that it was taking too long. *If children were in there . . . they'd be out by now. Right?*

He was about to go in after them when suddenly a figure slowly walked out of the entrance, cradling something in its arms.

It was Arianna, and in her arms was none other than little Karuli clinging desperately to her neck. A few seconds later children came bursting out of the Bastille, crying with joy as they searched for their parents. Mothers wept aloud as their children ran into their arms. They loudly praised God and the angels above, so overcome with joy that words failed them.

Arianna searched for Karuli's mother and found her weeping on the ground. Setting the little girl down, Karuli went to her mother and hugged her so tightly that she squeezed out a few more tears. The only words Karuli's mother could get out were, "Thank you," as she reached for Arianna's hand. A little choked up, Arianna nodded and went to find Gabriel.

Gabriel found her first. Running right into her, he picked her up and kissed her with all of the passion he could muster. Arianna could do nothing but release the tears she had been holding back for so long. Gabriel held her tightly, telling her how amazing she was and how proud he was of her. "You did it. You crazy, stubborn girl, you did it," he said over and over again.

"We aren't done yet," Ezekiel said, hopping down from his horse and patting Gabriel on the back. Gabriel nodded and wiped a few more tears from Arianna's face. "To Lárnach?"

Smiling a true genuine smile of triumph, Arianna nodded. "To Lárnach!"

EPILOGUE

I RESEMBLED THE MESMERIZING WAVES THAT rushed to shore, soaking my feet. The salty water resided reluctantly to its edge until it was finally pushed over the brink again. Graceful destruction. Terrorizing beauty. Sporadic obedience.

The sun hung high in the sky, warming my face as the sound of seagulls danced around me. I was filled with a joy I never knew I was capable of. All was right in the world. I could finally say and believe that I was happy, once and for all.

The weeks following the revolution passed by with many long-awaited changes. The queen's carriage was found a mile or so away from the battlefield. She had attempted to escape into the forest, but Gabriel had ordered for her to be tracked down and brought to me . . . alive. Naturally I wanted nothing more than to skin her alive before dismembering her piece by piece. But not even her death would satisfy me. Instead, I brought her to her sister, Parthena, but not without humiliating her first. I stripped the queen of her gown and forcibly scrubbed all of the makeup off of her. Once that was done, I cut all of her pretty auburn hair off and presented her to Parthena.

Parthena was surprised at all the events that had transpired while she was locked away. I told her of what had happened and explained to her how her people were waiting for her. Parthena smiled at that and soon after took her rightful place on the throne. Although Parthena was the polar opposite of Ophelia, she mercilessly condemned her sister to the dungeon. Unsatisfied with that, she demanded that Ophelia be denied food and water for five days. If she survived the five days then on the eighth day she would receive Parthena's scraps, and the pattern would continue.

Another change that occurred was the status of the Royals. After the storming of the Bastille the rebels demolished it brick by brick until it was nothing but a pile of rubble. After that they flooded Lárnach and slayed many of the Royals. They tore down shops, buildings, and even homes. The children were untouched, but the adults were fair game. The rebels took as many supplies as they could carry and brought them back to their villages so that they would be rebuilt stronger than ever.

The remaining Royals adjusted slowly to their new life in squalor. As reigning monarch, Parthena was fair to her people, even the Royals. With her new council, which consisted of some villagers and some former Royals, they developed a system of government that would attempt to please the majority while also recognizing the rights of the minorities. Parthena was accepted unanimously by everyone. It was time that Islocia had a fair and just monarch sitting on the throne.

As for me? How did I end up? Parthena offered me a position to stay in the palace, but I couldn't. I didn't belong there. So I made my way back to the coast to my shabby little shack. It was tough walking through what was once the Qingkowuat village. But I had a feeling that they were at peace, because as I walked through the village, small budding flowers began to bloom from the soil. I liked to think it was little Teta and Zakai blossoming wherever they are now.

"It isn't often that one gets to observe great beauty," Gabriel said, walking up behind me and wrapping his arms around my waist. I leaned into his warm embrace, inhaling his masculine scent.

"It isn't often that one gets to observe it in peace and recognize the joyful faces around them," I replied, laying my hands on top of his arms. I hadn't expected Gabriel to stick around after our war was over. But he did, and he cared for me so deeply that he left his former life behind to live a simple, quiet life with me.

"Do you see faces, Arianna?"

I chuckled, remembering a very familiar conversation I had o' so long ago. "Yes, I see faces. Happy faces all throughout Islocia."

"Are you happy?" he asked, turning me to face him. As I stared into his deep navy-blue eyes, I felt my heart ache in the most wonderful way.

"You are with me and Islocia is at peace." I smiled, stroking my hand down his face. "Yes, dear Gabriel, I am happy."

He leaned down and kissed me tenderly, holding me tightly as if he never wanted to let me go. Behind us the waves crashed to the shore, and seagulls lulled around in search for food. It wouldn't be long until we would join the others—Ezekiel, Bacchus, Moira, Colleen, and some of the other members of Sythos—for dinner. I was glad they stayed close by. My little family, together forever and free at last.

Quite an ideal ending to one hell of a journey.

"Not by speeches and decisions of majorities will the greatest problems of the time be decide but by iron and blood"

Otto Von Bismarck 1862.

Made in the USA
Middletown, DE
25 January 2022

59655089R00255